FREEDOM RISING

S.L. WEST

Pig Pen Publishing

ISBN: 978-1-7356323-9-1
Library of Congress Control Number: 2022900433

Pig Pen Publishing LLC
PO Box 2772
Bentonville, AR 72712
www.pigpenpublishing.com

To ALL my loves, little and big.

I have read of a world in which life gave you choice and hope; this is not the world I know.

1
The Journal

Sam:

The first light of the rising sun weaves through my burlap curtains and into my thoughts. With time not given permission to start yet, my alarm clock remains black and worthless, much like the familiar feeling of guilt and need contending inside me. I can't help but smile at the irony that the warmth of the early morning sun brings. It's as though the sun agrees with me, rebelling against The Order with its own declaration of defiance; "Screw you and your schedule. I rise and set when I want." At least that's how we talk in my head, the sun and me, but never aloud. It's comforting to know I have a comrade in all this, so when the daily guilt assaults me, the stronger need can continue to validate my choice. I have come to find solace in these lost morning moments filled with the freedom to indulge in such crazy thoughts and reading forbidden entries of a forgotten journal. These are moments I have quietly claimed as my own.

With Brylie's words splayed open across my chest, I think of how different my life was just three years ago. That's when I discovered the timeless hiding place of my great grandmother chronicles. Well technically, she was my great-

great grandmother, but I have come to call her GG. Chuckling at my own laziness, I hug her life-giving words close to me, willing her strength as my own. I'll never forget the day her world came colliding with mine. I was fifteen then and had lost my will to live…

Resting my head on my knees, I sit curled up against my bed on the floor. Tear stains streak my face as I fight to find the courage to do what I must. I have said goodnight to my family, or rather, my goodbyes. Now, all I need to do is reach up and grab my fatal cup of tea. It's shocking really, how easy it was to make everything happen. All I had to do was slip a handful of the toxic weeds into my pocket, then crush them into my nightly cup of tea. How was anyone to know I laced it with White Snakeroot from my morning rotation? Staring at the ominous cup sitting atop my nightstand, a tremble rolls through me in response to its challenge.

Three years working the rotation fields is more than enough time to learn the ugly truths of this life. I say life, but I'm not really living. None of us are, thanks to the tyrannical Sovereigns and their evil army of Singuri guards. With my clammy palms pressed into my weary eyes, another tear slowly rolls down my cheek; I hate this world with its masked lies. Drawing in a breath of the cool night air, I'm once again reminded of my differences as the same questions haunt me now as they do every other night: Why can't I just blindly believe like everyone else? Why can't I be content to live out my life schedule and do everything just as I'm told? Isn't that what's best for me? For humanity? Despite having that mentality drilled into me from my first breath, I still can't just believe because I'm told to. I wish I could. That would make my life so much easier. But no, I always have to question the reason of things. Even though I know there are no answers. There are never answers. Scoffing at my life, the acid of bitterness singes the back of my already tight throat.

"Welcome, to the New World Era, or affectionately called NE." The familiar words from my history class echo in my mind with new clarity. There is nothing welcoming about this world, at least nothing that lasts. How can there be, when there's no room for grace? A cynical laugh whispers through my parted lips as the bitterness boils hotter within me. Oh yes, welcome to the Era where choice has been stripped from you and with it, your freedom. No thanks, I'll pass. I've seen too much of your world already. Fifteen years of this hell is too long. Absent-mindedly, I rub my thumb across my forearm and feel the nothingness of the unseen chains implanted in me at birth; a computer chip detailing every aspect of my life, planned out for me by the Sovereigns. This is not security, its control, and I'm dying underneath the weight of it.

Resolved to be rid of this place, my trembling hand reaches out to claim my waiting cup, freeing myself from this prison with the poison it holds. An unbidden image flashes in my mind of my lifeless body being carried off to the incinerator by the mocking Singuri guards. They could care less that I'm gone. The harsh truth rocks me; even in my death, they get the last say. My hand involuntarily jerks with the cruelty of it all, knocking my cup over and emptying my escape onto the ground. "No!" My strangled cry is lost in the reality of my own stupid clumsiness.

Terrified, I watch as my liquid freedom runs carelessly across the floor; so much for my small act of rebellion, and any false courage that came with it. Sitting defeated in the silence and fearing what the morning will bring, I soon realize the tea isn't pooling; it's moving with a purpose. Hesitantly, I follow the trail on my hands and knees across the aged wooden floor until it disappears from me, hidden under my old, metal dresser. Now what? Moving the dresser is impossible. It's been secured in this same place for longer than I have been alive. Think Sam, think. Leaning my ear to the floor, I'm acutely aware of the eerie stillness that fills my room as the faint sound of a hollow thud tickles my senses. Nervous curiosity flows through my veins as I pull a pin out of my hair and push it into the crack of the floorboard, forcing its way around the edges. With one final shove, the pin is sent as far down as it can go, then tilts at an angle. The added pressure demands the board's submission as it suddenly pops! Removing the loose plank, electric currents tingle up and down my arms as a mixture of excitement and horror course through me. I reach inside to feel what might be hidden in this dark hole, if anything. There is something…something cold, hard, and smooth…

As my hand continues to investigate, I find what feels like a handle on top. Grabbing it, I pull, and out comes a thin, metal box. Resting it in my lap, my eyes scrutinize every detail of this hidden treasure. It's gray with spots of rust freckling its surface. Even through the layer of dust, I can see that it's old, like something time has forgotten. My fingers continue dancing along the edges, stopping only when they stumble upon the latch securing the closed lid. I can't move. My mouth becomes dry and scratchy, beyond what it has known from a long day working the purification fields; a field where the boiling humidity saps every drop of fluid out of you. My heart throbs in my ears as I consider my dilemma. Do I open the box and discover what's concealed inside, risking my own life, which suddenly matters to me now, or do I put it back, leaving it hidden in the unknown? I know one thing's for sure, surrendering it to The Order is not an option. I must protect my family from the suspicion that would follow.

Minutes pass by in what feels like an eternity of time before the hunger for a small bit of freedom takes control. Cautiously, I unhook the metal latch and slowly lift the lid of the box. An old musty smell assaults my nostrils, my nose crinkles in response to the unfamiliar scent. Peering into the opened box, my eyes settle on an object wrapped inside a worn piece of cloth. Gingerly easing it out, the weight of the mysterious item proves to be heavier than folded fabric alone. Unfurling the material, the smell becomes more pungent as I reveal a book within its layers. Brushing my hand gently across the old worn leather of its exterior, I note the feeling of difference in depth as it glides over the embossed cluster of dandelions in the center. My fingers walk along the darkened flyaways that travel further up the journal's cover, until they disappear, free from its edge. Drinking in the effect of the honey brown color of the leather accentuating the burnt umber tone of the embossed details, my mind races with the wonder of who created such a beautiful piece of craftsmanship. It's like nothing I have seen before. Then again, books aren't exactly allowed. They confuse the truth, so we're told.

Wild with hope, I unravel the securing cord of leather and open to the first page. With a sharp breath, I realize I'm holding a journal in my hands. The revelation comes as my eyes settle on a name, a name I'm familiar with: Brylie Marie James-Wells. Too many thoughts are whirling around in my head as my eyes read it again. How can this be? Brylie is my middle name, and Wells is my last. Why are they in this old journal? Eager to learn more about the woman whose name I share, I delve into the pages of the unknown, trying to discover how we are connected. I may not know her yet, but this Brylie person has just become my reason for living.

It's been one heck of a ride, getting to know Brylie, aka GG, one I almost didn't stay on after learning the truth of my family origin. Brylie lived during the time when freedom and choice belonged to everyone. She died during the division that brought about the Great War. As far as I can tell, she was around the age of twenty-three when she died, but not before she had a child in secret, my great-grandfather, Bennette James Wells. Surprise! That's also my dad's name. I guess that explains where Grandpa Jamie got the name. Anyway, Brylie was only sixteen when she became unwillingly pregnant with Bennette. My heart broke for her suffering in a way I hope to never know, then it hardened at the realization that my lineage is one of rape. But the way she wrote, with such conviction of her unborn son, calling him her hope, tore through my walls and poured courage and strength into me. Even now, as my hands knowingly flip to the familiar passage, the thrum of my heart steadies in anticipation.

...Even though this baby, my baby, was conceived out of a dark place, there's no way I could've gotten rid of him. The man who raped me was the evil in my life, not my baby. Bennette is my hope... I have decided the safest life for Bennette is to be raised by my parents, as my brother. I can still be with him and love him, and no one will doubt he's their child since Mom just suffered a miscarriage. He can be her comforter, and my hope... Yes, this is the safest life for him.

I can feel her convincing herself through the pages that she was making the right choice. It was her genuine words that drew me in and compelled me to keep reading. Brylie has a way of doing that, drawing me in. It's a strange feeling to admire her valor while at the same time being envious of the freedoms she had. Freedoms like keeping a journal. In my world, I don't have the liberty to have thoughts of my own, let alone write them in a notebook. But despite my internal conflict, I knew I had found a reason to keep living that night. I just had no idea how long that reason would last. Curiosity burns in me with too many unanswered questions and Brylie's journal connects me to the truth of our past. All history, my family, the world's, was erased or rewritten at the start of The New World Era. That night I was introduced to her world, a world of free choice, and I was connected to it. With all the newly discovered answers I had so longed for, I feared what would happen when I reached the end of Brylie's world. It wasn't until I got to know her, through the life in her words, that she truly rescued me with her courage. I need her strength to help me live the life of rules and schedules of my time, because without it, I would have been dead long ago.

I still have many pages to read, thanks to the strict schedule implemented by The Order, but I'm not fearing the end anymore. This slow walk through her life gives me the time to read and reread passages, allowing me to fully absorb and ponder them. Her dauntless response to her experiences gives me bravery I wouldn't otherwise have. I can't help but wonder if it was truly by accident that I found her journal, or if it found me.

2
Eighteen

Sam:

BEEP! BEEP! BEEP! Closing my eyes against the rude interruption, the obnoxious sound of the alarm announces that time can begin again. Six o'clock; my day no longer belongs to me. Pulling myself from my small bit of freedom, I quietly put my journal safely back in its hiding place beneath the old wooden plank. Resigned to the new day, I quickly grab my simple white T-shirt and light cotton pants from the dresser, knowing I cannot be late for my morning schedule. Taking the few steps down the barren hall, the smell of watered-down paint from the night before still lingers in the air. Having to stretch our white paint for the annual summer sprucing, it's easy to pick out the streaks in the new thin layer. Shrugging my shoulders, I know we did our best with what we were given, just as we do every year. Stopping in the middle of the hall, I wave my forearm in front of the scanner on the bathroom door. I'm clocked in for my morning routine with twenty minutes to shower and get ready for the day.

The door opens to the same bathroom I have seen

every day of my life: light grey walls, stainless steel toilet and sink, and frosted glass shower. Today, that's all going to change. Shaking my head free of *that* thought, I grab my toothbrush and turn on the sink, half tempted to not brush my teeth and greet my first unwanted kiss with morning breath. *How would he like that,* my mind defiantly challenges. I laugh at my empty threat, knowing full well I will comply. What else can I do?

Rinsing the minty foam down the drain, I steal a couple of minutes to look at myself in the mirror. Studying the image before me, I see the same reflection looking back at me: dark, unruly, curls, and dimpled chin. *Thanks, Dad!* My eyes are the only resemblance I see of Mom. In the mirror's reflection, her hazel orbs stare back at me, showing both relief and doubt in my slender physique. Most of the time I'm thankful for being unremarkable. This undesirable gift means I'm more likely to escape the eyes of the prowling Singuri; other times, I wonder what it would feel like to be pretty. Is there courage in beauty? I imagine GG was beautiful, just by the way she writes.

As the red-light flickers, my cheeks warm from the foolish notion of thinking I might see something different today. I throw my pajamas in the hamper where I know my mother will have them clean by tonight, since we can't leave anything dirty for fear of bacteria and sickness. Numbly, I scan my arm once again on the glass door, and I'm callously reminded of my prison as my personal information is displayed before me.

June 30th, 94 NE

Samantha B. Wells #2115: Female

Age: 18

East Sector: 227

6:05 am: Shower

Stepping into the shower, I swallow the bile that threatens to come up with the mounting anxiety that today brings. My eighteenth birthday. Birthdays are not events to celebrate as they once were; they are recorded to maintain the schedule of our lives and to make sure we conform and progress according to their program.

Age 5 – Start School

Age 12 – Start Rotation

Age 18 – Get Married

Age 21 – Start Reproducing

Age 70 – Death

Few make it to seventy. Death is common in my world, always justified, but common. Some die of old age or illness, but most from the stupid program the Sovereigns call life.

As the water turns on, I step in half dazed, allowing the tepid temperature to awaken my senses. I begin vigorously scrubbing my body trying to wash away the hate, but the only thing this chemically laced bar does is rid my body of dead skin and mites. The words of my grandmother bounce around in my tormented mind, *I cannot wait to turn eighteen! Finally, I'll be free to make my own choices. I'll be an adult and I can join the rebellion!* I wish I could rebel against turning eighteen, the milestone for adulthood. It's not the adult part that bothers me, everyone grows up; it's the "free to make my own choices" part and the forced marriage. In GG's day, marriage happened because you loved someone, not because it was a box to be checked off.

Love is something I know little about, and in marriage, it is almost non-existent. Thanks to the unfounded paranoia of The Order, limited time is spent with any single person outside your own family. It's viewed as rebellion. If we break this law, or any laws for that matter, we will be beaten or put to death. To further tighten the noose, if we witness or discover anyone not following the laws, we are required to turn them in or suffer the same fate. Because of this tyranny, there are few trusting relationships. Most people don't even bother trying to find true love. Fortunately for me, my parents did bother, and they found it. My home, inside the security of its walls, pushes the rules in very subtle ways. Not in a bad or troublesome kind of way, but in a way that has allowed me to have a glimpse into love. This glimpse is why today is so much more difficult for me, than it is for most others.

In just a few short hours, I will be taken from my family and home, leaving behind any sense of security and love I have ever known. I'll be forced to marry a man who is a stranger to me.

Just as the time I wake up and go to bed, the choice is not mine. "GG, help me through this day," I whisper. Leaning forward into the cleansing stream, I imagine my troubles being washed away with the water as it runs down my face, disappearing forever down the drain. If only it were that simple. All too soon the water stops, as though it's working against me too. Shoving my troubles aside, I step out of the shower and dry off as quickly as I can. Donning my day clothes, it's time to focus on the next step of my daily routine. Traveling lightly down the fourteen steps and another empty hallway, my feet make only a whisper of a patter on the newly sealed floor. My soft gait is something I have always been thankful for, often using it to sneak up on my sister or eavesdropping when I shouldn't be. As I continue my trek past the sparsely furnished sitting room, my eyes sweep over the oval knit rug in front of the fireplace, and memories of Mom's bedtime stories flood my mind. We would sit in quiet anticipation on that very rug, while Mom would sit in her wooden rocker that once graced her bedroom when we were babes. She would ignite our imaginations with stories made up from everyday things. A stick, a bug, or even a rock, it didn't matter what it was; the magic of her creativity made them all worth listening to. Sometimes Dad would join in, offering background noises or silly voices to other characters in her story. Swallowing the lump that crept its way into my throat, I push my eyes past the worn rug and over the small lumpy sofa as I force my feet away from the warm memories. *And this too shall pass.* GG's words spring to mind, speaking of the promise of better times to come. I hope she's right.

Pausing just outside the kitchen entrance, I think of my family's ability to accept this life, because it's what keeps us alive. I can never let them know about Brylie's journal; it would mean my death. If they ever found out, they would have to turn me in or suffer the same fate. We're not supposed to have any knowledge of how life was, just accept how life is, and believe it's for our betterment: like an android, programmed to follow. If we do not comply, then we are considered a virus to this otherwise perfectly functioning system and are removed. Though I would never say it aloud, I sometimes feel like a virus, wondering why I seem to be the only one who struggles with accepting this world. I keep waiting for these feelings to pass. They never do.

Closing my eyes, I pull close to me the courage of my GG. I need her today, more than ever. *I will not let them win.* It's a whisper of another memory of her words that I have repeated to myself many times over these past three years. Reminding me once again of her strength, the mounting weight threatening to crush my chest eases. I open my eyes and plaster a smile on my face before entering the room. The harsh whiteness of the kitchen compliments the cruel changes that today brings. Seeing my family already seated at our old wooden table, I take my place across from my little sister, Julia. She is nearing seventeen and is incredibly beautiful. She looks more like the grandmother I imagine, wearing our father's deep, brown eyes and our mother's smooth complexion and dark blonde hair. Her features speak beauty, and her body is strong with curves. My heart aches for her because she is too beautiful for our world.

An empty seat sets to the right of me. It's where my brother once sat and one of the only reminders we have left of him before he was shipped off to a neighboring city to be married. That's how The Order likes to do things; removing you from all that you know and dropping you in a new place surrounded by strangers. It's just another measure to prevent an uprising. Matthew is the most like our father, with his tall frame, average build, and always finding ways to bring a little humor into our home. His face is a near replica of our dad too. A frown tugs at the corners of my mouth. It's been four years since we have seen him, and now, it's my turn.

I look to my parents sitting on opposite ends of the

table. They were selected for each other and married twenty-five years ago. My family is not a bad family, compliant yes, but there is a quiet kindness here. Extra moments, simple as they are, are given to make sure we each know that we are loved. I'm going to miss them terribly.

As we eat in silence, my mind races around the irony of how my birthday falls on the first of two ceremonial days each year. If I had been born one day later, my marriage wouldn't take place until winter, December thirty-first to be exact, giving me six more coveted months with my family. The familiar disappointment leaves me paralyzed in my mess of emotions. Sitting and hoping for some kind of distraction, I fidget with the napkin in my lap. Almost as if my father can hear my thoughts, he looks at my mother with a small, endearing smile.

"Good morning, Anna."

She responds in kind, "Good morning, Bennette."

A simple gesture that's acceptable in our world, but the lingering smile my parents give one another is a gift meant only for them. It's then I notice the wrinkles of stress resting on my father's forehead, and the unshed tears in my mother's eyes. It's too much for my frayed emotions to see. I turn my attention to my sister in hope of a respite, only to find her sorrow-stricken face further threatening my resolve. The tightness in my chest returns with growing anxiety, revealing how close I am to having my own false sense of control dissolve. My hands turn clammy as the seconds tick by.

Ding…Ding…Ding…

Finally, the kitchen clock chimes, declaring breakfast time over. For the first time in my life, I'm thankful for a schedule to keep. Scooting my chair back, I start towards the steely gray sink, when my father interrupts.

"Sam, you need to go get ready with your mother. I will do your dishes."

There it is, so matter of fact and out in the open, the change that is coming. A wave of heat goes through me as I wonder how he can use *that* name to say something so calloused. Is he ready to hand me over so easily to a stranger? My jaw begins to ache as I strain to keep from spitting out such a question. Why does this surprise me? It means one less person to care for, one less person to send off into this world. After all, I'm now old enough to be on my own. Only, we are never on our own. We're all too busy living our schedules and fulfilling the program. My heart sinks, and just as quickly as the heat came, it's gone. Feeling depleted of my resolve, I surrender my dishes to my father and his hand brushes mine in a familiar way that settles my soul, reminding me of his love. If my emotions were not so crazy right now, I would have heard the strain in his voice when he offered this kind gesture. As my misplaced anger melts from my heart, I see this man as he truly is, a father giving up another child before he is ready to let go. Swallowing the lump in my throat, I can only manage a whisper, "Thanks Dad."

It's all he needs to hear, to know that I understand and still love him.

Squaring my shoulders, I determine not to disappoint or endanger my family. I need to be strong, especially for Julia's sake. It won't be much longer before she will be facing this day on her own. Our eyes meet, acknowledging the vow we've been taught in our family. "We rise and live together, or we fall and die together." Today, we rise.

Turning to my mother, I silently follow her up the stairs to her room on the opposite end of the hall as mine. As she closes the door, only one thought remains in the forefront of my mind…Who will the law require me to marry today?

3
Goodbyes

Sam:

Standing beside my mother looking at myself in her mirror, I'm now wearing the dress she gently laid out for me. My heart is beating so fast and hard it hurts. This is my wedding dress. If it weren't for what it symbolized, I would feel happy in this moment. She didn't give me just any dress, she gave me her favorite one, my favorite one; the dress that once belonged to her mother. I have studied the beauty of the delicate embroidery at the neckline and cuffs countless times throughout the years. It is not fancy, as that is forbidden, but it has something greater than elaborate embellishments. It has survived time. Slipping the fabric over my head, the soft blue material falls smoothly over my body, and lands perfectly where it should. Woven into the very threads of this beautiful gift is the courage of my mother and grandmother, who have both stood where I am now. My heart fills with warmth, making it nearly impossible not to cry. I had no idea she was planning to give me this dress today, but I'm so grateful she did.

"Thanks, Mom, it's lovely." It's all I can muster,

anything more and I will completely lose it.

She pulls me close, giving me a small kiss on the cheek as she holds me in her arms. "Your father and I were chosen for each other too, Sam." Her warm breath brushes against the side of my neck as she continues. "You eventually learn how to care for your husband and no longer think of him as a stranger. I was lucky because your father is a good man, and it was easy for me to learn to love him. I hope the same for you Sam." She finishes her encouragement with a gentle squeeze.

Hearing the wish emanating in her voice, my heart flutters. Maybe it will be the same. Maybe her hope can become mine.

We linger a moment longer, knowing it's all the comfort we will get. I breathe in my mother's scent: basil and lavender infused with fresh air after a cleansing rain. I wish I could bottle up her aroma and take it with me, drawing from her calm when I need it. I'm going to miss her, so very much.

Taking my hand, she guides me to the corner of her quilted bed, only a little larger than my own, and sits me on the corner, as she has done so many times before. My mother's experienced hands begin to work my hair into loose tendrils, delicately framing my face. As she pins back a stubborn strand, I can hear her smile in the soft chuckle from behind me.

"I have always loved your curls, Sam. I think they distinguish you, and in their own small way, they're beautiful and free."

Surprised by her confession, my own little chuckle escapes, which is a rare thing in this world. The reason she loves my hair, is the very reason I have always hated it. I have never thought of my hair as a symbol of freedom or beauty. I can't even run my fingers through it. Worse still, it brings attention to me in a world where you do not want to be noticed. Reaching up, I gently squeeze her hand, "Thanks Mom, I'll never think of my hair the same way again," I smile.

With a responding soft squeeze of her own hand, she returns to my locks and continues her magic. I feel the familiar gentle tugs as she works with my curls and the way they want to move, unlike my method of wrangling them into submission. This is why she has always done a better job than me. As the final pin is put into place and her masterpiece completed, she joins me on the edge of the bed. We sit looking at each other, recognizing this moment for what it is, a goodbye.

I watch as my mom pulls herself up tall and pats me on the knee before drawing us to a standing position. "All right, time to collect your things. Remember, only pack two sets of day clothes and one night. They will give you what you need before leaving the Hub. Since today is a purge day, don't pack any essentials either. You will have a new toothbrush and all your other needs waiting for you at your new home."

I smile at her last motherly direction before she sends me on my way, with each step leading away heavier than the one before. As I pass the middle door to the third room of our house, I wonder if Julia will stay in this room or move into mine, as I did when Matthew left. In a little over a year, the whole house becomes hers. Being the youngest, she will inherit the home to help keep track of our family line, and Mom and Dad will be shipped off to the unrewarding apartment complex, having outlived the need for so many bedrooms. Peeking into her empty room now, I find the same bland curtains on her window that adorn mine, and a metal dresser with a twin frame bed draped in an old patchwork quilt. *At least she can have my two blankets when I'm gone.* The sullen thought reminds me of the frigid winter nights when the chill is so thick upstairs it seeps through our blankets. It's during these nights that Julia would secretly slip into bed with me, and we would keep each other warm. I long for more of those nights.

A part of me wishes I could hurry up and get the agony of my impending departure over with, while the other part is soaking in every last second I have. Placing one foot in front of the other, I will myself towards my room. Walking in, I'm not too surprised to find Julia sitting on my bed waiting for me. We often spend time together in each other's rooms when the opportunity arises. She looks at me with her big brown eyes, and I see sadness and fear in them. Sitting down next to her, letting our arms touch, we sit in the silence. Words will not help now. Thinking of only one way to let her know that I will always be with her, I ease myself up and walk to my dresser. Pulling out a scarf from my winter drawer, one I know she's always loved; I walk back and hold it out to her. "To keep you warm when I can't."

Reaching out, she grabs it from my hand, then quickly jumps up and hugs me before running out in tears. She understands my goodbye. A large drop rolls down my cheek and I wipe it away, quietly scolding myself. "Now is not the time, Sam," I whisper.

With a deep breath, I close my door and grab the only bag I own. I will not be interrupted now. My family will leave me to pack on my own. As I gather my few articles of clothing and put them in a neat pile, there's one more thing I need to grab, my journal. Certain I can't leave it here, but not knowing where I'll hide it in my new house, I firmly decide, I don't care. I will figure it out when I get there. Doing what I have done many times before, I kneel and quietly lift the loose

floorboard and pull out the thin metal box. As I hold it in my hand, I pull the journal free knowing the case is too bulky to safely conceal. Replacing the old, familiar box back
into its hiding place, I secure the floorboard and carry the secret with me. Taking the fabric wrapped journal over to my bed, I stuff it between the layers of my folded clothes and put the items in my green canvas bag. Sealing the zipper and tightening the buckle on the top flap, I pull the strap over my head, resting it diagonally across my chest. I'm packed. There's nothing left for me to do except wait for my appointment…to get married.

Being left alone in the stillness of my room only allows time for my overworked emotions to run amuck in my mind. Why did I think I would enjoy this solitude? A gentle knock breaks me free of my lonely thoughts and Julia's head peeks around my door. I can see her eyes are red from crying, but she's in control of herself now. Quietly walking in, she hands me a departing gift, her scarf. I gladly receive it and secure it in the small pocket of my bag, content to wear it on every cold day of the year. I reach for her hand, and in a solemn love, we walk downstairs to where our parents are waiting. Just before reaching the front door, we unlock our fingers, yet another secret we must keep. I worry sometimes, if I'm a bad influence on Julia, having all these secrets with her. Then again, our parents allow us this secret. As we all walk out the front door, I turn one last time to say goodbye to this life I have lived in the East Sector. Tonight, I don't know where I'll be living. Forcing myself to no longer think of this as home but only as a number, I say goodbye to house E-227 and turn to rejoin my family.

Wordlessly, we walk to the bus stop where I'm to wait. The Hub is a long way from the house, so I can ride the shuttle today. If it were closer, I would have been required to take the journey on foot. My parents and Julia can't travel with me. They're working in the nearby fields for their rotation and must keep their schedules of the day, just as though it were no different from the rest. My schedule is the only one that's changed. Pushing the sour thought from my mind, I focus on my family. The best parting gift I can give them is a hope that I will find peace with whomever I'm assigned. My father gently squeezes my shoulder, a hug we give each other in public that won't cause scrutiny, my mother tenderly runs her hand along the side of my face, as though she's trying to memorize what I look like, and Julia squeezes my hand one last time. That's it…our goodbyes. I helplessly watch as my family turns and walks away, traveling down the dirt path, disappearing out of my life forever.

4
Him!

Sam:

Locked within myself, I mourn my loss as I stand alone on the platform waiting for my unknown future. The heat of the sun is already threatening to suffocate me as I stand beneath the useless shelter of the metal awning. My eyes eagerly absorb the world displayed around me as I have only been allowed up here a few times in my life. Scanning the fields, I can clearly see the layout of the town I call home, Paxton. The city is divided into four major sectors, each named after the four points of a compass. In the center stands a large tower high above the rest, where The Order resides. Outside the city base of each sector, the varying fields run the perimeter of our land, our means of survival. We're taught in school how to work and maintain the different fields until we become of age to be a part of the rotation, where we will remain until we die. Shielding my eyes from the glare seen even from this distance, I can make out the solid glass top of the massive tower. Safely tucked away in their nest, The Order watches over the people with a clear panoramic view of life below. The building literally serves as a reminder of our world revolving around them. With this visual truth, the disgust within me is overwhelming. The Sovereigns, the hierarchy of the government duo, live and breathe in that same tower. I can just imagine them sitting around a bunch of computer screens, with nothing better to do with their lives than to watch and dictate ours. They sit perched up there, directing the Singuri guards to the next bug they want to squash in their perfect system.

Speaking of the other half of this dynamic duo, the Singuri guard are here to make sure we comply or make our lives a living hell. Whatever suits their fancy for the day. Their single purpose is to uphold the program, and if you rebel, even in the smallest way, you will be put to death. The Singuri are taught that emotion is weakness and that The Order is above all else. I see them as more robot than human. They have to be, with the evil required of them.

Then, in keeping up the false pretense of equality, there is the entire other half, or maybe one-quarter, of the world's surviving population, the Simpletons. *That's me. Sam the Simpleton.* Laughing at my own stupid play on words, the truth of our lives settles over me and I drop my eyes to where I know the base of the tower resides, the main Hub. The Hub is the only part of the tower I have access to, serving as an updating center and medical facility. This is where I'll be going today. Following the stairs up the identical platform that awaits me on the receiving end of my journey, the connecting tracks taunt me. Above the city, multiple tunnels lead away from the tower to the substations in each sector. They're equipped with high-speed shuttles that transport the Singuri to where they are stationed, everywhere. I have never liked traveling in those death traps; and what joy, I get to ride in one today. With impeccable timing, the platform beneath my feet begins to rumble, announcing the incoming shuttle. As it slows to a stop, I am once again reminded of how much it looks like a black and silver bullet, more than a means of transportation. Running off solar energy, as almost everything in our world does, the body is comprised of a long sleek capsule. The roof is nothing but black solar panels that seamlessly blend into the steel sides of the shuttle. Again, death trap.

Tearing my eyes from the offensive contraption, I hesitantly climb up the steps and run my arm in front of the scanner. A number is displayed on the small screen and my assigned seat is given. I wish I could sit where I can be alone with my musings, but that would be asking for too much. Taking a deep breath, I walk forward and claim my seat while looking around me. I can't help but notice the shuttle is full of other young men and women dressed in their finest clothing and packed for the same future. Realizing I'm not alone in this venture pulls me out of my selfish behavior and I begin to recognize some of the faces around me. Wendy, who is four seats up and over from my own, sits with her braided golden hair on display just over the seats edge. Beside her is Amanda, whose own hair is pulled back in a bun, framed in delicate baby's breath. Directly across from them sits Eric, sporting his freshly buzzed head and crisp button-up shirt, smiling beside a very blushing Holly. *I don't want to see that.* My eyes jump to the seat behind them where I find Josh and Luke, who seem engaged in a spirited conversation. *I wonder what that's all about?* The foolish question sends an unwelcoming thought racing through my mind; I could be marrying one of them. My cheeks burn with the awareness of this very real possibility. Averting my eyes to the empty door for a safe space to recover, I freeze. The one person I absolutely cannot marry, just boarded the shuttle.

The familiar shift in the air causes the hair on my arms to stand, as Alex Orion makes his way to his seat. Seeing him now, brings fresh to my mind that horrible night six years ago…

Julia's soft breathing normally soothes my active mind to sleep, but tonight it just won't shut up. I have been part of the rotation for just over a month now, and what I have seen doesn't seem to line up with what I have been taught. I don't know. Maybe I'm just too new to understand how things work in the rotation. Matthew never seems to complain about it. It must just be me. It's always me.

Quietly slipping out from beneath the covers, I turn to my old friends, the stars. The best time to look at them is about an hour past curfew when all distributed power has been shut down for the night. With only the scattered, soft glow of the sparse streetlights fighting the dark of night, the stars always win. While victoriously bright within the four sectors, the city center is wide awake. With the solar reserves diverted to the tower, attached shuttle lines, Singuri Stations, and the incinerator, The Order remains in control. But I don't want to think about that.

Back to my friends. Pulling the edge of my tan burlap curtain aside, I gaze into the darkened heavens. It fascinates me how different the stars are every night. Some nights there are more than I can count, while on other nights, there are so few that the sky seems barren. I smirk with the knowledge that no one can control the powerful burning balls of gas in the sky. Stars are a bit rebellious, and I like that.

"VIRUS!"

The sudden yell jerks my body to attention. Sweeping my eyes across the street to the front yard of the Orion's place, I see Clay pulling his daughter out of the house by her hair. The lighting of the night casts shadows in a way that cause his contorted face to transcend rage and reflect evil.

"VIRUS!" He repeats, while throwing what looks to be a book on the ground.

Confusion twists my heart as it tries to understand the nightmare playing out before me. Why is her father hurting her? I want to scream, but to do so would reveal my own indiscretion. The warning bells are going off in my head, telling me I should go back to bed because something terrible is about to happen. But of course, I don't. I let my curiosity get the better of me and I stay rooted where I stand.

I watch, as the faint sound of the approaching soldiers draw near. I have never felt more unsafe in my entire life than I do in this moment. I can now hear the daughter, Joy, pleading with her father.

"Please, Daddy, don't. Please be quiet. I promise I won't do it again. I'm sorry..."

He won't listen. Instead, he spins on his heels striking her with so much force she falls to the ground, unconscious. Everything in their yard turns quiet again, until the Singuri arrive. A shock of bright light floods the yard as a spotlight is turned on. My brain is screaming at me now to turn away from this scene, but my body still won't comply. Paralyzed in fear, I watch as Clay shields his eyes with one hand, and with the other, points to the object he flung on the ground.

"It's there. Right over there."

Even from this distance, I can hear the fear in his once enraged voice. The lead soldier in charge of the scene picks up the offending item and sends the other guards to search the home for any further damning evidence. Thankfully, they come up empty. Releasing a breath I didn't realize I was holding, I know the lack of evidence is a good thing for his wife and two sons. It means they will *get the lesser of the two punishments. Without further proof, indicating the rest of the family's involvement, the Singuri in charge throws the book back on the ground, then lights it on fire. Without hesitation, he turns and shoots Joy where she lay motionless on the ground.*

The abrupt shock of the killing bullet rings through the night air wrenching a cry from my constricted throat. With my body suddenly awakened, my ears pick up the faint sound of Julia's muffled cries and my parents' footsteps running through the hall. The next thing I know, the lead Singuri is yelling out Joy's indiscretion so anyone within earshot can understand that she broke the law and was punished accordingly. One by one, he lines up the rest of the family and continues to shout out his charge against them, "guilty of harboring a virus". My door flies open behind me as my parents and brother barge through the entrance. Julia is scooped up into my mother's arms and carried off to her room, giving a false sense of security from the carnage outside. My father and Matthew cautiously approach me as I stand shocked at the window. My brain is trying to unsee what it has already seen while my heart hammers in a fast, erratic pace. Feeling flush, I am struggling to breathe.

"Sam, you're all right now. I'm going to go over there and help you come away from the window." My father takes a tentative step.

I hear his voice but don't understand why he's talking to me like a child. I look over at Matthew and then Dad. I am met with more confusion. Why are they looking at me like that? Of course, I'm all right. Joy is the one who isn't. Why would her own father do that?

"Why?"

The hot tears run uncontrollably down my face as I look back out the window. I don't know why I do it, but I do. As the monster begins his beating of the Orion family, I feel my father's arms wrap around me, trying to protect me from the horrifying sight lived out in the scene below. Normally his arms would bring security, but I do not feel safe. Not now. As my father pulls me from the vortex I have been sucked into, Matthew shifts his body in between me and the window, creating a barrier from the evil. The splintering of my mind feeds my raw emotions as a void opens inside me. I don't know what it is, but I can feel it. Something in me has died. The darkness that has latched onto my strangely beating heart pulls at me now. I never want to see my friends again...

A strange shiver draws me from my memory, only to find Alex Orion staring back at me. What I didn't know then was how devastatingly that night would affect my life for the next three years. Those events threw me into the hopelessness that led up to when I found Brylie's journal. I may not have had the strength to turn away from my fears then, but this time I do. Averting my eyes from Alex, I silently begin praying. Even though I'm unsure of His existence, I pray to a God my GG sometimes writes about. *Please, please, do not let me marry this man. I can't bear to wear his name.* It is by no fault of his own that I don't trust Alex. No one has trusted his family since that night.

5
Plum

Sam:

It's around nine o'clock when the shuttle finally stops and delivers us to our destination. Looking around, I see small children clinging to their parents' hands as they wait to be registered for school. Boys and girls caught between childhood and adolescence are here to get their rotation schedule. A blushing girl is waiting in line for her first female exam. All roads I have walked before.

As I make my way through the glass double doors of the main entrance, I'm met with the refreshing coolness of the lobby air. Despite every exterior wall being made of solid, tinted glass, the only cooling system within Paxton regulates the temperature of The Orders' headquarters. The unit is supported by multiple fans placed every fifteen feet along the steel beams to help circulate the air. Lesser fans than the ones adorning the Hub are the only thing that cool our stuffy homes in the smoldering heat of summer. Here, they're an added luxury.

Pushing through the crowd that has clustered at the entrance, I'm joined by a woman whose baby bump is just starting to show. I wonder to myself if she is registering her first pregnancy or her last. In yet another barbaric effort to control the population of the Simpletons, they sterilize us after giving birth to our third child, all the while claiming that this extreme action is in our best interest due to our limited resources and preventative measures of disease. If that were the case, then why do they allow themselves to have up to five children?

The expectant mother catches me staring in her direction and I shyly dip my head with a smile. She returns the gesture with a smile of her own. This small interaction is affirmation that I'm moving forward into a predetermined future. As I walk across the sealed concrete floor, I find myself standing in a wide-open space beneath four black and white signs hanging from the steel beams in the ceiling. Each sign is labeled North, East, South or West, showing which direction I should go. Making my way to the East Sector, I find a screen with a map on it showing the location of each area in the Hub. Seeing a scanner at the base of the map, I place my arm under it. Curiously, I feel a small prick in my arm as it's being scanned. *Did I really feel that? My nerves must be messing with me.* Shrugging my shoulders, I look at the corner of the screen where my name and personal information is displayed. I'm checked in. I then notice a small room lit up on the right of the map indicating where I need to go, room 3E. Committing the directions to memory, I search the large foyer for hallway 3. Unfortunately, I find it behind a cluster of Singuri guards. Loathingly, I head in that direction, leaving behind the sun filled foyer and step towards the oppressive hallway.

As I melt into the crowd of other people my age, I see some of them branching off as their black doors appear. Looking up, I see another sign, only this one has an arrow pointing to the left, listing 3D, 3E and 3F. Turning as instructed, I'm immediately met with the looming 3E door. *Wait! I'm not ready.* My pulse quickens, pumping icy fear through my veins. *I can't do this.* I know in my head I must, but all logic has left me. Frozen where I stand, a million thoughts course through my mind as the cold white walls close in around me. I need to get out of here. Confusion and resolve cause my entire body to tingle. As I shift my weight to my right foot in preparation to turn, my shoulder jerks as somebody bumps into me. The subtle collision jolts me back to my senses. If I don't show up, the Singuri will hunt me down and my family will be implicated if they can't find me. And if I run, I absolutely cannot be found. Where would I even go? I don't know who it was that bumped me, but they just saved my life and that of my family. "Thank you," I whisper to my nameless savior. Releasing my clutch from the strap of my bag, I rub the smooth fabric of my dress between my thumb and finger, reminding myself once again that I'm not alone. With one unsteady foot in front of the other, I take the last few steps and enter room 3E.

Standing just on the other side of the lifeless black door is a Singuri Captain flanked along the back wall by a small squad. There is no uniformity in their features, only in what they're wearing: a tan button-up shirt with matching militaristic pants, complete with a holstered gun and a shocking baton or whip, depending on their preference. Their black steel-toed boots offer a third option, if the former two don't have the desired effect. The only distinguishing marks, to determine their rank, are the number of black bars they have tattooed on the side of their neck. One bar means you are the lowest man on the totem pole, and five bars essentially defines you as a near god. The Sovereigns all have five.

As I scan their intimidating formation, my eyes note the grin on every single one of their faces. The humor playing on their lips accentuates the challenge found in their cold, dead eyes. There is no turning back now, for any of us. An excruciating hour later, the doors echo with a loud thud, announcing the check-in time has expired. The following click of the locking mechanism drives home our place in this world. Anyone who has failed to appear for their nuptials, without a satisfactory reason, will suffer the brutal consequences.

The continuation of the concrete floor is the only similarity to the foyer this room holds. There are no windows here but only solid plum-colored walls entombing us where we stand. *Why plum?* my exhausted mind wonders. The sound of an opening door draws my attention to the front of the room where a thin, lengthy woman from The Order appears. Dressed in a dark gray pencil skirt and a matching deep plum blouse, she approaches the podium, with the click-clack of her shoes reverberating within the room. She takes a seat behind a tall wooden desk. Recognizing the blackened wood, sealed with the Tung oil we work to express in one of the rotation fields, the extravagance of her desk serves its purpose. Shou Sugi Ban is a method of wood treatment that not only survived The Great Wars but became a symbol of hierarchy in our world. The Tung Tree itself was the peace offering that one of the founding members of The Order brought to the table when alliances were made. Every part of the tree is both beautiful and deadly, from its blooming flowers to its tempting fruit. The oil of its seed is what allows the success of the burned wood to survive over a hundred years. These trees are grown in the greenhouse field, contained behind the glass walls that provide the climate it needs to thrive. Due to its invasive nature and toxicity, these greenhouses are set on one end of the greenhouse rotation field while the citrus and fruit structures are on the other end.

Perched behind her elevated desk, she slams down her gavel in a demonstration of the power she wields, thickening the silence in the room with her unchallenged authority. All eyes are on her. As she looks over the crowd assembled before her, a mocking eyebrow raises in disappointment. The tamed feeling of defiance bristles in my gut. *Who does she think she is, sitting up there with her birdlike features?* Fighting the urge to remind her that she is no different than me or anyone else in this room, a swift mental reprimand puts me back in my place. *She is a member of the Sovereign, Sam, don't ever forget that.* Continuing to study her every detail, I concede to my stubborn self that her sharp features match the fierceness I had expected to see in someone from the Sovereign side of The Order. What I didn't expect, were her piercing green eyes and sleek dark hair. As she opens her mouth to speak, her stern and sophisticated voice easily travels through the room.

"Welcome. You have arrived at your eighteenth year. You may have noticed the large map in the entry where you were scanned and given the location of this room. What you did not realize, is that while you were being scanned, a small sample of your blood was taken."

"That's what I felt." I mumble to myself, earning a curious glance from the person standing next to me.

"This was done so we could cross match your DNA and fit you with the most compatible spouse," the bird lady continues. "We want to ensure we provide your offspring with the best health, and genes, that will have the greatest chance of success in our world. The program will match you with whomever it deems fit. You will have no say in the matter. Please understand, we are doing this for the continued survival of our race, and for you to have a chance at happiness."

Pft. Right. Do they even know when they're lying anymore? I look at my nosy neighbor to make sure I didn't say that out loud too. I'm good.

"Once you are matched, you will be married to your chosen. I will do so personally, here at my bench. After you both make a commitment to this match, I will use this encoder," she then holds up a strange, sleek looking device, "which will update your chip, and permanently tattoo the name of your spouse on your left ring finger. After this time, you will be given your living location, as well as new clothing and essentials to start your new lives. Consider this our wedding gift to you. Thank you, and best wishes."

No one speaks. We just stand there, obediently waiting for our futures to be decided for us. Replaying in my mind are her last words, "best wishes." Does she really think we believe they have our best interest at heart? I glance around the room and discover that some people do. I suppose that's easier to believe than the truth. I long for the time when warm wishes were real, not just thrown out there for the illusion of one's happiness, and wedding bands were worn on your fingers, not branding tattoos. Losing myself in the fantasy of another time, my entire body tingles as I swallow the gasp that threatens to break through my parted lips. She's already called my name, but I didn't hear who she called before me. Reluctantly, I begin my walk toward the bench and as I look around, I am met with faces of pity. Why? My stomach knots within me as the back of my obligatory husband comes into view. Everything is in slow motion as he turns to look at me. My heart drops at the revelation of the man standing before me. A stranger would have been better.

6
Her!

Alex:

I see her standing atop the rail station platform waiting for the shuttle to arrive. She looks so vulnerable as she twists the fabric of her dress in her fingers. I've never seen her wear that dress before. She looks beautiful. I've always thought Samantha was beautiful in her own right. Not the obvious, striking kind of beauty like her sister, but she has a subtle beauty that whispers in her soft features. I watch as she bravely turns away from her family and casts her eyes over Paxton. Waiting from my distant hiding place, I am struck by the glowing effect the sun has on her. *If only she didn't hate me.* My wishful thoughts have Clay to thank for that.

I can only be grateful that Clay isn't here to say goodbye, not that he would anyway. He left for the ocean rotation early this morning, leaving Micah on his own for school. Saying goodbye to my little brother was one of the hardest things I have ever had to do. As much as I'm going to miss him, I'll worry about him even more. It feels like it's only been Micah and me these past two years, after Mom died of a stroke. She was never the same after Joy was killed. Micah was only five when she was betrayed, so he escaped most of the physical punishment, but the memories still haunt him.

With the unrelenting rage rising in me now just as strong as it was then, I know I can never forgive Clay. Joy would have turned twenty-one this fall; had she not been killed by him. Unbidden images flash in my mind and my hand automatically touches the small scar on my brow, a constant visual reminder of my father's choice: law over his own flesh and blood. The consequences of that night have followed us all these years. I see it in the way people keep their distance and look at my father, as if he were the angel of death. But can they honestly say they wouldn't do the same? Clay, like many others, is a victim of his own weakness, believing the lie of a promised, peaceful life. I am not condoning his actions; in fact, I despise them. I despise how they took my sister away from me and I despise that we are forever marked by his choice. I'm only acknowledging the fact that most people would choose the same; many have. Aggravation rolls through me with this sobering truth. I won't be like them. I'm glad to be out of this place. My only regret in leaving, is that I can't take Micah with me.

I hear the shuttle pull to a stop and watch Samantha board the steps. Leaving my hiding place just below the landing, I rush forward to catch the shuttle before it can leave. With most people, I can shake off their condemning looks, but it's not as easy with her. With my small bag of belongings, I step on board and swipe my arm under the scanner. Looking up, I see her staring at me with the same judging eyes as everyone else. Feeling the weight of their discrimination, I clench my jaw, walk to my assigned seat, and lay my head back. Closing my eyes to the world around me, I think to myself, *here's to a new start, I hope.*

The shuttle pulls to a smooth stop and my eyes open to the Hub outside my window. I grab my bag and head to the undeniable future, entering it with no false expectations, just the reality of the facts. I don't entertain the idea of who I might marry, because the one person I would want to be my wife, can't stand me. I plunge through the crowd with the mindset of "the sooner I get this done, the sooner I can move on". Hustling through the front doors, I am met with a busy maze of organized chaos inside. Locating where the East Sector is, I find the map and discreetly pull my sleeve up to scan my arm. Revealing another faded scar, I quickly pull it back down again once the scanner beeps. Drawing my arm back against my side, I look at the map. There it is, 3E, the room where I need to report. I make my way through the crowd that has now gathered around me and head towards my destination. Walking down the long hall, I notice the soldiers positioned all around, looking like they're having a good old time. I bet they are. I can't stand them.

Setting my eyes straight ahead, I refuse to give them any pleasure. It's then that I see her standing in the middle of the aisle. *Why isn't she moving?* My heart skips. As I draw closer, I see a guard watching her with a sinister smirk on his face. He's waiting for her to turn around and run. That cannot happen. I inconspicuously navigate myself through the crowd and gently bump into her, hoping it causes her to walk. Though I desperately want to look back and see if my ruse worked, I must keep moving forward and play it off as though I didn't do it on purpose, for both of our sakes. Each forced step is unbearable, not knowing if Samantha is in danger. When enough space is between us, I peek over my shoulder and see she is moving again. Now it's my turn to smirk.

In the meeting room we are met with more soldiers

and a stern looking woman from the Sovereigns, a rare sighting. She is not impressive by any standard, but she was born into her position, just as I was mine. She takes a seat at her bench and begins to speak. I pay attention to most of what she says, but I'm distracted by her staccato voice. I catch the part where she said our blood was taken, then something about how we must agree to our match, and the tattoo. I have always thought the tattoos were strange, but our world doesn't believe in jewelry; it's frivolous and unnecessary. I only know about the rings because Joy once showed me a picture of them. It was hidden in the pages of an old photo album I had found, tucked away with the letters inside. We used to sit and read them together, learning about the world our government denies existed. It wasn't all greed and destruction as The Order would have us believe.

Ms. High and Mighty calls another name and the person standing next to me reports to the front. He's getting married. I stand there watching the simple proceedings take place, one after another. My fingers tap the side of my leg as the anticipation builds, I wish they would get to me already. Finally, I hear my name being called, "Alex Orion."

Obediently, I walk forward and stand in front of the woman seated behind her bench. As I wait for her to call out the name of the wife chosen for me, she hesitates as though she's trying to decide if the program is correct. Strange, seeing how it's their program and we're told to trust it completely. If it's never wrong, as they say, why is she doubting it now? As the woman pulls her glasses down to the tip of her nose, she looks out at the crowd and then back at me, and smirks. The hair rises on the back of my neck, *what's going on?* Replacing her glasses back up on her nose, she makes a note and casually calls out the name of my wife…

"Samantha Wells."

My exuberant heart races, squashing any prior concerning thoughts. I can't breathe. *Samantha Wells, my wife.* My mind exults in this rare moment of happiness. *I can't believe it. Against all the odds, she's chosen for me.* I want to shout for joy, but I know I can't. Forcing the muscles in my face to remain smooth and emotionless, I must keep my celebrations all within the mental realm. To speak them aloud would endanger us both. The truth of that reality smacks me hard in my heart, causing it to painfully skip a beat. She cannot get hurt! With absolution, I promise to spend the rest of my life protecting her, no matter the cost.

Soon, Samantha is next to me. I can feel the disappointment radiating from her. We listen to the words spoken to us and repeat the ones expected of us. I can see her jaw is set and determined to do what she must, despite her feelings towards me. The small measure of pain her reaction causes, pales in comparison to the pride I feel for her unwavering strength. For me, the pledge is easy.

After we complete the ceremony agreeing to our pairing, we are then announced as husband and wife. Our microchips are updated, and we are given our tattoos. I gaze down at the small tattoo displaying her new name, S. Orion, and I know her finger stings with the similar letters of, A. Orion. I'm acutely aware that she hates me and all that my name stands for right now, and I don't blame her. But I will work daily to earn her confidence, proving to her that the name Orion can be trusted again.

We are soon ushered into the next room and given our "wedding gifts" as well as our housing assignment, North Sector, house number 56, away from both our families. We join the rest of our group headed for the bus going in that direction. As we take our seat, I offer to hold Samantha's bags, but she refuses and clings tighter to them with a determination I can't help but admire. Not wanting to add to an already fragile situation, I decide to let her be and rest my head back against our seat and pretend to sleep. It's going to be a long and quiet ride to our new life. A life foreign to both of us.

7
Defense

Sam:

It's late afternoon when we arrive at our new house in the North Sector. I still can't believe I'm married to Alex Orion. *So much for praying.* My bitter mind scoffs at me as I incessantly fidget with my finger where the black ink burns into my skin, permanently declaring me *his*. Okay, so maybe it doesn't actually burn, but it might as well with all the anger ablaze inside me. I didn't choose Alex, and I don't want him! Desperation wraps its poisonous tendrils around my jaded heart. *Why? Why does it have to be him?*

As I walk up the unfamiliar dirt path to the front porch, the sun reflects off the steel number above the door, N-56. Frowning at the small number, I understand what it means. Another genealogical line has died with the last living heir joining their ancestors in the dust of this unforgiving place. This harsh truth serves as a simple reminder, it could always be worse. Alex holds the front door open, and I escape to the nearest room, locking it behind me. My face burns with emotional anger as I pace the floor while hot tears threaten to flood me once again. Tears of pain or tears of anger, I'm not sure. Probably both. I know I'm acting like a child, huffing about, and if I don't calm down soon, I'm going to pass out. Or do something that will get us both in trouble.

Sitting on the planked floor with my back propped against the only barrier I have between me and him, I begin slowly breathing in and out, in and out. With my back firmly pressed against the door, I take my first look around the room to see what surrounds me. A metal dresser, much like my old one, is grounded against the otherwise empty wall. To the right is a door leading to what I assume is the closet, and a simple wooden rocking chair sitting adjacent to the corner. As I turn my head, I see a double size mattress atop a simple wooden frame. My breath catches. I'm sitting in the master bedroom! *Oh no! I hope he doesn't think I'm in here ready to "fulfill our quota for children".* Jumping to my feet and pacing once again, "Hold up," I say to the suddenly hot room. "This," my hand gestures to the bed, "isn't happening." Forget burning cheeks, my face is now on fire! Anger is less of the problem compared to the sheer embarrassment smashing into me now.

I'm eighteen, but I have never been with a man. It's forbidden before marriage. Not that I ever wanted to, just as I don't want to now. I don't know what he's thinking, but he has another thing coming if he thinks we are going to *consummate* this coerced marriage. I have three years to come to terms with my need to be physical, with *him*. By that time, I'm expected to be pregnant with our first child or suffer through invasive exams to explain why I'm not and medication added to ensure that I can. I shudder at the mere thought. No thanks. I don't know how I'm going to be able to go through with *it*, not with the way I feel about Alex now. *Maybe I won't have to. A lot can happen between now and then.* The unfamiliar dark thought catches me off guard, but so does the lack of shame. I know I should feel guilty for thinking in such a way, but I just can't right now.

Bracing myself for a confrontation, I take a deep breath and walk out the bedroom door. With a rush of emotions whirling inside, I travel down the dimly lit hall, mentally noting the eerie resemblance of my old home. Determined to set the record straight, I march forward, towards the kitchen. I don't know what I was expecting to find when I reached the downstairs, but it wasn't this: Alex sitting at the table, with our dinner waiting. The aroma of delicious food awakens my taste buds and my stomach growls loudly, betraying my efforts of appearing in charge. A small hitch in the corner of his mouth, is the only giveaway that Alex heard my stomach roar. I quietly walk into the kitchen and join him at the table, sitting as far away from him as possible. Not wanting to acknowledge the three empty seats as another reminder of what's expected of us, I pick up my fork to silence my increasingly demanding stomach. *How long was I in the room for?* I wonder. I didn't even hear the clock chime telling me it was time for dinner. As I take the first bite, enjoying the savory garlic and rosemary chicken with rice, it occurs to me, I didn't cook this. Before I can stop the words from tumbling out of my mouth, I ask, "Where did this dinner come from?" As I wait for his answer, I mentally reprimand myself for talking to him beyond the necessary.

Alex looks at me a little amused, "What, a guy can't cook?"

In no mood for jesting, I defensively respond, "No! No, he can't, not in *my* house!" I don't really believe this, as my father would cook on occasion. I'm just so mad at him for…well…for being him!

Alex doesn't say a word, he just gets up from his chair,

and walks out of the room. A few seconds later, I hear a door slam.

"Well, that was easy. Now I only have to piss him off for the next three years." I say, quite pleased with myself.

I finish eating my dinner alone in a welcomed solitude. The chime goes off again, letting me know it's time to clean up. *Poor Alex, sitting in his room all alone, feeling dejected. The least I can do is clean his dishes for him.* Such are my condescending thoughts. I never knew I could be so rudely sarcastic, and I'm not sure how I feel about it. He did make dinner for us, and I didn't even thank him. Despite myself, I truly am starting to feel bad...a little. Great, now I *am* going crazy. I'm arguing with myself. Eager to stop my solo conversation, I stand and get to work on the dishes. Before heading up the stairs, I take a quick look around the rest of the house and find it's the same as any other: void of any color, yet sufficient for our needs. I can hear the memory of my teacher's lecture sounding off in my head, a speech on the life of a Simpleton…

"We are to live a clean and simple life, and for this reason we are known as the Simpletons. There is nothing noteworthy about us, except that we are equal in every way. We live in plain homes that look exactly the same, inside and out. The youngest child in your family will inherit the house when they are old enough to be married and start their own family. This way, the family line can be traced back to its point of origin. Each house is numbered, to register the location and the number of people living in them, a census of sorts. They are equipped with a single fireplace, for warmth in the winter, and a small cellar to store your food, after the rations at the beginning of each week and the harvesting of each season. There is a small fenced-in front yard at each home, with an added garden in the

back. You will be required to grow medicinal plants and herbs along the fence to help maintain the health of your household. Our homes and yards are made to look simple, to prevent envy and keep equality among us, ensuring a safe environment."

I find myself standing in front of the rug-less, empty fireplace with these last words echoing in my thoughts, *"a safe environment"*. At least that's what they want us to believe, and some do. I can't blame those who choose this false sense of security, it's easier than living as I do; longing for a world that no longer exists. Darkness surrounds me as the lights shut off, indicating the lights out hour. Frustration with myself and this entire wretched day emphasizes the absence of my family, nearly crushing me with exhaustion. Dragging my way back upstairs, I find Alex has taken occupancy in one of the rooms intended for children. Good. Overcome with emptiness, I head to the other vacant child's room. Tonight, no one will sleep in the master.

The next morning, my body feels heavy in the mattress while my mind relishes in the small victory from the night before. Feverishly working out a plan on how I can keep Alex away, none of my ideas are kind, but I don't care. I was forced into this situation, and now I'm going to make the best of it. While reading GG's journal, my eyes fall on the words that give me hope…

Despite the governments best effort to put a muzzle on the people, I refuse to conform to their ideals. I will always stand firm on what I know is true and right. They will not force me into their way of thinking and living. No matter the laws they impose on us, no matter the threats they make, I will remain me. They say people like me are full of hate, yet they are the ones drawing the lines of division. I can be kind *and* strong. I can dislike others' actions, *and* still love. I can be forgiving *and* hold my ground. I can have my own beliefs while others have their own, *and* not hate them for it. Can they? Sadly, the growing answer is no. What has happened to us, that we have lost the ability to allow free will among the people? Not even God Himself demands our commitment. He gives us that choice. While the authorities in this world progressively find new ways to take our choice from us. I watch as political correctness has become the muzzle over too many mouths. I will not be silenced. I will be the me I was created to be. Abba, help me.

Tucking her words deep into my heart, I can't help but realize the truth of my world being her fear actualized. Her words, *"political correctness has become the muzzle over too many mouths"*, paint a vivid picture in my mind. Having seen an old field dog who's surpassed its usefulness in a muzzle once, I am all too familiar with what she is saying. My heart splinters, knowing how GG's own heart would break because of my world. If she were alive today, she would see how the muzzle is no longer needed. The Order has all together removed the tongues of the people. Closing my eyes to focus on the positive strength in her words, "I will be me", I let them build me up. A plan begins to take form, and I mischievously smile; Alex won't know what hit him.

Armed with a concept of a plan, I'm more than ready

to face the day. Same routine, same clothes, same me, Samantha WELLS. With my armor in place, I walk downstairs and into the kitchen, Alex is already there eating his own breakfast. Smugly noting there is none for me, I smirk to myself and start for the small fridge.

"I'm sorry I slammed the door."

His apology catches me off guard, but I'm quick to recover. Not wanting to acknowledge him, let alone his apology, I mutely grab an apple and some bread and leave early for my rotation.

It's a stifling hot and humid day in my newly assigned four-week field rotation. With the distant marine layer trying to cool down the suffocating heat, we're left in a bath of thick, wet air. I'm miserable and drenched in my own sweat, straight down to my undies. And my hairband is lost in the massive frizzy puff ball atop my head. *That will be fun to find later,* my disgruntled thoughts continue to complain. My only solace in this gross day, is knowing the Singuri guards on duty are just as miserable as us. Unfortunately, they have me sifting the large rocks from the freshly overturned soil, while they stand by in the coolness of their covering, watching like a hawk. *I wonder what Alex is doing today.* The thought pops into my head without warning. *Why do I care what he's doing, just so long as he's miserable too?* Wiping the sweat from my brow, I blame the unwarranted thought on the heat. Trudging to the next mound of dirt I bury my hands in the hot soil, folding it into my sifter. As the smaller pieces fall to the ground, the large rocks and debris remain. My nose is filled with the sweet smell of soil, reminding me of my mother and just how much I miss her. My sullen memories are interrupted by the obtrusive sound of simultaneously blown whistles, loudly announcing the end of rotation. Tucking my mother back into the treasure box of my mind, I join the rest of the exhausted Simpletons as we make our way to the work bus. To everyone's relief, the day has gone by without any trouble. I think it's because everyone was just too uncomfortable to cause any.

My ride home on the work bus is stuffy and smells of body odor. *Yay, my favorite.* Drawing my eyes up from a particularly extra sweaty passenger, I notice an elderly woman watching me from a few seats up. *Why is she staring at me?* As I uncomfortably shift in my seat, she warmly smiles and holds up her hand, pointing to her own tattooed finger. My eyes widen as I realize what she's doing. I don't want her congratulations. I quickly tuck my hand away and hide it under my leg. Avoiding her gaze, I turn my face to absently look out the window. I don't want to think about *that*, now, or ever. As the bus slows to my stop, I unpeel myself from the torn vinyl seat and quickly walk past her, eager to get off. It may not be my home, but right now, it's better than the bus. I head down the remaining road between my house and the bus stop and pause just outside the edge of the perimeter. Peeking past the blackberries growing along the lattice of our front yard, I check to see if anyone is there. Noting the house is quiet, I breathe in a sigh of relief. Plucking a couple plump blackberries from the vine, I pop them into my mouth. The explosion of the tangy sweet juices satisfies my dry, swollen tongue. Climbing the stairs of the front porch two at a time, I can't wait to shower and be out of these dirty, sticky clothes; but first, water.

Wishing for more time in the shower to soak in the refreshing downpour, I begrudgingly take my own dirty clothes back to my room with me, determined to take care of them myself. I haven't seen Alex since this morning, but I'll make sure to tell him he can do his own laundry, if he doesn't figure it out first. As I shut my bedroom door, I hear the bathroom door close, and the shower turn on. Alex must have been waiting his turn. Taking this opportunity, I quickly, and quietly run downstairs and throw some leftovers together for dinner. I'll be dining alone in my room tonight. I don't care about the stupid rules right now, and *he's* not going to stop me. Hearing the shower turn off, I dash up the stairs and hide away in my room. See what he makes of that.

With a full stomach and an exhausted body, I curl up onto my bed and begin to doze off. Sometime during the night, I think I hear my door quietly open. When I turn to discover who's there, I only find my dirty dishes absent from the floor. *Alex?* I'm too tired to sort out how this makes me feel, so I allow sleep to claim me once again.

8
New Beginnings

Sam:

Waking to another morning lying in my own bed, I cherish this gift of space I've created for myself. Today, July 25th, greets me with a guilty sense of accomplishment. Except for our passing in the mornings and our evening meals, I have managed to avoid Alex nearly every day since being here. We seem to have settled into a life of living more as roommates who try to stay out of each other's way, than a married couple. At least I do. Occasionally, Alex will attempt to strike up a conversation with me, but I just ignore him. In the beginning, he would try to engage me every day; it was so annoying. But not anymore. Now, it's maybe two or three times a week. I think he got my message: NOT interested. So why do I feel a growing sense of guilt when I've done nothing wrong? I'm just being me, or at least a stronger version of me.

As my hand timidly traces the familiar embossed detail of the journal, my heart squeezes with loneliness. I haven't touched her words since I read the last passage five days ago. It still stabs at my conscience. Pulling the ribbon marker from its neglected place, I slip the journal open to my last visit with Brylie. Peering down at the challenging words of my grandmother's own reprimand, my stomach twists with doubt.

It's been a week since I found out the awful news, and to be perfectly honest, I don't think I've handled it very well. It's hard to accept something you didn't choose. Life is a real crapshoot sometimes. I mean, it can really hurt in unexpected ways. Then again, it can be more beautiful than you ever thought possible. I love Benny, beyond life itself. He is why I want another child, only this time with someone that I love, someone like Mitchell. But it would seem I can't...

My heart hurts too much and the anger threatens to consume me, then I remember my mom. It would be easy to be angry at life forever, but to what end. I can't change the circumstances I find myself in. I can either embrace them with all the good and the bad or continue to be angry about it and make life miserable for all of us. That's not what I want either. So Brylie, it's time to stop complaining about how things turned out and make the best of it.

My heart tugs at the sadness she would not allow herself to dwell on. Brylie could not have more kids after Benny. The unexpected grief that should have been hers fills my own heart with the possibility of the unknown for me. Infertility, or the inability to have more than one child, is not uncommon in my world. Just as the dirty bombs left their mark on the land, it also left scars in the human body. With each passing decade, the effects seem to have less impact on

the newer generations, but still exist. In GG's time, infertility
was not unheard of, but significantly less than after the fall,
aiding in the near extinction of man. When I think about her
problems and of those before me, my problems seem small in
comparison.

A tingling heat washes over my face as I reflect on my
recent immature behavior. My parents would be ashamed of
me. I'm ashamed of me. While Alex was trying to make things
easier, I allowed my anger to turn me into something ugly.
I've been too blind to see that I'm not actually living *as* me, I'm
only living *for* me. That is not strength, it's weakness. In the
words of GG, it's time to make the best of it and move on. But
how?

BEEP! BEEP! BEEP!

The wretched alarm goes off stealing yet another day
from me. "Well, not today," I declare to the morning. I'm not
sure how to undo the mess I've made, but until I figure it out, I
will follow Brylie's lead and try to be more understanding of
Alex. With this newfound determination, the rational side of
my brain kicks in. Truth number one: Alex was forced into this
marriage just as much as me. Truth number two: He's been the
nice one while I've been an insufferable brat. Okay that second
one hurt a little, but I guess the truth can hurt sometimes.

Hopping out of bed, I put my journal back in its new
hiding place, a hollowed-out space behind the baseboard in
my closet. I discovered its new home the first morning I was
here, when unpacking my few items from the East Sector. The
secrets these houses hold continue to astound me. With the
baseboard snuggly in place, I quickly gather my clothes and
head to the bathroom for my morning routine.

Refreshed and armed with a plan, I make my way to
the kitchen.

"Good morning, Alex." My voice squeaks, betraying my false confidence…*stupid voice*. Glancing in his direction, I see the surprised expression on his face when he looks up at me and responds, "Good morning, Samantha."

He doesn't know I wear the name Samantha as a form of armor. Sam is my name of love and strength, neither of which I feel here. Pushing my loneliness aside, I try again.

"What rotation are you working today?" Now I see a smile playing at his lips, taking note of how full they are.

"It's my last day of planting in the crop rotation today," he answers. "Tomorrow they're moving me early to the—"

Too distracted to hear anything else he's saying, intrigue pushes me to study him further, something I have never done before. My eyes move from his soft lips and discover a defined jawline and prominent cheekbones complimenting his honey brown eyes, eyes I could lose myself in if I'm not careful. Framed with perfectly dark, long lashes and arched eyebrows, I can't help but wonder how guys have all the luck. My cheeks warm with the new discovery of how attractive he is.

Freely admiring his features, my face turns ablaze as I realize he's silently looking at me. When did he stop talking? All too aware of him, I shrink inside myself with the painful clarity of how plain I am. As the heat creeps towards my collar bone, I quickly turn my back to him, busying myself with getting a drink of water. Though he doesn't make a sound, I'm alive to his presence behind me. What must he be thinking? Before I can find out, I hastily leave for my morning rotation. So, what if I'm early; I wasn't hungry anyway.

Working the livestock fields today, I welcome the solitude of open space. The coolness of the shade offered by the trees in the outer perimeter is a rare gift. Alone with my thoughts, I keep replaying the morning's events. I have never looked at Alex in any other way than with mistrust, and now that I'm aware of him, I don't know what to think. As the warmth of color creeps back into my cheeks, I feel foolish all over again. Concentrating on the task at hand, I walk the field searching out the White Snakeroot weed. Today alone, it claimed the lives of two more goats and a few chickens, something we can't afford with our limited livestock.

Unexpectedly, a Singuri guard brushes by me, escorting a young woman by the arm. As they're passing, I overhear a part of their chilling conversation.

"You will not taint my bloodline," he growls.

"I thought you loved me." I can hear the confusion in her voice as the look of pain weaves its way across her beautiful face. "What are you doing?" she continues as her eyes search the Singuri's face, seeking something I know cannot be found in him. "Please no. I won't tell anyone, I promise." Panic escalates in her voice as the guard continues to shove her towards the outer rim of the field. "Stop…Please! Somebody help!" Pulling against her captor's grasp, her desperate cries draw the attention of others nearby. But just like me, none of them move. As the guard jerks her towards the woods, she twists her body in another attempt to escape. It's then I see the little bump protruding from her abdomen, and I shudder at the realization that she's pregnant with his child. I want to run to help her and her unborn baby, but fear keeps me planted where I am. A tremble rakes through my body as I fight against myself to remain put. As her vibrant red hair disappears into the distance, silence hangs in the air with the weight of death pushing down on me.

My body feels heavy with disgust. Disgust for the

Singuri, disgust for her loving *him*, and disgust with myself. A loud shot rings out in the open field and I know her fate has been delivered. The sound reverberates through my bones as I'm once again reminded that despite the vastness of this open space, I'm still a prisoner within this world. The bitter truth is that her family will be left wondering what happened when she doesn't come home tonight because the Singuri won't bother telling them, not if she was pregnant with a tainted child. They will hide their deed, regardless of those of us who saw what happened. The Order knows no one will speak up against them. It's not right…any of it. My pulse throbs behind my eyes as I struggle to bury my emotions deep beneath the surface, where they can keep me safe. Slowly, I turn my head away and resentfully continue with my task. I don't want to be the next target.

The day drags on with the heat adding to the oppressive atmosphere. As lunch break rings out, it comes with great relief and hunger. I skipped out on breakfast this morning and in my haste to leave, I forgot to grab something for lunch. Finding myself hungry without any food, I sit beneath the shade and drink the cool water offered to us from the nearby pump. It won't be the first-time water will have to fill my empty stomach. As I sip the coolness of the underground spring, the sweet freshness soothes my parched tongue. Opening my eyes from my moment of rest, I discover before me, a plump pear. Hesitantly, I follow the aged hand up to find the smiling face of the older woman from my first bus ride in the North Sector. She silently nudges her hand towards me, gesturing for me to take her gift. Uncertainty gives way and hunger wins as I accept her offering with a friendly smile and nod of thanks.

Acknowledging our exchange as an open invitation,

she plops down next to me in the grass and strikes up a conversation.

"My name's Ruth; what's yours dear?"

Dumbfounded, it takes me a minute to respond, "Samantha." We don't usually talk with Singuri nearby, though it doesn't seem to bother her.

"Well Samantha, it's a good thing I packed too much food this morning, isn't it?"

Seeing the teasing in her eyes, I return it with a smile of my own as we both know there is no such thing as too much food. "Yeah, I must have forgotten in my hurry this morning."

Her calculated gaze reveals that she knows there's more to what I've said, but she doesn't press me any further. "So, you're pulling weeds today." She concludes as she plucks a stray piece of grass from my hair. "They got me collecting eggs and plucking chickens. I imagine by the time I'm done; I might just turn into a chicken myself."

Her careless chortle echoes through the thick air, and my heart pounds with fear of the repercussions it might bring from the nearby guards.

Sensing my panic, she stops laughing and looks me square in the face, cautioning, "Life's too full of death to be so serious all the time. You've got to root out fear, just like them weeds you been pulling all day. You've got to create your own happiness, Sammy, even in the smallest of ways." She pats my knee before using it as leverage to pull herself back up again and walks away.

Wide-eyed, I'm left gawking at the back of her retreating form. She, who lives each day on borrowed time, has told me to find happiness. No one, other than my family, has ever said anything like that to me before. Her gentle reminder sparks hope back into my day, another thing for which I'm indebted to her.

The rest of my shift goes by without any more major "incidents", and we are loaded back onto the bus at the end of our workday. As we travel down the dirt roads, my eyes grow heavy from exhaustion. The next thing I know I feel a gentle tap on my shoulder; it's Ruth, letting me know we're approaching my stop. Thanking her yet again, the bus abruptly jerks to a halt. As soon as I exit, the impatient driver takes off, leaving me behind in a plume of swirling dust. Fanning the dirt filled air from my face, I quicken my steps, anxious to be home and to cleanse myself of this rotation.

Walking in the front door, I notice Alex hasn't come home yet. Sighing with relief, I realize just how grateful I am to be alone. I still don't know what he thinks about this morning, and with today's events clouding my mind, I need to diffuse before even thinking about *that*. Better yet, how about I don't think about it ever again. I will put all thoughts of Alex away for good. That sounds like a great plan. Walking upstairs towards the bathroom, I feel my shower calling me even louder than before.

Standing beneath the water, I allow the warmth to ease my aching muscles and slow my racing mind, relaxing me of the day's tensions. When the water stops, I'm not angry with it, only thankful for the relief it brought. Taking my time getting dressed, I eventually head downstairs to start dinner. Before I can reach the kitchen, I see Alex sitting in the living room, waiting for me.

"Can we talk?" he calmly asks, despite looking exhausted.

"Sure," I nervously answer. Stepping into the living room, I stand in the awkward silence that fills the space between us. With neither one knowing what to say, I notice the muscles working in his jaw.

"Samantha," he begins, "I need you to understand that I'm not my father."

Shocked by the bluntness of his comment, I can only stare at him. He pauses to look at me. I wish he wouldn't do that. I try not to squirm with his eyes focused on me as he continues.

"I see the same look in your eyes as I do in so many other people. It's hard enough to live with judgment from them, but from you, it's unbearable."

Why would it be unbearable from me? Trying to wrap my head around what this could possibly mean, he continues before I can make sense of what he's saying.

"I understand you can't trust me right now. I only ask that you give me a chance to show you who *I am*. Please know, Samantha, I will *never* make you do anything you don't want to do."

Hearing the promise in his voice makes me feel even worse for the way I've been acting towards him. The shame of my actions force me to look down. I don't know how to respond. Here he is, making himself vulnerable, and I'm still locked away inside myself.

His voice interrupts my inner thoughts of judgment, "One more thing. If doing the dishes or making dinner upsets you, then I will figure out another way to help."

Looking up at him once again, I see a small smirk, ever so slightly turning up the corner of his...mouth. Looking to his eyes, I find the same teasing there and wonder how, even now, he's putting my feelings above his own? Knowing I need to say something, I force my conflicting emotions to form a coherent thought and meagerly respond with the truth.

"You're right…I'm sorry." What more can I say? I have no defense. With a nervous smile, I decide to take my first step toward peace with Alex. "Do you want to help me with dinner?"

He returns my smile with his own, and together, we head for the kitchen. Here's to a new beginning.

9
The Garden

Sam:

My insides feel like they're buzzing as Alex finishes up his breakfast. I managed to eat my eggs and toast in record time, which unfortunately now leaves me waiting on him. It's been a week since we've settled into a new kind of normal, though this morning's plans have me antsy.

"Are you all right over there?"

Alex's question pulls me from my mental planning. "Yes," I lie. "Why do you ask?"

Raising his eyebrow at me, he responds, "Well, if it was just your beautiful humming, I wouldn't think too much of it. But since your leg is causing the table to shake, I thought there might be something on your mind." He smiles, knowing very well that there is.

It's annoying sometimes, how well he can read me. "Okay fine," I confess, completely brushing past his comment about my humming. "I'm eager to get going on the fall garden. I didn't realize I was doing all that," I say as I wave my hand through the air. "Gardening was something my mother, sister and I would do together every year. I guess I'm a little excited to get out there and work on something that's my own." Quickly realizing what I said, I try to amend it. "I don't mean, 'my own, my own.' I mean, it's not anyone else's." He looks at me humorously. *Why am I so flustered?* "Ugh. That's not any better. What I'm trying to say is…"

"…that it's not *theirs*. I get it." His gentle tone assures me that he does.

A timid smile forms on my lips as I further confess, "I've been planning the garden layout in my head while waiting for you to finish." *Darn it Sam, can you say nothing right this morning!*

Laughing at my words, Alex scoots out his chair while grabbing his plate. "All right, I hear you loud and clear. Let's go work on that garden of yours." He finishes with a smirk.

"No Alex, I didn't mean for you to not finish your breakfast. I just can't seem to say the right thing today. Please finish eating."

Clearing his throat, his eyes turn up from the table to meet mine. "I already finished," his low voice answers.

Turning my eyes towards the table, I'm surprised to find his plate is indeed empty, but further surprised by the fact that my hand is slightly laying over his free hand on the table. When did I do that? Quickly pulling my hand away I scoot my chair out and respond with a nervous chuckle. "Well look at that, you're *finally* done. I'll go get the tools together while you finish up your dishes."

He shakes his head at me and chuckles. "I remember not too long ago when me doing dishes would upset you, but now—" he shrugs his shoulders.

Rolling my eyes at him with a smile, I walk out the back door of the kitchen without saying a word. The sound of his chuckle echoes behind me.

Working side by side with Alex in the garden feels good in an unexpected way. He pretty much let me plan out the entire garden, only requesting an additional potted chamomile plant for his room. He told me it reminded him of all the good things from his home. I didn't pry further but could only imagine he meant his mom. Knowing this little bit of truth about him made me want to plant my lavender next to his chamomile. I know, stupidly sweet, but that's how our garden began.

Kneeling in the dirt, turning the fresh soil over in my hands, my eyes brim with the memories of home. Discreetly wiping away the tear on my cheek, I glance towards Alex working across from me. Noticing the sweat rings along the neckline of his shirt and under his arms, I muse at the potential sight of us. With his body turned to the side and his head focused on the ground, I comfortably watch as the muscles in his forearms tense from the resistance of the deeper clay invading the topsoil. Pouring water from the bucket beside him into the parched hole, he turns the dirt once again, only this time it gives. Once he's satisfied with the tilled dirt, he kneels to the ground and begins to work the soil according to the needs of the plant. His experienced hands form a sturdy mound with a small well in the middle for the seed to be wrapped in the warmth and security of the earth. As he drops the seed in its cocooned home, my mind wanders into new territory with thoughts of potentially being wrapped in the security found in his strong arms.

As he moves down the row to the next spot, I continue watching him as he starts the process all over again. Without a doubt, Alex is gently confident, which is a complete contrast to who I thought he was. My heart stirs within me with wonderings of the man I am married to, but my head quickly intervenes with its own warnings of the world around us. Turning my attention back to the task before me, I draw in a steady breath of dampened, soil infused air and tuck my heart securely away where it can't be hurt. Returning my thoughts back to my happy place, I give myself to my garden.

A wolf-whistle screams through the air, shattering the security of my sanctuary. Turning my face up towards Alex, I watch as his body tenses from the offensive sound. Following his line of sight, I find a Singuri guard standing just on the other side of our fence, with his eyes focused on my crouched form.

"Can I help you?" Alex challenges. My heart skips a beat. *What is he doing?*

The guard smirks in his double pleasure. "There's nothing more attractive than a hot, sweaty woman hard at work, unless she's at your feet doing it." He laughs at his own not so funny joke.

Struggling to swallow my own rage at his disgusting arrogance, I can only imagine what Alex is doing to remain calm. That is until I see a malice laced smile slowly form on his lips.

"You would think that, wouldn't you," Alex retorts.

Alex! What are you thinking! My mind is yelling at him while my mouth remains shut. He knows this is nothing new from the Singuri. Why is he playing the fool?

No longer laughing, the guard draws out his electric baton from his belt. "What did you say, boy?" he spits.

Before I can stop myself from intervening, I jump to my feet and nervously laugh. "Alex, you can't just say that without explaining the rest of the story." With my heart pounding in my ears, my mind is rapidly working for an explanation. With both sets of eyes on me, Alex's looking confused, while the Singuri's looks intrigued, I casually walk over to Alex and place my hand in his before continuing. "When we were first married, I got mad at him for cooking and cleaning in what I claimed as *'my'* kitchen." Pausing to shake my head for effect, I resume. "Well, he turned it around on me and said it was his favorite place to watch his woman work." Another nervous chuckle escapes my lips.

A bead of sweat runs down the back of my neck as the scrutinizing eyes of the guard looks between Alex and me. "No, that's the second most attractive place for a woman!" He booms before laughing at another one of his not so funny jokes. I squeeze Alex's hand to make sure he gets my message as I force myself to laugh at the guard's degrading words. Alex only smiles. "Maybe next time listen to your woman," the Singuri continues, "and be wise with what you say to me. Otherwise, I won't hold back on either of you." The crackle of electricity in the end of his baton drives home his point.

Choosing not to speak, both Alex and I nod our heads yes, which seems to satisfy the Singuri guard even further. Turning on his heel, he struts away to taunt another unfortunate person. The moment he disappears around the corner I can no longer hold my tongue.

"Alex, what were you thinking?" I hiss.

"I was thinking he can't treat you like that," he retorts.

"I get treated like that all the time. Well, maybe not the wolf-whistle, but the degrading arrogance is a normal part of our lives. They're just trying to bait us to give them a reason to do what they really want." As my blood cools, my demeanor softens. "You should know this already, Alex."

We both know he does.

The silence stretches between us before his apologetic eyes lock onto mine. "When it comes to you, it's hard for me to stand by."

Now it's my turn to stay silent.

"But you're right. I'm sorry."

Wait. Can we go back to what you said about, "when it comes to me?" My mind needs more explaining. But I don't say any of this out loud.

"I don't believe you when you say you don't get whistled at."

"What?" I shake my head, clearing it of other thoughts. "I don't. I don't get whistled at." I factually state.

"I would be more than happy to fix that error in judgment," Alex teases.

"What do you—?" Before I can finish my question, Alex begins to whistle at me. Shocked and completely embarrassed, I throw my hands over his mouth while shushing him. "Alex stop! I don't want to be whistled at, you idiot!" A giggle escapes me.

His body tenses as a muffled "I'm sorry," tries to work its way past my hands. The feeling of his lips brushing against my skin sends nervous tingles throughout my body. The heat crawls up my neck as our eyes lock for a split second before I pull my hands down.

"Well, you should be," I tease back before turning and walking away. As I close the door behind me, I peek out to find Alex still standing in the spot I left him. His arms folded across his chest and his smiling face shaking at me. The sight of him makes my confused heart flutter.

10
Scars

Sam:

Walking back from a long day in the nearby fields, I think on the time since Alex and I were made to marry. It was only two weeks ago that we made amends and Alex made his promises to me. He's proven to be true to his word and incredibly patient with me in respecting my need for solitude. I find it's easier to talk with him now. I only wish I could focus more on the conversation and less on him, especially knowing he wouldn't give me a second look. It makes me nervous to be so aware of his presence. It's hard not to notice the subtle confidence about Alex. That's what draws me in and scares me.

Stepping around the final corner to our house, I stop dead in my tracks. Why is there a Singuri guard standing outside our door? As the blood drains from my face, my feet refuse to go any further, terrified to find the answer that awaits me. Did they find my journal? Did Alex? I think I'm going to puke.

The sound of Alex's groaning inside the house tears me from my near moment of sickness. "Alex!" All my selfish fears diminish, freeing my feet to move once again. Running inside to the unknown, I find him hunched over the kitchen sink, pale with pain.

"What's wrong?" I blurt out.

I see the knuckles on his clenched fingers whiten as he grabs the counter to straighten himself up, revealing a blistering red burn on his exposed side. Panic claws at me as I force myself to run back outside to the herb garden. *Think Sam, think… Lavender and chamomile to soothe and ease the pain, peppermint to draw out the burn, and tea tree to help prevent infection. Aloe will have to wait.* Ripping the herbs from their mother plant, I dart back inside to prepare my poultice. As I grind the leaves in my pestle, I notice the guard has left. Good.

"So…what happened?" I manage to choke out.

"It's nothing really," he tries to casually answer but the pain is still evident in his voice. "I wasn't paying close enough attention to the steam coming off the hot rocks, and it bit me."

I can see there's more to his story, but I smile at his little joke anyway. If he's not ready to talk about it, I won't force him. Walking over to join him, I see his body stiffen with the anticipation of what's to come. "This is going to hurt at first, but it will help prevent infection, and lessen the pain and swelling." I don't know if my words bring any comfort to him, but my babbling helps calm my nerves. Scooping a good amount of poultice on my fingertips, I lean down towards the wound, "Alex, I'm ready, are you?"

He nods, releasing the breath I didn't realize he was holding. I feel its warmth brushing the top of my head, causing a new set of nerves to kick in. *Stay focused Sam. Focus.*

As my fingers gently set to work, he sharply inhales as the wound protests to any kind of touch. "I'm sorry," I quickly respond. "The lavender and chamomile will help with the pain, and the peppermint will cool the burn." It's nervous chatter, I know, but I need something to focus on. I pause, realizing for the first time, Alex is without a shirt. It's not exactly what I had in mind for this experience, not that I had anything in mind. Avoiding his face, I continue my pointless explanation. "I added tea tree to keep the infection away, but we still need to change the dressing often and in between changes, give the burn some air so it can dry out and we can apply aloe vera to encourage healing." Spewing the information out a million miles a minute doesn't help the fact that he already knows all this. We sat in the same class in school. I wish I could go somewhere and hide.

"Thank you," he offers. "I think I can feel it working already." His hot breath caresses my head once again.

The nearness of his face to mine does little to help my concentration. "Liar," I tease back. "But thanks all the same."

He laughs at my feeble attempt of a joke. At least my discomfort can bring him a reprieve from the pain.

Taking a deep breath, I prepare myself for what comes next. "I'm sorry Alex, but I have to examine your wound more closely. Are you okay with that?"

He goes rigid again, and I assume it's because of the pain he might feel. "Sure."

Carefully, I allow my eyes to lead as I take a closer look at his side, noting some irregular marks. Following them all the way around, my chest tightens as I realize these strange marks are faint pink scars, marking his entire torso. Involuntarily, my hand reaches out, curious to see what they feel like. He inhales at my touch but doesn't stop me. I continue to trace the next mark, and then the next, and the next.

"What happened?" I whisper.

He silently slides his hand over mine, covering his secret wounds beneath them. His large hand nearly swallows my own, his touch creating a conflicting warmth within me, a warmth I want to welcome and fight off at the same time.

"My father betrayed my sister, and I was punished for it."

His words cut through my opposing emotions with the harsh truth. He doesn't have to say anything more for me to understand. Closing my eyes, I try to shut out the memory as my mind races with a million different things I want to say. *I'm sorry this happened to you. I'm sorry I wrongly misjudged you. I'm sorry I was such a jerk.* But none of them escape me. All I can manage is a soft, "I'm sorry."

Then, as though I'm the one hurting, he pulls my hand from his scar and gently presses it against his lips. In that moment, I am no longer able to fight the warm feelings inside of me. My skin tingles as I welcome his unexpected kiss. I'm not angry with him, instead, I invite his comfort. As he pulls away, searching my eyes, for what I'm not even sure of, I find myself doing the same.

Ding…Ding…Ding…

The chimes of the clock break this unfamiliar moment, and we gently pull away from each other. Unprepared for what just happened physically, and in my own heart, I try to change the subject onto safer things.

"You should probably get cleaned up, while I work on dinner."

"I can help—"

"No, no you can't," I interrupt, needing to be alone right now. "Because Alex…you stink."

Seeing through my taunting, he smiles and puts his

hands up in surrender.

A nervous laugh escapes me as he turns to leave the room. Safely alone now, the nerves and panic I worked so hard to push down are forcing their way out, and my body begins to quake. The water purification fields are the most dangerous rotation we have within the city. When the recycled water is filtered through the chemically treated sand and sent over the boiling stones, the hot steam coming off them is deadly. The smooth black stones rest on top of a solar material that absorbs the heat from the sun and reflects twice the amount back onto the rocks. Many people have fallen into the rocks and died a horrible death. That could have been Alex. I shudder with the fear of what could have been, and in that moment, I realize I do care about what happens to Alex Orion. He is a part of my world now.

It's been two and a half weeks since Alex burned himself, but the possibilities of the "what-ifs" are still fresh in my mind. Even now, as I prepare a new poultice for him, my dreams from last night threaten to steal my calm. It was a horrible nightmare where I found myself working in the purification fields. The day was almost over when a bored Singuri guard pushed Alex into the hot stones. I watched as his body flailed in the boiling water and his screams were muffled as his throat filled with lava. The guards stood around laughing and taking bets on how long it would take for him to die. I screamed and tried to claw my way to save him, but no one could hear or see me. I was insignificant. I was invisible. As Alex was sinking beneath his boiling grave, the taste of bile filled my mouth. Waking up with an urge to vomit, I quickly ran to the bathroom, making it just in time. I hate how this life not only steals your waking days, but your dreams too.

Forcing the nightmare from my mind and entering his room, I see Alex standing in front of the window. Unprepared for such a sight, I pause, admiring the effect the warm light has on his bare skin. My eyes fall over the healed lash marks along his back and I'm struck with the understanding that I hate his father for causing him pain.

"Good evening, Samantha. How are you?"

My face flushes with embarrassment at the realization of being caught. *Fantastic.* Thankful for the cover of the evening light, I innocently walk over and carefully inspect his burn. There's new red skin already forming a dry protective layer over the wound, which is good.

"I'm fine, how are you feeling?" *Too hurried Sam, now he knows you're nervous.* I glance up at him to see if I'm right, only to be met by his smiling eyes. Grabbing the aloe infused ointment, I begin smoothing it over the new skin. I can sense him watching me as I work.

"I'm good," he pauses, "though I think your attentive care has a lot to do with that." His low-pitched voice doesn't travel far before tickling my ears. The nearness of him shakes me as I finish my increasingly difficult task. *Why am I so aware of him?* Quickly gathering up the supplies, I fumble with the gauze, nearly dropping it into the wash basin. Clearing my throat, I place the items in his hands, feeling the edges of his fingers slightly curling around mine.

"Since you're doing so well, I think you can manage

on your own from now on. Just don't forget to use the compress first, and then the aloe," I quip.

As I turn to walk away, he tugs my hand and pulls me back towards him.

"Thank you, Samantha." His voice is low and tender, awakening me to his own insecurity.

I feel my armor falling away as I offer him a little piece of me, "It's Sam, you can call me Sam."

"Thank you, Sam," he whispers into my hand as he gently kisses it, pulling me even closer now.

My heart races as my eyes seek to find the ruse. This can't be true. But when my eyes find his, my heart flips in understanding; it is true.

He takes a small step towards me, drawing me into his arms, and I let him. "Thank you," he repeats. Only this time, I know he means more than me taking care of him.

I wordlessly nod my head against his chest, overcome by the familiar scent I have come to know as Alex Pressed against his bare skin, I close my eyes, immersing myself in woodsy chamomile as it wafts off him beyond the peppermint from his dressing. It floods my senses and I feel safe here, enfolded in Alex's arms.

"Sam," he repeats softly, trying out my name. "I like it."

I laugh, at least that's what it was supposed to be, "Thanks. My sister gave it to me when she was three. She decided Samantha was too long to 'lub', so she called me Sam, and it's kind of stuck in my family ever since."

I feel the breath of his laughter on my head. "Well, thanks for sharing it with me," he offers as he slowly releases me and shifts his body away.

What did I do wrong? I wonder, already missing the

nearness of him.

"My brother Micah did something like that, only he was four. One night, when our mom was tucking him in, she told him she loved him. He stopped her and very seriously asked, "What about when you die? What happens to your love then?" A look of pride and adoration flutters across Alex's face. "His mind has always worked in bigger ways, so this wasn't too out of the ordinary for him. Mom just leaned down, and very seriously told him that she would love him forever and always, not even death could stop love."

Respecting the space he needs to visit this memory, I stand in silence, as I listen about a woman I never knew, and desperately wish I had.

He smiles as he continues to tell the story. "Well, Micah's little brain heard what she said, and he told our mom, 'I love you Mom, forever and always… even after you die.' I remember her stifling a giggle before brushing his wild hair out of his face and leaning in and whispering it back. It became their little thing, until she died." He runs his hand through his hair, as though to smooth the pain from his memory. "He still tells her every night that he loves her, even after she died. Then, I became his safe place, and it became our thing too."

Struggling to find the right words to this immensely personal moment, I fidget with the edge of my shirt. "It's hard being away from them, isn't it?" It's more of a statement than a question that needs answering.

He quietly nods his head with a somber smile.

Understanding the comfort of solitude, I slip out of his room and solemnly walk to my own. With memories of Julia's bubbly personality, my parents, and Alex swirling in my mind, I decide now is a good time for us to be alone.

Retrieving my GG's journal, I lie on my bed, desperately needing her wisdom. I open the pages, turning them to the familiar passage I'm seeking…

Today I discovered the man I'm going to marry! I say discover because I have known him my whole life. Can you believe it? I guess love sometimes has a funny way of creeping up on you. I always imagined love would come like a summer's rain, suddenly and exciting! But that's not how it happened with Mitchell. No, He was patient and kind. He was willing to wait for me and invest in "us", before there was even an "us" to invest in. He knows about Bennette and is excited to be his Father. I only wish Mom and Dad were here to see us get married. I'll soon be Brylie Marie James-Wells, and Benny will be, Bennette Lee James-Wells. I know it's long, but it's a strong name, filled with love. How did I get so lucky? It's funny, I would've never imagined spending the rest of my life with Mitch, but now I can't imagine my life without him…

Her words turn in me as I consider how impossible it is, that she and I live in two completely different worlds and times, yet we share the same story. My feelings have changed so much for Alex since our marriage that it frightens me. I wrongly misjudged him for so long, thinking he was like his father, but he's not. Alex is kind, thoughtful, and strong. I'm not just talking about his physical strength, there is a quiet confidence about him as well.

I wasn't planning to give Alex my name tonight, but I'm glad I did. When he called me Sam, it felt natural; it felt right. I have never had the courage to be so intimate with anyone before, but it was easy with him. My hand warms at the memory of his tender kiss and I softly touch my lips, remembering the longing I felt to feel his lips on mine. I don't know if I love Alex, but I do know I care for him, and I'm open to the idea of love.

11
Viruses

Sam:

THUMP! THUMP! THUMP!

As the pounding on the front door pulls my foggy brain out of sleep, I impulsively jump out of bed. Forgetting about my grandmother's journal, the loud thud as it falls to the floor, awakens every nerve in my body. With its awakening comes the fear, and then the panic. Scooping it up, I race to the closet and quickly pull back the baseboard. As my trembling hands clumsily shove the book into its hidey hole, my fingers fumble with the task it so desperately needs to complete. As I finally secure the board in place, Alex speaks.

"What's going on, Sam?"

My chest aches with the increased pounding of my already erratic heart. He saw me! The anxiety of uncertainty threatens to paralyze me with its tingling spreading beyond my chest and into my arms and legs. Slowly, I stand and turn to face his judgment. Where I thought anger would reside, I am met with an expression of betrayal. "I'm sorry," I whisper. It's all I can manage before the debilitating fear reaches my legs and anxiety prevails as the victor. Frozen in place, I'm helpless prey to the incoming Singuri whose thundering footsteps are now making their way up the stairs. With a panicked look, Alex's eyes dart from me to the floorboard and then back to me again. An almost primal expression shifts into place as Alex grabs me and pulls me away from the closet. I was wrong about him: he is just like his father. My delicate feelings for him fracture in this moment of clarity. *How could I be so naive?*

Instead of forcing me in front of him for the ultimate betrayal, he positions himself in front of me, shielding me from what's coming. The door flies open and the Singuri break into my room. Alex's body goes tense, revealing muscles I didn't know he had. My terrified mind desperately wonders if his physique is intimidating to the guards at all.

"Is there something we can help you with?" Alex sarcastically challenges.

This again…has he gone mad? Eyeing him with my unasked questions, I realize he's deflecting the attention from me and onto him, and it works.

Without a word, the nearest guard steps forward and strikes the side of Alex's face with the butt of his gun, knocking him to his knees. As the blood trickles from the newly formed gash along his brow, they jerk him to his feet laughing. And then they grab me. The moment their hands touch me, Alex fights against his captors, shoving one into the wall and throwing his elbow into another.

"Get your hands off her!" he growls through the throng of new guards surrounding him.

His demand is met with a solid strike to the gut, toppling him to the ground.

"He's mine!" The proclamation comes from the guard on the receiving end of Alex's elbow. As he approaches Alex's prone body on the floor, he kicks him in the stomach.

"Leave him alone!" I cry.

Turning his sickening grin towards me, he simply starts laughing. Then without warning, I feel the sting of his hand across my face, leaving a burning sensation on my cheek. As the slight taste of metal invades the corner of my mouth, I'm certain my lip is split too.

"Look at these two. Aren't they quite the mouthy pair," he taunts, and another round of laughter fills the room.

"Maybe they need a lesson in manners," he continues. He steps back towards Alex, who is now forced into a kneeling position by two other guards. With the quietness of the onlookers' anticipation, the buzzing of his electrified baton hums through the air as he prods Alex with it. Helplessly, I watch as his body jerks and contorts to the current being pushed through him.

"Stop! Please!" My pleading only encourages the devil to point the baton at me.

"See, now I thought you would have learned your lesson from watching your boy here experience this fun little toy of mine." A mixture of hunger and amusement gleam from his hollow eyes. "But I guess all you Simpletons are really just that stupid." He waves the unlit baton in front of my face before his devilish grin sends its own warning of electricity through me. Drawing his weapon down to the hem of my neckline, he caresses it against my exposed collar bone. With his eyes leading the path, he slowly begins to draw it further down. My skin burns from the unwanted touch.

"ENOUGH!" The lead Singuri barks. "If you don't get it together BOY, I will be using my baton on you in places the sun don't shine! Now put it away!"

Deflated of his anticipated fun, the devil puts his

baton back in its holster at his side and begrudgingly complies with his orders.

"It's bad enough that we have to haul his semi-conscious body down the stairs, don't add hers." His commander continues. "And since you created this problem," he tilts his head toward Alex's slowly recovering form, "you can haul him to the shuttle."

Before I can relish in this turn of events, he speaks up again. "And I'll be right behind you, keeping you, and her," now tilting his head in my direction, "in line." His commanding tone leaves no room for questioning. The devil guard falls into line, with one hand grabbing Alex's arm, pulling him toward the door.

As the Commander walks up next to me, his overwhelming presence makes my blood run cold. "Move it," he commands. Fearfully, I obey.

"Where are you taking us?" I desperately ask, already knowing I won't get an answer.

Dragging us outside, we are joined by a small squad of guards. The Commander organizes a perimeter around us and begins parading down the street. We are being treated as though we're an example for others to learn from; but no charges are being called out. I don't understand why they're doing this. We haven't done anything wrong, that they know of, at least. Then it dawns on me, they're The Order; they don't need a cause. With no other options, we continue moving forward, heading directly for the Singuri substation. As we round the corner, my insides twist with the recognition of the sleek, silver shuttle with an unmistakable 'O' on it. This shuttle is used only by The Order. My breath catches as my legs freeze. This just went from bad to impossibly worse. The Commander beside me shoves me into compliance. Climbing aboard the shuttle feels like we've just climbed into our own coffins, which is probably not far from the truth. As the devil guard pushes Alex into a seat, I sit next to him, grabbing his hand for strength.

"Are you okay?" I whisper.

He doesn't answer, but he also doesn't let go of my hand.

I can only guess at his thoughts now that he knows my deadly secret. The unexpected weight of loss settles over me as we sit in silence, awaiting the shuttle's deliverance to an unknown end. Desperate for understanding, my mind feverishly reflects on the past few minutes, and I realize, they didn't search the house. Confirming that they must not know about the journal, my heart settles its hummingbird pace, relieving the ringing in my ears. Despite continuing to replay the events over in my head, the reason for the Singuri remains a mystery.

All too soon we find ourselves in the heart of The Order and come to a stop at the top of the watch tower. *We're not supposed to be up here,* my frantic mind acknowledges. Alex and I are escorted off the shuttle and down the open corridor towards the looming building ahead. As we enter the terrarium like foyer, my eyes continuously scan the area for a possible escape route. Terrified, I only see glass windows surrounding the entire circumference of the room. As we draw closer to the center of the room, my eyes settle on a giant statue of a scroll, with the names of each founder boldly etched into it. Alex and I look at each other, silently communicating that there is something more going on here. Nudged on, we're led to a room like the one we were married in, only this room is grander in every way, and more sterile than the previous one. Stumbling on my next step, my brain is trying to grasp what my eyes are seeing.

"What are…How did…"

My unfinished questions are silenced as the horror of finding my family standing in the middle of the room sinks in as truth. They must have brought them in before us. Scanning each one of their faces, my heart drops at the sight of Julia. She has a bruise on her cheek, her hair is disheveled, and the strap of her dress is torn. An unspeakable rage fills me and all I want to do is protect her from these monsters. Forgetting everything around us, I run to her, throwing my arms around her mute form in an attempt to shield her. As she numbly stands there the same devil guard commands us to separate, but in this moment, he is nothing to me. As he draws near to forcibly make us comply, I hear Alex growl, "Leave them alone." I'm stunned at the fierceness in his voice as each word rolls with authority through his clenched jaw. Glancing toward him, I watch as his warning is met with yet another blow, only this time to his kidneys. Curse the devil guard! As Alex's body folds over in pain, I hold Julia even tighter with the blood-lust eyes of the guard boring into me.

"That's enough!" The stern voice of the Singuri Commander echoes throughout the room. "I'm done dealing with your mistakes!" Pulling his own electrified baton out, he shocks the troublesome guard in the groin. Collapsing him to the ground, in what I can only hope to be excruciating pain, I fight hard to keep my face stone still. "Get him out of my sight," he commands another Singuri in the wings. Jumping into action, he signals for a fellow guard to help him scoop their downed comrade from the floor. The looks on their faces tell me they're familiar with his pain. The disheveled devil guard looks from Alex and then to Julia and me. It's then I notice a scratch mark across his face that I hadn't seen before.

As he shifts his challenging gaze from me to his Commander, I watch him struggle to contain the furious rage building inside. With one last look of disdain, he forces himself to comply with his orders. Directing his attention and energy ahead, he turns and slowly hobbles away.

Free of his oppression, my mind turns its attention to the Singuri Commander. He knows what's behind the scratch on the devil's face. Something big happened tonight before we met up here and I need to know what it is. Locking eyes with me for only a split second, I catch a glimpse of what would be a shadow of remorse in any other person, but not him, he's a Singuri. He looks away from me as he clears his throat, not giving anything away. Frustration and fear compete for first place in my emotions as I shift my gaze to my parents. Fear takes the lead as I see rage burning in them like I have never seen before. More frightening is the pain that overshadows it. I slip from Julia to my parents, hugging my mother first and then my father. He flinches. Something's wrong? It's then I see the blood staining the back of his tattered shirt.

"What happened?"

As his hands clench into fists, my mother answers for him. "Before they collected us, they went for your brother." She stops to swallow her already dry mouth before continuing. "Matthew knew something wasn't right, so when they came to collect him and his family, he tried to stop them…" Her hand flutters to her mouth as a look of despair fills her eyes. I hadn't even thought of Matthew and his family; it's been so long since we've seen him, and they're so far away. Looking into her eyes searching for the words she can't speak, the anguish of understanding settles in. They killed him, along with his wife and kids too.

"No." The word soundlessly escapes my lips as my

heart pounds within me, over and over, pumping the hate to every part of my body. I look at my father, and then to Julia in her tattered state. Now I can see the complete picture of the pandemonium playing out in my head.

"I'm going to kill them." The words quietly slip out under my breath, a venomous promise I intend to keep.

I don't know when or how, but Alex is standing there beside me, gently holding me back from the red that has filled my vision as my hate for The Order grows. Gripping my arms tighter, I hear him whisper in my ear, "not now Sam. In time." His promise snaps me out of my haze, and I look at him questioningly, *what do you mean, in time?* I can see he knows something I don't, and I want to demand he tell me, but now is not the moment. Biting my tongue, I rest myself in his confidence and slowly defuse my desire for revenge.

The door opens and in steps a panel of Sovereigns. All dressed in the same deep plum color. I recognize one of the members as the woman who married Alex and me.

"What's she doing here?" I ponder aloud.

"I was just thinking the same thing." Alex agrees.

Prompted by the guards, we all turn and face them. The man in the middle of the bench begins to speak.

"I imagine you're wondering why you're here; we are wondering the same thing ourselves. During the new DNA testing for marriage, an interesting thing happened that required us to open our old records. Upon review, we discovered this isn't the first time an irregular reading has cropped up in your line. We could not assume it was an anomaly, which is why we took samples from you this evening."

What? They did? I look over to my family again, only to be met by their focused faces, prompting me to return my attention to the Sovereigns.

"It would seem, Mr. Wells, despite your last name, you are a descendant of The Order, and by blood, so is your family."

What? My head begins to spin. *How can that be?* As we all stand there, too stunned to speak, another member of the panel speaks up. Despite the unmasked anger that tints her voice, I recognize her immediately.

"We would like an explanation of how this came to be. This simply cannot go unchecked."

With the shocked silence looming before us, my father finally steps forward, "I don't know." Insufficient as it is, it's the only answer he has to offer.

Unpleased by his response, the panel begins discussing among themselves the different possibilities and solutions. Then it dawns on me; I know. The night my grandmother was raped, she didn't see her attacker. It must have been a descendant of The Order. *What do I do?* I can't tell them I read this in her journal, or they'll kill us all for sure. If I don't tell them, they might still kill us, or they might not since we are descendants of their precious line. Debating over what action to take, a gavel slams down, ceasing my indecisiveness. I'm too late. They've already come to a verdict.

"Since no one can account for this curious turn of events, we must deal with the situation as though it could be a virus. You will be escorted to the compound of the Singuri guard where a further investigation will be carried out and a solution to the matter will be determined."

Yeah right, an investigation. We've already been labeled a virus, and we all know your solution for that, a sentence of death. Mom, Dad, Julia, Alex, and me are all surrounded by armed Singuri guards. My mind goes numb with the knowledge that we're about to die.

I barely feel my feet moving as we're led back to the shuttle and delivered to the guards on board. My parents sit together and Alex, curiously, behind them. Julia sits across the aisle and up a couple seats, distancing herself from them. Knowing this will be the last time I see her; I settle in next to Julia holding her close and acting as her barrier from what's to come.

"I love you Jewels," I whisper to her as she rests her body into the curve of my arm. As her eyes fall shut, I sit still so as not to disturb the small bit of peace she has found with me. As my eyes wander over to Alex and my parents, I see them discreetly whispering to one another. Remorsefully, I wonder if they're still trying to figure out from where the tainted blood came. Averting my eyes back to Julia, I see the swollen bruise on her cheek, and fear what this night took from her. Turning my thoughts to our surroundings, I look out the window, fruitlessly trying to see where we're going. It's no use, the shuttle is moving too fast for me to make out any shapes in the dark.

As the time passes, my hope dies more with it. I sit thinking about the last time I was on the bus, and my prayer. I know things didn't turn out the way I had wanted, but neither did Alex. I don't know what else to do, so I follow Brylie's lead and pray once again.

The shuttle glides to a stop and I see the incinerator only a few hundred feet away. With my heart pounding, I nudge my sister so we can exit the shuttle, ready to run. I watch curiously, as Alex quickly pushes himself before us, while my parents wait behind. Something is happening. As we stand, my father leans over and whispers, "I love you girls. Look out for one another." With a swift kiss on our heads, he steps around my mother, allowing her in front of him.

Confused by what he said, I pause to look at him before scooting out in the aisle in front of my mom, but then her strong hands begin shoving us toward the door. Everything is happening too quickly; I can't make sense of it all. Simultaneously Dad rushes the rear two guards while Alex knocks out the engineer. Mom starts screaming for Alex to go while pushing Julia and I out the door with him, and then locks it shut with them still inside. Through the glass she quickly tells me, "I love you," and turns to charge the guards who are now overcoming my father. I watch through the door as my parents' wrestle with the guards, keeping them from sounding the alarm. Panic overwhelms me, and I begin screaming, "NO! Please! You have to come with us!"

Alex pulls me away, "Come on Sam, we have to run."

"Alex! My parents!" I scream in shock.

"SAM! You have to help Julia. We need to run, NOW!"

The intensity of his voice awakens me. I grab my sister and we run for the trees. No one speaks, we just run as fast as our legs will carry us. My lungs burn as we push forward into the cold, dark night. Minutes or seconds pass by, I don't really know. Two shots ring out in the silence of the night, followed by the sounding alarm. This could only mean my parents are dead. My breath catches as I struggle to block this knowledge from my mind and keep running. I don't have time to grieve now. Pulling Julia along with me, I follow Alex blindly through the woods. With nothing but the moon to light our way, I'm amazed to see Alex moving with such ease, moving like he's done this before. My muscles scream in protest, and my lungs are on fire from the unfamiliar exercise. I ignore them both and force myself to keep going, eventually they turn numb

With the sound of the alarm long lost in the distance, Julia pulls away from me, "Sam, I can't go anymore."

Her breathless plea pulls me to a stop. Looking over, I find her lying on the ground curled up in a ball, her body shaking in small spasms. Unable to speak, I crouch down next to her and look at Alex, my eyes pleading with him. Understanding her need, he looks around and cautiously concedes to rest for the night. Sitting near Julia on the ground, I can now see her eyes are red and swollen from crying, reminding me of everything we have lost today. I can no longer be strong for the both of us and I crumble into tears of my own. Feeling everything I wasn't allowed to feel before, our sobs become a united song of muffled sorrow. I want to scream with rage, but I can't; that could give us away to any Singuri still searching. I watch as Julia's tears of mourning turn into tears of anger. She looks at me crying, "They hurt me, Sam," confirming what I feared. Hearing her pain reignites the fire in me and shoves aside my own grief. Pulling her close, I gently rock back and forth, trying to soothe her. I know I can't take away this pain, but I wish with every fiber in me that I could. As her body relaxes into a depleted sleep, I feel the weight of her pain bearing down on me. I curl my body protectively around hers and slip into a fitful sleep of my own.

12
The Ocean

Sam:

"I'm sorry, but I think we need to start moving." I awaken to Alex's soft voice just as the sunlight starts to peek over the horizon. Blinking away the heaviness that refuses to let me go, I stretch my legs in defiance to its hold. My eyes open to discover a blanket of leaves carefully covering Julia and me as we slept. *Alex.* Warmth radiates from my heart in response to his kindness but slowly ebbs away as my waking mind begins piecing together the events from the night before. Images flash through my head of him leading us into the trees and my parents charging the guards. Why would they do that? My heart squeezes to near crushing as another memory plays in my mind. A memory of Alex and my parents talking right before—

"You knew, didn't you?" My accusation is barely above a whisper as my confounded mind can't decide if I'm angry with him or my parents for their death.

"Yes." His steady eyes never leave my face as he confesses his sin to me.

With the weight of his words, these once sheltering

leaves now feel like a thousand knives of betrayal pricking into my skin. My confusion burns with the need for an explanation.

"Why?"

Shifting his body closer towards me, I instinctively lean away. I see the effect my action has on him as his shoulders fall under the weight of it, but I'm too hurt by his betrayal to care.

Dropping his gaze, he slowly releases his own breath of regret. "They wanted me to tell you to keep rising, and that you would know what it means. I'm sorry Sam."

My strangled heart ruptures at the message in their final words. Turning my face away to hide my falling tears, I look down at Julia as she sleeps. With the soft morning glow illuminating her face, I drink in her peacefulness as understanding comes; they fell, so we could rise.

Oh, Mom and Dad, it hurts. I hear you…but it hurts.

Sliding my body softly away from Julia, I force my aching muscles and heart to function. Tiptoeing away, I signal for Alex to follow. "What's the plan?" I ask just out of earshot of her.

Afraid of making too much noise, he walks closer to me as he answers. "We keep heading towards the ocean where the refugees live in hiding. We can find shelter with them."

Colored with suspicion, I look at Alex, realizing there's so much I still don't know about him. "How—?"

"Ocean rotation," he answers, already knowing my question. Picking up a small stone and turning it over in his hand, he continues. "When we worked the ocean rotation, we wouldn't always fish and scout for things, we would find people, too." The struggle on his face is easy to read, as he picks through his memories trying to decide what to say next.

"Sometimes they would already be dead when we found them, and other times the Singuri would shoot them, but only after interrogation."

The chill shooting through my body reflects the distant look on his face as the gruesome depiction paints itself in our minds.

"I'll never forget the way their blood stained the sand…" He shakes his head trying to clear it of the unwanted image, and as the memory shifts into something different, a smile begins to play at the corner of his lips. "Every once in a while, though, someone would be lucky enough to get away. The Singuri would make us hunt them until it was time to leave, completely wasting our day of rotation." He chuckles then, and I join him. Wasting Singuri time is always a win. "We could never figure out where they went to hide," he continues. "But once, I did find someone. She wasn't much older than my sister was, when they took her life, and the fear in her eyes was the same as Joy's. I found her hiding in a small pile of driftwood and seaweed and encouraged her not to be afraid. I told her I was going to draw the guards away and instructed her to stay hidden. I could see she was terrified I would give her up." His jaw tenses with the very idea of it and with renewed conviction, looks at me.

The intensity in his eyes calms my captivated heart as the honey-colored windows into his soul reveal the passion of the man standing in front of me, and with this revelation my prior feelings of betrayal melt in the understanding of him.

"Sam, I could *never* do that, to her, or to anyone." The unforgiveness in his voice is unmistakable and I recognize his declaration for what it is; he is not his father.

"I believe you." My quiet voice is a wisp dancing loudly in the thickness of this pivotal moment. I watch as my affirming words lift the heavy weight I placed on his shoulders only moments ago, as he offers me a gentle smile.

Turning his face in the direction of the ocean, he continues his story. "I don't know if she did as I instructed because she believed me, or because she was too scared to do anything else, but as she lay silently in her shelter of driftwood, I turned away and sprinted towards the ocean." A mischievous look of humor fills his face as he concludes his tale. "Let's just say, I decided I needed a bath, and took a dip in the ocean."

I can feel the shock on my own face, quickly followed by the heat of blushing at the very idea, "Naked?" I ask incredulously.

Now he's really laughing. "Yeah. The Singuri were equally surprised. They didn't like my idea much, but rules are rules, and they had to follow in after me. It was the best community swim I've ever taken!"

With the many different images swirling around in my head, my mind settles in on one with three or four guards trying to catch a very naked and slippery Alex in the ocean. It's too much to keep from chuckling. As the sound of our laughter pierces the veil of tension, the disbelief of his actions further confirms my theory of his lack of fear for the Singuri. How is that possible, to be free of fear from such devils.

I would have never known about this other life by the ocean if Alex didn't tell me. I understand now, why my own father and brother wouldn't talk about it either, or why I wasn't allowed to go. The women are not permitted on the beach rotation. We must work the miserable cotton fields instead. I never imagined people living in secret at the shores though.

My thoughts are broken at the sound of Julia crying

my name. "Sam…where are you, Sam?" She's afraid I've left her. Dashing to her side, I begin smoothing the hair from her battered face, revealing bruises more prominent than the night before. "Shh Julia, it's okay. I'm right here. Shh, you're safe." Speaking in a soothing voice I continue to stroke her head as she opens her eyes and looks at me, then at Alex and back at me again. Whether her nightmare was only in her dreams or in the reliving of it, I continue to comfort her.

"You're okay Julia, it's just me and Alex. You're safe with us." I calmly reassure her.

As the sleep ebbs from her eyes, she finally wakes up enough to see I'm telling the truth and grabs onto me as though I'm her lifeline.

Alex and I exchange a look of compassion for Julia, and an understanding of our mutual hatred for The Order.

"Sam, do you think it will ever get better?" she quietly asks.

I can only think of one answer, and it's not my own, "Yes…I do. You are worth so much more than what you feel right now. Just remember that Jewels, okay."

She nods her head and weaves her fingers into mine, just like we used to do back at home. Only for a few moments, do we steal the sounds of the morning to ourselves. The crickets are starting to fade from their nightly symphony, seeking shelter from the newly awakened birds searching for their morning meal. Their chirps communicate to each other in a friendly good morning song, or a happy exclamation of their recently devoured delight. The breeze dances through the leaves of the high branches, releasing a few remaining drops of dew. It truly is serene in the woods, but even I know, the serenity doesn't last long out in the open.

"You ready to go Jewels?" I gently nudge her with my

whisper.

Closing her eyes one final time, she takes in a deep breath of the fresh morning air. "One more minute," she answers with a smile.

Smiling down at her sunlit face, my heart squeezes at the familiarity of our parents etched within her beautiful features. "Okay Princess, it's time to go." She smiles as I use the familiar name our brother, Matthew, used to call her. Julia was his Princess, and I was his Darling girl. Tucking the sweet memory back into its treasure box, I can't allow that pain right now.

"All right Darling. If you say so." Her smile widens with recognition.

She slowly starts to stand, and I rise with her. "Okay Alex, I think we're finally ready."

Taking the opportunity to tease Julia one last time, she only glances at me, then turns her attention to Alex, indicating she's ready.

Walking hand in hand, we follow Alex's lead. As he continues to confidently guide us on a trail only known to him, I watch as he handles the hike with ease. "How are you in such good shape?" I blurt out. Not believing I just said that out loud, I curse my curiosity for always getting me in trouble. Maybe I wasn't loud enough for him to hear?

Alex simply looks at me from over his shoulder and grins, so much for hoping he didn't hear me. Turning my gaze to the treetops, I study the eucalyptus and evergreen trees towering over us. The effect of the branches filtering the rays of light that find their way through is almost magical. As the exposing sun continues to climb its way up into the sky, the magic begins to fade, and I begin imagining noises around us.

"How much longer until we reach the ocean?"

"It's about another mile or so," Alex answers. "Are you both okay?"

"Yeah, we're all right." I try to disguise my growing anxiety as I look to Julia, "We're just eager to see the ocean, right Jewels?" Smiling, I gently squeeze her hand, reminding her that I'm here and she returns my smile with one of her own.

I feel the cool air changing with a sweet unfamiliar scent riding in its breeze. Alex was right; it's not much further ahead. My pace quickens with each step closer to the cliffs. I can hear the ocean growing louder with its odd rumblings, reminiscent to the sound of distant thunder. As we break through the tree line, spread out before us is the most captivating vision I have ever seen. A never-ending span of blue hues, and white, reflecting the shimmering sun off the constantly moving surface. I'm mesmerized by the rhythm of the waves, rolling and tumbling with so much power. They do it again and again, looking as though they're racing to be the first to shore. As it fades into a calm sheet over the sand, I'm in awe of how it gently retreats back onto itself once again. The ocean I see is nothing like the one Alex described. I stand on the edge of the cliff, breathing in this beautiful vision of freedom.

13
Mary

Alex:

"Alex, thank you for loving her enough."

These are the last words Ben Wells spoke to me before he and his wife were killed, and I know what he meant by them. I love Sam enough to help them die so she could live, and most likely lose her at the same time. In fact, he was counting on it, and he was right. Knowing my part in Sam's loss has created a furious guilt inside me, but I will gladly take it if it means she lives. If there was any other way to get her and her sister out alive, I would have done it, but there wasn't. Her parents knew this truth before I did and made me promise to take care of them, an easy promise to make.

I allow my eyes to drift to her small frame standing on the cliffs' edge. One would think there's not much to her, looking fragile enough to be carried away by the wind. But I know better. I've seen how Sam wills herself to be strong even when she doesn't feel strong: like in the rotation fields that grind you into the ground, or the classrooms where they teach us that we're nothing, in the hall at the Hub when she didn't run, our forced marriage and her apology, even in the forbidden embrace she gave her sister in front of the Sovereigns and their guards. Each memory flitting through my mind speaks of her remarkable strength. Now, on the heels of her parents' death, she carries the weight of both her and her sister's suffering on her shoulders. I know she doesn't realize how special she is, which only makes me love her more. To lose her would be like taking the air I breathe. She's a part of me now, more than ever.

As she pulls her arms around herself, I step closer, silently offering my support. We both stand here, inches apart, watching the waves continuing to tumble over each other. The ocean breeze catches the loose hair at her temple. She reaches back to tuck them behind her ear, and I breathe in the sight of her. My heart beats for her alone. Slowly leaning back into me, she rests against my chest as her head tucks perfectly beneath my chin. "It's beautiful, isn't it?" she nearly whispers.

I practically hum in agreement, because to me, she's more beautiful than any ocean.

I long to stay here absorbing this new wonder with her, but the uncertainty of where the Singuri are demands we find the refugees soon.

"We should probably go. I don't know how far behind us they are." My voice is low and apologetic.

Understanding my meaning, she reluctantly pulls away. Putting a faint smile into place, she walks over to her sister, catching her by the hand, and playfully asks if I'm ready. There she is, being strong again.

As we walk along the top of the ridge, I spot the thin trail leading down to the shore and we begin our descent, careful not to slip and fall over the edge. As the bottom draws near, I hear multiple footsteps approaching.

"Hurry! We need to get to the beach before we're

seen," I warn.

Hastily taking the last few steps into the safe covering of the cliffs, we hear them standing just above us.

"Search everywhere! We don't leave until they are found!" The guard barks out.

Racing through my mind are the memories of all the people they did find. I can't let that happen to us. I won't let that happen. I lean forward to pick up a rock, the only weapon I have, and I hear a soft whisper from behind us.

"Psst. Over here."

Cautiously turning, I vaguely see an older woman standing in the shadows of the cave.

"Quickly, follow me," she urges.

With nowhere else to go, we sink into the deep hole of the bluff, discovering a faux wall made of a reflective barrier that looks, and somehow feels, much like the actual earth outside. She slides it open, allowing us into the safety of its hollow. It's cool and damp inside, also dark, very, very dark. The only light we have is from the odd torch this stranger holds as she leads us forward through a maze of tunnels, with the sound of the ocean growing farther away. The levels in our path keep changing as we twist and turn our way into the unknown. What did I walk us into? As we round another corner, I can finally see light dancing inside the cave walls. I hear a sigh of relief escape from Sam as the narrow tunnel opens, allowing me to walk protectively beside her and Julia. The closer we get to our destination, the more prominent the light becomes. As the woman leads us through an opening, it spills into a large cavern filled with people. As my eyes adjust, I realize they have all stopped what they're doing and are looking at us, equally unsure of the situation.

"Where are we?" I finally ask her. Just then, two men

who carry themselves as the Singuri enter the room. From the corner of my eye, I see Sam pull Julia behind her. "What's going on?" I demand.

"Relax. We're on your side." So says the liar.

Noting the faint scar on the side of his neck where his identifying tattoo should be, I highly doubt it. "You don't look like it. You look like one of them." I spit back, tilting my head in the direction we just came from.

Neither of us say anything as we suspiciously eye each other. I must have passed his inspection because he continues to explain.

"That's because I used to be, but I haven't been for a long time. You have nothing to fear from us. You can trust me when I say you're safe here."

Trust him. Is he serious? I look back at Sam and Julia, then to the crowd now gathered around us and realize we don't have much of a choice. "Okay, let's say I believe you. What is this place?" I need answers, and he seems to be the one who has them.

Relaxing with me, he offers, "I'm Thomas, and this is Shane."

I look to the side of him and find the man he is gesturing to, another shadow of the Singuri.

"You're in the caverns of the refugees. This is our home. We've all been where you are now, running for your lives. I know you're wondering how that can be, since I was Singuri, but please allow me to explain."

I begrudgingly nod my head in consent.

"I have never agreed with The Order, or the life of the Singuri. About four years ago I started smuggling people here that were marked for death. Shane and I both worked the same shift, so we were able to keep it hidden for some time, that is, until about a year ago. I'm still not sure how, but we were discovered the last night we were bringing people out to safety, and we've lived here ever since. Every day we look for more survivors, and today, Mary found you." He indicates to the woman who led us here. Turning the questions around on me, he protectively asks, "Now it's your turn. Who are you and why are you here?"

Before I can answer, Julia belligerently yells, "Because of you and your kind! Taking whoever and whatever you want! And then making up some stupid lie to kill my family!" She lashes out at him, but Sam holds her back, and all I can do is watch as Julia's anger gives way to bitter tears. The room is dead silent, as the reality of her situation hits home for more than one person here. They know her pain.

Thomas watches her with a shameful rage evident on his face, "I'm sorry…" he gruffly manages, then turns and walks away, taking Shane with him.

Sam comforts her sister, as Mary leads us to another room in the cavern where they serve food from a large open fire pit. My eyes follow the smoke rising from the fire, tumbling up to the ceiling into an air vent.

"Aren't you worried about it being seen?"

She smiles at my worry, then answers, "Oh no, Honey, we're too far into the hillside for them to track it here. The smoke usually disperses throughout the underground inlets, before it can get that far," she shrugs her shoulders, "but if any does escape, it's masked by the thick fog and smell of the ocean. The same goes for warming fires, though we usually just cuddle close to keep warm." She says the last part with a chuckle, as she winks at me.

Now that she's talking more, I notice Mary has a slight accent, much like my old neighbor, whose ancestors originated from what used to be the southern United States, though I'm not supposed to know anything about that.

As we continue walking, Mary shows us around our new living quarters, informing us that the caverns were once used as a bunker during the Great Wars. First, we're shown the little alcoves that randomly branch off from the many tunnels serving as private sleeping quarters. Some of the openings are covered by a linen cloth while others are left open to the hall. There are small lights strewn along the upper walls, utilizing the same solar energy as above, lighting our way through the maze. Moving on, she takes us to the water room, and my jaw drops as the sight unfolds before me. An inviting waterfall flows from the mouth of the rocks above. Spilling down into a smaller size pool, occupants enjoy the blue green waters as the steam rises from the surface. I notice some solar stones in the bottom of the swimming hole, and my hand instinctively touches the newly healed scar on my side.

Following the pool with my eyes, it flows into a subtle stream, where I imagine it leads to the sea. Though the air is thick with moisture, I can feel the coolness coming off the waterfall, a welcomed change from the heat permeating from the surface of the pool. As I take it all in, Mary begins to explain.

"This is our only freshwater source. We collect our drinking water using buckets on a pulley system above the falls. Down below, we shower and wash our clothes, sometimes at the same time." She chuckles again at her implication. My eyes travel up to the ceiling where I find a crudely made pulley system of old harvest buckets hanging down from a rope, leading to the edge of the cave wall. My eyes continue further down to the smooth rock surface beneath the waterfall. "We make our own soap using resources from the sea and the surrounding vegetation. It's not the best stuff, but it'll do the trick. Over to your right are some alcoves we use as a place to relieve ourselves; we only ask that you rinse and empty your buckets, downstream."

I can't help but chuckle with her this time.

Moving on, Mary takes us to see the training room, explaining that it's for those who want to learn combat skills, and only those who want to learn. In the middle of the room, I see a couple raised platforms with two occupants practicing their sparring, and beyond that are what appear to be targets. Feeling a twinge of excitement, I'm anxious to practice the defensive moves I gleaned from watching the arrogant Singuri train. What was supposed to serve as an intimidation tactic, taught me skills I shouldn't know. *Idiots.* As we cycle out of the gym, I already know this is my favorite room.

Mary leads on and introduces the next room. "And finally, here is our work area. This is where we create things to help make our lives easier underground. It also serves as our medical room; with what little supplies we have. Most of our remedies are natural, just like they were up top."

Looking around, I see the room is lit by lanterns mounted on the walls, allowing a steady light as though it were daytime. As we round the corner into the second compartment of the room, I see Thomas standing over a makeshift table: there's a map sprawled out and a small group of people gathered around him. I can't see the details of the map, but it looks old with markings drawn all over it.

"This is where we plan our scouting missions, and whatever else Tom and Shane are working on," Mary says. Just then, Tom's head turns as he hears his name. He grabs something from the table and starts walking our way. As he gets closer, I can see what he holds in his hand, a device much like the one they used during our marriage ceremony.

My eyes narrow, still not trusting him, "What's that?"

"We need to remove your ID chip and the tracking device imbedded in it," he explains. He holds out his arm and shows me the ID scar. Eager to remove the invasive tracker, I stretch my arm out and feel a sharp pinch as the device plunges a large bore needle into me.

"How come they didn't find us in the woods when we were escaping?" I ask, mad at myself for not knowing they were tracking us.

"They can only track you so far before our transmitters block the signal; that's why they haven't been able to find us yet."

I flinch as the handheld device begins to burn and then beep, indicating my tracker has been removed. I study the small scar already forming on my arm.

"Once the chip has been removed, the laser seals off the wound to prevent bleeding and infection. You're free and clear now," Tom patiently explains.

Following my lead, Sam steps forward to have her chip removed. She's being brave for her sister again. As her procedure finishes, it's Julia's turn, and with Sam's guidance, she hesitantly steps forward. Uninvited, Shane walks up to offer his assistance and I automatically don't like how eager he is to help. Sam and I share a glance, silently agreeing that he's not welcome here. Tom, who seems more sensitive of Julia's situation, declines his offer, and quietly hands the device to Mary. Noting the considerate thought as something a true Singuri would never do, I can see the difference in Tom. Unfortunately, I cannot say the same for Shane. It's obvious he didn't like the rebuff and saunters off like an idiot, and Tom watches completely unfazed by him. As Mary finishes with

Julia's arm, she concludes our tour.

"Well, that's it, our home sweet home." She says with a smile. She's easy to like.

While Sam and Julia are ushered back to the waterfall room, I decide to hang around with Tom and get a feel for how things are around here. As Tom and I walk around the room, three things become very clear to me. First, and most important, is the fact that Shane does not seem happy with the way things are. He craves more power. Second, Tom is surprisingly a good guy, and someone I think I might be able to trust. I can understand why the people would look to him for leadership. This leads me to my third observation. Tom is the one running this place and seems to have some plans under way. As we head over to the table, I intend to ask him about it, but before I can, Shane walks over and positions himself between us.

"We're needed in the medical area," he interrupts.

Tom looks at me apologetically and excuses himself. As they walk away, Shane looks over his shoulder with an intentional warning that clearly states, *back off!* Obviously, he's trying to establish himself as the next in command and wants to make sure I know that I'm not welcomed here. *That's too bad Shane*, I think to myself; *I'm not a Simpleton so easily intimidated.*

14
Caverns

Sam:

Sitting alone in an alcove, I study the newly formed scar on my forearm. When we arrived at the caverns, Tom told us about the tracking devices that were implanted in our ID chips. I should've known The Order would do something so violating. Thinking through the past twelve days, I cannot believe the change our lives have taken in such a short amount of time. Alex, Julia, and I are now living underground among strangers who share a similar story of survival, fleeing the brutality of The Order.

My heart hurts in knowing how much my family would've loved this place, especially the waterfall. The first thing Julia and I did after our 'grand tour' was soak under the downpour of the water, allowing it to wash away the filth of our journey. I'm thankful Julia is safe with me. I have seen how this place has allowed her the freedom to slowly come to life again. As Julia and I settle into our place here, Alex has been busy discovering the ins and outs of the caverns and meeting with Tom. Despite the scar on his neck, which once boasted his Singuri rank, Alex seems to think Tom is trustworthy. He doesn't say much about Shane. Personally, I have a hard time trusting either of them, especially Shane, who still sports his two-bar tattoo.

Alex showed me this amazing map of the Old World the other day. There were lines drawn to show the new borders of our current world, and parts of the earth completely marked out that no longer exist. When I first saw the map, I was astounded to see how much bigger the world was before the wars, and just as upset to learn that more of the world survived than we were led to believe. Unfortunately, I didn't get to study the map as much as I would have liked because Shane interrupted us. He seems to be good at that more and more lately. His intrusion left me curious about the circled question marks dotted along the expansive blue surfaces of the oceans. Alex said he would take me back another time to look at the map when Shane's away from the cavern. I'm contented in knowing I'll get another chance to study it. I want to learn everything I can that The Order refused to teach us and unlearn the lies that they did teach. I still can't believe how much they withheld, or how much is really gone. We truly are lucky to be alive. It's staying alive that seems to be the hard part now.

Though I prefer to keep to myself, I understand the wisdom in knowing my surroundings. I have pushed myself to meet the people I'm in hiding with and have discovered there are survivors from nearby towns that I never even knew existed. I suspected the world was bigger than what The Order led us to believe, but I have only ever known of Paxton, my hometown, and Kent, where my brother was shipped. I was kept in the dark about the others. Whitley, a town established further inland, is bordered by Riku and Biton. Biton is the newest town to crop up in the last five years. Apparently, we're doing a good job repopulating the earth. Kudos to us, I suppose. Tom says The Order doesn't like for the Simpletons to know just how many towns there are, because if we knew our numbers, we might fight back. He said the fear of an uprising is the true reason for the Simpletons being sterilized. Though I was mind-numbingly angry at this truth, I couldn't help but laugh when he told me this. I can't imagine an uprising. There are too many people who believe the lie of equality, and the rest are too afraid to think differently.

Tom is the leader of the Refugees. I have learned a lot about him in my efforts to get to know those around me. He's twenty-seven and according to the Singuri way, was married at nineteen, then widowed at twenty. I didn't press him on such a sensitive topic. I thought it was bizarre how he used the term 'widow' since he also told me how the Singuri live reckless lives and don't claim family in The Order, only bloodlines. He explained how all Singuri start the training academy at the age of ten, and begin active duty when they are fifteen, and never retire. This revelation only emphasizes my belief that the Singuri are more robot than human. Though Tom, and his father, might just be an exception to that belief. As it turns out, his own father never liked the coldness that was demanded of the Singuri guard, so he secretly raised Tom to respect Simpletons as his equal. Again, he surprised me with this insight. I thought all Singuri were hungry for power, much like Shane. But I must admit, Tom seems like a decent guy. It doesn't mean I trust him; it just means I think he's better than the Singuri. A perfect example is how he doesn't use the knowledge and power the Singuri gave him to rule over others. Instead, he uses it to teach them how to survive. Despite his best efforts, I can still see the years of regret that he carries with him, haunting every decision he makes.

In the evenings, Tom teaches self-defense, weapons, and hand-to-hand combat. Alex participates in these lessons, and he continues to surprise me with his uncanny ability to learn so easily. It took me a little longer to jump in on the training, as I was torn between my excitement to learn and my lack of trust in anyone here. At first, I would only spar with Alex, allowing him to teach me what he had learned. He's a natural teacher; I only wish I could say I was a good pupil, but I found it hard to concentrate. The more time I spent with Alex the more confused I became about him. Instead of learning from his corrections, I would get lost in his gentle touches or guiding hand. Every time he got near, it was like I was hyper aware of him, and my brain couldn't retain anything else. He would try to teach me how to block a punch and all I saw were his sweaty, strong arms. When he would correct my unstable stance, my skin would radiate under the touch of his hands. I was turning into a pathetic mess. Ultimately, I had to swallow my pride and ask Tom to teach me instead. Alex was a little hurt at first, but then Tom clued him in on why I made the change. Now he just smiles at me when we practice. *Thanks a lot, Tom.*

"Hey, you got a minute?"

Startled at the sound of Julia's voice, "You scared me half to death!" I reprimand, as her smiling face pops around the corner of the entryway.

"Sorry," she giggles, then shifts nervously, "but are you free?" The hidden undertone in her voice reveals she has something important to say.

"For you, always," I answer, patting the space beside me.

With a timid smile, she comes in and sits down, fidgeting with the hem of her sleeve.

Allowing the stillness to linger, I patiently wait until she's ready.

"I wanted to talk to you about the night we were taken, if that's okay," she probes.

A small part of me wants to tell her I'm not ready, because my hatred is still simmering beneath the surface, but if she needs to talk about it, I will listen. "Sure," I force myself to respond. Bracing for the horrors of that night, I take a quiet breath and allow her to lead the conversation.

Transforming before my eyes, I watch my sister fold inside herself as she pulls the inner strength needed to relay what's in her heart. She doesn't look at me, only at her fidgeting hands. "They came to the house late at night and used that stupid device to take the samples from us. We didn't know then that they were going for you and Matthew too." She pauses and chews the inside of her cheek, as she wrestles with what she has to say next. "The Singuri who took our blood samples waited to do mine last. After Mom and Dad had theirs done, they were taken outside, and I was left alone with him in the house. At first, I tried to fight while his hand smothered my mouth, but then he hit me so hard I thought I was going to pass out. I wish I had… He pinned me down and told me if I screamed, he would kill them, so I silently let him take me." Her quiet tears slip steadily down her soft cheeks as her pain rips at my soul.

Oh Julia, I am so sorry, my mind cries out before she begins again.

"When he was done, he smiled at me and said, 'That's a good girl' and patted me on my swollen cheek." She closes her eyes against the vileness of this beast while my mind plots its revenge. My stomach churns with hatred and I force myself to swallow the bile in my throat.

"He then took me outside with Mom and Dad. They knew right away what had happened. Dad lost it and charged after the guard, but he knocked Dad to the ground with his electrified baton. That's when the guard laughed and told us about Matthew and his family. Mom began weeping, and I stood there frozen." Her face mimics the memory of the overwhelming horror of that night, transporting me there with her. Then it shifts into a shadow of pride. "I wish you could have seen Dad. He got up and tackled the Singuri guard to the ground. I have never seen him so consumed with rage as he punched the guard over, and over again." She shakes her head in the disbelieving awe we both share in her memory. "That's when the head Singuri came over and ripped Dad away. I don't understand why he didn't just shoot Dad then, but when he saw me, he shoved Dad to the ground. The monster who hurt me was demanding Dad's death, but the Commander told him to shut up, that he had already done enough damage for one night. Then, to appease the Singuri law, Dad was lashed for attacking the guard. From there, we were taken to the tower, and you know the rest." Suffocating silence settles over both of us. *I do know the rest.* Gently reaching for her hand, I hold it in mine, "Jewels, I'm so sorry I wasn't there." It's all I can say. I can't undo the wrong that's been done to her, or to our family. I can only help her through it, and one day, I will find that guard and kill him.

Falling into my thumping chest, the sobs that rack her body shudder through my own. "I just don't understand. Why Sam?! Why did they do this?"

As she cries into me, the guilt of knowing the answer to her question is suffocating. But I can never tell Julia; it will only endanger her more. I must bear this secret alone. Wrapping my arms around her quivering frame, I weep with her. Together, we weep for her injustice, we mourn the loss of our parents, and our brother and his family. Finally, we cry for all the things we can't put into words. We cry until there's no tears left and as the night wears on, her sobs eventually slow down enough to allow her to fall asleep in my arms. Tonight, she is safe with me. Tomorrow, I'm asking Tom to teach me how to shoot a gun.

I wake in the morning to find Julia already gone. She must have snuck out while I was sleeping. Pulling myself from the pile of blankets, I throw my clothes on and head out to find Tom. As I walk past the kitchen, I see Julia with Mary and a group of kids I've seen her hanging out with more and more. Her resilience is amazing.

Rounding the corner, my body collides with Alex, and I'm momentarily distracted by our proximity.

"Sam." Alex confidently smirks at me with his annoyingly cute, quirked eyebrow. "Can I help you?"

With his hand against my back, I feel the heat spreading from his fingertips. "Actually, I was looking for Tom." I feign more confidence than I feel, as I step past him to find the bemused culprit of my increased discomfort. "Hey Tom, I was looking for you. I was hoping you could show me how to shoot today."

Tom looks at Alex, while Alex is looking at me. I'm not surprised my question has caught them off guard, as I have been intentionally avoiding this part of our training. I wasn't ready for it, but that was then.

"I'm ready to learn now, if that's okay with you?" I didn't so much ask, as I questioned his hesitation.

"Well Samantha, if you think you're ready, then I'll be glad to teach you. But can we have lunch first?" he teases, dissipating any residual tension.

"Lunch? I slept that late?" I ask no one in particular. "Yeah, that's probably a good idea. I should eat too."

They look at me realizing for the first time that I just woke up. Though neither one of them say anything, I can see the unasked questions on their faces. With the curious silence lingering around us, we all turn and walk back toward the kitchen together.

Mary, Julia, and the kids are gone now, but in their place is Shane, the last person I want to see. As we sit down to eat a simple lunch of fish and toast, Shane gets up and sits next to Tom.

"What are you guys doing today?" he asks.

I know he doesn't really care about what we're doing, but he does care about *who* we're doing it with.

"I'm taking Samantha to the gun range while Alex works in the medical room today," Tom replies.

"I can help you at the gun range. That way you don't have to jump between two people in instructions," Shane eagerly offers.

He thinks Julia's going to be with us. What an idiot. Like I'd let him anywhere near her. Just as I'm about to tell him what I think about his offer, Tom interjects.

"Aren't you up for the scouting shift today?"

I watch the frustration on Shane's face as he acknowledges his prior responsibility, "Yup."

"Well, you should probably get out there, just in case a refugee comes looking for help," Tom prods with an air of authority. *Good for you, Tom.*

Shane slowly stands and throws a glare in my direction before sauntering away. I doubt my poorly concealed smirk will help improve his sour mood, but I don't really care. I will say, I'm starting to like Tom the more I hang out with him.

As we go our separate ways, Alex wishes me luck on my training and then runs off to the strategy room. *Hmm, I thought Tom said he was working in the medical room today?"*

"All right Samantha, are you ready?"

With Tom's question, a surge of excitement and nerves course through me. "Yes!" I say a bit too loudly.

Tom chuckles before leading us to a weaponry room I didn't even know existed.

"Where did we get all this? And where do I start?" I can't hide the eagerness in my voice as my eyes take in all the different types of guns, a collage of colors and sizes. My eyes fall to a second case, filled with tactical knives and self-defense weapons. The hunger to learn consumes me.

"Impressive, isn't it," he muses.

More like intimidating, but to Tom, I only answer, yes.

Even with my ability to remember things easier than others, my head is whirling with all the new information: 9mm versus a 22, pistol versus revolver, AR-15, shotgun, 45 caliber, M4, automatic versus semi-automatic, hollow point versus full metal jacket, shotgun shell versus buck shot. Then, there's cleaning and maintaining your weapon, the safety features and responsibility of your weapon and the choice you make when discharging it. There is so much to learn my head feels like it's going to explode. By the end of the evening, I have learned about various weapons and their functions, then I'm tested by Tom on my knowledge of them. He seems satisfied, maybe even a little impressed. Now I can pick one to shoot.

An unfamiliar giddiness tingles all over me as my eyes scan the locked case for '*the one*' I'm going to choose. I know I'm not ready for anything big, so at least that narrows it down some.

Hmm…revolver or pistol? I contemplate to myself. My eyes continue to search until they land on a black piece that seems to be calling my name. "How about this one?" I anxiously point to the smaller size pistol near the end of the case.

"And what is that one called?" Tom tests me before allowing me to touch it.

I confidently smile. I know this answer. "It's a Glock 42."

"And?" He presses.

"Glock 42, or G42, is a .380 semi-automatic pistol, with a six-bullet mag capacity. *Unless*, you have an extended mag, which allows for two additional bullets, making a total of eight rounds." I wink at him teasingly.

Tom smiles and nods his head in approval as he unlocks the case. "Now remember, the smaller size does not mean it will have less of a bang. The kickback when it's fired will be bigger than a larger gun because there is less metal to absorb the shock from the bullet firing." He hands me the unloaded weapon and allows me to familiarize myself with the look and feel. It feels right.

"Yes, this is the one," I confirm with a grin.

He hands me the magazine and instructs me to load it with six hollow point bullets for practice. I'm frustrated at how my fingers continue to fumble over something that looked so simple when Tom was doing it. If I want to shoot it, I must be able to load the dang thing.

"Good. Now there's no safety switch on this model, so what do you have to do, or not do, when it is loaded?"

Another stupid question Tom, can't I just shoot it already! That's what my mind is yelling and undoubtedly, what my face is showing, but instead, I answer his question with the respect my weapon demands. "I must keep it disengaged, or the chamber unloaded, and most importantly, keep my finger off the trigger until I am ready to fire."

He smiles at me proudly. "Good job. I think you're ready."

I keep myself from doing a giddy little dance as Tom leads me over to the shooting range section of our training center.

"All right Samantha. I want you to practice the 'aimed shooting technique' for now. It's perfect for the beginner who is still learning how to use their gun sight. Focus on the front center sight using your dominant eye while closing your other eye. As you focus, the front sight will line up with the back two and they will become fuzzy, and your front sight will be clear. Line it up with the center of your target. Take in a breath to offset any imbalance and as you release your breath, pull the trigger."

Okay, I got this. Stepping into place, my stomach twists in nervous excitement. As I raise my weapon into position, I make sure my hand is clear of the back of my gun. I close my left eye, allowing my prominent eye to focus, and everything falls into place just as Tom described. With my sight centered on my target, I draw in a breath and squeeze the trigger as I exhale.

BANG!

My arms jerk up as I jump from the loud kickback of my first shot. Despite Tom's warning, I wasn't anywhere near ready for it. "Oh, wow!"

His muffled laughter finds its way through my protective earmuffs.

"You cannot tell anyone about this. Especially Alex." I give him a warning look.

He knows I'm referring to his past betrayal. "Fair enough. I promise," he concedes.

"Thank you," I smirk. Returning my attention back to the untouched target at the end of the range. *I can do this.*

As it turns out, I can't. At least not very well. The anticipation of the loud bang kept throwing me off and I didn't hit anywhere near the center of the target. After my poor performance, Tom and I come to an agreement; I will devote time to my physical and weapons training, as long as he teaches me how to shoot a variety of guns and throw defensive knives. There would be no more of the 'whenever I feel like it,' approach. Had I known what I was committing to, I would have thought twice about it, then probably still agreed. It makes me feel like a bad-ass learning how to defend myself, or in this case, my sister. Maybe she will let me teach her how to use a knife. I think she'll be ready for it by the time I know what I'm doing, and I think it will help her feel less vulnerable.

The long hours of training have been hard on my body, but in a good way. With only a couple weeks in, I know I have a long way to go yet, but it feels good to not feel so defenseless anymore. As I sit in the warm pool allowing my thoughts of revenge to entertain me, I hear someone slip in across from me. Peeking through my slit eyes, I find Shane sitting there, looking at me. The hair on the back of my neck stands up as I realize the room is empty. I must have dozed off.

"How are lessons going?" He disingenuously asks.

"They're going really well. Tom said I'm a natural," I lie, feeling uncomfortable being alone with him. I can't tell if he's buying it.

"Really? Maybe some time I can join you, and see this natural talent of yours," he challenges.

"Maybe." *That's never going to happen.*

He smirks. "And maybe you can bring Julia. I can teach her how to fight," he glances at his hands and arms before continuing "and how to handle a weapon."

That arrogant… Easing out of the water, I grab my towel before my anger gets the better of me. I turn as casually as my incensed body will allow, to make one thing absolutely clear to him. "I will teach my sister *everything* she needs to know, and you— you will leave her alone." Forcing myself to walk away, I can feel his eyes burning into the back of my head in response, and I know this isn't going to be the last of him.

15
The Challenge

Sam:

Tom has been training me hard for just over a month now, and I welcome the change it's making to my body. Not only have I gained muscle mass, but I know my way around a gun and how to utilize a knife in a way I never knew before. I used to feel unable to defend myself, whereas now, I feel strong and confident in the skills I've learned since being here.

I approached Julia about teaching her how to handle a knife. At first, she was a little hesitant about learning to use a weapon, but then I showed her how I could hit a target without looking like a complete idiot. After the look of shock wore off, she was eager for me to teach her. She's not ready to learn any hand-to-hand combat yet. I think knowing how to defend herself with *something*, will make her feel more confident and ready to learn eventually. I told Alex about my run in with Shane and he was not happy about it; that makes two of us. I recently agreed to let him spar with me again, and if I'm being honest, I've missed Alex. My prior struggles are under control now, though they still sneak up on me from time to time. For someone who has always kept the idea of love and attraction as a myth, it has been incredibly hard to navigate my feelings and responses to this very living and growing reality.

"Come on Sam, you're faster than that," Alex goads.

I don't think he realizes how much that fuels me. Stepping to the side in our dance of countermoves, I see his smug face wink at me. Then again, maybe he does realize how much his goading fuels me. As we circle around each other, I lunge, landing a shot into his gut, forcing myself to ignore the resistance of his sculpted stomach. He gives me a half smile and I swing high, narrowly missing his face. He grabs my arm and pulls me into a tight defensive hold. I can't move as his arms hold me close; my pulse quickens. Before I can sort through another mental assault, he lets go of me and takes a step back, gesturing for me to try again. How am I supposed to focus after that? I search my mind for anything I can use to defeat him. Aside from a cheap shot to the groin, I have nothing. Alex is bigger and stronger than me, and though I sometimes get a shot in, my arsenal of moves isn't advanced enough to take him down.

"You can do this."

He encourages me with such fervor; I can't help but smile at his confidence in me. It's then I notice a slight falter in his step. Is it possible that I have the same effect on him that he has on me? Charged by the possibility, I take a tentative step forward, allowing him to capture me again. Only this time, I pay attention to his heartbeat, feeling its elevated rhythm beating against my back. Is it because we've been training, or because of me? I can feel his breath on the top of my head, reminding me of another night. I turn my face to look up at him. There's no mistaking the quickening pulse in his neck. As he loosens his hold on me, I twist my body around so I'm standing face to face with him, with only inches between us. I look into his eyes, trying to read what he's feeling; this is foreign territory for me. Always believing it was a one-sided struggle, I stand there, realizing neither one of us wants to move. He leans in closer, and my heart pounds as I stand my ground. Acknowledging my unspoken permission, he closes the space between us. At first, it's a gentle, unassuming kiss. He's careful not to push me, and I'm too nervous to delve deeper into this new feeling.

Alex gently pulls away, with his forehead resting on mine. "Is this okay?" he whispers.

The vulnerable tone in which he asks, reveals to me he's nervous too. Words forsake me, so I nod yes, causing our heads to move in unison. We chuckle. "Can I kiss you again?"

I whisper, "yes," and he leans in. Pressing his soft lips against mine, I feel the sureness in his kiss. The intensity awakens my senses and they come alive. I allow his lips to melt into mine as I reach my hands up to the back of his neck, then traveling down his strong shoulders. He responds to my touch with goosebumps that emerge on the surface of his skin beneath my fingertips. With his hands now on my waist drawing me closer to him, I feel his touch tracing the curve of my back. Excited fear explodes from the corners of my mind; I'm not ready for this! Panic swells within me. Not knowing how to stop what I started, I abruptly pull away, leaving him looking wounded and insecure.

Wanting him to understand, "It's not you, Alex…" I try to explain, but don't know how. Closing my eyes to the warring of insecurities and desire within my tightening chest, I feel his hands gently cupping my face. "It's okay," he whispers, then lightly kisses the tip of my nose.

Relief washes over me, as I cover his hands with mine.

He understands what I'm afraid to put into words. "Thank you," I murmur.

We slowly drop our hands in the quiet current that still lingers between us. Hesitantly, I turn away from him and leave.

In the privacy of my sleeping quarters, I silently berate myself for allowing desire to drive me forward, and my doubt for holding me back. I'm a mess. Even in my discombobulated state, my admiration for Alex grows with his response to my mixed messages. Why can't I trust *this*, whatever *this* is, between us. Frustrated, I grab fresh clothes and head to the falls. I think a cold shower will help in more ways than one.

The next morning, I wake up with yesterday in my thoughts, my fingers lingering on my lips, wondering if Alex is thinking about it too.

"Time for practice, you ready?"

I hear his voice from the other side of the dividing curtain, sending my heart into stupid mode. Vainly attempting to smooth out my morning curls, I swiftly tidy my personal appearance and bed. Why my bed? I don't know. It makes me appear more put together than I am on the inside Foolish? Probably, but I can't help myself. Taking in a quick, soft breath, I nonchalantly answer, "You can come in, Alex." Desperately hoping he can't see my nervousness; I look up to find a playful grin on his face. "What?"

"What's my punishment today?" he teases.

My many failed attempts at fighting with him yesterday pop into my mind. Then of course, there was that kiss. The warmth blooming in my cheeks attest to my insecurities and disbelief as I wonder what he means.

Bending down he kisses my forehead, "I have a plan, just trust me," he whispers. And in that whisper, any doubts I had of him, and potential regrets, melt away.

Secure in his confidence, I allow him to lead me to wherever this new plan takes us. As we round the corner of the tunnels, I find Tom waiting with a torch in his hand; this can only mean one thing, we're headed outside. Panic rises inside of me as this dark refuge that once felt ominous has now become a cocoon of security, and we're going to leave it. My feet stop while my mind wrestles with the longing to be outside and the fear of being exposed.

"What about the Singuri? Aren't they still looking for us?"

"They gave up on finding you a while ago and shouldn't be back for another couple of weeks, when the next ocean rotation takes place." It's Tom who offers the reassuring answer.

Satisfied with his explanation, my mind settles on the happy realization that we're going outside. "Lead on," I assure them with a smile.

Alex takes my hand and pulls me close as we begin our journey through the many twists and turns.

"Alex," I whisper. "I need to learn how to make my way through the tunnels. Do you know them?"

He squeezes my hand as he answers, "Are you asking to be alone with me in the dark, because my answer is – YES." I can hear him chuckling as he finishes his sentence. Playfully frustrated, I punch him in the arm. "Ouch." He teases. "Yes, I know my way through the tunnels, and yes, I would love to teach you. How does tomorrow sound?"

Not willing to let the opportunity pass, "Sounds great! Can I bring Julia?" I ask, knowing I will need a distraction as much as she needs to learn.

Before Alex can answer, Tom chimes in, "If you need

more company, I will be happy to escort you," he jokes.

I shoot a glare at him in the dim light knowing he's referring to my prior struggle and inability to focus when I am around Alex.

"Shut it Tom," Alex chides on my behalf. "I think Sam's right, Julia should learn her way around here. It would help her feel safe."

I don't argue with Alex, because once again, he understands. "Thank you," I say.

Hand in hand, we continue to travel deeper into the tunnel. Gradually the damp earthy smell melds into the aroma of the sweet, fresh ocean air. I deeply inhale the cleansing scent. My heart leaps with the memory of it. With only a few more steps, Tom leads us to the end of our travels. He stops before a keypad that looks strikingly like the ones from the city. I never noticed it my first time through. I watch as Tom punches in a code to disarm the security and stand astonished as the faux cavern wall reveals itself as it begins to open. He must see my curiosity, because he explains, "This is how we get in and out of the caverns, and it's how we keep unwanted guests out. When we come back through, I'll have to punch in the code again, or an alarm will go off, alerting everyone of intruders."

"That makes sense," I acknowledge. "I wasn't sure how the security worked. Don't get me wrong; the tunnels are their own kind of labyrinth, but it's good to know extra measures have been taken."

Tom smiles at my admission before turning to lead us through the opening. As we emerge from the darkness and onto the shore, the light from the sun nearly blinds me. As my stinging eyes slowly adjust, I'm surprised to find a small group of people already waiting on the shore, including

Shane. My stomach knots as I study him from across the sand, with his eyes focused on my sister.

"Julia!" I call out, breaking his unwanted attention. As she turns to me with a beautiful smile and waves back, Shane turns with his own look of annoyance.

"I'll see you later," she hollers, as Mary beckons for her help with a rambunctious little boy. Before Shane can turn to follow her, my eyes bore into him with my silent warning, *I'm watching you.* He simply smiles at my warning, chuckling it off as he turns his back to me. My blood boils!

"Something bothering you?" Alex quietly asks from beside me.

"He is," I practically growl as I nod my head in Shane's direction.

Following my line of sight, I feel Alex go tense next to me. "Did he hurt you?" he asks through clenched teeth.

Stunned by the intensity of his words, I quickly amend my comment, "No, no, he hasn't. I just don't like him, especially the way he watches Julia."

Alex relaxes a bit before answering, "I know what you mean; I don't trust him either. I've already talked with Tom about it. That's one of the reasons why we decided to do our lesson outside today. He wants to watch Shane out in the open and see how he reacts to our training, and to her. He's also asked Mary to keep an eye on things."

My heart softens for this man standing next to me. He's looking out for Julia too, and so are Tom and Mary. Relief calms my protective heart, knowing Shane is under a watchful eye. I suddenly remember Alex's comment from earlier. "So, what's this great idea you have for today?"

He smiles at me. "You'll see." Then he throws me over his shoulder, shouting, "We're ready when you are, Tom!"

Tom, who I can barely see around Alex s waist, starts laughing at us. As I squirm to free myself from Alex's hold, the redness burning through my body is not caused by the sun, "Alex! Put me down!", I demand. The ripple of laughter in his strong back is felt through my hands as I brace against him. All I can do is dangle over his shoulder as he continues to tromp forward. He sets me down and pecks me on the cheek, before capering off to join Tom. Giggling, I shake my head at his boyish behavior, knowing that whatever they have planned, it has him in a good mood.

Tom motions to Alex to gather everyone around him and begins to explain, "Hey everyone, thank you for joining us today. I know you're wondering why we've asked you to come outside for training. Allow me to explain. It wasn't that long ago when we discovered Alex, Sam, and Julia out here. I have since found them to be invaluable to our cause. As we continue to grow, the need to train has become even greater. Alex had an okay idea for this." Everyone snickers at this friendly teasing. Everyone except Shane, who stiffens at Tom's continued praises. "All right, maybe it was a better than okay idea," Tom continues. "He suggested we train in tactical defenses against each other and given the open space and the softness of the sand, he thought it would be best to train out here."

A sense of pride swells within me as his words ring out through the air. Tom motions to Alex, who steps forward, to continue the oration.

"Please understand that we only want to teach you how to defend yourselves, if ever the need should arise." Alex gestures to a circle drawn in the sand and continues. "We'll all gather over there and compete against one another. Feel free to join us. However, if you don't want to participate, enjoy the beach and the much-needed sunshine before it leaves us for the winter." He smiles. "Oh, one more thing, I call dibs on Sam, so hands off!" Everyone laughs at his joke as I feel myself turning red once again. Looking at him with a stare that says, *I'm going to kill you*, Alex smirks, knowing he's in for it. Glancing around, I watch the people divide into two separate groups and I can't help but notice Shane's face exuding jealousy as he watches Alex. Pretending to forgive Alex for my embarrassment, I protectively make my way over to him, and we join the others at the circle. Julia isn't ready for close contact yet, so she rejoins Mary to help with the children. A conflicting sigh escapes me as Shane joins our group, eager to have his turn wrestling with Alex.

One by one, Tom matches us up with an opponent close in size, except me, I'm paired with Alex. True to his word, no one else gets to wrestle with me. At first, I was a little uncomfortable fighting in front of others, but as I'm learning how to avoid punches as well as making them count, I'm feeling more confident in my abilities. I'm definitely not the helpless girl I was when I showed up in the caverns.

Stepping into the ring, we begin our dance of sidestepping, swinging, and blocking. "Quit taking it so easy on me," I tease Alex.

He looks at me, one eyebrow raised, "Okay, but you asked for it." With my next swing, he grabs my hand and swiftly turns me around into his arms. I can't move. That same stupid move gets me every time.

He whispers in my ear, "Now what are you going to do, Sam? Not that I mind being this close to you." My heart pounds with the proximity of his body to mine. My mind tries to decide if I want to kiss him, or if I want to drop him. Closing my eyes, I take a deep breath, remembering an old maneuver Tom first taught me. Quickly, I widen my stance, exposing one of his legs, and I thrust my hips back while simultaneously bending down. I grab his leg and pull as hard as I can. His feet come flying out from beneath him and I reposition myself over his fallen body, striking my elbow toward his face. Alex dodges my blow, and flips me over onto the sand, now positioning himself over me. I try to wiggle my way free, but his hold is too tight. I look up and see him smiling, "Good moves, but not good enough." He shouldn't have said that. Playing to his confidence, and our current position, I stop struggling and look him square in the face, "I don't know, I rather like our current situation," topping it off with what I hope is a flirtatious smile. I feel his elbows loosen their hold on my hips. Not missing my opportunity, in one swift motion I straighten my legs, shooting myself out from under him, and strike him in the side of the face with the heel of my hand. Then, repositioning my body once again, I pin Alex back into the sand.

A look of shock and pride stretch across his face. I hear him groan in surrender.

As my adrenaline wears off, it's then I notice the red mark across his face, and I panic.

"I'm so sorry. I didn't mean to hit you that hard." I tilt his head to the side so I can take a closer look. "I should have been more careful."

Ignoring my attempt to inspect the damage, Alex's hand covers mine as he turns to face me again. "Don't be sorry Sam, those were some impressive moves," he pauses and winks at me, "maybe even persuasive," he adds, then starts laughing.

All around us, there's an eruption of howling and clapping. Apparently, we drew a crowd. "Good job,

Samantha!" I hear Tom call out above the rest. My skin turns hot all over as I become overly aware of my body still straddling Alex's. Scurrying to get up, I extend a hand to help Alex from the sand and I can see he truly is impressed with me.

"I always knew she had fight in her, it was just getting her to see it in herself," Alex boasts. In that moment, hearing his words of acclamation, redefines a part of me and the way I see myself. Reaching my hand to his face, I smooth my fingers down the mark I left on his cheek.

"Are you okay?"' I ask tenderly.

"No," he answers with a twinkle in his eye, "but I will be." He swoops me up into his arms and charges for the ocean.

I yelp as the tingling cold water washes over us and I tighten my arms around his neck as the ocean's pull tugs on me. He draws me closer to him and I smile to myself with my mother's words crashing into my mind, *I was lucky, because your father is a good man. It was easy for me to learn to love him. I hope the same for you too, Sam.* Alex is a good man…and I think I'm falling in love with him. My heart flutters as this unexpected realization surprises me.

"Is this better than your last community swim?" I tease in his ear.

I feel the deep rumble within his chest, as his smiling face turns towards mine. "Absolutely," he confirms. Leaning closer in the nearly nonexistent space between us, he kisses me with such conviction, a shiver of desire pulses through my body. I lean into his kiss, adding a fervor of my own.

"It's about time!" Julia teases from shore.

The passionate spell is broken and I'm suddenly very aware of everyone around us. Looking up to see who else might be witnessing our display of affection, I find Shane standing a little too close to Julia. Any residual heat from our kiss is completely dispelled with the ice now running through my veins.

Alex senses the shift in my body as I slide out of his arms. "What's wrong?"

I nod my head, "Look. He's hovering again." Alex already knows who I'm talking about before his eyes find Shane. "I despise him, Alex. I despise the hunger he has for Julia."

Understanding my need to protect her, he takes my hand and walks us over to join in their conversation. The relief in Julia's face is evident as she takes my other hand and playfully asks, "Is it true, did you really beat up Alex?"

Before I can answer, Alex interjects, "Utterly and completely. And she's welcome to do it again any time." We all laugh at his taunting, all except Shane. He's silently fuming at our interruption, but I could care less.

Seeing an opportunity, Shane looks directly at me and challenges, "It must be comforting to know that your husband is so easily beaten. What are you going to do when someone like me comes along?"

Seething under my skin, I bite my tongue. What does he mean *when someone like him comes along?* Trying to keep my composure, I ignore his comment and turn my attention to Julia. This only annoys him further.

Unsatisfied with my lack of response, he turns his attention to Alex, "Maybe you should practice a little more, so she doesn't have to worry about such things. Or are you afraid to fight someone who might actually challenge you?"

I can tell Alex is tired of Shane's arrogance, and amazingly, somewhat amused. "Really Shane, there's no need for all this. If you want to wrestle with me, just ask." Adding the final touch, Alex winks at him.

Shane is not a fan. "Let's say I do; would you fight me right now?" he challenges.

Accepting the invitation, Alex retorts, "Sure, practice makes perfect, right Shane?"

I can't believe how relaxed Alex is; he doesn't seem worried at all. But when I look over at Shane and see the satisfaction growing in his eyes, it makes me uneasy. He's getting what he's always wanted; a chance to tear Alex apart.

As we make our way back to the circle, my heart begins pounding so loudly I wonder how no one else can hear it. Julia has come with me this time, having witnessed the unfolding tension in the air. I hold her hand as Alex gives me a quick peck on the lips before he confidently turns to face Shane.

"Before the match begins, may it be known, we fight until someone is down, not until someone concedes," Shane declares.

Understanding the current situation, Tom joins us and interjects "…and I will referee the match, to make sure things don't get out of hand in the heat of the fight."

Shane doesn't seem happy about this development, but he is in no position to argue. As Tom stands on the other side of me, we watch the fight begin. They circle one another, waiting for the first punch to be thrown. Shane moves first. Eager to hurt Alex, he swings and just misses the side of his face, where I hit him earlier. Alex ducks, sending a fist into Shane's gut, causing him to gasp for air. Backing away, Alex stands down, giving him a chance to recover. I can hardly breathe as I watch it all unfold before me. Without warning, Shane bounces back and attacks Alex with full force, punching him in the ear from behind. Dazed, wondering where the cheap shot came from, Alex turns, only to be struck in the jaw. He covers his face while crouching down, dropping his elbows to protect his torso. I watch as Shane lays into Alex, punch after punch, unleashing his fury. I angrily wonder why Tom hasn't called foul. I can't take it anymore! I grab Tom's arm, squeezing it, for fear of what's to come.

He calmly leans over and quietly reassures me, "Just watch, your Alex is a good fighter. He's wearing him down."

My Alex. Tom's words plant firmly in my heart. Trusting him, I force my eyes to stay open. Immediately regretting it, I am met with the smug look on Shane's face, directed towards Julia and me. Fire burns through me, and more than anything, I hope Tom is right. Stealthily, Alex shifts out of his protective stance, setting his sights on Shane. With a calculated step forward, Alex jabs him in the ribs, followed by a side hook to the jaw. *Now he's not smiling*, I think to myself. I watch as the impact of Alex's punches lands heavy and hard into Shane. There's a controlled fury I see in Alex, and it's a little frightening to watch. Shane stands there in near defeat, as the fourth blow is delivered, a brutal shot to the nose. As his blood gushes down his lips, Shane falls to the ground holding his face. The rules he set forth, demand Alex to strike again. Instead, Alex looks down at Shane, and refuses to hit him.

"I will not strike you while you're down. I concede the match." He spits the words out as he turns and walks away.

Everyone is watching in stunned silence as they realize Alex would rather forfeit the win than continue beating on Shane. In doing so, he has won something far greater than the match; he has won their respect. The spectators look to Tom for a response, and he doesn't disappoint.

"According to the rules set forth by Shane, Alex has lost… but, according to *my* rules, he is the true winner." An eruption of applause breaks the silence.

Beaming with pride, I look at Alex and see Mary working a solvent into a small gash under his eye. Tom looks over at me, almost as if to say, *see, what did I tell you*. His pride mirrors my own. I can perceive now how close he and Alex have become over the past month and a half. Today, I am more thankful for that than ever.

Making my way over to Alex, I honestly wonder if there's something wrong with me; *why am I not bothered by Shane's beating?* Pushing my concern aside, I place my palm in his, drawing his trembling hand to my lips, "You did good, Alex," I encourage, before kissing the top of his bruised knuckles.

He looks at me as though I'm the only thing that matters to him. I will never understand how a man like him could want someone like me.

Mary turns her attention to Shane and takes him back inside to tend to his more serious injuries. Tom follows closely behind, escorting Julia and the children back to the cavern. My heart skips with encouragement to see her finally finding her place in our new home. As they disappear into the faux wall, Alex and I stay behind to welcome the dusk on our own. With the final sliver of sun resting beneath the horizon, Alex pulls me close, and I welcome the warmth of his arms. Leaning against his chest, I feel the thumping of his heart on the back of my head as we watch the stars begin to dot the night sky.

16
Confessions

Sam:

As I sleep, I feel the warmth of another body next to me. Rolling over, I find Alex sleeping beside me. Studying the lines of his face, my vulnerable heart wonders if he loves me. My eyes continue their unabashed perusal as they travel along the curve of his neck, then to his broad shoulders and down his arms, remembering the power he carries in them. I reach out, placing my hand gently on his chest. I want to feel his heart beating, its rhythm draws me in closer and closer, until our bodies touch. Longing to feel his arms around me again, to feel safe, to feel loved, ever so lightly, I kiss his lips. Alex opens his eyes. I see the same fire in them as my own. I weave my arms through his, whispering. "Hello, Love." It's the first time I have called him that, and I mean it with everything in me. He smiles as though I have just given him the world. Reaching his arms around me, he begins tenderly kissing me. First, he brushes the top of my head, then down the side of my temple, onto my cheek. His breath tickles my ear as he makes his way down my neck. My senses are alive as I reach my hand up into his hair. I turn my face to his, finally our repressed passions meet in our kiss. My hands explore his strong shoulders, as he draws me closer by the small of my back, our bodies melting as one…

Startled, I awaken to the touch of Alex smoothing a curl away from my face; it was only a dream.

"Sorry, I didn't mean to wake you." Looking around in the dark, I realize we're back in the alcove. I must have dozed off.

"How did I get here?"

He smiles and explains, "We were watching the stars, and as you were telling me about the freedom you find in them, you started snoring," he shrugs, "so I carried you back here to snore in private."

"I do not snore!" I teasingly push him away. I remember looking at the stars, and being so close to him, I felt protected and cherished. "I'm sorry, I didn't mean to fall asleep."

Rolling back onto his side with a smirk, "It's okay. I enjoy watching you sleep." His smile broadens as he continues, "What were you dreaming about? You looked really happy."

Feeling the color rising into my cheeks, I cover my face. Of course, I remember, but there's no way I'm telling him. Offering a distraction, "What were you doing when I woke up?" I ask as my finger traces down the side of his face.

Now it's his turn to look a little embarrassed. He gently tugs one of my curls down, watching it bounce as he lets go. "Do you know how long I have wanted to do that?" he chuckles at himself.

I can only laugh at him and the irony of my loathsome curls.

He pulls me into his arms again, and whispers, "Sam,

can I ask you something?"

Resting my body against him, willingly and foolishly, I answer "Yes."

It feels like time has slowed down, as he struggles with what he's going to ask. "What were you hiding in the closet?"

There's no accusation or judgment in his voice, even still, my body tenses at the surprise of his question. I had forgotten he saw me.

"It's okay Sam, I'm not mad at you," he reassures, "I was just wondering, because I don't want you to be afraid to tell me."

He sounds so genuine I know I can't keep this secret from him anymore, not if I want us to work. I close my eyes, trusting the man I know him to be, and confess my longest kept secret.

"It was an old journal that belonged to my great-great-grandmother. Her name was Brylie Wells. She wrote about her life and the world she lived in, her struggles, and victories." I hesitate for a moment, before deciding to tell him *why* I found it. "I snuck some Snakeroot home with me the night I found it. I was in a very dark place then, but this journal saved me. It's how I have survived these past few years." His arms tighten, drawing me in closer with the understanding of the implication in my words. Absorbing his comfort, I plunge forward with the terrible truth. "My grandmother was raped when she was not much younger than Julia. I'll never forget her courage when she decided to keep the baby She called him her hope. She gave birth to Bennette Wells, my great-grandfather. I didn't know at the time I read her entry, but I think he is where our bloodline crosses with The Order."

Now empty of my secrets, I feel terrifyingly

vulnerable as the silence between us grows deafeningly loud. He probably doesn't know what to think of me anymore. I'm just a big lie to him. Suddenly I feel dirty from my confessions.

"I'm sorry, Alex, I didn't know. I'll understand if you don't want me anymore." I feel my heart twinge at the thought of him not loving me.

He leans forward and kisses the top of my head, "You have nothing to be sorry for; I love you just the way you are, Sam."

This is the first time he's said he loves me, and my terrified heart calms with the confession of his words. I roll over to tell him I love him too, but the look on his face stops me. I see a deep pain, unmasked, in his eyes.

"What's wrong, Alex?" I ask, worried I've hurt him.

With an unsteady voice, he begins his own confession, "My sister and I used to have a book, an album actually. We would secretly sit together after lights out, looking at the pictures and reading the letters that were tucked away inside." He swallows the lump in his throat before he can continue. "That's what she was coming to do, the night my father betrayed her. She made me promise not to say anything. All I could do was watch as she took the blame for my discovery."

His eyes are lost in a faraway memory, and my heart breaks for him. My words alone are not enough for this moment. I pull his hand to my chest, allowing him to feel the pounding of my heart. "I'm sorry," I whisper. His eyes are closed, as if to focus, trying to find a measure of comfort within my heart's rhythm. "I love you," I quietly confess.

His eyes open, gazing upon me, and in the place of pain, I see hope. "Thank you." He rests his hand over mine as we lay there, souls open for the other to see.

17
Dirt Wars

Sam:

"Knock-knock, can I come in?" Alex's voice weaves through the linen divide of my sleeping quarters, drawing my mind from the reminiscing thoughts of last night.

"Sure," I calmly respond despite the butterflies in my stomach.

Stepping through the curtain, my butterflies seemed to have done a collective flip as Alex's once silhouetted frame comes into full view. His still damp hair from his morning shower reveals a fresh trim that's cleaned up his typically tousled hair, without taking his charm away. His faded t-shirt clings to his chest reminding me of how it felt to be held in his arms. I barely notice the rest of his ensemble of cargo pants and work boots when Alex clears his throat drawing my attention back to his face.

"Good morning, Love." Alex's voice carries a tone of teasing satisfaction that matches his quirked eyebrow.

"Good morning to you too, Alex." I tease back as my nervous heart flutters at the image of him.

"What? Did a good night's sleep bring you to your

senses?" He jests, but I can see his confidence is now fractured by a fear of doubt.

"Never, you're stuck with me now," I hold up my hand bearing his name, "It's a good thing they gave us these, now you can't trade me in." I smile at my own cleverness.

He walks over, entwining his fingers with mine, "I wouldn't have it any other way," his lips caress my knuckles before kissing the finger with his name inscribed on it.

"I wouldn't either." *Not now*, I add mentally. I know it's true, more than anything else I have known in my life.

"Sam, are you awake yet?" Julia's intruding words are like a splash of cold water drawing me back to the present. She's looking for me.

Untangling myself from Alex, I answer, "Yeah, I'm in here." She pulls back the curtain, a little embarrassed to see Alex with me.

"I was wondering if you were going out with the group today," she hesitantly inquires.

Looking back to Alex, I connect his fresh appearance this morning and realize he's going out with whoever this group is. "Alex, what is she talking about?"

Throwing his hands up in surrender, he answers, "I was going to tell you, but I got a little, distracted." He looks at me with a smirk. "Tom is taking a group out scouting for medical supplies. You can come with us if you want, that is if you don't mind being around a bunch of smelly men. Except for me of course. I smell good." He sniffs himself.

I chuckle and shake my head at him, "No thanks. I think I'll just hang out here with my sister." Turning my head towards her I continue, "I've kind of missed you lately." She perks up at my words, and I can see she has missed me too.

"All right then, I'll leave you two alone for some

'sister' time, while I hang with the boys." Alex concludes as he leans down to kiss me on the top of my head.

"Have a good day," I whisper, noticing a slight look of relief on his face. Reaching my hand up, I gently pull his face down, and truly kiss him goodbye. I no longer care if Julia sees us. It's good for her to see a healthy kind of love.

When Alex pulls away, he confidently smiles, "If it's anything like that, my day's going to be fantastic "

Julia and I both laugh as he turns and struts out the door.

After getting dressed, Julia drags me to a small room that's hidden in the back of the kitchen. She's excited to show me her favorite place within the cavern.

"Surprise!" She exclaims, as she points to a nearby garden box. "Look how they grow, even though we're underground."

Following her hand, I see plants and herbs growing despite their surroundings. Wondering how they can grow without the sun; it becomes clear that each garden bed has a dancing light. Looking up, I discover, hanging from the center of the room, a glass lantern with a small flame burning inside. Connecting the dots, I study the planters once again, noting the solar material once used for boiling stones is now lining the inner sides of the garden boxes. The reflecting light provides each plant with the much-needed warmth and nutrients to grow. *Amazing.* They used something intended for death, to bring forth life.

"It's stunning," I exclaim.

"I know," Julia agrees, "and we get to plant today!" Her eyes shine with excitement. "We'll be spending our afternoon with Mary and these precious gems she brought with her to the garden," Julia informs me.

This is not what I wanted to do when I woke up this morning, but the joy emanating off Julia makes me excited too. I look around at her "gems" befitting my Jewels, and realize I never noticed before, how some of the kids look and behave differently from other children I have seen. The Order would terminate these kids because of their differences.

Julia catches me watching them with a quizzical look, "Aren't they beautiful? Mary said it's something called Down Syndrome. I don't know how anyone could see such innocent happiness as something wrong." As she continues to watch them in complete adoration, one thing becomes clear; Julia finds her solace amongst the kids.

"You're absolutely right, Jewels, they are beautiful." The love I have for her pours over to these precious children in my smile. In return, a couple of the children beam their own smiles at me and the light of pure happiness from them is enough to make this garden room flourish.

We join the small group and set to work on the task assigned to us by Mary. As Julia turns the rich soil over in her hands, I remember how, like me, she loved gardening at home with Mom. Working side by side with her now makes my heart smile. Mom would be proud. Wiping a drop of sweat from her brow, I notice Julia looks troubled.

"Are you okay?" I ask with concern.

"Yeah, I'm fine. I was just thinking about something."

"Anything you want to talk about?" I urge, dropping a few more seeds into the soil. I watch her forehead crinkle between her brows as she turns her private thoughts over in her mind.

"Sam, do you love Alex?"

Taken back by her personal question, I try to explain what I don't yet fully understand myself. "Now, yes…but at first, I hated him."

She tilts her head questioningly.

"It wasn't because of anything he had done, but because I judged him so incredibly wrong. When The Order first gave me this," I hold up my hand, showing her my tattoo, "I despised it as a label of ownership. I felt like I was branded against my will." A little laugh escapes me at the irony of it all, earning me a concerned look. "I'm okay, I promise. I just find it comical how something that represents everything I hate about this life, now represents almost everything I love about my new life." I look directly at her, so there's no room for doubt. "I could not have picked a better person than Alex Orion. So yes Julia, I love him, more than I ever thought possible."

With her tear-filled eyes looking back into mine, I feel like the worst sister imaginable. A large tear rolls down her face leaving a trail for others to follow. How could I be so insensitive to her struggles? "I'm sorry Julia, I didn't mean to upset you."

She wipes away her tears, leaving a dirt smudge across her cheek, "You didn't upset me, Sam. I'm happy that you were lucky enough to find love…lucky like Mom and Dad."

My own eyes sting with tears that I refuse to cry. She's right. I am lucky. "Thank you," I whisper. "Now, let me clean the dirt off your face." Smiling, I reach over and brush my hand across her cheek only to worsen the smudge. "Oops, sorry," I laugh, "I think I made it worse."

She scrunches her nose at me, and without warning, wipes her hand down the side of my face, leaving a streak of dirty fingerprints. My mouth fallsopens in disbelief.

"You sneaky little…" throwing a handful of dirt at

her, we both start laughing. The dirt war is on! Globs of soil fly as this once serene garden oasis turns into a battlefield between Jewels and me.

"Julia! Sam!" Mary's stern voice cuts through the jovial atmosphere. We stop, dirt clod mid throw, and turn to look at Mary. The look on her face clearly says she doesn't think we're very funny, and no wonder, we've started the children in on the fun. Before Mary can say anything to either of us, the dirt clod that was left in mid throw just moments ago, pelts her in the shoulder. Mary's mouth drops open and I can't stop from laughing. The offending mud obviously came from Julia because of where she's positioned, so when Mary gives me the motherly glare, I innocently point to Jewels.

"Traitor," she rightly accuses me.

Before I can respond, a dirt-ball hits Julia in the arm and another in the back of my head. The shock of Mary retaliating is vastly overshadowed by the ensuing dirt war that explodes in the garden sanctuary. In the end, the battle is won by the children in their devastating blow of filling two buckets with dirt and dumping them over mine and Julia's distracted heads. Our surrender came at the cost of head-to-toe defeat. It was a fantastic memory made and tucked away in my treasure box.

Covered in dirt, Julia and I head off for the falls. As we stand beneath the cool water, allowing it to clean the dirt from our bodies and our clothes, the ambiance shifts in the absence of laughter. The joy of our dirt battle isn't lost, it's just muted by the reality of our lives.

"Sam."

Julia's voice draws me from my own reflection, and I turn my attention to her.

She looks at me with sad, yet hopeful eyes as she

continues. "Do you think I will ever be able to trust again, trust enough to fall in love, like you?"

The vulnerability in her voice breaks my heart for her and the nightmare she endured. Seeing her painful hope, I know I must answer her. "Yes." Pausing, I choose my next words carefully. "I think love will find you when you're ready for it. You never know who your heart will choose."

She looks at me and smiles then, finding encouragement in my words. "Thank you."

After we're done cleaning up, we meet with Mary and the others for dinner. Alex hasn't returned yet, and I'm starting to get anxious.

"How long do they normally stay out on these scouting trips?" I ask Mary.

She doesn't seem too worried as she answers, "They usually come back around this time. It shouldn't be much longer now, Honey."

Her words soothe my anxiety, and the prospect of seeing Alex soon fills me with peace. I like Mary, she reminds me of how I imagine my grandmother would be, 'sugar and spice', as GG would've said.

Looking over at Julia, I see she's with the children again, and they are eagerly gathered around her. As I lean in closer, I can hear her telling one of our favorite childhood stories.

"...Ms. Dandy, the dandelion, was a flower who loved to stand tall in the sun. There was one thing our flower friend could not understand. Why was that mean ol' cloud always picking on her? One day, when she was enjoying the sunshine with her friend, Casey the Caterpillar, the cloud came overhead and blocked all the wonderful warmth. Frustrated and sad, Ms. Dandy mustered up the courage of a lion, and asked the cranky ol' cloud, 'Why are you always picking on me?' And do you know what the cloud said?"

In unison, the children all answered, "No!"

I smile as I watch this living memory of our childhood play out before me as Julia continues the story. "Well, the mean ol' cloud told the brave little flower, 'I'm sorry, I thought you might be hot. I wasn't trying to pick on you. I was just sharing the coolness of my shade.' And then the cloud turned from fluffy white, to a very sad grey, and he began to weep, raining down on Ms. Dandy and Casey the Caterpillar. Poor Mr. Cloud was sad. Our flower friend had hurt his feelings. He wasn't a mean ol' cloud after all. He was just misunderstood. Feeling sorry, Ms. Dandy apologized to the cloud. 'I'm sorry' she said, 'I thank you for your shade and your rain. They both help me to grow.' And just like that, Ms. Dandy the Dandelion, grew high up into the sky, all the way to Mr. Cloud. He stopped crying and was a very happy white cloud indeed. He forgave Ms. Dandy, and the three of them were friends from that day on. You see, Ms. Dandy learned two very important lessons that day. One, never judge someone because you can't understand them. And two, forgiveness will always free your heart to grow." The children all begin to giggle as Julia stands up, reaching her arms as high as she can, showing them just how big they too, could grow.

My heart overflows with pride at the sight of Julia, as I remember our mother telling the same story. For her to tell it now, only means she's working on forgiveness in her own heart, a lesson I would do well to remember. As I discreetly wipe away a tear, I hear a commotion coming from the tunnel. Sensing something is wrong, I shift my body between Julia and the kids, and whatever is coming.

Tom is the first to enter the room, and he's bleeding

from two large cuts on his left arm and one on his leg. He begins barking out orders when two more men follow in behind him, one of which is carrying a young child. They must have found more survivors. I shudder when I realize Alex isn't with them. *Where is he?* Time stands still as I watch more faces come through the tunnel and none of them are him. Growing increasingly anxious, I begin pacing. *What am I going to do if—* my foreboding thoughts are cut off as Alex emerges from the mouth of the cave. I can breathe again. My calculating eyes examine him; he's covered in dirt and blood. My heart beats faster, fearing he's hurt. When comprehension catches up with my eyes, everything I see comes into focus. Alex's arm is wrapped around another smaller person. It's Micah, his brother.

"Thank God," I say aloud. They're safe.

Alex looks up at me, and I see the array of emotions he is trying to hide. Anger. Joy. Regret. Sorrow… I don't know what happened out there today, but I do know it's deeply hurting him. I run over to them, first embracing Micah, as though he were my own brother.

"Micah, you're okay. You're safe now," I comfort him, longing to reach through the blank expression on his face.

I can feel how thin he is, as he weakly wraps his arms around me. Alex's own tired body heaves a sigh of relief as he transitions Micah into my arms. Mary quickly comes over to help me and begins to tend to Micah. Relinquishing him to her nearby care, I turn my attention back to Alex. I have so many questions to ask, but now is not the time. I grab his hand to let him know that he's not alone. I can feel the dried blood on his knuckles, and it takes everything in me not to look down and draw attention to his wounds. As Alex feels my touch, I see the muscles in his jaw loosen. We sit there, allowing our hands, and the silence, to be enough.

Once Mary is done cleaning and bandaging their wounds, we take Micah to the kitchen to get some food. Instinctively, I find myself wanting to take care of him. Micah is barely eleven years old, though he looks smaller. Alex once told me of how surprised his family was when they found out his mom was pregnant again. He was so happy to have a little brother. Alex always felt more like a father figure, instead of a big brother. Knowing he carries so much guilt for the pain his brother endured; first when the Singuri came, and then in his own absence. I can't imagine how he's feeling now.

Encouraging Alex to eat, I grab food for the two of them and sit quietly beside them. Alex only picks at his food, while Micah devours his; more evidence that he hasn't eaten in a while. Alex's shoulders slump as he pushes his plate away. I won't push him to eat. I wouldn't have much of an appetite either. Looking over at Julia, my heart squeezes to see her so healthy and safe. She is recovering unbelievably well from her trauma. I sometimes forget just how strong she is. Right now, she's tending to Tom's wounds. In the delicate way she is caring for him, I can see that my little sister is learning to trust again. Tom is a good man.

Not too far away, a wolf is lurking. I see Shane watching them, with a look of contempt oozing from his face. He must have felt me looking at him because he turns his attention to me. Good. Let him look, and may he be smart enough to read the fire in my eyes.

18
Growing Pains

Sam:

With the increased population of the caverns, Micah, Alex, Julia, and I have been sharing our own little cavern home for over a week now. It is one of the many dirt and stone rooms cut out within the massive cave walls. It's also larger than the single ones we had before. It offers a small alcove, giving a semblance of privacy for Alex and me, one small desk with a simple wooden chair for us all to use, and beds, made up of piles of blankets on the ground. It's a little crowded with four people, but Alex and I both agree that we want to keep our siblings close. It's funny how we have grown into our own little family, broken, but together, made whole. Finding time alone is a bit trickier now, but we know it won't be like this forever. Julia is feeling more and more confident, to the point where she is ready to get her own space nearby Once we get all the new refugees firmly settled in, she will be moving out and into an adjacent alcove. I'm not sure how I feel about that, but I won't stop her.

With the influx of so many new faces, I wasn't entirely surprised when Julia asked me to start training with her.

Today is day four.

"Okay, Julia, remember, plant your feet first, then rotate your hips as you thrust your hand forward. Keep your fingers up and your hand flexed backwards so the palm is the point of contact."

I watch as she repeats my words into motion against the freestanding punching bag.

"Good. Now for more force, make sure your elbow follows the same line of path as your palm."

Making the subtle adjustment, Julia attacks the bag again.

"Better!" I chuckle. "You really are impressive Jewels. Do you remember how to do an elbow strike if you don't have room to do a full heel palm strike?"

"Please, don't insult me, Sam," and with that, she swiftly adjusts to the elbow strike. After a couple of blows, she spins around, almost in a dancing motion, and throws out an alternative elbow strike. I continue to watch my sister alternate the different moves she's learned, and I notice a shift in her demeanor. What was a fun and an unsure dance is now a torrent of emotions. Her face twists into one of bitter pain. I lean into the bag to counter her force, and silently encourage her healing. With each punch she releases another injustice that has plagued her body, mind, and soul. Each strike lands, breaking that link of chain that has kept her from freedom. Stronger and stronger she hits with wild rage until the last of her spent aggression drops from the edge of her chin into a mixture of sweat and tears. With nothing left to give, she stands there looking at me, and I at her.

"Wow, Sam, had I known this would make me feel this good, I would have started training a long time ago." She chuckles half-heartedly.

Happy to follow her lead into a distraction, "You say that now, but wait until tomorrow, when you *feel* all that 'good'."

She rolls her head in exaggeration and groans at my response.

"Already feeling today's workout, are you? Well, come on then old lady, let's go soak in the hot pool."

With bright eyes, she bounds up next to me, "Let's go!" She grabs my hand and begins pulling me in that direction.

Winding our way to the water room, we pass only a handful of people in route. "That can't be," I whisper, "the lighting must be playing tricks on me." My feet come to an abrupt halt as my mind begins to believe what my eyes are truly seeing. Not far from where we're standing, I see a new refugee, with flaming red hair.

"What is it, Sam?" Julia's concerned voice is an echo in the back of my mind as I step across the open space.

"Excuse me, beautiful, pregnant woman with red hair."

"That would be me, but my name's Irene," she chuckles as she turns her full attention towards me.

"Sorry, I'm just surprised and beyond happy to see you." Her confused expression to my response urges me to further explain. "You don't know me, but I was working the fields when you were dragged away..." As my voice tappers off into silence, a quiet understanding settles between us and Julia discreetly excuses herself; she knows of the story that I'm referring to.

"I'm so sorry I didn't run after you to help. I wanted to, it's just—" The shame is overwhelming, and I can't bring myself to finish. The confession would confirm my cowardice aloud.

Irene gently places her hand on my arm, "Please, don't be sorry; it wasn't your fault. I would have never forgiven myself if you did chase after me and something happened to you. Besides," she chuckles as she rubs her belly, "as you can see, we got away."

Turning my hopeful eyes to her face once again, my own smile awakens to meet her greeting one. "I'm glad you did, so very glad." Even with this good news, I can't help but wonder, "But how? I heard a gunshot."

With a fierceness I have only seen once before, Irene looks straight at me, "Never underestimate a mama bear," she finishes with a smirk.

Disbelieving this small happy ending I get to experience, joy breaks through my typical restraints and I pull her into an embrace, which she heartily returns in laughter.

Not wanting the reunion to end, I invite her to join Julia and me. Unfortunately, she was on her way to the medical room for a checkup. Before departing, we make plans to meet up tomorrow for lunch. It's a strange feeling, when you meet someone, and you instantly know they're going to be an important part of your life. That's how I feel about Irene.

It has been three weeks of practicing self-defense with Julia. She is infinitely more confident with the idea of fighting back; so much so, she's moved into her own space. Well, it's kind of her own space. Micah splits his time between Julia, and Alex and me. He's the little brother we never had.

Turns out, Julia's phenomenal in her sparring abilities, taking more naturally to it than I did. Her growing skills have already led to her sparing with Tom and Alex a few times a week, much to Shane's frustration. We've talked about him and his not-so-subtle comments and actions. How did she put it, she's 'prepared to kick his ass, should he try anything'. I laughed so hard when she said that to me. It was a shock at both hearing her say the word ass, and the mental image of her beating the crap out of Shane. With the same perspective as our mother, we've never been ones to use bad language. There's a whole wide world of vocabulary to use. *But hey, I hear you, Jewels.* She's also never been a violent person, and still isn't, but Julia won't ever go down again, not without a fight.

"So, Tom seems like a good guy." I try to broach the subject.

She smiles back at me, though we are in the middle of sparring. "Yeah, he is. Now focus on training me."

I laugh. She's not getting off so easily. "He's kind of cute too." I wiggle my eyebrows at her for added fun.

She lunges at me, but I sidestep and get her in a headlock.

"Well, don't you think so?" I press.

Grunting in frustration, she concedes, "Fine. Yes, I think he's cute and yes, he's a really great guy."

I drop my grip from a headlock down into a big bear hug. "See, that wasn't so hard, was it? And in case you're wondering, I approve."

Suddenly, she widens her stance and drops down, grabbing my legs, pulling them out from underneath me. A move I know all too well. "I don't need your approval, there's nothing going on," she retorts.

"Not a fan of my comment I see." Sweeping my leg out and around her, Julia drops down next to me. And now we're both on our backs, laughing hysterically.

"What's so funny?" Tom asks from a distance.

We turn our watery eyes to the rooms entrance where we find Alex and Tom walking in and looking bemused. This only makes us laugh harder.

Alex just looks at him, shaking his head, "Sometimes, it's better not to ask." He quips.

I love his wittiness. "What do you guys want, can't you see we're in the middle of training?" I playfully wink at him.

His eyebrow shoots up, "Yeah, we can see that." He smiles at me. "I guess you're not interested in going topside for a little swim then, are you?"

"Now? It's nearly the end of fall!"

"A warm front has moved in, and we wanted to take advantage of this last bit of good weather." It's Tom who offers the answer with a jovial smile.

Ah, a familiar summer day that commonly visits during this time of year. Looking to Julia for an answer, I ask, "Well, Jewels, what do you think?"

Without hesitation, she answers, "Yes, yes, yes!", and we all laugh at her enthusiasm.

Jumping up, I go to offer my hand in help, only to find Tom has beat me to it. "Who won?" he inquires.

"I did," we both say in unison, earning a collective laugh from all of us.

As we make our way through the now familiar path of the winding cavern, I notice Micah isn't with us. "Where's Micah?"

Weaving his fingers into mine, Alex kisses the top of my hand. "He's hanging out in the work area today. He said he wants to make something for underground." I can see the pride shining off him, as it always does when he talks about his brother.

"I'm glad he's found something that interests him. He's a pretty smart kid."

Alex looks at me, a little stunned, "You can see that already?" Unexpectedly, he pulls me to a stop, while Tom and Julia continue moving ahead. Unsure of his emotions, he looks at me, "Thank you, Sam, for loving my brother the way you do."

Caught off guard by his sentiment, but also understanding his reservations, I reach my hand up to the back of his neck, the tips of my fingers in his hair. "He's my family now, too." Wanting to alleviate his worry with these simple, honest words, I see the concern fall from his eyes. This man, I have only just begun to learn, is more than I ever hoped for. Pressing my mouth gently to his, I kiss him, leaving no room for doubt.

"Hey, you guys coming or not?" It's Tom, teasing us from the darkness ahead.

Smiling, with our lips still touching, Alex turns his face to the side, "Yeah, yeah, we're coming." Hand in hand, we amble our way through the dark, familiar tunnels.

I don't think I'll ever get used to the sudden shock of the sun blinding me when I first exit the cave. We have our false sunroom down below, but it's nothing compared to the warmth or brightness of the real sun. It's intoxicating.

With Julia and Tom scouring the beach for shells, I lie on the blanket with Alex in the sand. Feeling his gaze on me, "what are you doing?" I ask, through closed lids.

"Oh, just wondering if you're ticklish," his playful voice answers.

Though it would be nice to feel his hands again, my unsettled stomach forces me to lie. "No, not really," I casually answer.

He's not buying it. I can hear the challenge in his voice as he responds, "Really?" Before I can react, I feel his fingers tickling along my sides. Laughter bursts from me as I beg him to stop. To my humiliation, Alex freezes, looking at me in disbelief, "Did you just…fart?"

Burying my face in my hands, I wish I could hide my redness as it travels down my neck and onto my collarbone. "It's your fault," I blame. "I asked you to stop, and you didn't." I think he's too stunned to say anything because silence only greets my accusation. Uncovering my face, I chance a look at him and see he is smiling. "Stop! It *is* your fault. Besides, I do *not* fart, I toot. Thank you very much," I state.

At this, he throws his head back in laughter, and my humiliation is complete.

Turning my covered face away from him, I feel the coolness of his shadow falling across me.

"Sam," he turns my face back towards his silhouetted frame above me. "It's all right, we all do it." He kisses the tip of my nose playfully, then confesses, "Why do you think I try to wake up before you every morning?" He winks at my shocked face.

"Alex!" Now we're both laughing. His admission is meant to console me, and it works. I had no idea.

Moving past the little 'incident' I ask Alex if he wants to go swimming, since the ocean is calm and welcoming today. As we enter the retreating waters, a shiver runs up my body, and I realize it's colder than I expected. Alex rubs his hands over the goose bumps that have formed on my arms, sending another shiver through my body that has nothing to do with the cold.

"Do you want to go back to shore?" he asks.

"No way." I splash him in response.

"Oh really," he scoops me up and runs deeper into the waves, plunging us both under the icy surface.

The frigid water steals what little remaining breath I have left, as Alex's arms tighten around me. Breaking the surface, I gasp in playful shock and cry out, "Julia! Help me!"

Without hesitation, she runs in after us and jumps on Alex's back, knocking us all off balance. We land in the cold waters once again. As the three of us find our footing, we hear Tom's boisterous laugh from the shoreline. Looking one to another in silent agreement, we head straight for him. Ex-Singuri or not, the guy didn't stand a chance against all three of us.

With the seasons shifting and not knowing how many more opportunities we will have like this; we spend the rest of the day playing in the ocean and soaking up the warmth of the sun. At one point, Julia challenges us to make sand angels, in lieu of snow angels. We gladly oblige her challenge. As the tide rises, the cool ocean breeze settles in. I can't help but remember a similar day from the pages of my grandmother's journal, one we now get to live. The smile beaming from my face is only rivaled by the sun with the knowledge of this truth.

Alex's quiet gasp turns my attention is his direction. "What is it? Are you okay?"

Reaching out, he tucks a wayward curl behind my ear, "You're so beautiful, it sometimes takes my breath away."

My concern melts away with his declaration of something I thought I would never be. My cheeks blush from the unfamiliar praise. A shy smile is my only response.

Alex gently takes my hand, leading us back through the dimly lit tunnels, he whispers to me, "I have a surprise for you."

With a smile on his lips, my curiosity is piqued, "What is it?" I ask.

He simply shakes his head no; he's not going to tell me.

Feeling giddy from the possibilities, I try a different tactic. "Will you at least give me a hint?" I ask, in my attempt at flirting.

He looks at me with that incredibly cute, raised eyebrow of his. *Ugh, I swear he knows he's charming.* Now I know Alex won't budge, he's having too much fun with this. That's fine, two can play this game.

Pulling away from Alex, "Come on Jewels, let's beat the boys to the falls, and wash this sandy, salt water off." She laughs at me as I grab her hand, and we run off towards the faint, glowing light ahead. As we round the last corner, we nearly collide into Shane.

"Watch where you're going!" He snarls, before he realizes it's us. "Oh, sorry. I didn't know it was you." His eyes land on Julia in the familiar hungry way.

I answer for her, "Don't worry about it. We'll be on our way." Then, in the most perfect timing possible, Tom and Alex scamper through the tunnel opening. Shane glares at them, and then at us. I can feel the heat of his anger permeating off of him as he turns and storms away. Julia and I snicker, then take off for the falls again.

For obvious reasons, it probably wasn't the best idea

to shower with Tom and Alex, even fully clothed, but I'm in a hurry. There's a surprise to be found out. Taking advantage of the 'washing your clothes at the same time' option, I pull Julia and I off to our own side, so we have some semblance of privacy. I'm not completely without rationale.

Julia starts lathering the back of my shirt. "Hold on, I have an idea," she informs me. The excitement in her voice leaves me unsure of where this is leading, but before I can ask, she turns around and begins wiggling her back against mine in a ridiculous effort to clean us both at the same time. I bust out laughing, happy to see her silliness thriving again. Grabbing onto the opportunity, I join in and start wiggling with her. I've missed this comical, care-free side of Jewels. As we slide up and down, my knotted mess of curls snag and unsnag on Julia's tank top.

"Ouch!" The involuntary screech is quickly followed by more wiggles and giggles, but not before an alarmed Tom and Alex peek over to see if we're all right. Judging by their stunned faces, I don't think they were prepared for what they saw. This just makes Julia and I laugh even harder.

"Geez, Sam. Can't you just take a shower?" she quietly teases while poking me in the ribs. We both giggle at her private joke.

"Now that you mention it Jewels, no, I'm finding it really difficult right now." My retort is swallowed by more laughter. Alex and Tom are looking at us again. "Don't think I didn't notice your little stolen glances too," I whisper.

She turns pink and buries her face into her hands as she realizes she's been caught. "It does matter to me, Sam." She mumbles through her fingers.

Perplexed, "What do you mean? What matters?" I ask.

Looking me straight in the face, she boldly explains, "I

don't need your approval, but I do want it."

Understanding floods through me as I truly look at her, my little sister, who looks so grown up and vulnerable, all at the same time. I reach over and pull her into a hug, whispering, "You have it."

It's been a long time since I've seen my sister smile like that, and it encourages my heart to know her healing has reached a new depth. I only wish our parents where here to share this moment with us. As the thought comes to mind, I make a silent promise to them; I will do everything in my power to keep her happy and safe.

19
The Surprise

Sam:

With Julia and Tom off to dinner, Alex and I are alone in our room. I try sitting at our little desk, but my legs won't stop bouncing. I watch Alex, as he grabs his emergency bag and retrieves the elusive surprise, covered in an old, tattered cloth. *Wait, I know that cloth.* My hand covers my mouth as realization sinks in.

"Is that my GG's journal?"

He quietly hands it over, allowing me to find out for myself.

I fold the worn cloth back, and there, in my hands once again, is my journal. I hug it close to me, as though I am embracing a loved one.

"How did you get this?" I whisper.

Alex shuffles his feet before answering, "On our last supply run."

Aware of when he means, I grab his hand and gently run my fingers over his newly healed knuckles. This is the first time he's been able to talk about it.

"Tom worked the whole trip around our old house in

the North Sector. It was still empty, so I was able to slip in and out without any problems."

Still in shock, I ask the obvious question, "He knows?"

Nodding his head yes, he continues, "He's okay with it. He thinks you should have the journal. That's not where we encountered a problem. After the house, we went to a small medical station a couple of blocks away. As we were leaving, I bumped into my dad and Micah."

How can that be? I ponder to myself. *They don't live anywhere close to our old house.* The questions must be evident on my face because Alex answers.

"I couldn't understand it either, until I saw who they were with. Turns out, they were part of a small group of prisoners, sent to work the North Sector that day. I couldn't just leave them, Sam. I couldn't. So, we improvised. "Tom and Shane took out the two Singuri guards, while I quickly freed the prisoners. Before we could escape, two other patrolling guards stumbled across the scene and sounded the alarm. My dad hastily gave me Micah and told me to do better than he did." He pauses as he grapples with the memory. "Then, a crazy thing happened. So crazy I still can't understand it. My dad picked up one of the guns and ran in the direction of the oncoming Singuri. He yelled at us to run, and we did. All of us...He fought Sam, he fought to save us."

Turning his face away from my knowing eyes, I steady my own emotions with a deep calming breath. His hidden tears drop on his grey t-shirt, staining it a darker, gloomy grey. Longing to take his pain from him, I step closer and draw his hand into mine. Placing it tenderly over my heart, I hold it there, willing my comfort to be his. He turns and buries his face into my neck, unleashing the dam that only moments ago, he was afraid to let me see. Silently I hold him as he cries from a pain, only somewhat familiar to me. The loss of a parent I know full well, but not the reconciliation of one. My parents loved me unconditionally. Alex's dad…that's a different story. Wrapping my other arm around him, I whisper the one truth I've learned through my own pain, "It's going to be okay."

20
Sand Beds

Alex:

I can't believe I cried in front of Sam; I feel like such a baby. I knew I needed to tell her everything, but I wasn't ready for the emotional assault that came with it. I will do better by her. I will be stronger for her from now on.

"Hey, you haven't heard a word I said. What's on your mind?" Tom's words cut into my internal reprimand.

"Sorry, Tom. Rough night," I quietly answer.

"Anything you want to talk about?"

Yeah, plenty, but how do I tell him that I cried? "I told Sam about our last supply run," I hesitantly reveal.

He looks at me, cautiously nodding, "How'd that go?"

"As good as can be expected, I guess." A lame answer, I know.

"So, what's troubling you then?" he presses.

I can't even look at him this time, "I cried like a big baby, while she just stood there and held me." Saying it out loud just makes me feel like a bigger idiot.

"I see," he slowly answers, "and now what, you feel like a fool?"

It's a question he already knows the answer to.

Shifting his body towards me, "Let me tell you something, Alex, being raised as a Singuri, we are taught that crying is weakness, and to turn such emotions off. When my wife died, I couldn't cry for her. When The Order took my daughter because she was born, 'differently,' I couldn't cry then either."

I look at him; I had no idea.

"Yeah, I had a family, but you wouldn't know by looking at me. That's the residue of the Singuri guard on me. I have always had to bury my pain, deep inside. If I shed even one tear, I would've been deemed faulty, and they would kill me and anyone I had left to care about."

I offer him the only solace I know, "I'm sorry, Tom, I didn't realize…"

"I don't want your apologies, Alex," he calmly shakes his head. "That's not why I told you. I want you to know that it's okay to cry. Pain. Suffering. Loss. They're all real and valid emotions. Feel them, respect them, cry over them, and then heal from them. It takes more courage to do that, than to bury them inside. Only a coward buries what he cannot face. It's taken me a long time to understand that truth, but I finally do." He pauses, allowing time for his words to sink in.

His words contradict everything my father ever said or lived. My mind grapples with this new perspective of what it means to be manly.

"You hear me, Alex?" Tom nudges.

I silently nod my head yes as my mind continues to tumble through my memories. In the rawness of Tom's confession, and my own feelings, I can't make sense of it all. "I just don't understand. My dad was the one who turned my sister in. No matter how much she begged and cried, he wouldn't listen. Then, there he was, picking up a gun to protect Micah and me."

Tom clasps my shoulder as a brother would, "It sounds like your dad lived with a lot of regret, a companion I know very well. I'm willing to bet the choice he made years ago, haunted him all this time. There was nothing he could do to take it back, so at the first sign of hope, he entrusted Micah to you, and did the one last thing he could. Now, you must decide if you can forgive him, and move on."

I know he's right. It's just going to take time. "Thanks, Tom." It's all I can say, before the quiet settles in.

"Hey guys, what're you doing?" Micah's bubbly voice breaks the short silence as he walks into the room.

Tom answers, giving me a few extra minutes to pull myself together. "Nothing much buddy, what about you?" I can see the brotherly relationship they've created, and I'm happy for them.

"Oh, you know, making sand beds." He looks so excited about his invention, but I'm concerned with what it means.

"Oh yeah, what's that?" He looks at me as though I'm a complete idiot.

"Well, it's a bed, made of sand. Come on, Alex, it's not that hard."

We all laugh at his response. He truly is my brother. "Where is this 'sand bed' exactly?" I ask, even though I'm pretty sure I already know.

"My room." He states. "I realized the other day how comfortable the sand was, and I thought, why not bring it inside and sleep on it. So, I did, and it's way better than the hard floor." I can see he is quite proud of himself.

"And guess what?" he asks me.

"Hmmm. I don't know, what?" He's really excited now.

"I made one for you and Sam too." He's smiling from ear to ear.

"You did. Wow! Thanks bud." I can see Tom hiding a chuckle. He's not getting away so easily. "You know what? I bet Tom would love to have one too!"

Tom looks up at me through slit eyes, quickly thinking of a way to get out of his new predicament. "You know, he's right. Unfortunately, I don't have time to do it today. Sorry, Micah. Actually, I should get back to work before I get in trouble with Mary." He turns to escape.

Completely missing Tom's dodge, Micah chimes in, "I can do it for you. Alex, do you want to help? I can show you how to do it."

The eagerness in his voice matches my own. "Absolutely. I would love to help!" I offer. "See you later, Tom. I've got plans with Micah..." Smiling, I turn and walk away, leaving Tom to his own mumblings. This should be fun.

True to his word, Micah leads the way to show me his wonderful idea. Along the way, we run into Sam, and she asks to tag along. Micah is more than happy to have her join.

"Okay, first things first. We need to find some good driftwood. Two long pieces and two shorter pieces. We're going to make a bed frame."

Jumping right into his orders, we set off to find the supplies. At one point, Sam looks at me questioningly. "You'll see," and that's all I tell her.

Finding what Micah has asked for, we bring the materials back to him.

"Okay, now we take them inside and tie them together. Follow me." Smiling at how much he's enjoying this leadership role, we follow him back inside to Tom's room. As he explains what we're doing, Sam tries to hide her laugh while I swallow my own chuckle, but for an entirely different reason. Once the frame is put together, Micah tells us to wait for him at the tunnel opening, while he runs to get something. Sam and I don't mind waiting, alone.

"Hey, I wanted to say thank you, for last night." I still feel foolish about it, but I want her to know it matters.

She doesn't say anything. Instead, she cups my face with her hand, leaning in with a gentle kiss. *How am I so lucky?*

"I take it back. I thank you for...right now." Pulling her close, I kiss her again as we slink away into the dark entrance of the tunnel. It's been a long time since we've stolen a moment for ourselves. I need to fix that.

"Ahem…are you guys done yet?" Micah's little voice interrupts our moment.

Laughing, Sam and I pull away.

"Thank you," Micah offers and leads on. He brought out a blanket that was cut in half and sewn into 'blanket cases' as he calls them. "Fill them up halfway, otherwise, they're too heavy. Then we'll carry them back to Tom's room and put them inside the frame on the ground. He's going to be so excited!"

"Yeah, he is!" I affirm with equal zeal. Sam shakes her head at us, chuckling. I love her smile.

A half hour and four blanket cases later, the deed is done. According to Micah, 'Tom is going to sleep like a baby tonight.' Satisfied with our work, he darts off to the main cavern in search of Julia and the other kids, leaving me and Sam trailing behind him.

"Well, that was fun. I almost want to hide in Tom's room, just to see his reaction." She winks at me.

I love when her mischievous side comes out. "I'd rather spend time with you. What do you want to do?" She looks around, "Hmmm, so many choices. Let's see…" She's having fun with this.

"Hi, Sam. Hi, Alex", Irene says to us with a coy smile as we pass her in the tunnel.

I notice the look exchanged between them and wonder what it means. Before I can inquire, Sam casually asks, "So, do you want to go shower? All this sand is making me itchy." Without missing a beat, she skips off towards the falls, and once I recover, I chase after her.

21
Long Awaited

Sam:

Our clothes are wet and clean when we finish at the falls. To my annoyance, the room was full today. I can't tell if Alex is disappointed or not. Sometimes, I feel like there's no doubting he wants me, but then there are other times, where I just don't know. Slipping out of my wet clothes, I wring out my hair and nervously wrap the towel around me. I haven't braved going out in my towel yet, though many people do. I normally have a change of clothes with me, but not today. Today I ran out without thinking clearly, and now I have to walk through the cavern like this.

You can do this, Sam, no one's even going to notice you. I mentally prepare myself. Stepping out of the privacy of the changing alcove, I'm aware of two things. One, Alex is still in his clothes, and two, he is staring at me. Biting my bottom lip, I feel my cheeks turning red.

Quickly, I shuffle past Alex and all the background faces in the room; I'm getting out of here, now! As I walk into our room, I stop short of our sleeping area. Laughing, I see Micah has made us a bed too. So caught up in the humorous secret, I don't even hear Alex come in, until he clears his throat.

"Um, you forgot your clothes." The uncertainty in his voice is only eclipsed by his nervousness. With my back still turned towards him, I grasp the top of my towel to ensure its security. "Thanks," I quickly respond. Needing to change the subject before my heart pounds out of my chest, I blurt the first thing that comes to mind. "I didn't know Micah made us a sand bed, too." Probably not the best thing to point out right now.

His soft laugh has me turning before I can stop my stupid curiosity, and sure enough, I see his signature smirk. My stomach flips. I wish he wasn't so handsome when he did that. Emboldened by my weeks of conversations with Irene, I allow myself to explore these new stirrings. I drink in the alluring effect his full lips have on me. Subtly, his smile shifts into something more. All too aware of how alone we are, and unsure of what to do next, our eyes meet with each other's unspoken desire. My cheeks flush as Alex takes a tentative step closer. I take a timid step towards him. He drapes my wet clothes on the back of the chair, leaving his hand there like an open invitation. I rest my hand on his, a quiet reassurance. Drawing my other hand to his lips, tenderly, he kisses my fingertips, setting every nerve on fire. Goosebumps rise on the back of my neck as my fingers remain on his enticing lips, igniting the hungry flame inside me. Craving more, I slowly pull our hands down and take the last step forward, kissing him in a way so there's no mistaking how I feel. His hands move to my hips, pressing me closer. All restraint abandoned, I eagerly reach for his shirt, struggling to get the wet fabric off. He reaches up and helps me pull it over his head. Then his arms wrap around me, enfolding me against his damp, bare chest. A burning desire swells inside me as his lips lightly brush my cheek, caressing the edge of my mouth. He moves down, kissing my neck, lingering at my collar bone. Then he retraces his steps until his lips land perfectly on mine. All I want is Alex! I want to know him, in every way possible. Pressing my body further into his, my hands find their way along the familiar scars across his back. I feel his muscles responding to my touch, and it empowers me. Drawing my face into his hands, he breathes, "I love you." Looking into his warm eyes, I see this man loves me. Knowing the one thing I can say to make him understand how I feel, I whisper "I love you, Alex Orion." The name I once hated. The name he asked me to give a chance. The name I now wear on my finger proudly. "I love *you*." He tenderly kisses me one last time, before the serenity of the moment gives way to our passionate desires.

22
Betrayal

Sam:

The loud, harsh sounds of the warning alarm awaken us from our blissful sleep. Alex and I jump out of bed, hastily throwing our clothes on in the chaos of the unknown. As we grab our emergency bags, Julia runs in.

"What's going on?" The terror is evident in her voice.

"I'm not sure yet, but I'm going to find out," Alex says. I'm glad he's taking the lead. "Grab your bag, and Micah's too, we're headed to Tom's."

We travel close and fast through the chaos of the cavern, until we run into Tom in the work room. Micah is standing right next to him, with a familiar blank look on his face. He seems to have checked out.

Instinctively I go to him, "Micah, it's Sam. Everything's going to be okay." Gently rubbing his back, I continue speaking slowly and clearly, to make sure he understands. "I need you to stick close to us, okay Micah?" Grabbing his hand, I steadily walk him over to Julia and place his hand in hers. "Here, you hold tight to Julia, and don't let go. I'm going to step over with your brother and Tom to figure out a plan. Now remember, don't let go of Julia's hand." I squeeze their joined hands one last time before releasing them from my own. Micah is still in his own protective world, but Julia nods at me with a quiet understanding; she will keep him safe.

Without time to waste, I turn towards Alex, "Okay, what's the plan?"

Alex hands me a gun, my gun, and I take it without hesitation. Tom steps into the role of a well-trained soldier, as he barks out orders, "Mary, you take the children and exit out of the north tunnel. Julia, Micah, you two go with her. Shane, you do a sweep of the main cavern, and make sure everyone is out, then—"

"Tom," Alex interrupts, "Shane isn't here."

In a singular moment, I watch disappointed clarity cross Tom's face, and my stomach twists with the bitter hatred of the truth. *Shane, what have you done?*

"Alex, you follow me, and we'll clear the main cavern. Sam, I'm going to need you too. Are you up for it?"

Without reservation I answer, "Absolutely, what do you need me to do?"

He pulls the chain from around his neck and hands me the dangling key. "Grab the world map and all the plans we have in the medical closet. It is crucial that no one gets a hold of them. If need be, burn them. Do you understand?"

The intensity of his voice leaves no room for question, and I nod my head yes.

Before I leave, I slip a small knife into Julia's hand and quickly give her a hug. "Keep your eyes and ears open Jewel's, you got this. I'll see you on the other side of the tunnel."

She grabs me before I can go, intently looking at me, "Rise together or fall together, Sam. I'll be waiting."

A smile of pride swells within me; she is so much more grown up than I realize. "Rise together, then. See you on the outside." I quickly kiss her on the cheek and leave her and Micah with Mary, knowing they will be safe.

Tom and Alex take off down the tunnel towards the kitchen area while I dash to the medical room. My sweaty hands fumble with the key, as the lock seems stuck and won't budge. I wipe them on my jeans and try once more. Instead of yielding and giving me the prize inside, the key snaps under my demand of submission. Panic bubbles inside me. "It's okay. Everything's going to be okay." My reassurance only goes as far as the words escaping my mouth. Beyond that my panicked lungs cry for fresh air as spots dance before my eyes. Closing out the world, I shut my eyes and breathe deeply, counting down from ten, an old childhood trick my father taught me when anxiety threatened my safety. *Five, four, okay Sam, you can think this through. Three, two, what do you have that can force the cabinet open? One.* With my countdown complete, the answer comes. Aiming my pistol, I fire the first shot and then the second, both landing side by side on my intended target. Darting to the newly breached cabinet, I quickly holster my gun and grab the sleek leather storage tube containing the vital documents. Before I have time to turn away, I hear *his* voice behind me.

"I think those belong to me, *Sam*." The M of my name is punctuated with all the hatred he holds for me.

Turning to face the wolf that's been lurking all this time, I find Shane with his treacherous hand outstretched towards me. "Funny, I'm pretty sure they're mine. That's why they're in my hand." I sneer back.

He laughs at me, while stepping closer. "You know, I have never liked you, *Sam*—"

"It's Samantha to you." I remind him of his refused attempt at trying to call me by my personal name. With our eyes locked, I casually shift the strap of the leather tube, securing it behind me.

He laughs smugly before sneering at me. "You're awfully arrogant for someone so plain." His curled lip softens, "Now your sister, on the other hand." He sucks the air in between his teeth, sending fire up my spine. "Now she's someone I could like. All. Day. Long." He pauses as though he is suddenly aware that Julia and I are not together. "Where is she by the way…with Tom?" He spits the name out like venom.

Working to control my rage, I know I need a clear head for what's coming. "She's safe, away from you. And if you were smart, you would stay far, far away from her." As I grind out my warning, I ever so slightly shift my weight, preparing to defend myself. "But then again, you've never really been that smart."

The veins popping out in his neck prove I've hit my mark. Teeth bared, Shane lunges for me. Sidestepping, I put into action my plan of attack. First, I punch him in his tender nose, ensuring I break it this time. Second, I swiftly follow up with a quick firm knee to the groin. He buckles over in stunned pain. Third, I run for the north tunnel. It's in this final step that I nearly collide with a Singuri guard at the mouth of the north tunnel. Fear grabs hold of me for a split second before I realize there's no other choice but to fight. I take a step back, raising my arm to protect myself from his oncoming blow. I hesitated too long, and his fist strikes me in the ribs. Pain shoots through me as I feel a crack at the point of contact from his knuckles. I don't have time to recover before he hits me again, dropping me to the ground. I narrowly roll out from under his foot, right before it crashes down next to my head. As I roll, I feel the hard metal of the gun tucked against my lower back. The gun! Grabbing my weapon, I aim at the Singuri. He lunges at me, and I feel my gun go off in unison with the sound of his own. He tumbles to the ground. I'm not sure of what's happened. As the guard's body slumps over my own, I feel the warmth of blood seeping through my clothes. *Did I shoot him, or did he shoot me?* Just then, Alex, Tom, and a group of others burst through the tunnel. Alex's eyes widen with fear, as he frantically runs to me.

Pulling the guard off, he exclaims, "Sam! Are you all right?" His hands travel my body, desperately searching for my wound. As he touches my ribs, I flinch. He gently lifts my bloodstained shirt to see where my pain is coming from. The fear in his eyes shifts into that of relief as he sighs, "No bullet wound. Thank God." He looks at me earnestly then, "Sam, I need you to get up."

I nod my head, as clarity floods my mind. I tuck the shock of my battle with the Singuri guard away. *I shot him. He is dead, and I am alive. Yes, I can get up, and I can keep moving.*

As we run through the north tunnel, with each shallow breath I take, it feels like a thousand needles stabbing me in my side. *It could've been worse!* Alex is beside me the whole way, and Tom is in the back, making sure everyone gets out safely. As we emerge from the tunnel, I'm surprised to find a solar transport bus, waiting in an old, abandoned building.

"Where are we?" I quietly ask.

Leaning in closer, Alex answers, "We're in the outskirts of the meadows. This is an old Singuri post. Tom has been working on this back-up escape plan ever since he noticed a shift in Shane's behavior."

Shane. I remember. I fought Shane. "Alex, I ran into him, inside the medical room."

He looks at me more closely. "Did he hurt you?" he growls.

I can't help the smile that crosses my face as I answer, "No. I hurt him."

Alex looks at me in astonishment. "First, the Singuri guard, and now Shane…I always knew you were amazing." He kisses me atop my head, a familiar comfort to me now.

As we travel down an old road under the cover of night, my heartbeat slows down as the adrenaline of survival tapers off. Gladly giving Tom the leather canister, I find my way to Julia, needing to see with my own eyes that she's okay. Sitting in a seat with Micah asleep on her shoulder, I drink in the undisturbed view of my sister's peaceful calm. I smile as I slide into the seat across the aisle and grab her hand.

"You all right, Jewels?" I ask.

She takes a moment before answering, "Yeah, I think I am." I understand what she means.

"Thank you, for watching out for Micah. It means a lot to Alex, and to me." She squeezes my hand as I continue, "Sometimes I forget just how grown up you are. You did amazing tonight, Jewels. I'm very proud of you."

She looks at me and truly sees my messy state. She leans in and says, "We rise together, Sam," proclaiming our victory.

Kissing her on the cheek, I put my forehead against hers, "Rise together."

It is our unbroken promise to one another.

23
Secrets

Sam:

It's dark by the time we arrive at the safe house, and I've had some time to think about everything that happened. I killed a man today! I'm not sure how I feel about it. I know he was evil, and trying to kill me, but I took another life. That's not something to take lightly. Then there's Shane, the man I wish I did kill. As long as he's alive, I will never feel at peace. Julia has become a sick trophy to him. He won't stop pursuing her, not until he has her. So, the next time we meet, I'm putting him in the grave.

I should've known the peace wouldn't last, not with me around. When my life settles into a semblance of harmony, something happens and completely rocks it. I was happy and content living underground, but maybe that's why it had to happen. Shane's betrayal forced me to remember the world outside. It made me see how I was truly living, as a rat. We were all rats, flushed out of our dark, timeworn tunnels. It's easier to see now, being above ground in the light of truth. Even still, I will always mourn the loss of my first, truly safe home.

It was a short, restless night before we awoke to another long day of traveling ahead of us. According to Tom, we should reach our destination tonight. As I board the bus, I look around and find Alex with his arm around his little brother. Nearby Julia is sleeping against Tom. My heart aches with the knowledge of my good fortune.

Mary nudges my leg to get my attention. "Come sit here and let me take a look at that side of yours." It's not a request.

I ease myself into the seat next to her and gently lift my shirt so she can inspect the damage.

"Yeah, that's a good one, or a bad one, depending on how you look at it." We snicker at her joke. Mary always has a way of lightening the mood. "Looks like a couple fractured ribs, Honey. When we arrive, you get cleaned up, and then come find me. I'll take care of you, you hear me?" Reaching up, she gently pats me on the cheek.

Smiling back, "Will do, Mary," I promise. She's a good person, but I get the feeling there are secrets behind the teasing and tender care. Even still, I've grown to love her. Mary's firm but spunky at the same time. She's always ready to impart wisdom, even if it comes in the form of a question. Though a little younger, she kind of reminds me of Ruth, from the crop rotation. She is defying the odds, and The Order. *I wonder if all old people become like that.* I laugh at my own musings, knowing Mary would not appreciate me calling her old. *I wonder what's become of Ruth.* Sneaking another look at Mary, I notice her lips pressed together in a frown, an uncommon look for her.

"What's the matter?" I gently ask, as my hand finds hers.

She shakes her head gloomily, "We didn't all make it out."

For the first time since we've been on this bus, I look around. It's only now that I notice the missing faces of some of the children.

My heart plunges, "Mary, I'm so sorry."

This strong woman, my pillar, leans into *me* and for the first time I see a crack in her armor. What pains has she endured that have allowed her to become this amazing woman? My heart breaks with hers. Mary, my warrior of strength and humor, is crying. My hand instinctively tightens around hers, as we both silently mourn the loss of such innocent lives.

My grandma's words come flooding back to me:

Tonight, the leaders have voted to end the lives of any child that does not fit their standard of normal. My heart breaks as I realize the depravity our world has fallen into. Why can't people see the truth? This is not for a better future: it is for a more controlled future. Well, I will not go quietly. I will fight and my Ben will know, we fight together, and we rise together."

A stubborn tear rolls down my cheek as I reflect on one of her last few journal entries. Grandma Brylie knew the truth then and died fighting for it. Is that to be my fate? If it is, I will embrace it, so long as the ones I love are safe.

Jolted awake, I stop myself from nearly falling off the seat. *I don't remember being here,* my sleepy mind briefly panics. Looking up, I find Mary snickering at me.

"Easy there, don't wanna add another broken rib; two's plenty." Mary winks at me and my heart warms with her getting back to her old antics.

With the reminder of my injuries, the familiar needle sensation returns with a fire. She's right, two is more than enough. I gently ease myself into an upright position and rub my eyes, not believing it's dark already. "I slept that long?" I ask no one in particular.

"Sure did, kiddo," Mary amusedly answers. "See, we're already here," she points out the window, "I thought I was going to have to wake you up, snoring as loud as you were—"

As I look out the window, Mary's taunting words become distant as the intrigue of what's outside becomes clear. With only a half moon to light up the night, the darkened outline of multiple structures reveals what appears to be another town.

"...If it wasn't for the less than smooth stop our driver made, I thought for sure I was going to have to shake you awake. He spoiled all the fun."

Mary's chuckle draws my attention back to her, just in time to see her playful smile before she turns to rejoin the kids.

Looking out the window again, I study the mysterious silhouette before me. The seat gives way as another person slides in beside me and the familiar scent of woodsy chamomile fills my senses.

"Where are we, Alex?"

"We're in Neva, a refugee town," he answers.

I turn to face him, with more questions in my eyes.

"Tom started it almost six months ago. He's kept it hidden from everyone, until recently, when he told Mary and me."

I know it shouldn't, but his explanation feels a little like a betrayal. Was Tom meeting with him about this place all the times I was meeting with Irene in the mornings? He knew and didn't trust me enough to tell me. Swallowing, I feel like the same burning needles in my side, are now tormenting my heart.

"How do the Singuri not know about this town?" I manage to mutter.

This time, when he looks at me, I can tell something's wrong. He pauses, taking in my own shift in mood before answering. "The Singuri don't look at land they consider useless and dead. Neva sits on top of a marsh. In the winter, it freezes over with the snow, but during summer, it can be a deadly bog, completely useless. When Tom was with the Singuri Guard, he was sent out here to scout for new land. It was deemed dead then, but he recognized the potential it could have, the potential of being a safe haven..."

Okay, sounds good so far, but... "What is it you're not telling me now, Alex?"

Not missing the subtle jab, he apprehensively answers, "Well, to make this town happen, and to keep it hidden, Tom has been in touch with some old 'like-minded' friends."

Absorbing this new information, I think on his words, 'old, like-minded friends'. Then it hits me. "The Singuri?" I ask in astonishment. "How can he trust them? Worse still, how could you not tell me about this place and the monsters running it?" I angrily whisper to keep our conversation private, since the bus is full of people. The accusation is out there. No taking it back now, and I don't want to. I feel mad, frustrated, hurt, betrayed...so many different things at the same time. I can't stand to look at him right now

"Sam." He says my name with such pleading, "I'm asking you to trust me. I need you to trust me. I don't have time to explain just yet, but I will, later. Right now, I need to get off the bus with Tom and meet with the council of Neva. I'm asking you to please wait until you hear everything before you make any kind of judgment. Can you do that for me?"

It's hard to hear him through the ringing in my ears and the fire that's currently consuming me. *Trust him? Wait without judgment? He didn't trust me after he judged I wasn't trustworthy enough to know of Neva. Can I do that for him? I don't want to do anything for him, ever again.* Closing my eyes against the conflicting feelings of my own vulnerability and my desire to punch him in the face, I need to be alone; I need to think. With my eyes closed, in my own private mental room, I reflect on the last few months. *All I have known Alex to be, has been goodness and truth. He could be deceived, but unlikely, because he is intuitively smart. And Tom, he's been a solid man, true to his word. If he was anything less than trustworthy, I would've never let him near my sister. So, are they deceived, or am I?* With a release of calming breath, I open my eyes and look at Alex. He's scared. My heart twists at the sight of him. "Okay, I'll wait." It's all I can say with the pain of his secrets still so fresh.

With a sigh of relief, Alex thanks me, pausing before he leaves. "I love you," he whispers, then turns and walks away.

I watch as he and Tom get off the bus. Alex lied to me. Well, he didn't exactly lie with his words, but he kept this massive secret from me. How am I supposed to take that? It's too much to sort out right now. Pushing this new information into its own box, I tuck it away with the rest of the ones I don't want to unpack.

I make my way up the aisle to Julia and Micah. I happily find Micah engaged in conversation with Mary and the other children. He appears to be fully recovered from the stupor he was in during the attack. *Thank God.* Looking to

Julia, I cautiously ask, "Did Tom tell you anything about this place?"

She looks at me with her wrinkled brow and nods her head yes. She's clearly uncomfortable with the idea as well. "It'll be all right, Sam." She's talking to me, but I know she's talking to herself too. "I trust Tom and he says they're trustworthy."

Wow! When did their relationship take such an important turn? I want to argue that Tom once trusted Shane and look at how well that turned out. But, if she, of all people, can take Tom's word for comfort, I most certainly will not rip that away from her. Keeping my lone concerns to myself, I simply nod my head in false agreement with her.

24
Neva

Sam:

The buildings I saw outlined in the dim moonlight were huts built up on stilts. I can see why The Order would call this land dead. The bubbling marsh beneath makes me feel like I am suffocating most days.

Accompanying the smothering air, there's no usable land for crops. Ever resourceful, the residents have figured out a way to grow them in greenhouses on stilts. Unfortunately, living in the marshy bog water are one of the few terrible pests that survived the wars. Mosquitoes! They're everywhere! I absolutely hate them, and because they seem to love me, I am now learning how to make a new bug repellant. I use the same eucalyptus and tea tree plant as before, only now I add something called lemongrass. It smells citrusy and helps tremendously with the bugs around here.

We are free to burn in the open, as the land was reported to have hot pockets that spontaneously combust. This lie Tom fed to The Order is kept alive by random burns.

The second night we were here, Alex explained to me about Tom's past. The Singuri guards that helped him, have all fled The Order and now live here. The ones that could, brought their families, which is such a foreign concept. I still have a hard time wrapping my head around it, but I see them, the old Singuri guards, and their families. They interact with the rest of us as their equal, which only shows how blindly wrong I was about the reality of my world. Not all Singuri are evil, just like not all Simpletons are good. With a divided force, I can now understand why The Order is so paranoid of an uprising.

The huts can only comfortably fit two. Alex and I have our own, while Julia and Micah share one at the end of the same dock. We have a connecting boardwalk between our two huts, which makes us all feel more at ease. It's interesting to me, how they worked the heating into each hut to ward off the cold of the piercing winters. The bog gives off a natural gas and these geniuses figured out how to harness the heat of the gas through a chimney. The flue runs from deep within the bog, straight up through the floor of each hut, and finally out through the roof for ventilation. The inner house portion of the flue widens, containing an interior box that's lined with hot stones, serving as a stove for warming and cooking.

In the two weeks we've been here, I have learned it's a completely different way of life in the Neva swamplands. It is off the maps and probably one of the safest places we can live. I often wonder about my family and what they would think of these different places that Julia and I have called home. I can see mom and dad thoroughly enjoying the ocean, but Matthew would have loved the bog. His curious, scientific mind would be in heaven right now. I hate knowing that I'll never get to see them again.

It's been a long day harvesting from the swamp. I feel disgusting and wish I could just soak under the refreshing falls of the cavern. Instead, I get the luxury of rinsing off with a hanging bucket of water. All pessimism aside, it's not that bad. We wash with a eucalyptus, lemongrass water infusion. It was a pleasant surprise when I discovered the 'indoor' plumbing they rigged through the same pipe design that runs through the floor and into our stove. Turns out, there's a smaller pipe within the lining of the larger pipe that draws water from the bog below. The water is cleaned as it passes through the heating element, much like our purification fields, and is then ready for use. For the cooler water, they run a secondary pipe back down through the bogs surface and bring it up again coming from a different nozzle. I don't know all the technicalities, but it's impressive. I'd say the only downside is having to empty the dirty water before hanging the little bathing tub on the exterior wall.

Tip toeing in from the shower area outside, I notice Alex has already drawn a bath for me. He must have done it before he left for his meeting. It's been weird between us since we arrived here. I'm pretty sure I'm the cause of it. Even though Alex was right about Neva and its occupants, I still feel the sting of his secrets. He hasn't tried to pursue me in any way physically, instead, he's been patient and kind. I don't know what to think right now. I miss him and the feel of his lips on mine, but I'm also not ready to go there again. It's not just Alex though, it's me. I'm different now, and I know I am. I just don't know what it means. I have done things I have never imagined I could do. I feel stronger, but I also feel more dangerous. Not wanting to think about this anymore, I push the tattered boxes of my thoughts from my mind.

Pulling the privacy blanket closed, I drop my small towel from my body and slide into the inviting bath. Closing my eyes, I force myself to focus on the way the hot water eases my sore muscles. Feeling each knot release, is enough to allow my body and mind to relax, slipping into an almost sleep.

Knock! Knock!

Foggy brained, I quickly jump up and mumble, "Hang on, I'm coming." As I wrap the towel around me, the front door lurches open. With my feet still in the lukewarm tub and my head popping over the top of my makeshift privacy curtain, I'm caught looking into the startled blue eyes of Neal.

"I- I'm sorry," he stammers as he turns his body around, so his back is facing me. "I thought you said to come in," he finishes apologetically.

Feeling his incredible discomfort from where I stand, "Do you always barge into homes that don't belong to you?" I tease with a giggle.

He nervously chuckles from the door.

Neal is a tall, well-built Simpleton from Paxton, but that's pretty much all I know about him.

Securing my towel around me, I slide the curtain back and tell him it's safe to turn around.

Seeing the blush slowly crawl up his neck inspires my own flush of confidence. "So, what are you doing here?" I ask, stepping around the curtain.

He fidgets with his ear as he answers, "Oh, um, Alex told me to stop by later, to grab an extra blanket, um, for my mom," he stammers.

I can't help but smile at his unease as I walk to the bed and grab a blanket from the drawer beneath. Unnecessarily smoothing any wrinkles from the folded quilt, I hand it over to him. A small tingle runs up my arm as my hand brushes against his, a feeling I haven't felt, since the last time I was caught in a towel. The memory deepens my flush colored cheeks. I look at Neal as he takes the blanket. Our eyes meeting only for a second before he quickly turns, thanking me on his way out the door. Not sure of what just happened, I plop down onto the bed, feeling confused and ashamed.

When Alex returns later that night, I tell him about Neal's visit. I dare not say anything more; I don't understand what the *'anything more'* actually was. As I lay in bed next to him, I know I find comfort in having him close by, but I also know we've changed. I look at Alex in the light of the night and visually trace his familiar features. His angular jaw, tense even while he sleeps, accentuates the fullness of his lips. Lips that still appeal to me, but the longing is absent. His dark hair is now long enough to rest on his forehead as I watch him sleep. My heart stings with the knowledge that I still care about Alex, but I don't desire him. Not the way I used to.

What is wrong with me, GG? I haven't spent time with her since being here. I feel too much like a stranger to open her journal. I'm glad to have GG close though, thanks to Alex who brought her back to me. With that one thought comes flooding in all the other kind things he's done. Closing my eyes, I whisper in a trembling voice, "Thank you". A warm tingling spreads throughout my chest. With the feeling of something small blooming again, I look at Alex. How can I feel a small something for him while I'm awake; then as I sleep, I dream of Neal in a way I once dreamed about Alex. Even my sleep confuses my already muddled heart. Allowing exhaustion to pull me in, my restless mind surrenders.

I slowly wake to the sound of Alex making breakfast. Quietly, I study him with my freshly opened eyes, enjoying that he hasn't seen me yet. I remain silent, watching the all too familiar scene play out before me and I can't help but smile.

"Hey, didn't I already tell you, no man cooks in my house?" I tease.

He shakes his head and mocks me, "I'm sorry your majesty, please forgive a simple man of his ignorant ways."

I start laughing and it feels good; it feels familiar. As I stretch out the sleepiness, Alex wishes me a good morning.

"Morning," I say through a yawn.

He chuckles again, then hands me a cup with an unfamiliar warm, dark liquid in it.

"What's this?" I ask

He looks excited as he answers, "Coffee. Try it. It's *so* good."

I take a sniff of the rich smelling aroma and decide if it smells this good, then it must taste good. Fully expecting a pleasant surprise, I carelessly take a big drink. I was wrong.

"Alex! This is disgusting. You like this stuff?" I accuse, a little too harshly.

He looks at me, honestly surprised by my reaction. "Yeah, I really do. You don't?"

"No, I really, truly, do not like it. It's bitter, and just…wrong." I respond.

Looking disappointed over the stupid coffee, he hands me my plate of food and sits on the foot of the bed. "Thanks for making breakfast though," I say with a halfhearted smile.

"Welcome." He quietly responds as the awkwardness settles in again. We eat our breakfast in silence.

"Well, I have a meeting with Tom and the council this morning, so I need to get going now. I'll see you at lunch?" I can hear the dread and hope mixed in his question. Dread that I'll say no and hope that I'll say yes.

I don't say anything, instead I shove a bite of food in my mouth and nod my head yes at him. A small hopeful smile tugs at his mouth before he leaves, without a kiss goodbye.

We're broken, and I don't know how to fix us. I'm not sure if I want to.

25
Space

Alex:

My mind is not on this council meeting, it's on Sam. She hasn't been the same since we fled the cavern. She's built a wall between us that I don't know how to get over, let alone break. I know I should have told her about Neva sooner, but I didn't know we were going to be attacked, at least not yet. I'm afraid I'm losing her, and that thought is unbearable.

"Alex, what do you think?"

Sarah's question breaks my depressing train of thought.

I didn't hear a single word that's been said since the meeting started. Tom must recognize my troubled face because he jumps in.

"My apologies, Alex has not been brought up on the newest developments in The Order yet. I will make sure he is caught up before our next meeting. With that being said, maybe we should call this a wrap and actually do something productive today," he teases.

The other council members all snicker at his little joke. I can always trust Tom to help me out. As we all say our goodbyes, I decide it's time to talk to Tom about what's been going on.

"Hey, thanks for that. My mind's been a little distracted lately."

"Anything you want to talk about?"

Maybe. Probably. But where to begin… "I think something's wrong with Sam. I know there is, I just don't know *what* it is. Ever since we left the caverns and came here, she has been distant. I know she's hurt I didn't confide in her about Neva, but I was going to the day we got attacked… Sometimes, I get a glimpse at how she used to be, how *we* used to be, and then it's gone. I'm afraid I'm losing her, and I don't know how to stop it."

I wasn't planning on pouring it all out, but it feels good to share this burden with someone else. Tom doesn't answer for a few long minutes, but I'm used to this response by now. He takes his time, measuring the words he hears and then usually gives sound advice.

"Alex," he pauses, "I think maybe you should give Sam some space."

This is not what I want to hear.

"I think Sam is hurting and confused. From what I understand from Julia, she has had a lot of changes in her life. I don't just mean you."

My shoulders slump. This isn't going the way I wanted.

"Relax, she loves you. I know this, not only because Julia told me, but because I see it. Alex, she has lost all her family, except for Julia. She was forced into a marriage she didn't want, at first. Then her sister was attacked, in the worst way imaginable. A person like Sam, feels responsible. Then there's the caverns. She was learning to feel safe again, and that was all ripped away. She had to fight for the first time in her life, and she had to kill someone. Now she needs to be able to sort them out on her own. You once told me you asked Sam to give you a chance to learn to trust you. Well, I think it's time you give her that same chance and trust her. Things aren't going to be the same, Alex. Not after what you have both been through. You'll be better and stronger, but you have to allow time for it to happen."

I sit, numbly listening to his words. I don't like his advice, or the fact that he's probably right. I don't want to be away from Sam; it physically hurts me just thinking about it. But this is not about me, it's about her. If she needs space, then I'll give it to her. Slowly, I breathe in the truth of what needs to be done and exhale my resolution to do it.

"Okay, Tom. I'll do it, but I'm going to need your help. It's going to hurt like hell, but I can do it for her, and only if she wants me to. I'll ask her this afternoon and offer to move out, and maybe stay with you, if that's all right. I don't want Micah to be too confused by it all, or Julia to know, unless Sam wants her too."

Tom nods his head in agreement.

"Thanks," I mutter.

I have a plan, now I only need the courage to follow through with it.

Tom clasps my shoulder, ensuring me that I'm not alone.

Lunch time rolls around all too quickly, and I'm not ready to see Sam. I slowly make my way to the hut, and I remind myself of Tom's words.

I open the door to find Sam dressed in a simple cotton dress. With the light casting through the window behind her, I can see the silhouette of her figure. She is breathtaking. My voice hitches as I try to pay her a compliment, "You look beautiful."

She smiles in response, and my heart soars at this small possibility of hope. I sit down hardly noticing the fish she cooked and set before us.

Okay, Alex, you must do this now or you're going to wimp out, I mentally prepare myself. "Sam, can we talk?" I cautiously ask.

She looks at me hesitantly but nods her head.

Clearing my dry throat, I press on to what needs to be done. "I'm sorry I wasn't there for you in the cavern, and I'm sorry I didn't tell you about Neva." I pause to collect my thoughts; the next part is not going to be easy. "I can see things are different between us. I feel the wall you've built, and I don't know how to get through it. When I try, it seems to only makes things worse."

She sits silently, not refuting my words. *It's true then.*

Taking a deep breath, I continue, "I was wondering," *just say it Alex,* "do you want some space, apart from me?"

Though it pains me to say the words, I know it's the right thing to do. As I watch Sam sit there, for what feels like eternity, she finally looks up at me. I see both pain and relief etched in her beautiful face. A tear escapes her moisture filled eyes and slowly rolls down her flushed cheek. Everything in me wants to reach out to hold her, but I know I can't. I need to stay where I am.

As Sam opens her mouth to speak, her voice comes out as a quiet whisper, "Yes." It's all she can say as the storm rolling inside her threatens to pour out.

I close my eyes as her "yes" punctures my heart, plummeting it from the new heights it dared to soar with a small bit of hope. Before this moment, there was always room for doubt, but now that has died away. There's a silent pause between us as neither of us knows what to say next. I need to make this as easy on her as possible, so slowly, I begin to speak. "Okay… I can stay with Tom at night and maybe some with Micah. I don't want him to know right now, he's still too fragile. I'll only grab my stuff for a couple days at a time and swap them out occasionally." Even as the words are coming out of my mouth, I still can't believe this is really happening. I don't want to leave her, and I don't want her to feel like I'm abandoning her either. "Sam, if you need me, I'm still here. Always."

I want to say so much more, but I know it would only be selfish. I quietly stand up, grab some clothes, and stuff them into my bag. I turn to look at Sam one last time, and whisper, "I love you," as I close the door behind me.

26
New Life

Sam:

I can't believe what just happened. Trying to make an effort, I borrowed a dress from Irene, one I knew Alex would like. I guess he did, but now I'm alone. My heart can't reconcile it all. *How did I let this happen?* Of course, I already know the answer to that, and so does Alex. *I'm damaged.* I thought he would always be there for me, but he asked if I wanted some space.

He did say he would be there for me if I needed him. My thoughts are a jumbled mess, and my emotions are even worse. Wasn't I just longing for the very thing Alex gave me, to be alone? But as I lay here, in our bed, the loneliness is overwhelming. Drawing my knees up to my chest, I begin to cry. It starts out slow from the pain of his absence. It then grows into a deeper aching sob, releasing everything that's happened over these past few months. I can feel the cold chill of the approaching winter settling into my now spacious hut. With no one around, I'm free to cry, and feel the ugliness of what I have become. As my suppressed emotions wash over me, I allow myself to be pulled into sleep and I welcome its embrace.

I wake up in the morning with my eyes puffy from the night before. I slept soundly, for the first time since we left the caverns. My body has forgotten what it feels like to truly rest, and it wants more. As I roll over, someone knocks on the door.

"Sam, can I come in?" It's Julia. *Does she already know?*

"Yeah," I croak. My throat feels raw, just like everything else in me.

She walks through the door, eyeing me suspiciously. "Are you okay, you sound terrible."

Relief floods me as I realize she doesn't know about Alex and me. Quickly I come up with an answer, "I don't think so, I think I'm sick." I really am sick, just not in the way I'm leading her to believe.

Concern crossing her brow, Julia comes over and gently places her hand on my forehead, just like our mother use to do. "You don't feel warm, but you do look and sound terrible," She teases. "I'll make you some soup, and a couple compresses to help you feel better." As she grabs me a cup of water, she continues, "I will bring them by later, but for now, I want you to drink this, and then go back to sleep."

When she offers me the cup, I can't help but smile at the motherly role she has assumed. She'll be an amazing mom someday.

Accepting the drink, I relish in the coolness the water brings to my dry throat and hum my relief. Julia looks satisfied with my response and gently kisses me on the head before leaving. Following her directions, I have no problem rolling over and sleeping my pain away.

I spend the next three days hiding away in my hut, feigning an illness that is only of the heart. Mary frequently stops by with Julia and Micah, who seems to be taking an interest in medicine. He looks worried about me, which makes me feel even worse for lying. I suspect Mary has an idea of what's going on, but she doesn't let on. She only recommends that I find my way outside in the sun before it disappears completely for the winter. When they leave, Julia typically stays behind, making me a replacement compress and doting on me. Today, however, I think I'll take Mary's advice.

"Julia, do you want to have lunch outside with me today?"

She looks at me with a smile on her face, "I would love to."

As we take our food to the outside bench, Julia sits quietly next to me. I watch as she nibbles on her sandwich and secretly long to have the calm resolve I see in her.

"Julia, you are truly amazing. You seem to have settled into Neva seamlessly, but that doesn't surprise me. You've always been able to find the good in things."

She looks at me thoughtfully, then answers, "Sam, you know you're amazing too, right? You are amazing, and you are good. Don't forget that. I can't imagine my life without you in it. I love you, Sam."

Drawing her into a tight hug, I realize she understands more than I thought. "You always seem to know what to say, Jewels. Thank you. I'm glad you're with me, and I love you too. Always." She is the first person I've hugged in a long time. I miss this.

"Ahem," we turn to see a bashful looking Neal, standing next to the hut. His striking blue eyes feel heavy on my self-conscious mind. "I was supposed to come tell you, Irene's in labor."

"What?!" Julia and I yell simultaneously as we immediately jump up, and start running for Irene's hut, leaving our unfinished lunch for the birds. As we approach the door, we can hear Irene panting to Mary, "Where are they?"

Without further hesitation, we burst through the door. "Here we are." I exclaim through quickened breaths. "Sorry, we came as soon as we heard."

She looks at me with a pained smile, "You're out of breath, like you're the one laying here trying to give birth."

We all laugh, as I note my need to get back into a fitness routine.

"How can I help?" I ask, resolved to think of someone other than myself.

Irene looks at me, "You can come stand beside me, and hold my hand. Julia can help Ms. Mary in any waaaaaaay—" She's cut off by a contraction, and I feel her squeezing my hand as she breathes through it. "In any way she needs," she finishes.

Irene is a resilient woman, that's for sure. As the minutes tick by, so do the contractions and the severity of her pain. The time approaches, and Mary instructs Julia and I to hold each of Irene's legs.

"Okay, Honey, it's time to push. Your body knows what it's doing, so listen to it. The next time you feel a strong contraction, I want you to push as hard as you can. You hear me?"

Irene nods her head, with only enough energy to reserve for what's to come. I wipe the sweat from her forehead, before grabbing her leg again as she pushes through the next contraction. Time stands still for a glorious moment, between the restrained cry of Irene, and the cry of her baby.

"It's a boy!" Mary announces.

She wraps him in an old sweater, turned baby blanket, and hands him over to Irene. She's crying, as she draws her newborn son against her chest. "He's beautiful," she whispers.

I feel tears running down my face as I witness the birth of a new life.

"What's his name?" I quietly ask.

She looks at me with a questioning smile, "I was thinking of calling him Samuel, Sam for short. If you're okay with it?"

I'm shocked. I mean, I know how I feel about Irene. She's my most cherished friend outside of Julia. We've grown close from all the time we spent together in the cavern, but only some here. I have not been a good friend lately, hiding away. I need to change that. "Absolutely! I would love it." Leaning over, careful not to squish little Sam, I gently give Irene a hug.

As Mary threatens to give us, 'a good ol' what for' if we don't give Mom and babe their rest, we finish our congratulations and leave. Laughing at another one of Mary's funny little sayings, Julia and I head back to our huts. Not wanting to return to the solitude just yet, I stop her outside my door, "Jewels, do you want to stay with me tonight? I think Alex is hanging with Micah," I lie, knowing full well that's where he's staying.

She looks at me, a little suspiciously, then answers, "Sure, sounds fun."

"Great," I nervously reply. I'm nervous because I didn't just invite her over so I wouldn't be alone. I invited her because tonight I need to tell her about Grandma Brylie. If I'm going to have any chance of moving forward and out of my own dark hole, I need to start by showing her the truth.

Sitting around the metal tub soaking our feet, I try to calm my racing nerves as I finally broach the subject. "Julia, I have to tell you something, and it's going to be hard for me to say, but I think you should know."

She looks at me apprehensively, then nods.

I go into detail over my attempted suicide and the journal that saved me. Julia just sits listening, with absolute calm. I know she is absorbing every word because a lonely tear slips from her cheek when I tell her I was going to kill myself. She doesn't even flinch when I reveal to her how our bloodline was tainted by The Order. I can't decipher if she's in shock, or if she's angry. Now that it's all out there, all I can do is wait.

Julia closes her eyes, and simply asks to see the journal. I haven't opened the pages since we fled the cavern. As I hand her the cloth covered treasure, she unfolds the fabric, and tenderly opens the pages. I watch her, as she lightly brushes her hand against the old written words Then she begins to cry. It's not a gut-wrenching cry, but it's a deep, unfamiliar cry and I'm not sure what to make of it.

"Julia, are you all right?" I ask with concern.

She takes a moment before answering, "Yes, I'm good Sam. I'm actually really, really good." A smile spreads across her face, as another tear falls from her closed eyes.

I feel horrible for not sharing this piece of our lives with her sooner. She could have been finding her own comfort this whole time, but I was too afraid. "I'm sorry I didn't show you sooner, I was foolish, and selfish and—"

She gently places her hand over mine, rescuing the nightgown I was twisting tightly in my lap. "You have nothing to be sorry for, Sam. I understand why you did it, and I'm not mad at you. I just thank you for showing it to me now," then she leans in to hug me. As her arms encircle me, her forgiving strength pours into my weakened soul.

"Will you show me the story of Bennette?" she asks with wary anticipation.

Julia, you are a beacon of light in this dark pit of mine. I nod my head yes as I draw back from her embrace and pick up GG's book. Flipping the pages to the familiar passage, I read Brylie's words of confidence and hope. As the story unfolds, I watch a new peace wash over Julia.

The darkness of night slowly fades into the warm pinks of the early morning, as Julia gets to know our grandmother, and I return to an old friend. This is the second time her journal has saved me.

27
Winter

Sam:

The bitter winter had settled in for four long months and my isolation became lonelier than I ever imagined. Julia, Irene, and baby Sam were my only little flickers of hope, as I desperately tried to cling to something good. My life was consumed with late night readings and hanging out with Irene and little Sam. But now, as spring settles in, I welcome back my old comrade, the sun. I didn't realize how much I missed our early morning chats, until I found myself alone in the cold lifelessness of winter days. Ah, but now the sun has returned, and with that comes the thaw and new life. Speaking of new life, little Sammy's cry draws my attention back to him.

I look over to Irene as she adjusts herself to nurse her son and am struck again with the absolute, pure love that is found there. She looks down at her son while he's eating and chuckles. "Settle down or you're going to spit it all back up again," she warns with love. It's moments like these that keep me coming back as often as I do. I know Irene's body is fully healed, but I still use it as a reason to hang around and help as much as I can. Today has been a quiet one, with Samuel nursing and sleeping most of the time.

As we sit at the small table in the serene atmosphere, Irene casually asks, "Have I ever told you about Samuel's dad?"

Pop! There goes the serenity. Shocked by the mention of someone I see only as a sperm donor, I can only shake my head no.

"As you know, I was already married to an unkind man. This wasn't anything new to me, since my own father was abusive. I never felt loved, or like someone who could be loved. Then one night, when John was drunk, he struck me down in our front yard. There were two patrolling Singuri guards who walked by as he struck me. That's when I met Marcus." She looks up at me, "Did you know that if you beat your spouse in public, you can get arrested, but if you keep it behind closed doors, they just ignore it?"

I nod my head yes. We all know how the game works for The Order. Look the other way, until you can't. I imagine his drunken rage is what drew the attention of the Singuri, and not Irene.

She continues, "As the one guard went to my husband, Marcus came to me. After he helped me to my feet, he gently ran his hand along my bruised cheek. I was never touched so delicately before. As his eyes were examining me, I thought I saw something in him that I mistakenly perceived as compassion. I know that sounds crazy, but you must understand, he was *kind* to me. Then the next thing I knew, Marcus had John by the throat, threatening to end his life if he ever touched me again."

This is a shocking revelation for sure, and it doesn't make sense with the man I saw dragging her off to the woods. "Then why did he try to kill you?"

Irene gives me a crooked smile before she answers, "Because he's a Singuri, and I'm a Simpleton. I foolishly believed he loved me as I believed I loved him. I had nothing to compare real love with. I couldn't see that his protection and kindness were just instruments to keep me to himself. What I regarded as compassion in him, was, unbridled passion. He wanted me and so he had to have me, but not forcibly. Oh no, his ego had to make me want him too. From the beginning, it was a game I didn't know I was playing. When I found out I was pregnant, I knew the baby was his. John hadn't touched me in months, abusively or intimately. I was so excited when I found out, but I wasn't sure how to tell Marcus, because of who we were.

"As time went on, and we continued our romance, I would ask him little questions about kids and having a family. He always gave me the right answers but would also ask if I was taking the herbs to prevent pregnancy. I was, when I got pregnant, but not after I found out. Just another sign I missed in my naive heart of his true intentions. As my stomach started to grow, I knew I couldn't hide it for much longer. I didn't want John to raise my baby, and Marcus had promised me a better life. I thought I knew his answer, before I told him about Samuel. We were in love after all." She rolls her eyes at the foolish idea. "I was wrong. As he was dragging me off into the woods, my distraught mind could only understand one thing, my baby was in danger. It was strange, how the opportunity presented itself. When he drew his gun, I could see the conflict on his face; I don't think even he expected it. In his small hesitation, I pleaded for one last kiss goodbye. My humility must have appealed to whatever was conflicted inside of him, because he pulled me in for one final embrace. As he poured the last drop of his passion into the kiss, I bit his lip and kneed him in the groin. It was easy to take the gun from him then. That was the shot you heard."

My heart grows for Irene, "You're a pilar of strength, you know that?"

She smiles at me, and then peeks down at little Sam. "So, you see little one, you were born out of love."

The adoration is evident in her voice, and the look on her face tells me she finally knows true love.

While she tenderly nurses her son, we hear a knock on the door.

"Come in," she answers, as she shifts the light blanket over her.

Tom and Alex enter, carrying in a beautiful, wooden rocking chair with exquisite details carved along the headrest. The dark, smooth planks for the seat and back offer an invitation of comfort. *Impressive craftmanship*, I mentally conclude. As my eyes travel from the chair to Alex, I can't help but linger. It's the first time we've been this close since he moved out of the hut.

"It's stunning." Irene's voice cuts into my thoughts.

"It truly is," I agree, turning my attention back to the chair.

Smiling, Tom speaks for them both, "We're glad you like it, because Alex made the chair. I only came to help deliver it, in hopes to catch a glimpse of your little Sam," he confesses.

"Alex! You did a great job. Thank you so much." Irene gushes.

Amazed by another unknown talent of his, I sneak another look at Alex and see a humble smile on his face. *I miss him*. This realization makes my heart pound with a buried longing.

As Irene adjusts herself and pulls Samuel out from underneath the covering, she hands Tom the small blanket and gestures for him to take the baby.

"Here, he needs to be burped," she teases.

I watch, as this once hardened Singuri guard melts into a sensitive father role. A role from which he was once deprived. As Tom gently rubs Sam's tiny little back, he starts to squirm, making little grunting noises. A loud burp escapes his small mouth, sending laughter throughout the hut.

"Well done, Tom, you're a natural." Irene compliments.

I see her well-intended words causing a subtle look of pain in Tom's eyes. A look you would only notice if you knew his story.

Tenderly, Tom kisses Samuel's rosy cheek, then hands him back to Irene. "Thank you." Clearing his throat, "we need to get back to the council room for our meeting."

Irene gladly receives her son again, and Tom looks at me, "Sam, you're welcome to join us, whenever you're ready," he invites.

Somewhat surprised, I calmly answer, 'Thanks, Tom, maybe next time," and I truly mean it.

When Tom turns to walk away, Alex briefly pauses to look at me. Neither one of us knowing what to say, I offer a timid smile before he turns and walks out the door. Confused over the exchange, I can't help but remember a time when I was *his* Sam.

Noticing the shift in the atmosphere, Irene asks, "What was that all about?"

Looking across the table at her, I don't even know where to begin. My eyes must show my painful confusion because the next thing I know, Irene's hand is resting on mine.

"It's okay, I don't need to know. Just trust that whatever is going on here can be worked out, *if* you love him. You need to ask yourself: Do I love Alex? Not because he's a great guy. Not because he's your husband, but because you choose him. Hell, maybe you didn't even choose love, you just fell into it with him. But if you haven't," she pauses until I look at her again, "that's okay too. If you don't love him, then you need to let him go, for your sake, and for his."

There's nothing but stillness and the pounding of my heart in my ears. Time seems to have stopped as the question suspends in my brain. *Do I love him? Do I love Alex Orion as I once professed, or do I need to let him go?* With only the thought of letting him go, my brain begins to function again. Images of our past play in my mind: my cruelty when we were first married, his patience and kindness towards me, his terrifying burn and the healing that came with it, the Singuri charging in at night and Alex shielding me, his forgiveness of my betraying journal, the gift of bringing it back to me, the confession of his conflicting pain towards his father, the deep ache I felt for his pain, and the stolen moments and glances meant only for him. My hand reaches up to my heart, feeling the memory of his touch resting there.

I know the answer to her question…

"Are you okay?" Irene asks.

I feel her hand squeeze mine as I remain silent. I know I need to talk to someone, but I don't want to spoil this time for her and her new baby. So, I calmly squeeze her hand back and coolly answer, "Thank you for asking, but we just miss each other." It's not a lie, but it's also not the full truth.

Reading between the lines of silence, Irene accepts my answer without pressing me further; she is truly a good friend. Ushering me out of her hut, claiming she and Samuel need a nap, Irene hugs me one final time before closing the door.

Retreating from her serene home, my calm resolve lasts maybe ten steps before I start running in a new direction. I know exactly where I need to be.

"Have you seen Julia?" I ask, walking into Mary's hut unannounced.

"Well, it's nice to see you too, Sam. What if you saw more of me than you were bargaining for, barging in like that?" She teases, with a smile on her face.

"Sorry, Mary, you're right. Let me try again." I step out and then knock on her door.

"Just a minute, let me put on some clothes really quick. I enjoy walking around in the nude when I'm all alone, in the privacy of my own hut!" Mary doesn't care who might hear her loud teasing as she taunts me once again.

Unable to hide my laughter, "Mary, can I come in?" I ask through chuckles.

"Sure thing, Honey. All decent now."

I walk back in shaking my head, "Hi, Mary, it's good to see you. NOT, all of you, just you."

She snickers at me.

"So, how have you been?" I offer with a smile.

"Well now, that's more like it," She teases. "I'm good. Thank you for asking," she says, with a sparkle in her eye. Ms. Julia is teaching the kids in the greenhouse today. She's become quite the good little teacher." Mary proudly declares.

I smile at this idea knowing she's always been good with children and has a heart for them too. I nod my head in agreement as I ask, "Can we talk?"

She looks at me, and silently pats the seat next to her.

I nervously sit down. As we both wait in the silence, I take my time sorting out what I want to ask. With a deep sigh,

I decide to jump all in and start with my greatest fear.

"Mary, do you think someone can be so damaged, they're beyond help?"

She studies my face with her comprehending eyes before she honestly answers.

"Well, Honey, I think that has everything to do with the person. If they want to change, or forgive, or whatever it is they need to do, then I'd say, they're not beyond help. But, if the person doesn't want to do those things, and only expects everyone else to, then I'd say, it's not looking so good."

She doesn't push me for more information, she only waits.

"Do you think I'm damaged beyond help?" I whisper.

Silence. A long pause of horrible, confirming silence. I can't look at her. It's me who doesn't deserve Alex, not the other way around. I feel a gentle hand under my chin, nudging my face to look at her. Allowing my head to be tilted up, I keep my eyes closed in fear of the judgment I'll find in the wake of her silence.

"Well now, who ever said you were damaged?"

At the sound of her reassuring voice, my eyes slowly open and I am completely unprepared for a teary-eyed Mary. Cradling my face lovingly in her hand, my own reservoir of tears spill over, slowly rolling down my cheeks. I stare into the face of a woman who loves me like her own flesh and blood. She is just another person I don't deserve.

Her thumb wipes away a tear as her voice finds strength once again. "I certainly didn't say you were damaged. I know Julia and Alex didn't, and well, Tom knows better...so it must've been you," she wisely concludes.

Heaviness steals my voice. I can only nod my head as shame bears down on me.

She wipes my tear-stained cheek as she reaches her other hand to the opposite side of my head, tilting my face at full attention so I can't turn away from her.

"Samantha Orion, you hear me now. You are not damaged. You are hurting, but you are not damaged. You are a survivor. You have lost a lot in your young life, and you've been forced to make decisions that not many people have. Now listen here, *You. Are. A. Fighter.* You fought for your sister, you fought for your life, and you continue fighting for each day you're living, but you need to learn to pick your battles. Too much fighting isn't good for any one person." She pauses, allowing me time to process everything she's saying. "Sam, I know you and Alex aren't together in the same hut."

My breath hitches in surprise.

"Don't look so shocked. I notice things. What you need to understand, Sam, is that doesn't mean you're not together. That man still loves you, and I can see you still care about him. I also know you don't want to stay in this rut, or you wouldn't be talking to me. Honey, it's time to let go of the things you can't change and learn to grow from them. They don't define who you are; they only add to who you are becoming. You, my dear, are a beautiful, strong warrior."

I have never heard Mary speak so much at one time. The weight of her words washes over me as I claim her affirmation as my own. A new round of fresh tears freely flows with each soul cleansing sob that I cry. Mary pulls me into a hug, and I melt into her, releasing everything I have bottled up.

"How do I fix it, Mary?" I ask between sobs. "I miss him."

She speaks into my ear, "Let him in, and trust that he still loves you. Not with an untested young love, but with a mature steadfast love. Keep in mind, Sam, your love will be tested and challenged for the rest of your lives. But you get to grow together, if you choose to."

I hold her tight, "I do. I do want to grow old with him," I cry.

She gently pulls me away and looks at me with her little smirk, "Then why are you telling me? You should be telling him."

I take in a ragged breath knowing she's right. Brushing away my tears, I sit up tall. "Thank you, Mary. You're the grandmother I've never had," I whisper, kissing her on the cheek before I turn and walk away. I have plans to make.

28
Reconciliation

Sam:

It's been four days since I've talked to Mary; four days
to figure out what I want to say to Alex; four days and I'm still
pacing the small space of this hut. Abruptly, I'm interrupted
by Alex's knock on the door. I breathe deeply to steady myself
for what's to come. Nervously biting the inside of my cheek, I
open the door.

"Thanks for coming," I say.

"Thanks for inviting me," he responds.

There's an awkwardness in the air as I gesture for him
to have a seat at the small table, where I've prepared another
simple meal of seasoned fish and rice. My nervous doubt
assails me: *maybe I should have made something different this time,
considering our last failed meal together. But it's not like we have a
ton of options.* I internally rationalize my own anxious
thoughts.

Alex whiffs the air as he steps in and a pleased sound
escapes his lips, "Mmm," he smiles, "smells good." As his eyes
shift from the food and settle on me, the heat of his gaze
rushes up my neck and into my cheeks; I still get butterflies

when he looks at me.

"Thanks," I offer. "Do you want to sit down?" *How am I ever going to get through this night?* As we both take a seat at the table, I nervously tug on the end of one of my curls. Twisting the lock around my finger, I look at him and find a smile flickering across his face. He watches as I release my curl and it bounces back to its original spot. *Oh, right. He likes that.* Motivated by this little truth, I take a quick breath and jump right in.

"First, I want to say thank you, Alex. Thank you for giving me space… I wanted to hide the person I feared I was becoming, because I didn't know who she was. And because I didn't want to hurt you." He leans forward to say something, but I put my hand up to stop him.

"Please let me finish, or I might not be able to do this." He settles back into his seat, allowing me to press on. "Second, I want to say I'm sorry. I was hurt by the secrets I thought you were keeping, and I never gave you a chance to explain. I was such a mess and so afraid. I was afraid of what I did in the cavern. I was afraid of this place. I was afraid of losing everything again. But instead of losing it, I pushed everyone away… Alex, I don't want to be away from you anymore, it hurts too much. I want to let you in, but I'm terrified. So, I'm asking, can you be patient with me? I would like to take our time getting to know one another. Only this time, I want to do it for ourselves and not for our circumstances. Just you and me. Can you do that?"

I feel like I just emotionally threw up, leaving me raw and helpless in the succeeding silence. Braving a glance at Alex, I'm met with an intensely unnerving gaze. *I wish I knew what he was thinking.*

Ever so slowly, he answers with a smile, "Yes." Those

three simple letters carry so much meaning.

I slide my hand across the table grabbing his and raising it to my lips, I tenderly kiss his fingers as he did mine, many months ago in the North Sector. It seems a lifetime ago. As I look at him, with his warm eyes searching mine, I feel the familiarity of the home I once found in them. I welcome him back into my heart.

Alex doesn't leave tonight, he sleeps beside me, in our bed once again. I feel the warmth of his body next to mine. His rhythmic heartbeat lulls me into a deep peaceful sleep.

In the morning I wake up to a familiar scene, Alex cooking breakfast. My heart smiles with the recognition of this simple act, and I decide right then and there, Alex can make breakfast for the rest of our lives; as long as he's with me.

"Mmm, smells good," I smile.

He turns, looking at me with a smile of his own, "Thanks, I hope you don't mind?"

I can hear his lingering doubts and immediately want to squash them for good. "Not at all. If you want to spoil me with breakfast every day, I give you permission."

He chuckles, readily accepting my olive branch.

"Is that bacon I smell?" I ask in disbelief as my mouth salivates at the thought.

"It is, with some fresh eggs and a side of fruit," he answers over his shoulder. He's spoiling me.

Feeling giddy and anxious, I dive into a nervous chatter. "I have missed bacon so much. I would've sacrificed the clean, fresh air for pigs in the caverns, just to have some. Did you know we have a drove of them, here in the bog? It works out nicely, because they turn up the orange candy-root that's trying to take over the marsh. Who knew? Pigs, they're helpful *and* taste delicious."

He looks at me funny, with my nonsensical ramblings.

"Don't worry, I've only missed bacon, *almost* as much as I've missed you."

He laughs. "I'm glad you cleared that up, I was getting a little worried." We both laugh at the ridiculousness of the situation. It feels good to be bantering again.

Alex and I settle into our new normal. We don't have a lot of free time together, considering we still want time with Julia, Micah, and Sammy. It's become a routine for us to go jogging around the boardwalk every evening before dinner. My lungs burn and I am reminded that it's good to be active again. Rounding a corner, I spot Neal and Irene out for a walk with Sammy. I can't help smiling at them and their new little family.

Alex cuts into my thoughts, "Do you feel up to sparring again?"

It's been a long time since I've practiced, so I eagerly answer, "Yes, but where?"

He smirks at me, and I know he's excited to show me something.

As we slow our jog down to a walk, we stop in front of a long structure, one I haven't noticed before.

"This is the council room," he explains. "We don't just meet here to talk; we also train here." Eager to show me inside, Alex grabs my arm and pulls me through the front door.

"SURPRISE!" A loud chorus of voices greet us. I instinctively jump back. Startled and confused, I look around and see the smiling faces of Julia, Tom, Mary, all the children, Irene and Neal, who's now holding Samuel.

Turning to Alex, I quietly ask, "What is this?"

"It's your birthday, Sam," he quietly confides.

It's already June 30th? I can't believe we've been gone for a year. What about the new year, or Julia, Alex, and Micah's birthdays? Was I so out of it I have no memory of them coming and going? That can't be. I look over at Sammy and notice he's not a newborn anymore. My face burns at the realization of my selfishness. Time is too precious to lose. Resolving to correct my behavior, I smile at everyone. "Thank you so much, it was truly an unexpected surprise." I turn to Alex, giving him a threatening look that earns a round of laughter. Then I realize, it's not just my birthday. Reaching down, I grab his hand as I turn back to our friends, "Today is also our one-year anniversary," I proudly announce.

Everyone shouts out congratulations! I look to Alex, finding joy exuding from his face.

"Thank you," he whispers.

I lean in, placing my hand on the side of his face, "No, Alex, thank you," and my lips longingly meet his.

The room erupts in hoots and hollers, disrupting the moment, and causing my face to turn a deep shade of red.

Beaming, Alex projects, "All right, that's enough. I thought we were celebrating."

I catch Julia's quiet comment as we walk by, "You'll definitely be celebrating later," she teases.

I shake my head and keep walking, though internally I'm freaking out a bit. Alex and I haven't been intimate since the caverns. Tonight was the first time I truly kissed him, and it was in front of a group of people. *What if he is expecting that? Am I ready? Are we ready for that level again?*

After the party, Alex and I stroll along the boardwalk, enjoying the sounds of the night. We sit on a bench outside a new, vacant hut and look up at the stars. It's been a long time since we've done this.

"Do you know why they've been building more huts?" I ask Alex.

"I haven't heard anything, but I imagine they want to be ready for any new refugees."

That makes sense, though I still can't wrap my head around this other world we currently live in. "It's amazing how this whole life exists outside of The Order. It makes me hopeful."

"I know what you mean," he says as he holds my hand.

Hearing the change in his voice, I look over and find Alex gazing at the stars. I study his face, noting the stubble he's forgotten to shave the last couple days. "Alex, are you ok?"

He closes his eyes, with his face still turned towards the sky, "Yeah, I am." He then turns to look at me, "I can't help but think of all the people who are still oppressed by The Order. They deserve a chance at this life too."

His mind is always on others. Squeezing his hand, I lean up and peck him on the nose, bringing a smile to his face.

29
Proposals

Alex:

I spend another morning making breakfast for Sam, this will never get old. Our lives are vastly different now than they were three months ago. It leaves me amazed at how different our love is. I was preparing for her to tell me it was over, but instead, she asked if we could take it slow. I would give her eternity. Dating Sam has been the easiest thing I have ever done. Though I admit, it has been hard at times to not pursue more than a kiss. I don't think it's one sided either, but we both agreed to see how we do without sex. I wouldn't say it has ever been easy for me, because I know I am irrevocably in love with Sam. However, being with her, in this way, has shown me the absolute love she has for me. Watching her now, there's only one question that comes to mind—

"Stop watching me eat," she protests, interrupting my thoughts.

"You would deny a man his favorite pastime," I quip as her laughter strengthens my heart. "Sorry, I just can't help it, you're too beautiful in that dress," and she is, in that dress, or any other. I see a subtle hint of pink on her cheeks, reminding me of the effect my praise has on her. I reach my hand out, gently touching the blush that's blooming, "I mean it, you are beautiful." She rests her head in my hand, and I see she finds courage in my words. I will always build Sam up into the woman she truly is.

Sliding my hand away, I lean down and kiss her cheek, still warm from my touch. "I would love to stay here all morning with you, but we have commitments to keep."

"I know, you're right," she concedes, and scoots out her chair. "Let me change into my work clothes, since we have a date working the bog today. Don't forget, we have a council meeting tonight."

"Actually," I grab her hand, pulling her back towards me. "I ran into Tom this morning when you were still sleeping. The meeting tonight has been bumped up, so, we don't have to work in the swamp today." I pause, as she tries to conceal her pleasure in hearing the news. "I know you're happy about it, so there's no use in hiding it," her smile widens, "but I personally feel robbed. I was looking forward to seeing you in the mud." I raise my eyebrows at her and smirk.

She punches me in the arm before scolding me, but her laughter ruins any illusion of anger.

"You know, I don't think you realize how strong you are," I say, as I rub my arm for emphasis.

She stops laughing, and leans over, lightly kissing my arm. With her lips still against my skin, "I'm sorry," she whispers.

Closing my eyes against my growing passion, "Sam," I whisper back, "do you even know—"

She cuts me off with a fierce kiss. As she pulls away, I see a playful smile.

Taking a deep breath, I answer, "Yeah, that about sums it up," and she giggles as she walks to the door.

"Something to look forward to," she winks at me, then walks out. I love when she's like this.

Dumbfounded, I wonder if she knows of the plans I've made for tonight. I grab the door, closing it behind me, and run to catch up with her.

Still feeling dazed from her kiss, I nearly bump into Tom as we enter the hall. "Oh, excuse us," I say

Tom just looks at us, then gestures for us to follow him. I can see by his set jaw, something's going on. Sensing the change in the atmosphere, my demeanor shifts into one of business.

"What's happened?" I ask.

"I'm not entirely sure, but we're about to find out," he answers cryptically. Now I start to worry.

Entering the council room, we find the others are already seated around the table. I pull a chair out for Sam and then take my seat beside her. She started coming to the meetings a couple weeks ago and I'm glad she did. She belongs here.

"Thank you for coming." It's Adam who greets us. "I only wish I had good news to report."

From my peripheral view, I see Sam shift her body to attention. We both recognize the seriousness of his tone preludes to another change.

"We are getting reports that Paxton is under lockdown. After the most recent changes made to the DNA testing, The Order has been 'cleansing' the Simpletons. We now fear it's spreading to the nearby towns. Our inside guards have done all they can to facilitate the rescue of as many people as possible." As he pauses, the grim expression on his face tells us that the number of casualties is high. "With the caverns no longer safe, we only have Neva and Digby as sanctuary for all the refugees. We will be receiving refugees in approximately one week, and we're already running out of room. Digby is another safe haven town located about a day's drive, east of here. It's almost at capacity as well."

"What about Harlan, should we consider opening its doors? I'm sure there are some of us who would go there." Tom offers up this unfamiliar town. I can tell by the look on the other members' faces, that Tom just divulged information he wasn't supposed to share.

"Harlan?" Sam questions. "I thought there was only one other town, Digby?"

I nod my head in agreement, as this secret is news to me as well.

Tom looks from her to me, then explains, "It is the only other town, but Harlan is not a town—"

"Tom," Sarah cuts him off, "what are you doing?"

Looking deliberately at each member of the council, Tom begins, "I'm offering a solution. You say we need more room. I say Sam, Alex, and the rest of the people here are trustworthy. When we tell them about Harlan, you will find over half the people here will want to go. We've asked them to trust us. Now we need to be willing to trust them with this," he concludes.

Silence fills the room, as the council considers Tom's words.

"What do you propose?" Adam asks.

Turning his attention back to me and Sam, Tom explains, "Harlan is the headquarters of our rebellion. By the sound of it, the one your grandmother helped to start."

I hear Sam gasp, as this new information shocks

everyone in the room.

"How do you know about Brylie?" she warily asks.

Tom shifts before answering. "The night we fled the cavern, I overheard what you and Julia said to one another, about rising together. I asked Alex about it on the bus, and he told me it was a family promise you carried on. That's when I first suspected a connection. Then, when you showed Julia the journal, she started telling me about Brylie. Please don't be angry with her; she was just so excited to be connected to someone who understood her struggles." Sam gives him a reassuring nod before he continues. "Sam, from everything I have learned, I think Brylie was part of the original rebellion. 'Rise together, or fall together,' is the mantra of our cause."

She sits stone silent as the meaning of Tom's words sink in.

"Sam, what do you have to say?" Adam questions.

I watch as she stands with a newfound courage and addresses the council. "It's true. What Tom suspects must be true. It all makes sense now," she pauses, as she searches through her memory of the many journal entries she has scoured. "I've read of her protests and rebellious uprisings from when her enemies were first coming into power. I didn't connect the dots before. Those enemies must be the founders of The Order. If your motto is truly what Tom says it is, I have the journal entry of exactly when she wrote it. If you have a rebellion compound hidden, then I say yes! I absolutely want to go. Also, Tom's right. There are many who will go with us."

I have never been more proud and terrified than I am now. I rise and stand next to Sam, showing a united front. I say, "Rise or fall, we do it together." In a show of unification, she puts her hand in mine.

"Thank you," Adam offers, "I couldn't agree more."

Carried by the momentum, Tom interjects, "Then I think it's time we make a plan." With that comment, the room turns into a frenzy of ideas and resolutions.

It's late into the night when the meeting finally comes to an end. Sam and I walk back to our hut, lingering under the stars to steal a moment of normalcy to ourselves.

Drawing her close to me, I whisper into her beautiful mess of curls, "I thought you were brilliant tonight."

She turns her face to look at me, "I still can't believe it's true. My Grandma was a founding revolutionist. She never ceases to amaze me," she muses.

Leaning in with a savoring kiss, "I know what you mean," I whisper.

After a long moment, she slowly pulls away, smiling at me, "Not yet."

As her hand finds mine, I innocently tease, "What? I only wanted to kiss you," and it's true.

She shakes her head at me laughing, then pulls me along to our hut.

When we enter the door, Sam abruptly stops, and I nearly bump into her.

"What's this?" she asks, pointing at a banner hanging in the middle of the room.

"Julia," I say under my breath. *She must've done this. I should've never told her that I was going to do it tonight.* I try coming up with an alternate explanation when Sam interrupts my feverish mind.

"Why does it say, 'Congratulations Sam and Alex?' Congratulations for what?" she wonders.

There really is no way around it. I have to tell her the truth. Shuffling my feet, I ask Sam to sit down. She looks at me reluctantly but does it anyway.

"Well, before we had the meeting, I made other arrangements. When the meeting went in the direction it did, I decided not to follow through with the other plans. I didn't realize Julia would do this," gesturing to the banner, "so I didn't think to tell her not to." I know I'm rambling, but this isn't how I had imagined this going.

"Alex," Sam draws my attention, "You're making zero sense right now. Can you please say it in a different way? It's just me."

I sit next to her on the bed and take a deep breath, reigning in my heart. "Sam, that's just it. You have never been, 'just Sam' to me. I have loved you long before we were married. When The Order matched us, I couldn't believe my luck. I knew you despised me, but I was determined to show you I was different. Back in the caverns, when you first told me you loved me, I felt like the richest man in the world." As the turmoil of my memories rise to the surface, so does the deep ache they left behind. "Then I had to let you go, and I felt like the most destitute man in the world." As I choke out the words, she grabs my hand and humbly kisses my palm. Drawing her hand to my chest, I place it over my steady beating heart. "When you asked me if we could take it slow, I felt my heart come to life again. Being with you is like breathing; natural and effortless. My love has changed from when we were in the caverns. It has gone through some rough growing pains, and it's stronger because of them. I know you didn't choose me, Sam, not at first. I have always wished I could make that right." Keeping her hand pressed against my chest, I shift my body, so I am kneeling before her. "With Julia's approval, and my love, I'm asking you, Sam Wells, if you will marry me...again?"

She looks at me with tears in her eyes and I worry I've

said something wrong. Then, unexpectedly, she throws her arms around me, kissing me over and over while she exclaims, "Yes, yes, yes, an infinite number of times over, yes!"

Her joy is contagious as I scoop her up, aching to be closer. My yearning grows into need, my voice comes out low and deep, "I love you," I profess, "I have loved you forever, and I will love you always."

She reaches her hand into my hair, pressing her lips to mine. I love the way her desire feels as she kisses me deeper, again and again. It would be too easy to let the night carry us away. Hesitantly, I set her softly away from me, with my forehead touching hers, "Not yet," I whisper with a smile.

A quiet, unsteady laugh escapes her lips as she exhales deeply, "Thank you."

In this choice of restraint that we've made, something more than passion grows between us.

30
Family

Sam:

I didn't think anything could surpass the knowledge of my rebel roots, but Alex's profession of love transcended it far beyond what my heart could believe. He surprised me with his proposal in the best way possible. He made it easy to say yes. As sure as I am of his unwavering devotion, so is my absolute love for him.

I slip out of bed, still wearing my cotton shorts and one of Alex's stolen t-shirts, and tip toe my way to the kitchen. Today, I'm making breakfast for him. Bending over to put the large, flat, hot stone into the stove, I hear Alex from the bed.

"Now that's a great view to wake up to."

Shaking my head, I tease, "You're lucky I'm holding this rock in my hands."

"Well, that depends. Are you going to throw the rock at me? In that case, I'm not lucky at all. If you are implying that if your hands weren't full, then you would put them on me, then I'm pretty lucky." He laughs at his own wit, and I can't help but join in.

"Well, why don't you come here and find out," I

challenge.

"Oh no! I prefer the safety of our bed and the view," he winks at me, "By the way, you look cute in my shirt."

I didn't really think much about how it would look when I put it on, only about how it would smell. Now that I know, I will have to tuck it away for future use.

"I'm glad you can see past this mess of curls I have going on," I divert.

"Your 'mess of curls' is one of my favorite things about you. Also, your long legs, which are currently teasing me from the bottom of my shirt," he adds.

Biting my lower lip, I see the mutual hunger in his eyes. "Yeah, it's probably best you stay over there while I cook breakfast," I confess.

He falls back into bed as my words sink in, and I chuckle at his response.

Breaking the moment, there's a knock at our door. "Who is it?" I call out.

"It's Julia—"

"And me too," Micah pipes in.

Then in unison they ask, "Can we come in?"

Looking to Alex apologetically, he nods.

Tucking his shirt into my shorts so you can actually see them, I mouth the word, 'mine' to Alex as I tug on his shirt. He shrugs his shoulder and bobs his head up and down with a goofy grin on his face.

"Come in," I say, through my chuckle.

Without further delay, they come bounding in through the door like two eager kids waiting for dessert. "Well," Julia impatiently gestures to her sign.

"Obviously you already know the answer," I tease.

She throws her arms around me, bouncing up and

down with her congratulations.

Laughing at her enthusiastic joy, I peer over Julia's shoulder. Micah walks over to his brother, stretching out his hand, offering him a congratulatory handshake. *He's such a funny, little man.*

Once Julia calms down, she turns and hugs Alex. Then Micah hugs me, with the biggest smile on his face.

"I'm glad you're my sister, for real now." His simple words catch me off guard, but the depths of them touch my heart, and I hug him tighter.

After all the congratulatory greetings are over, we sit down for a family breakfast.

"Julia, do you mind hanging around afterwards?" I ask.

"Not at all. I would love to spend some extra time with you, before Alex steals you away for good," she teases with a wink.

Micah pipes in, "Does that mean you'll have some extra time this morning too?" directing his question to Alex.

"It sure does, but since you beat me to the punch, I'll just ask now. Do you want to go fishing with me today?"

Micah's eyes light up with the idea of doing two of his favorite things, hanging out with his brother and fishing.

"Well, yes, but I want to be back in time for the opening of the new greenhouse tonight."

There's no mistaking his excitement about the citrus greenhouse he requested to have built.

With the recent mysterious illness that has cropped up within the community, Mary and Micah have worked endless hours trying to figure out what was happening and how to treat it. They found that the illness seems to respond well to fruits and veggies, especially citrus. As for the source, we can only guess that it's coming from the mosquitos, another reason to hate them. A commonality to those who are sick is they had multiple mosquito bites. Poor Mary was one of the initial victims. She spent two weeks recovering in her hut. She was not a good patient. I chuckle at the memory of her scolding me for making her stay in bed when she was itching to get out and move again. Mary is a great caregiver, just a terrible patient.

Surprisingly, it was Micah who took over the treatment of the ill. He has blown us all away with his ability to retain information and understand it so perfectly. His mind works in a very different way. It allows him to identify problems and find solutions from speculative ideas. He is a bit socially awkward, but his mind is a beautiful thing to watch unfold. Alex told me that he's always been that way. Micah was quiet for most of his youth and didn't speak much until he was five years old. Prior to that, he would only answer yes or no to questions. Even then, it would come as a nod. His mother knew how to communicate with him the best. His father just liked having a kid who wouldn't bother him too much. When their mom died, Micah latched onto Alex even more than he did before. That's when their relationship really took off. Before then, Micah would hardly hug him. But when it came down to Alex and their dad, he knew Alex was the safe choice. He has since told him he always felt safe with his brother, but Mom was his favorite.

I don't know how I so easily became someone Micah could trust, and hug, but I will be forever thankful. I know he was lucky to be rescued from Paxton before The Order figured out his differences. I can't bear to imagine his fate if they had. I do know, because of their blind ignorance, they would have missed out on a very beautiful and intelligent mind. Micah is a pearl among gems; he doesn't shine the same but has his own kind of beauty. The same can be said of the children they deem virus ridden by Down Syndrome. Those sweethearts are diamonds among the gems, shining with such pure joy and happiness. You can't help but feel better just being around them.

Pulling myself from my thoughts, I see Micah awkwardly hugging his brother. My heart squeezes at the sight. They are truly beautiful in their relationship. Spotting me looking at them, Micah swiftly pulls away. I ruined the moment.

"Well, let's get going already," he instructs Alex.

"Okay, okay, can I at least kiss my fiancée-wife first?" he retorts. We all laugh at the odd title I now hold.

"If you must, but I'm going outside," and with that, Micah walks out the door.

Alex just laughs at his brother and quickly gives me a peck goodbye, "I'll see you later tonight," he promises, and then he's out the door.

Julia's busy washing the dishes when she smirks, "That Micah! He sure is something else."

"He sure is," I agree with a smile. "Jewels, why don't you come sit with me at the table. I can finish those in a minute."

Settling into her seat, she looks at me cautiously, "You know, you use that name when you have something really good to say, or something you think is going to be hard for me to hear. So, which is it today?"

I didn't realize I had a tell, but she's not wrong.

"Well, I think a little bit of both. Have you seen Tom today?" I ask, wondering what she might already know.

"Only for a couple minutes. I ran into him this morning, but he told me he was too busy and would find me later. Why? Did something happen?"

I can hear the worry in her voice, and quickly ease her fear, "Tom's okay, don't worry. I actually need to talk to you about Grandma Brylie." She leans in with relieved interest. "We had our meeting last night and some changes will be happening soon. What you need to know is that Brylie was one of the founding revolutionists to the uprising. The enemies she fought were actually the founders of the existing Order."

I watch as a look of shock crosses Julia's face. She abruptly changes into a roar of astonished laughter. "Of course she was," she exclaims. "I mean, why wouldn't she be? The zeal she had for life and the fire to fight the evil she constantly encountered; it all makes sense." As her laughter fades into a smile of pride, Julia looks at me and asks for our grandma's book.

I hand it over and watch as she flips through the pages, looking for something I must have missed. Finally, she settles on a passage and encourages me to listen.

Today was lost in mere moments, while the fall of humanity took its time. Everywhere people are demanding to be heard, yelling, "I am right!" Problem is, not everyone has the same idea of what right is. That doesn't seem to stop stupidity from growing and transforming into ignorant hate. This once small rift of differences has now created a chasm in which free will is becoming obsolete.

Somewhere in the haze of these self-proclamations, right has become wrong, wrong has become right, and now, good has become blurred in the name of war. My fear is, from this war, the greatest casualty will be freedom since trust has already fallen. Neighbor is plotting against neighbor, government against government, and now nation against nation. It won't be long before paranoia sets in and takes care of the rest. I fear for what may rise from the ashes when these foolish cocks are done fanning their feathers in a display of superiority. Why can't they see that knowledge without understanding is egotism, which can only produce the child of supremacy. I will continue to fight against this evolution that insists anything less than their definition of perfect is unacceptable. Ben will know the truth, no matter what it costs me. Even if I have to pay with my life...he will rise.

Julia reads Brylie's words as if they were her own. I watch in awe. The same conviction plays out in the animation on her face as I hear the fervor in her voice.

"Sam, how could we have missed that? I mean, we couldn't know her enemies *then* are the same as ours *now*. This is just crazy!"

I laugh at her excitement, "I know exactly how you feel. I just went through all of that," I motion my hand in a circle, as though to encompass her, "in front of the entire board of councils."

Her jaw drops open in disbelief, "They know?"

"About that…there's another conversation we need to have." Julia sits there with a controlled patience I can only dream of having. I tell her about the meeting that took place the previous night, and the choice set before us.

"Jewels, I want you to make the decision you feel is

best for you. Of course, I want you to always be with me, but that's just because I'm selfish." We both smile at my self-admitted flaw, "but I want you to be happy, wherever you are."

She looks at me somewhat confused, "Then you should know my answer already. I will only be happy where you are."

"You mean me *and* Tom," I tease.

She only shrugs, knowing that I'm right. I wonder what she'll do when the day comes that Tom and I are not headed in the same direction. "How are things with the two of you, anyway?"

"Slow. Very, very, slow."

"Are you okay with that?" I know I am, but I can't tell if she is.

She considers my question before answering, "Yeah, I think I am. At first, I was terrified of trusting any man ever again. Especially since Tom was a Singuri guard, so there's that." She laughs at the irony of it all, then looks at me seriously, "He was never one of them though, he's too good."

She's right, he is too good to be that evil.

"It gets easier to figure out my feelings and fears the longer we're together. That's strange to say…together, but we are. He's incredibly patient with me. Sometimes I think he's more afraid to try anything than I am. I get it. He's lost a lot too. Then there's me… I'm damaged goods."

"Jewels," I reach out, cupping her face in my hand, "don't, for one minute, think of yourself as less because of what someone else did to you. Tom doesn't see you as damaged; he sees you as a gift to be treasured. He is taking it slow because he respects you, and he's probably afraid. Afraid of not just hurting you, but afraid of getting hurt himself. And you're right, there is you. There is wonderful, beautiful, strong, courageous, you. Julia, you're my hero."

Her silent tears roll down her cheeks, wetting my hand as my heart breaks for her struggle. "Thanks, Sam, I needed that reminder. I never thought of Tom as being afraid; he's so confident and authoritative in all he does. I sometimes forget that he's a softy underneath that tough exterior. Have you seen him around little Sammy?"

We both laugh as I shake my head yes. Big, burly Tom wrapped around little Sam's pinky is quite the sight to see.

That evening, the council held a grand meeting with all the residents of Neva, informing them of the incoming refugees. They also updated everyone with what's been going on outside our bubble. As Tom predicted, many of the villagers are ready to leave and join the rebellion in Harlan. Many were also upset by the secrecy from the council. I can understand the frustration. The revelation about my grandmother was left out, as decided by Julia and me. We didn't want any extra attention, good or bad. It's funny how all my life I felt I was meant for more, but I always doubted myself. I still do, but now with these new enlightenments of my grandmother, I can't help but feel fueled to carry on her cause.

31
Home

Sam:

"Sam, earth to Sam. Did I lose you again to daydreams of your wedding?" Julia teases.

Refocusing my attention back to the matter at hand, I lie and tell Julia that she caught me. I don't want her to be disappointed with my wandering thoughts, as she has assumed the role of my maid of honor. She insists on doing things the same way they are described in Brylie's chronicles from her wedding. I have asked Irene to be my Bridesmaid, and Alex has asked Neal to be his Groomsman, reserving the privilege of Best Man for Micah. These four people will stand with us, as witnesses to our mutual love and union. Tom will be the one to marry us. I would have asked Mary to be a part of the ceremony, but she told me she would have none of the attention and much preferred to be with the children. It's a good compromise because I would love to have the children there.

Seeing an opportunity to boost morale, the council decided to cancel all work for the day of our wedding. Which means there will be too many eyes watching us; I will suffer their gaze, so long as Alex is at the end of the aisle. Not having much time before the new refugees arrive, the town pitched in and organized everything. With Julia and Micah at the helm, they were able to get everything done in just one day. So today, July 3rd, is our true wedding day. With Alex being sent off to get ready in Tom's hut, I stay behind in ours.

"I'm so nervous," I confess. "Where's Irene? She's running late."

Julia looks at me with a mischievous smile as she answers, "Never mind where she is; just hold still while I work on your curls."

I laugh at her as she tries to figure out how to make this one particularly stubborn ringlet conform. "The secret is to just let them be how they want to be, and work *with* them. That's something I learned from watching Mom."

She tenderly lays her hand on my shoulder, squeezing it as a familiar hug we once knew from our father. "I'm sorry Mom and Dad aren't here, Sam. I know they would be happy that you found love. I know I am."

I smile up at her, "You're right, they would be happy, but don't be too sad for me Jewels, because I have you."

Just then, Irene walks in with a dress delicately draped over her arms; she reaches out, gesturing for me to take it.

"A gift from Julia and me."

My throat catches, as I recognize the dress. It's the one I borrowed from her when I asked Alex I we could take things slow; when I knew I couldn't be without him. The once simple, tank top neckline, has now been replaced with a soft, sheer material that cuts just below the collarbone. It gracefully falls into two billowy sleeves, each one detailed with a delicate white embroidery. My eyes follow the beautiful pattern that has hues of cream, ivory and white. They travel the length of the dress down past the hem, onto the new sheer fabric, that now runs the length of the floor. The bottom of the dress opens to a flowing illusion of woven ivy and flowers drifting in the breeze. I recognize the pattern as reminiscent of the one from my old wedding dress, my mother's dress. As the tears well up in my eyes, I caress each leaf of the ivy and delicate flowers adorning this remarkable gift.

"How?" is the only word I can manage to ask.

Irene responds. "I know how much you and Alex like this dress. I wanted to make it my wedding gift to you."

Not wanting to wrinkle the dress that now drapes over my arm, I reach my hand over, and grab hers, "Thank you," I choke out.

"Irene taught me how to embroider so we could both work on the detailing. We began a few weeks ago, when Alex first started talking to me about asking you to marry him." Julia laughs at this new bit of news, "It took him long enough to ask you."

Sounds like him, always willing to give me time. I smile.

"Mary donated the sheer fabric from the remnants of her own wedding dress. It was a family heirloom and she wanted you to have it. She also wanted you to have this." Julia reaches out to Irene and hands her a box I didn't notice she was concealing. They're both grinning from ear to ear as they hand me yet another surprise. I don't know how many more my heart can take.

My nervous hands gently pull the lid off, and my breath catches at the sight of a stunning headpiece. I gingerly pull the woven flowers from the box, and I'm intrigued by the attached fabric. It's made of a fine mesh with delicate bead like clusters of material, interlocking them together. I have never seen anything like this before.

"What is this?" I ask in awe.

Irene answers with a snicker, "It's called fishnet. Mary said you caught yourself a good one, so you should wear it." She chuckles.

I join in her laughter, "Of course she did. I'll have to thank her when I see her. This really is too much for her to give," even though I know in my heart, she wouldn't have it any other way.

"Thank you, both of you, for these amazing gifts. I will treasure them always." I can't help the tears from coming, which in turns makes Irene and Julia cry too.

"Stop, before we all walk out there red eyed and puffy." Irene chides. "Now let's get you into this beautiful work of art, shall we?" And with that, she takes the dress from me and unzips it. Julia holds the other side as I carefully step into the fabric. The dress is pulled up into place, and it falls perfectly onto my body. The fabric compliments my figure without being too tight. The way the added sheer feels against my skin is almost as mesmerizing as the way it teases the eyes with a hint of what lies beneath. I can't help but chuckle, knowing Alex is going to be taunted all night. Irene places the band of woven flowers slightly off to the side of my head. I stare in the small mirror at my reflection and smile. The image reflected before me steals my breath away; I genuinely look bridal.

We all stand there looking at the bride I have become. Julia reaches back into the box, with a glint of laughter in her eyes, she holds out another piece of fabric.

"I missed something?" Reaching out and taking it from her hand, "What is it?" I ask, confused by the small item.

Julia leans in closer to answer, "Mary said it's called a garter, and you put it up on your thigh. She said it's for tonight," then she winks at me as she pulls away giggling.

I can feel the color rising in my cheeks as it dawns on me what she's talking about. "Julia!"

Now both Irene and Julia are laughing at my expense. Conceding to the idea, I ask them to help me put it on, and they are more than happy to oblige.

As we complete the finishing touches, it's time for me to face the waiting crowd.

When the door is opened to my hut, I'm met with a beautiful sight of all the work the villagers have done. It was a good idea to give them something else to think about. My eyes take it all in. I find the walkway lined with a garland made from the wildflowers and greenery of the swamp. Cattails are placed at the end of the rows, made up of individual chairs everyone brought from their own homes. Before stepping out to start my journey, Julia steps beside me. She hands me a bouquet of Queen Anne's lace and willowy fern leaves.

"It's beautiful, thank you."

She looks at me and smiles. "Okay Sis, are you ready?"

I nervously nod my head yes as Julia takes my hand. Like so many times before, we walk hand in hand, down the boardwalk. She leaves me at the back of the gathering to continue down the aisle on my own. I can't see Alex, but I know he's at the end, waiting for me. He's always waiting for me. Preparing myself for the full attention of those gathered to celebrate. I stand up straight and put one sandaled foot in front of the other. Halfway down the aisle, I see him standing there. His eyes focused only on me, as mine are on him. His mouth opens with a silent gasp, slowly followed by a smile beaming with pride. How this man loves me so much still amazes me. With everything we've survived, I understand love a little better now, and I absolutely love Alex.

He comes into focus, and I see he's wearing a pair of light tan slacks, with a white cotton button up shirt, and flip flops. He looks casually handsome. Once I reach him, he steps forward to take my trembling hand. It fits comfortably in his. With this feeling of home, my nerves subside instantly. We rewrote our vows, different from the mundane ones we were forced to recite with The Order. Tom asks Alex to say his vows, and I can barely hear him with my heart beating out of my chest.

"Sam, I love you and I vow to be patient with you. I will support you and be strong for you when you need me to be. Being your sparring partner, I know you're plenty strong yourself." The crowd laughs at his teasing as Alex rubs at his jaw for dramatic effect. "You never cease to amaze me with your humble strength, desire to take care of those you love, and the depths you are willing to fight. I vow to always be by your side, no matter what comes. I have loved you with a young love before you were mine. Now that you have chosen me, I am free to love you without reservation. Thank you for the gift of your heart, I will treasure it. I promise to love you forever and always, even after you die." We both laugh at the secret term of endearment, and we see Micah smirk with the familiarity of his own words. "With my whole heart, I receive you, Sam, as my beautiful wife."

As his words wash over me, I feel the conviction of his love as this truth becomes my own. Without any introduction from Tom, I begin my own vows.

"Alex, I don't think I will ever understand the love you have for me. When we were first married, I was terrible to you because I thought you to be someone different. Even then, you sought to put me above yourself. You have truly loved me with a patient and sacrificial love. Because of this, I have learned of the kind of man you truly are. You are patient, you are kind, you are humble, and you never ask for more. You are always happy with what you have. You are fierce, in a different way than me of course." Now everyone laughs at my taunting. "I love that we can laugh. I love that we can tease each other. I love that you light up when you see me. And that you love my stubborn curls." Another chuckle from the crowd. "I love being loved by you, and I love, loving you. I love that no matter where we go, you are my home. I vow to stand with you, and to love you forever and always, even after you die. With my whole heart, I receive you, Alex, to be my husband." I conclude smiling.

I watch as a small tear slides down Alex's face. Reaching up to wipe it away, he does the same for me. We both laugh at the tender gesture we offer to the other. With our hands gently resting on the others' face, Tom announces one more vow.

Our eyes lock as we proclaim our borrowed vow in unison. "Where you go, I'll go. Where you stay, I'll stay. Rise together or fall together, I'll do it with you."

"I believe this is the part where they say, 'you may now kiss your Bride'," Tom concludes with a chuckle.

"Oh, believe me, I will," Alex proclaims.

Not wasting another moment, we both lean into one another, whispering 'I love you' right before our lips meet. Our kiss starts out slow and gentle, relishing in this tender moment of unity. Then it deepens with the promise of our future. How a kiss can be both gentle and deep is a beautiful, perfect mystery.

An eruption of applause and cheers finally separate us, and I'm left torn on whether or not I'm glad that we're not alone. Celebrating the reception in the Council Hall, Alex leans in and whispers, "You look stunning."

With a coy smile, I lean into his ear and whisper, "You should see what I have on underneath."

Alex's step hitches, as the thought of my words sink in. Then he shakes his head with a smile.

As the reception winds down, I don't think I have ever felt more tired and nervous, as I do now. Our guests line up in a row on either side of us, creating a path for Alex and me to walk through. We travel down the human lane and are surprised by the soft white flurries of the cattails, flowing down like snow. Alex grabs my hand, and we dash through to the other side as the fluff settles into my hair. The reception fades into the distance as Alex draws me further into the night.

"Where are we going?" I finally ask. The suspense is overwhelming.

"Just trust me," a favorite response of his. And I do.

Rounding the corner, we get into one of the patrol Jeeps, where I'm surprised to find a couple bags already loaded.

"I asked Julia to pack yours, and then Tom loaded our stuff. I wanted to take you off site for our own time together. Everything's already been taken care of."

"Really? Where off site?" I ask, trying again for a clue.

Alex looks at me and smiles, his favorite game to play. Okay, okay, I'll just have to wait for the surprise.

Needing to stay within the safe boundaries of Neva's outer perimeter, we don't drive far before Alex stops at a gathering of large eucalyptus and ash trees. He comes around to my side of the Jeep and scoops me up into his arms, carrying me towards the cluster of trees. I'm awestruck at the sight of the interior of this oasis. Entering the cluster of trees, I see an open hut, of sorts. The roof is the same as the ones back at the camp, but the walls are missing. In place of solid material, they are made of delicately draped canvas and mesh covering. There are three dimly lit solar torches spaciously placed along the perimeter of the room, giving off an ambient glow. Inside the circular room is a quaint seating area, off centered on one side, while the other is adorned with a low-profile bed. As Alex sets me down beside the bed, I feel his body next to mine. His husky voice whispers in my ear, "You were saying?"

Chills shiver through me as I nervously bite my lower lip, fully understanding his meaning. It's been a long time since we've been together, and my heart aches for him now. Twisting my body around, I lean against him, pressing my mouth against his. Feeling the warm fullness of his lips on mine feeds this newfound desire in being his wife. While my fingers work feverishly at the buttons on his shirt, he gently works the zipper down my spine, tickling each vertebra as he passes. The fabric falls to my feet, he steps back to take a long look at me. The moment he finds the garter his mouth slowly lifts into a smirk. Not a teasing smirk, but a 'come hither before I pounce', kind of smirk. I nervously giggle.

"I told you to wait and see what I had on underneath," I hum teasingly.

"And it was well worth the wait." He counters, with an even bigger smile. "*You*, were well worth the wait." Closing the gap between us, with our bodies moving as one, he gently lays me down on the bed. "I love you," he whispers into my parted lips, fueling my hunger. All else is lost to the symphony of what burns within us. Tonight, I am my beloved's, and he is mine.

I lie in the stillness of the early morning with my body

pressed against Alex. A trail of goose bumps dance on my skin where his fingers caress up and down my exposed back, sending shivers up my spine. Reminiscing about last night, it felt different from the nervous hunger I'm used to feeling. There was a new kind of desire. His passion was gentle, and deliberate, allowing me to feel the way he loves me. Last night was so much more than in the caverns. Last night, Alex felt like home.

Turning my face up towards his, I whisper "Thank you."

"You're welcome," he jokes.

I bury my head into his bare chest, "That's not what I mean," I clarify as I playfully nudge him.

Drawing my face into his, he whispers, "I know," then gently kisses me back into bliss.

Longing to have him feel what he professes to know, I press my lips deeper into his. "I love you," I breathe, easing my body over his. The morning belongs to us.

32
Bonds

Sam:

We were given two blissful days to ourselves, before returning to the marsh. The new refugees are scheduled to arrive in four days. Before we leave, Alex and I pack up the salvageable items of the hut, then set it on fire. We can't leave any evidence of life for a possible patrol team to stumble across. The flames lick up the sides of the support beams and I'm reminded once again of how much our world evolves around The Order. On our drive back to the village, we set a few more fires to keep up the appearances of an unstable and dead land.

We barely make it in the door before Julia and Micah come knocking. With one last, longing kiss, Alex turns to open the door.

"We missed you so much. And…Tom kissed me, or I kissed him." Julia confides in us.

"Yeah, and it was so gross," Micah chimes in.

Alex and I can't help but laugh.

"Tell you what, Micah, how about we leave these two lovely ladies alone. You and I go get something to eat. I've worked up quite the appetite since I've been away." He winks at me before leaving with his brother.

Feeling my cheeks burn, I shout after him "Yeah, you better run!"

"It's good to see you two together again," Julia smiles.

"Thanks, Jewels, now tell me all about this elusive kiss."

She enthusiastically jumps right into the story of how she kissed Tom after we left for our honeymoon. "He walked me home and hung out for a little bit after Micah was settled. We were just sitting there, talking about you and Alex, then I just leaned over and kissed him."

I sat there flabbergasted. "What? How did he respond?"

"At first, I wasn't sure what he thought. He just sat there looking stunned."

I bet he was, I stifle my chuckle.

"When he didn't say anything, I stood up and went outside. I was humiliated." She covers her face in her hands, reliving the embarrassment. "Then Tom followed me outside. It felt like forever before he joined me, but eventually he did. I apologized for assuming he would want to kiss me and asked him to just forget about it. We kind of just stood there in awkward silence. But you know Tom, he thinks things through, while I practically died in anticipation."

Poor Julia, I bet she was a nervous wreck, and poor Tom, I bet he was thrown off his axis completely.

"AND???" I prompt after she takes too long to continue the story.

She beams at me, and I know she must be getting to the good part. "He came and stood behind me, wrapped his arms around me, and said he was sorry. He was just pleasantly surprised and didn't know what to do. He confessed to wanting to kiss me for so long but didn't know if I was ready. When I turned to apologize for taking his moment, that's when he drew my face up to his and told me to stop apologizing. Then, he leaned down and kissed me. I mean he *really* kissed me."

Her eyes are aglow with the memory, and mine are wet with tears. I'm elated for her. Pulling Jewels into a big bear hug, we fall onto my bed, laughing with joy.

"I love him, Sam."

My laughter stops as I think about my baby sister being in love. She looks at me, waiting for my response. "Julia, I am truly happy for you. Tom is someone I respect and I'm confident he will take care of you, should we ever part ways."

A shadow of concern crosses her face, as she thinks on this very real possibility. She shrugs her shoulders, "No, I don't think that will ever be a problem. Haven't you heard? We're all living together, forever!" She shouts, then tackles me.

I laugh at her quirkiness and think of how opposite Tom's calm is to her silliness. It's a good balance for them. He's in for an entertaining ride, that's for sure. Julia rolls off me, breathless from her own exertion. "So, did you enjoy your time away?" She winks at me.

"Well, you know…" I start to tease. Then realizing what I said, "I mean, no, you don't know, right?"

Julia's cheeks turn a deep shade of crimson I didn't even know was possible. "No, I don't know!" She practically yells at me.

"I'm sorry, Jewels, I didn't mean to upset you, but maybe we should talk about this now."

She holds her hand up to stop me, "No, no that's okay, Mary has already told me *all* about it, and she's given me herbs, for when I'm ready, which won't be for a *looong* time. That's something Tom and I talked about after our kiss."

I scrunch my nose at her.

"Not just sex, so don't look at me like that. We talked about all of it. What I've been through, what he's been through, and how we're going to approach it. I don't know, Sam, I kind of like the idea of waiting until I'm married, like Grandma Brylie, when she was given the choice."

Unable to refrain myself, I roll over and hug her again, "I love you, Jewels."

She just laughs at me, then starts to fill me in on everything I missed while I was gone. As the evening turns into night, we both fall asleep in the comfort of my bed. We curl up next to each other, like we used to do in the cold winters.

In the morning, I wake up to Julia sleeping next to me with a blanket draped over us. Rolling over to the edge of the bed, I spot a note strategically placed on my nightstand. I pull it open and read:

Good morning Love,
I came in last night and found you both asleep. I didn't want to wake you, so I threw a blanket over you and camped out with Micah. If I'm not in his hut, it means we're out building the last few huts for the incoming refugees. Come find me when you can.
Love you,
Alex

I fold the note back in half and tuck it away in my drawer. This is the first letter I have received from Alex. I know it's silly, but I'm going to keep it forever. With a rush of emotions, I decide to write my own letter for Alex to find later. Maybe he will enjoy it as much as I do.

Julia and I pack a lunch before heading out to meet the guys. We round the corner to the secluded new extension of the boardwalk and Julia stops in her tracks. "Seriously, how are we supposed to get anything done with that," she points, and I follow the direction of her finger.

Alex, Tom, and Neal are all working on a hut, shirtless, in the hot sun. Micah, cute as he can be in his own bare chest, is handing them supplies as they call for them. Then, from out of nowhere, Irene pops up, "I know, quite the sight! Right ladies? I'm thinking they are feeling pretty good about themselves these days." She chuckles at her more than accurate joke. "Now how about we give them their lunch."

I admire Irene's sense of humor.

"Okay fine. We can watch for a few more minutes." We all laugh at her bantering, which draws the attention of Micah.

"Oh hey, when did you guys get here?" He hollers and the other three look up.

They're all smirking at the fact that we were just gawking at them.

"Never mind, we've been caught," Irene mischievously whispers. She shouts back at Micah, "We just got here, brought some food if you're hungry."

Julia and I both mouth our thanks as we slowly walk the last bit of distance to the end of the pier. I watch as Alex tosses the others their shirts, before putting his own back on. He walks up to me, suspicious of my grin.

"Did you really just get here?"

"I will never tell, but I will say," as my finger tugs at the hem of his shirt, "you really didn't have to put that back on for my sake."

He shakes his head at me, "who said it was for you? Maybe I was thinking of Mary, or did you not see her standing behind you?"

My cheeks flush as I turn to look for her, only to find she's not there. I hear Alex laugh behind me and I know I've been caught.

I reach out and playfully push him, then walk away. I join the rest of the group, leaving his boisterous laughter behind me. Alex catches up and stands next to me. I feel his hand on the small of my back, lingering lower than usual. He's really not making this easy on me. Julia hands us our food and we sit down with everyone else.

"Hey, Tom, how many refugees are we expecting on the ninth?" I ask.

"Around three hundred."

Nearly choking on my food, "I didn't realize there were so many," I admit.

"We didn't either, but from what we understand, only half of them plan on staying here, while the rest want to move on to Harlan."

I nod my head in understanding. "Well, that's good. We should have enough room then. What about Harlan, can it handle such an influx in people?"

I can see the pride in Tom's eyes as he answers, "Yes, it certainly can."

I find myself feeling more excited about Harlan than I was before. We leave in four days, just after the new arrivals get here.

After lunch, we all continue working on the new hut. It now sits vacant, awaiting its new occupants.

Julia and Tom head off in their own direction, while Micah joins Alex and me in our hut for dinner. Irene and Neal ask if they can catch up with us after they go get Sammy; I miss the little guy. We sit and enjoy a simple meal of crawfish soup when Irene clears her throat. "I'm glad you let us crash your dinner tonight," she teases. "Neal and I wanted to talk with you guys before things get really crazy around here."

I don't like the feeling that's creeping into my gut with her words.

Alex responds, "You know you can always talk to us." I shake my head in agreement.

Irene reaches over and grabs my hand as Neal continues. "Well, as you know, there's a slew of refugees coming in soon. Irene and I have been talking a lot about what we are going to do." He pauses, then Irene jumps in, "We've decided to stay here, in Neva. I don't want to raise Sammy in the middle of a revolution compound. He needs a sense of security and home. I feel like we've found that here." She looks over at Neal, who smiles at her adoringly. They really are in love with each other. "Sam, can you forgive me for abandoning you?"

I jump up and hug her, "You're not abandoning me," I reassure her. "You're protecting your family and I would never fault you for that." I pull away and look at her. "I will miss you every day and selfishly wish you were with me. We all know I have a selfish streak." They all laugh at this known flaw of mine. "But I could never be mad at you. My life will always be better for knowing you. And besides, when we're done kicking The Order's butt, first thing I'm doing is coming to find you."

She laughs at my promise, "Thank you for being such a good friend."

Even in her embrace, my heart sinks. I don't know how I'm going to get by without her. I'm already dreading the absence I'll feel when she's gone.

With the night drawing to a close, Micah heads back to his hut and Irene and her little family leave too. As Alex and I settle in for the night, he pulls me into his arms, "Are you ok with all this?"

"I'll have to be," I answer honestly. "I'll never stand in the way of Irene's happiness."

He squeezes me gently, "Sam, you keep making comments about how your weakness is selfishness. But that right there, proves just how unselfish you are." I reflect on his words; he might have a point.

"Thanks," I offer as I snuggle further into his embrace.

Alex holds me while I quietly cry myself to sleep. When the night claims me, I dream of Harlan, and I dream of Irene. She's in Neva, and it's burning to the ground. "How did this happen?" I scream out to her. She answers with one word, "Traitor!" I try to close the distance between us, but my efforts are in vain. She is always just out of reach. I can do nothing but scream and cry as I watch the entire village going up in flames. "NO!"

I wake with a start, and Alex jolts up next to me. Looking around frantically he asks, "What's wrong?" Finding no threat, his eyes settle on me. I watch as his startled panic melts into concern. He reaches out and touches my cheek, wiping away a tear I didn't even know I cried. "Are you okay?"

I can't answer him over the massive lump in my throat. With the images fresh in my mind, I bury my face in his chest and cry.

He gently holds me, tenderly stroking my head while my tears turn into sobs. The last thing I remember before falling asleep is Alex rubbing my back, telling me everything was going to be okay. I sleep peacefully for the rest of the night; I welcome it over the nightmare.

33
Moving Forward

Alex:

I stir to the sudden movement of Sam next to me, jolting up prepared to fight. Looking around, I find nothing. "What's wrong?" There's no answer. I look at Sam to make sure she's all right. That's when I see the look of terror on her face, with wet marks staining her cheeks. "Are you okay?" I reach my hand out to dry her tears away.

She doesn't answer, only buries herself into me and cries.

I don't know what she was dreaming about, but I can imagine it has to do with Irene. Stroking her hair, I wish I could take her pain away. A part of me is angry with Irene and Neal for choosing to stay. But the better part of me understands. Sam was so brave for them tonight. I could see the pain it caused her to learn she was losing her closest friend, and Sammy. Feeling her cries turn into deeper sobs, all I can do is give her the same comfort my mother once gave me. I pull her close and gently rub her back in long, smooth, circular motions. "It's going to be okay, Sam. I'm always going to be right here. It's going to be okay." Minute's pass and I repeat the same motion over and over again until her body finally relaxes, and her breathing slows down. Lessening the frequency of my verbal assurance, I continue to rub her back in circular patterns. The exhaustion of her emotions drains the last of her effort to stay awake. I feel Sam's body slacken in my arms. She's fallen asleep again, thank God. I lay here feeling the rise and fall of her back know she's drifted into a deep slumber. Propping my chin atop her head, my eyes land on the nightstand and notice a folded piece of paper. Carefully sliding out from beneath her, I quietly snatch the folded note and carefully slip outside. Using the light of the full moon, I begin reading:

Dear Alex, or should I say, Beloved,
I just wanted to say thank you for my note. I know it's small,
but it brought me joy today. I also wanted to say thank you
for loving me. You drew me in and from your love, mine
grew. I don't know that I will ever be deserving of your love.
Because of you, I have experienced something that is almost
unheard of today. With the many uncertainties of tomorrow, I
know I'll be fine with you by my side. I love you, Alex Orion,
forever and always…even after you die.
Yours ~ Sam

Reminiscing over her words, I smile. *I like that she called me Beloved.* Folding her letter back, I look out over the marsh. "Please, God, let me be the husband she needs. I love her more than myself. I need to keep her safe. That's it. That's all I ask." I feel a little foolish for talking with a God I don't know much about, but from what Sam has read to me, He sounds like someone who would listen. Shrugging, I turn to go back to bed. Before I do, I pull out another piece of paper, to write a love letter to my troubled wife.

Dear Love,
Thank you for your note. It's funny how something so small can make a big impact. I loved your letter; I only wish you would stop feeling like you need to be deserving of me. Samantha Orion, you are just as deserving of my love, as I am of yours. Neither one of us started this life together with a true sense of love. We have grown and so has our understanding. I will always be with you, no matter what comes. I love you just as you are. I'm the lucky one to be loved by you in return.
Loving you forever and always, even after you die.
Your Beloved
P.S.
I hope you don't mind me using your full name; I've missed it. I know you grew up being called Sam by the ones you loved, but I grew up falling in love with a girl named Samantha. Maybe we can compromise?

Folding it in half, I place the note in her drawer. Easing myself back into bed, I breathe in her earthy, lavender scent. The familiar smell immerses me into a calm only she can bring. I drift off dreaming of the day she first captivated me.

The next morning, it was hard to leave Sam after she told me about her nightmare. I reassured her that everyone was vetted before coming to Neva, but I wanted to meet up with Tom to confirm this. When I arrived at his hut, Julia was already there. Deciding it would be good for her to be involved too, I disclosed to them Sam's dream. Tom didn't seem too concerned about it, having full confidence in the council overseeing the filtering process of the incoming refugees. It was Julia who persuaded him to reconsider the process. She said Sam has always had little dreams growing up. They were like déjà vu or a shadow of things to come. They were always non-consequential and easy to overlook. Every now and then, she would have one that hit too close to reality. None as horrific as her nightmare from last night though. We all sat in silence, not knowing what to make of this news. Ultimately, Tom conceded to Julia's urging and agreed to arrange for additional security.

I discovered Neal and Irene agreed to become members of the board a couple weeks ago. This means they had made their decision to stay long before telling Sam. It's hard for me not to be angry again, knowing this detail, but I try to put myself in their shoes and not cast judgment. It's half past twelve, and Sam was supposed to meet me at noon for lunch. Excusing myself from our impromptu meeting, I set off to find out what's wrong. I approach our hut and hear a strange sound coming from inside. Opening the door, I find Sam hunched over a basin, throwing up.

"What's wrong?" I ask as I walk towards her.

She puts her hand up to stop me, "I'll be fine, just don't come any closer. I don't want to get you sick."

Ignoring her command, I walk over and gently begin rubbing her back. "Not a chance. If you're sick, I want to help you." I see her pale, clammy face as she sits up from the bowl. "Here," I grab my pillow and stuff it behind her back. "Why don't you lie down a little, but not all the way." As I help guide her against the newly propped pillows, concern works it way into my heart. She looks terrible.

"Thanks," she pauses to swallow. "I'm sorry I didn't make lunch."

I can't help but snicker at her apology, "I'll forgive you, this time." She laughs, then lurches forward, dry heaving into the empty bowl. As soon as her body relaxes, I offer to make some peppermint tea, eager to take care of her. I work at the stove, and I feel her watching me. "What? Am I doing something wrong?" I ask.

She chuckles, "No, I just haven't fully appreciated the image of you in the kitchen before."

Shaking my head at her remark, "Appreciate all you want, Love," I wink.

"Thank you, I think I will" she quips as I pour the boiling water into the cup.

Bringing the tea to the bedside stand, I kiss her head, "No thanks needed," I reply. My eyes drift over the top of her head and notice a new letter, lying unfolded next to her. I smile as she tries to casually cover the paper with our blanket and divert my eyes. I won't ruin the surprise.

Once I'm done eating and Sam finishes her toast, she begins to worry about not being better in time to greet the refugees. I remind her that the new arrivals will not show up for another two days. They need to travel in the cover of darkness so she will have plenty of time to recover; this seems to ease her mind.

"What did Tom have to say this morning when you talked to him?"

"He's going to set up additional security and has agreed to push out our departure by another day. We leave on the 10th now"

I can see the relief and approval on her face.

"Sam, I should tell you, he also said that Irene and

Neal have agreed to be new council members for Neva. They decided a couple weeks ago."

She's silent while the truth of their decision settles down on her. We agreed to no more secrets, no matter how small or insignificant they seem. But I don't see how telling this one is going to help.

"If we had a kid, would you want to stay behind?"

Her question throws me off with the image of us having a child. I desire to have a family with Sam more than anything, but now is not the best time, considering we're about to join a rebel uprising. I suppose that's the point of her question. Choosing my words carefully, I honestly answer, "One day, I hope to have as many children as we want. Whether that's one or ten, I don't know, but now isn't the best time to start. I don't want to condemn Irene and Neal for staying because that's how they believe they keep their family safe. But you and me, we're too much like your grandma. I would rather my children see me fight and die for my beliefs, than hide away, shielding them from danger. Both actions are a form of protection. I can't say if one is better than the other. I think it comes down to who you are."

Satisfied with my answer, she starts to get up from the bed. "Whoa, where do you think you're going?"

She looks as though she's annoyed to even answer this question, "We need to pack, remember."

"No. I will pack our stuff. You just sit here and point me in the right direction." I smile at her knowing she won't be angry with my compromise.

"Okay, fine. I'll stay here while you do all the work," she agrees with a smile.

"Hey now, you still need to point, that's work too. Important work in fact." I'm full on smiling at our ridiculous banter.

"You're absolutely right," she chuckles.

It doesn't take long for me to pack up all our stuff as we work together with our point and pack method. We don't have much, since most of it was already here and will be left behind for the new tenants. It's weird to look around and imagine someone else living in our home. That's just it, this isn't our home, no more than the caverns were. With the extra day, we now have four nights left here, then it's onward to the revolution.

34
Hello and Goodbye

Sam:

Having lost the last two days to recovery, I was worried I'd miss the arrival of the new refugees. It was a strange sickness that went as fast as it came. *I must've been exhausted*, I conclude, dismissing the issue entirely. Anxious for the new residents to arrive, which should be any minute now, I check my watch for the hundredth time. As Alex stands beside me and holds my hand, I recall our previous conversation. It was enlightening to hear him talk about having a family that night. But ten kids…I don't know if I want that many. It's nice to have the option though. Looking over at Alex, I can only smile. He's going to make an amazing father someday.

The rumble of the approaching buses draws my attention back to the present, and my heart pounds with anticipation.

"All right, everyone get ready," Tom shouts.

Alex pecks me on the cheek before going to join Tom while I meet Irene at the table. Julia has opted to stay behind with Micah and the other children, since Mary is still not feeling well. Unfortunately, this means, she too will be staying in Neva. She promised to join us in Harlan once the refugees are settled and her health is back to traveling condition. She intends to allocate her duties over to Irene before she leaves. Mary professes that she's looking forward to bossing everyone around in Harlan. Even though her delay is temporary, her absence adds to my selfish burden. I have come to love Mary and Irene like family. This separation is going to tear a piece of my heart out.

A bus stops in front of us, with another two trailing just behind it. Thanks to my dream, Tom set up an additional screening station with scanners to detect tracking devices. Though I'm surprised to see them take my dream so seriously, I won't argue because it brings an extra measure of comfort. The first two buses open their doors and the first to exit are the elderly. By elderly, I mean people in their late fifties to early sixties. This age range is an accomplishment from where they're coming from. As each person steps off the bus, I can see hope settling on their exhausted faces. Not far behind them are the children. My heart splinters at the sight of their clothes and terrified, innocent faces. Rage surges through me. *Curse The Order for stealing their peace.* The last occupants to deboard the buses are the adults who have taken charge of the children. Some are parents, while others fill in the space for parents long gone.

The third bus comes as a shock to me. As the passengers begin offloading, a gasp escapes my lips; it's full of Singuri guards and their families. Tom and Alex are quick to go over and greet them, while I wrap my head around this new revelation. I can understand why they traveled in a separate bus, because even knowing what I know now, it's still intimidating to see them. I can only imagine the confusion the

Simpletons are feeling.

Since our escape from Paxton, I have learned not all Singuri are evil. It's still hard to trust something you have been raised to fear. I watch as Tom explains to the new arrivals this difficult truth, reassuring them that everything will be okay. Only a few complain but are quick to comply when they see the equally distraught faces around them. Alex ushers the children over to where Irene and I are waiting to scan the newcomers, just outside the entrance gate. We thought it would be more comforting to have two women welcoming their unsure minds.

As we work through the long line of anxious people, a young girl holding a tattered teddy bear walks up to me and asks if her mommy is here. When I look up to the guardian with her, I see the sadness in her eyes as she silently shakes her head, no. I don't want to be the one who crushes this little girl's hope in miraculously finding her parents in this new place, but I know I can't lie to her either. Offering a distraction, I reach out and touch her stuffed animal's head and compliment her on how cute he is.

"What's his name?" I gently ask.

"Teddy." Her voice is soft and shy as she answers.

"Do you want me to scan Teddy first, so you can see how it's done? He seems like a brave bear."

She smiles at me and holds her bear out. I gently take him from her trusting hands and explain to Teddy about how I got my tracker out and now I'm free. I ask if he would he like me to see if he still has one in him. I hold the bear close to my ear, as I remember my own mother doing, and respond to his pretend answer. "You got it, Teddy! I'll be very careful. You are such a brave bear." With those words, I scan him, and he comes up clean. "You see the green light, that means Teddy is free and clear." I offer the bear back to the anxious little girl. "Thank you, Teddy, and thank you, young lady." I smile at them both.

She smiles up at me in return. "My name is Lilly."

"Well nice to meet you, Lilly. I'm Samantha, but my friends call me Sam. So, you can call me Sam too."

She smiles at me calling her my friend. Giving me her unspoken permission, Lilly extends her arm out to me. As the device travels along her forearm, it beeps red. Her eyes turn huge as she's figured out that red must mean bad because green means good. *Damnit. I really didn't want her to have a tracker.*

"Okay Lilly, can I show you something?" Not waiting for an answer, I show her my arm and where the chip was once hidden beneath my skin. She looks at it with curious interest. "This is where my tracker was before my friend Tom took it out. It only took a few seconds, then I was freed. I need to do the same for you. I know you're brave because Teddy told me so." She smiles at our little secret. "When I put this device over your arm, it's going to tickle and maybe feel like an itchy sting, but it will be over very fast. Are you ready?"

She squeezes her bear tighter, then nods her head yes. She watches the instrument and I quickly distract her before the needle plunges into her skin. "Do you want to see something silly?" When she looks up at me, I pull one of my curls and let it bounce back up. Lilly giggles at the motion and asks if she can try. Relieved it worked, I gladly let her pull my curls until the tracker is removed and her wound is sealed.

To my surprise, Lilly leans in and hugs me. "Thanks for helping me. I don't want Teddy to think I was scared," she whispers.

"It's okay to be scared. I still get scared sometimes, but

just like you, I'm brave because of my friends," I whisper back.

She smiles at me once more, before being ushered on. I look up to find Alex staring at me. By the look on his face, I suspect he watched the whole thing play out.

I smile at him, "Back to work, Orion, you're slacking."

"Yes, ma'am," he teases and turns to rejoin Tom.

There weren't any more trackers found among the refugees. No one seems to know how Lilly's was overlooked. Thanks to the hidden jammers on both buses and around the perimeter of the safe zone, The Order was not able to find us. I love it when their own technology works against them.

Sorting through the mass influx of people, we do our best trying to find everyone a place to stay. The elderly are grouped together in the council hall for the next two nights and everyone else is dispersed among the available huts. Tom gave up his lodgings and is staying with Julia and Micah. That should make for an interesting couple of nights. Many of the people who are going to Harlan have also opted to bunk with others until we leave. Alex and I don't have room in our hut since it's full of everyone's supplies for the upcoming trip. Turning to leave, I see Lilly going home with Irene, offering me another reason to be thankful for them staying.

As we enter the hut, Alex swings me around, and fiercely kisses me.

With my head in a fog I ask, "What was that for?"

"Sometimes I'm overwhelmed by you." He kisses me again, and whispers, "You're going to be a great mother someday."

My breath hitches at his praise. I've always feared becoming a mother. His words are a consuming fire to my doubts.

Leaning in, he murmurs, "I'm not saying start a family

right now, but maybe we can practice."

I would laugh at his comment if it wasn't for the feel of his throaty voice against my ear, doing funny things to me. "Mmhmm," is my only capable response.

He laughs softly. What is this man doing to me, to make even his chuckle sound sexy?

"Alex," I breathe.

"Yes, Samantha," he answers.

I love the way he says my name. "Kiss me."

He responds with a small brushing of his lips against mine. The heat from where our lips touched leaves the rest of my body feeling cold.

"More," I whisper.

I feel his mouth smirking on mine before he answers my desire.

It's been another long day of meetings with the transition of the new refugees into Neva. Those leaving are in the final stages of packing for our departure tomorrow. Opening the door, I'm met with the stillness of our empty hut. It's not our hut anymore, it belongs to someone else now. With the undeniable truth of what tomorrow brings, the quiet becomes deafening. Tomorrow I say goodbye to another home and another way of life. First it was my childhood home, then my home with Alex, then the caverns, and now. our little hut on the end of the pier. With all my pent-up emotions of the last few days surging to the surface, I'm glad to find myself alone. No longer able to keep it all in, I put on one of Alex's shirts and crawl into bed. Curling into a ball, I quietly cry as I let go of those I leave behind.

35
Queen Anne's Lace

Alex:

Standing just inside the doorframe, I'm now glad I decided to go with the quiet approach. With the fresh flowers in my hand, my heart pulses for the woman I picked them for. Queen Anne's Lace, or in flower language, a sanctuary. That's exactly what I strive to be for Sam. But if I'm honest with myself, she's equally my place of refuge. Observing her sleeping form, I can see the red puffiness around her eyes and know she's been crying. Tiptoeing my way across the room, I deposit the Queen Anne's Lace into a cup and place it on the nightstand for her to see in the morning. Gingerly, I climb in bed and curl my body around hers through the blankets. "I love you, Samantha Orion," I whisper. Feeling her body relax into mine, I breathe her in, again and again, until the night claims me too.

36
Departure

Sam:

"Load it up!"

As Tom yells out instructions, everything becomes surreal to me. Not long ago I was agonizing over the change my life forced me to take. Today, I welcome it with open arms. The only hard part is leaving Mary, Irene, and little Sammy behind. As we load onto the newly arrived buses, an old part of me is terrified of the journey that lies ahead. That part is slowly becoming more silent.

In case we encounter any Singuri on the road, we've disguised ourselves as prisoners in tattered clothes and unkempt appearances. Tom has joined us as a prisoner, since he's well known among the Singuri. He has equipped each bus with five pristine, uniformed Singuri guards: two in the back, one in the middle and front, while the last drives the bus. Had he attempted this same strategy a few months ago, I would've stayed behind, but since being in Neva, my eyes have been opened to a world of espionage and intrigue.

"Move out!" It's one of the guards in disguise who yells out the order. As the motor comes to life and the bus lurches forward, I wave one last time to the family I leave behind. With the dust swirling behind us, I swallow the lump in my throat and sit down, determined not to look back again. The splintering of my heart resembles the sharp pins and needles I felt in my fractured ribs. Only this wound is much deeper. As Alex finishes up the headcount, he takes his seat beside me, and the presence of his body brings a sense of home to my everchanging world.

We travel over roads long forgotten to time. The overgrowth from abandoned landscapes and broken homes are randomly placed along our route. I imagine what it once looked like when the towns were thriving and wondered how many families lived here. Maybe it was like the place my grandmother lived? Looking at the rubble around us, I can't help but feel a glimpse of the fear these people felt when their world fell around them. How can something so big, fall so hard?

"Everyone be on alert! Have your restraints ready! We're about to turn on a road still traveled by The Order. If we run into trouble, bind your wrists, keeping it loose enough should you need to break free." Tom barks out.

His words linger in the air, adding to the tension threatening to suffocate us all. We slip our hands through the unrestricting rope as the bus makes a sharp turn. We travel down a barren road that stretches endlessly before us. We are completely exposed here. On either side is nothing but dry, cleared land. The scars of war are evident on its surface. Not even time can erase the damage done. I now understand why they call this land forsaken; nothing but death resides here. A sinking feeling settles into my gut, with an intense urge to throw up. I swallow down my bile, for fear of causing panic among the other passengers. I see, scattered among their faces, the same unease I feel in my stomach. I search for Julia and find her leaning against Tom's shoulder. He refused to leave her side and so strategically he placed them towards the back, to hide his identity and her beauty. Even with her dirty clothes and messed hair, Julia still shines too bright for our world. Another wave of nausea rolls through me and I'm barely able to stop myself from losing it. I close my eyes and focus on my breathing: in and out, in and out, in and out. The sensation slowly eases away. When my eyes open, I find Alex watching me with a look of concern written across his face.

"I'm all right. I just need some fresh air," which just so happens to be the one thing I can't have right now.

He gently cups my face with his bound hand, rubbing his thumb up and down my cheek. My nerves settle, despite my stomach continuing its silent protest.

"Patrolling motorcycles ahead! Everyone be ready!" The driver announces the looming confrontation. He reaches for the switch hidden under his seat to turn the tracking device back on. We pull on our bindings creating an appearance of false constraint. Tom slouches in his seat, shifting his body in front of Julia, both reducing his size and her visibility. Alex and I duck our heads, as any good prisoner would do, preparing to avert our eyes from the devils lurking.

The bus slowly rolls to a stop, where two motorcycled Singuri await. As they dismount, one guard goes to the bus behind us, while the other boards ours. As he mounts the bus, he pauses to speak with the driver, who seems to have all the right answers. Then turning, he looks down the rows, scrutinizing each passenger. His steps are slow and intentional, reminding us that he is the one who holds the power. As his eyes gaze over the many dirty faces, I feel him stop just short of our row. "It's quite the pathetic group you have here," he taunts, "with the exception of a couple pretty little things."

My heart pounds, as I fear he has noticed Julia. Instead, I feel his hand brush my hair away from my hidden face. Alex tenses beside me as relief and disgust take their turn in occupying my mind. The realization that he's talking about me wraps itself in a blanket of horror. He slides his calloused fingers up and down my cheek, as he studies my face. I feel exposed and violated by this prowling creature. The tension in the air is too thick. The idea of this man touching me any longer is more than I can take. My body lurches forward as I vomit at his feet. The guard jumps back but not before some of my stomach contents splatter on his boots. Snarling his disgust, he calls me a filthy name that I don't care to retain in my memory. I'm glad I threw up, both for the relief I now feel and for the deterrent it brings. Alex struggles to stifle a laugh, while the angry guard hurries towards the door.

"Take care to have them medically cleared when you first arrive. We don't want their filth spreading." He wipes his hand on his pants, as though I have just given him some invisible germ. Good.

No one looks up until we hear the motorcycles roaring to life and speeding away. Alex is immediately undoing our restraints, "Well, that's a new tactic," he teases.

"I'm only a little sorry," I manage to smirk.

I can see underneath his smile, the rage he's working to control.

I rest my hand on his. "I'm okay," I assure him.

"But what if you weren't, Sam? I couldn't just sit here and let him—"

"I know, but he didn't. Besides, I'm pretty sure he would've changed his mind if he got a good look at me. But I puked on him instead."

We both laugh at my ill humor.

Alex draws me closer to him. "Sam, I know you don't see it, but you are beautiful. The guard was at least smart enough to see that, but foolish enough to act on it." I feel his chest rise and fall with the controlled efforts to calm himself down. Feeling empty of energy, I allow his breath to lull my racing heart into a slow, rhythmic beat. He's always made me feel safe. Alex is my sanctuary.

Unfortunately, we don't have time to clean up my mess, so Alex and I move to one of the few empty seats while I mumble my apologies to the other passengers. The driver switches the tracker back off as he turns the motor on. We travel for another hour in tense silence before the bus turns onto another hidden road. We drive down the abandoned trail alone, until the day begins shifting into night. Having only snacks and no rest stops, there's a collective sigh of relief when we reach our first destination. A deserted farm offers shelter for the evening. Looking around, in the glow of the pink fading light, I can see the land is healing here. There are small signs of new life with the patches of green grass spotting the expanse of the barren fields. We unload and get everyone settled into one of the broken-down barns, while the buses are concealed in another. We hold a small council meeting under the covering of the awning outside, while the rest of the travelers try to get some sleep. Tom wasn't expecting there to be any patrols on this route and is suspicious of the possible change in the Singuri routine. We decide to set up a watch for the night, switching out teams every three hours. Tom and Alex are the first to volunteer. Since we are leaving at the first light of dawn, we only need four more participants. If we leave on time tomorrow, we are set to arrive in Harlan sometime in the late afternoon, early evening.

Tom and Alex make their final round and Julia sits next to me. She offers me a cup of chamomile ginger tea and bread. With my stomach still in knots, I wasn't feeling up to eating at dinner time. But now, this bread tastes like heaven. We sit quietly under the stars listening to the sound of chirping crickets and an occasional croaking of a frog. Micah's sleeping form stirs from time to time, with the tenor sound of a nearby toad.

"It's a beautiful melody, isn't it? Reminds me that life is still fighting." Julia's words draw my attention to her. "I was just thinking the same thing," I smile.

Finishing the last bit of tea and bread, my body is ready for sleep. Lying back between Micah and Jewels, I succumb to the lullaby of nature around me.

37
Harlan

Sam:

The morning comes with the anticipation of Harlan ahead. We were able to clean out the bus and open a few windows overnight, allowing some fresh air in as we slept. Except for the excitement that's charged the atmosphere, I'm feeling back to my normal self. The bus tumbles down the neglected roads for hours before we approach a valley tucked away at the foot of a disfigured mountain range. We carefully drive down the hole-ridden dirt path, weaving through the deserted valley. Tom directs us into a shadow between two exceptionally deformed mounds. As we draw closer, I discover the shadow is disguising an old, unstable looking tunnel. I don't understand why Tom would turn us off the valley road down a dark, insecure hole. But then I remind myself that he knows where we're going, and I don't. As we drive down the creepy dark passage with only our headlights revealing the limited path before us, I fight the urge to ask how much longer. When the bus finally rolls to a stop, I watch as Tom walks out into the headlights and then disappears into the darkness. A feeling of unease settles over the passengers as the sound of approaching footsteps draw closer. Tom boards the bus with an unfamiliar woman, who directs the driver which way to go. I feel Alex shift next to me. I turn to ask him what's wrong and discover him staring at this new passenger. *How could he look at her like that?* "See something you like?" I accusingly question.

Rather than denying my not-so-subtle accusation, he looks even harder. If that's even possible. "I think—"

He's cut off by Tom's announcement, "We've arrived at Harlan!"

The mystery woman deboards the bus, leaving my husband's craning neck leering after her retreating form. *Jerk.*

"I need everybody to be patient as we unload the buses," Tom continues, though at this point I don't know if I can be patient. "I know you've all traveled a long distance and are eager to get off the bus and go to bed. Please hang in there a little longer. We are almost done. Thank you."

As everyone settles back into their seats, Tom walks towards Alex and me. "Sam, I hope you don't mind, but I need to borrow Alex for a few minutes."

"Not. At. All." I seethe. Okay, so maybe I don't have my anger as under control as I thought I did. Both Alex and Tom are looking at me like they're afraid of what to say next. Taking a deep breath, I slowly exhale. "It's fine," I lie, "I'm just tired. Go do whatever it is you guys need to do."

"Are you sure?" they simultaneously ask.

"Yes," I affirm.

Buying my false front, Alex gives me a peck on the cheek, "Thanks, Love. Find me when you get off, okay?"

I nod my head, "Mhmm." I answer, and then they turn to leave.

Unfortunately for me, sitting near the back means I am

one of the last to get off the bus. When I finally deboard, I'm met with the flickering light of the torches in the hands of those who came to welcome us. Picking my way through the crowd, the eerie glow casts dancing shadows across the faces of many well-wishers. Avoiding the unwelcome illusion, I turn my eyes to the top of the crowd in search of Alex once more. Spotting him beside Tom's towering frame, I slip between the uncertain strangers around me. I stop in a little alcove to watch Alex as he engages the company of those who appear to be the Elders. Even from this distance, it's easy to see his confidence while he speaks to them. His body language never shies away, rather, he meets them equally in smiles and a bold handshake. Once all introductions have been made, I follow them, keeping my distance, as they shift off to the side of the entrance gate to continue their semi-private meeting.

I watch this exchange continue and wonder who these leaders are. *When did Alex become a member of their inner circle?* Off to the right, my eyes catch a now familiar form prowling towards him. My breath stops, as this unwelcome figure leans into his ear and whispers something. The snuffed fire that was burning in my belly just moments ago, reignites with a new purpose. *Who is this woman, and why does she think she can take such liberties with him?*

Alex turns to see who has invaded his space and my fury burns brighter as he foolishly doesn't step away. Instead, he stands there gawking at her. Oh, she's beautiful, I didn't miss that. I don't think anyone could. She's around my age, maybe a little younger, has olive skin, deep brown eyes, and a figure that a Singuri Guard would drool over. *How could he not notice her?* Even still, my heart stings.

As I prepare to interrupt this private moment between them, she throws her arms around Alex. To my disliking, he greets her with equal enthusiasm. *Who is this girl, and why does Alex look so happy to see her?* Pulling away from their embrace, Alex holds her at arm's length, staring at her in a pleasant disbelief. Turning my eyes to the stranger who has captivated all my husband's attention, I find delighted desire within her own. Clearing my throat, I finally interrupt, "Alex?"

As if pulled from a trance, he turns his beaming face towards me. "Sam! You're never going to believe who this is!" His enthusiasm fans my internal flames to roaring.

I look from him and then to her, as though it's the first time I have noticed this woman. I smile at her, one of which she returns in the same tight fashion. *Oh, she doesn't like me either then.*

"You're right, I can't guess," I fake my nonchalance. "Who is she?"

"This is Amber! The girl I saved at the beach," he jovially explains.

Looking at her face once again, I see a confident, exotic woman, not a scared child. She would have been beautiful, even back then. Why did Alex keep that from me?

"Nice to meet you. I'm Samantha, Alex's wife." I smile sweetly at her.

As this bit of news sinks into her wanting eyes, her smirk fades into a slightly concealed scowl. "Nice to meet you," her silky voice offers. "I look forward to getting to know you better, and Alex, while you're here." She continues, "I always wanted to meet my brazen rescuer."

On the tinkling of her delighted chuckle, the memory of their meeting comes back to me. Her "brazen rescuer" as she calls him, was Alex running completely naked into the ocean. My body turns hot all over. As she discreetly lays her claim, I quietly wonder if she can see the flames within my eyes.

"Well, we have to go to the Welcome Meeting and figure out where everyone is going to fit in here." Alex's intrusion couldn't be more perfect.

Temporarily forgetting the object of this new territorial game I find myself in, I turn my attention back to him. "I'll meet up with you and fill you in on everything," he concludes as he pecks my cheek for the second time in a matter of minutes.

And just as quickly as the bud of inclusion sprang up in my heart, so did the shear of his words prune it away. Not as confidently as I was before, I answer, "Okay. I'll see you later then."

Alex looks at me for only a moment before Amber draws back his attention. She loops her arm through his, and with a smug look, pulls him away.

Alone, I numbly watch their retreating backs as the truth of the 'we' he spoke of moments ago takes root. *We have to go to the Welcome Meeting*, echoes in my head. We, not as in Alex and me, but we, as in Alex and Amber. Begrudgingly, I admit to myself that they do make a finer looking couple. Maybe that's the truth of it then. Maybe I'm the one who's been tricked. Maybe all this time, Alex has been dreaming of reuniting with her, as she clearly has been for him. Maybe I'm second runner up, simple, and easy to love, easy to keep secrets from…and easy to leave.

My stomach twists in knots and the sudden urge to throw up has me darting for the nearest dark corner. Pressing my clammy face against the coolness of the stone wall, I mentally note that we're underground again. Slowly inhaling and exhaling the fresh cool air, the knots in my stomach begin to loosen and settle.

"Are you okay?" an unfamiliar voice asks from the shadows.

Gasping, I instinctively take a step back, "Yes," I lie, while casually reaching for my hidden knife tucked securely at my side.

Stepping from the shadows I'm faced with an older man. He is impressively built and dressed in something reminiscent of the Singuri uniform. It's like nothing I have ever seen before. He walks forward and my eyes recognize something familiar about him. But I can't quite place it. Before either of us can say anything further, I hear Tom's surprised voice from behind me.

"Dad?"

Wait, what? Did he just say—

"Dad is that you? I thought you were still in Paxton."

My hand falls away from my knife as I watch the older guard smile from ear to ear.

"I was, until a few days ago," he responds, "I ran into a couple patrol guards yesterday. They reported two buses full of prisoners headed to Biton." He lifts his brow in a knowingly way. "I intercepted them and traveled non-stop to come here. Now The Order thinks I'm MIA, but don't worry, I've already got that figured out."

I can't organize my thoughts fast enough to keep up with all the new information swirling around me. First, Tom's dad is alive, and by the looks of it, he's someone important. Which, by default, means Tom is important. Second, he intercepted the guards from yesterday, potentially saving all our lives. Third, Alex is still off talking with mystery girl, in some apparent meeting, which brings me to four. If there is a meeting, wouldn't Tom and his dad be there? What did she tell Alex to sneak him off like that?

Thoughts of Alex are pushed aside as Tom sidesteps me and embraces his dad. It's an odd sight to see; two large Singuri men, hugging.

As I try to wrap my head around this turn of events, Julia appears at my side, taking it all in. "Did you know?" I ask her.

"That he would be here? No."

Leaving the rest unsaid, I understand then, that she knew he was alive. Wondering what other secrets she might have; I can't help feeling hurt by another secret kept from me. *Why didn't she tell me?* Then again, I haven't told her everything about Alex, and apparently, he hasn't told me all his...

"Sam, what if he doesn't like me?"

My mouth agape, I turn to look at her. *Who wouldn't love Jewels?* As her pleading eyes reveal her vulnerability and fear, I squeeze her hand. "Then he's a fool, and I don't think Tom would allow such mutiny."

Giggling, she squeezes my hand back.

"This is Sam and Julia," Tom introduces us, interrupting our little exchange. "And this is my father, William Everett."

William shifts his body towards us, and I see his identifying tattoo displayed on his neck; five bars. I swallow my gasp as I connect the dots. I recognize the name Everett as belonging to one of the founding members of The Order. It's rumored, that among the Sovereigns, there is a generation of leaders who stand above the rest. They are known as the Belay descent, and Everett is in that line.

"I thought your name was Thomas Jones?" I accusingly ask Tom.

"Jones is my mother's maiden name," Tom explains,

"one I assumed after fleeing Paxton. Just as you don't desire the fame that comes with your grandmother's legacy, I don't desire mine."

I look from Tom to his father and then to Julia. She knew this too. Feeling queasy again, I slowly pull in a deep breath, refusing to throw up. *Not in front of them.*

"I imagine this all comes as a bit of a shock to you," William says. "I apologize for the secrecy and hope to have the opportunity to earn your trust. I have heard a great deal about you and your dear sister, Julia. I look forward to getting to know you both, and your Alex as well." He nods behind me, acknowledging 'my Alex', who has suddenly appeared.

My head is in a fog of emotions and information. He knows about us, yet I know nothing about him. None of this insanity is news to Julia, except the part where he called her dear. Compartmentalizing the massive amount of new information, I push this new box back in the corner of my mind to rummage through another time. Clearing my head of its jumbled state, I'm finally able to offer a sensible response.

"Yes, it is a shock, to say the least." I snort as I shake my head. "I would be lying if I said it didn't feel like another betrayal. But we all have our own secrets." A look of approval passes between ol' William and me. "I also look forward to getting to know you. Unfortunately, you already have the advantage of knowing about my existence."

Laughter breaks the tension that crept in during our impromptu circle sharing time.

"To make up for my advantage, allow me to show you around," William offers, taking the first step in trusting one another.

With Julia's hand still in mine, I cozy up next to her. To anyone else this would look like a normal thing for us, but for me, it gives me the space I need from Alex. He's not my favorite person right now, not after he ditched me for Amber. As a group, we follow William through the maze of the underground compound. He guides us with familiarity and ease. As we travel the corridors, I can't help looking between him and Tom. I feel like I'm looking at Tom in thirty years. They are both tall, and confident, with a warm demeanor. They both even stand the same way. If William is the predecessor to Tom, then I already know I will like him. Continuing to weave our way through the tunnels, we pass through a training room and medical bay, which is notably stocked better than the caverns. We are then ushered through the mess hall followed by a quick stop at the bathroom quarters. At least here they have something resembling a shower and toilet. From there we go down a long hall that has multiple inlets from different directions. We come to a stop in front of two large doors. They are made of the same singed wood technique that Alex used on Irene's rocking chair. My heart stings with the subtle reminder of my friend and little Sammy.

William reaches his hands out, slowly pulling the heavy doors open, revealing what's inside. My heart stops as my eyes are met with an impossible indoor oasis. Somewhere above, the sunlight streams in, feeding the lush green grass that grows on top of the rich soil. There must be at least forty acres hidden down here. My eyes follow the path stretched before us, discovering a familiar pattern in the fields. "The crop rotation," I whisper.

"Very good, Sam." William praises me, so easily using my nickname.

"Thanks, *Will*," I smirk my response. Those closest to us shake their heads and chortle at our exchange. I'm glad we can seamlessly slide into this relationship, seeing as though Julia will likely become his daughter in-law.

Returning my attention to the rotation fields, I note the watering system in place. Stemming from the large pond in the center of this sanctuary, there are streams of water irrigating the fields, like veins. It's a work of art by itself. The pleasant chirp of a bird draws my ears to the sound of other wildlife within this sanctuary. The croak of frogs in the distance reminds me of our stay at the barns last night. The buzzing of bees captures my attention. Turning my head, I spot the eager workers anxiously returning to their hive boxes. Next to the bee corner are rows upon rows of flowers. I easily recognize chamomile and lavender among them. A kaleidoscope of butterfly's flutter from one nectar source to the next. The returning sound of a bird's chirp tickles my ears, drawing my attention to a nearby tree. Within the branches, I watch my singing companion land in its nest. *Amazing!*

"How?" I hear Julia breathe the single question that I imagine we all have.

Will answers, "There are many tunnels and caves that we have yet to explore in this compound. We stumbled across this refuge five years ago. We think it's fed by an underground stream, which, as you've seen, we've harnessed for the fields. The thriving wildlife already existed before we got here, so we're extra careful not to disturb them too much, or over harvest from the fish and other animals. As you can see, we have chickens around the perimeter of each crop field. They not only provide us with eggs and meat, but they eat the bugs which attack our vegetation. We tried to have pigs, but they disrupted too much of the natural habitat and we had to get rid of them. Some of us were more eager than others to be rid of them because of their smell."

I laugh, because I know I would fall into the category of those who wanted to keep them.

"For now, we have chicken, fish and rabbit, as well as the food we grow." Snapping an orange off a nearby tree, he offers it to Julia, who graciously accepts. I can see he is smitten with her already, and judging by the look in Tom's eyes, his world has just been made perfect.

"This isn't the only oasis out there," he continues. "The others are above ground and are heavily guarded. The Order has been seeking them out for years and keeping them for themselves. They have been slowly building up a new life on the backs of the Simpletons; this is one of the reasons we fight against The Order. What was originally planned to help a dying world, has become a selection of survival."

Perfect. Oasis. Bubble. Popped!

My eyes travel to the beauty that lies before me, and my ears burn from the truth of The Order's oppression. The euphoria that once enfolded me with life, resurrects a righteous anger within me. My heart hammers with the injustice of what the Simpletons' lives have become. My parents, Matthew, Ruth. They were all a mere means to The Order's end.

"They've turned us into slaves," I growl between my teeth.

All eyes are on me as I break the silence that once surrounded us.

All the years of my self-doubt, thinking I was the problem. All the wasted energy on trying to conform to their outline of what makes a successful human…All just so they could stockpile hidden troves of natural resources like the one we're standing in. A tremor rolls through my body. "No more." I pause to calm the splattering of emotions exploding inside me. Releasing my breath, I look to the familiar faces around me and speak louder. "No more!" I repeat. "It's our time to stand up against them and rise!" Captivated by the dormant passion that has stirred awake inside me, I failed to notice the stillness that enveloped us during my call of action. From out of this calm came a thunderous roar showering down from above us. Turning my face, not up to the open sky this time, but to the perimeter above, I see what my eyes failed to notice the first time. A platform running around the edge of the oasis. It's on this platform that rebels have gathered and answered their call to arms. Not sure of when or how they even got there, I see hundreds of them, dotting the rim of the canyon. Just as my voice carried up, theirs carries down with the cry of their chant, "Rise Together!" The rhythm springs my heart to life, pounding louder and faster with each chant. "Rise Together!" The excitement of the promised change ahead pulses through my veins. "Rise Together!" William turns, with a huge grin plastered on his face and arms outstretched to the circle above us, "Welcome to Freedom Rising!"

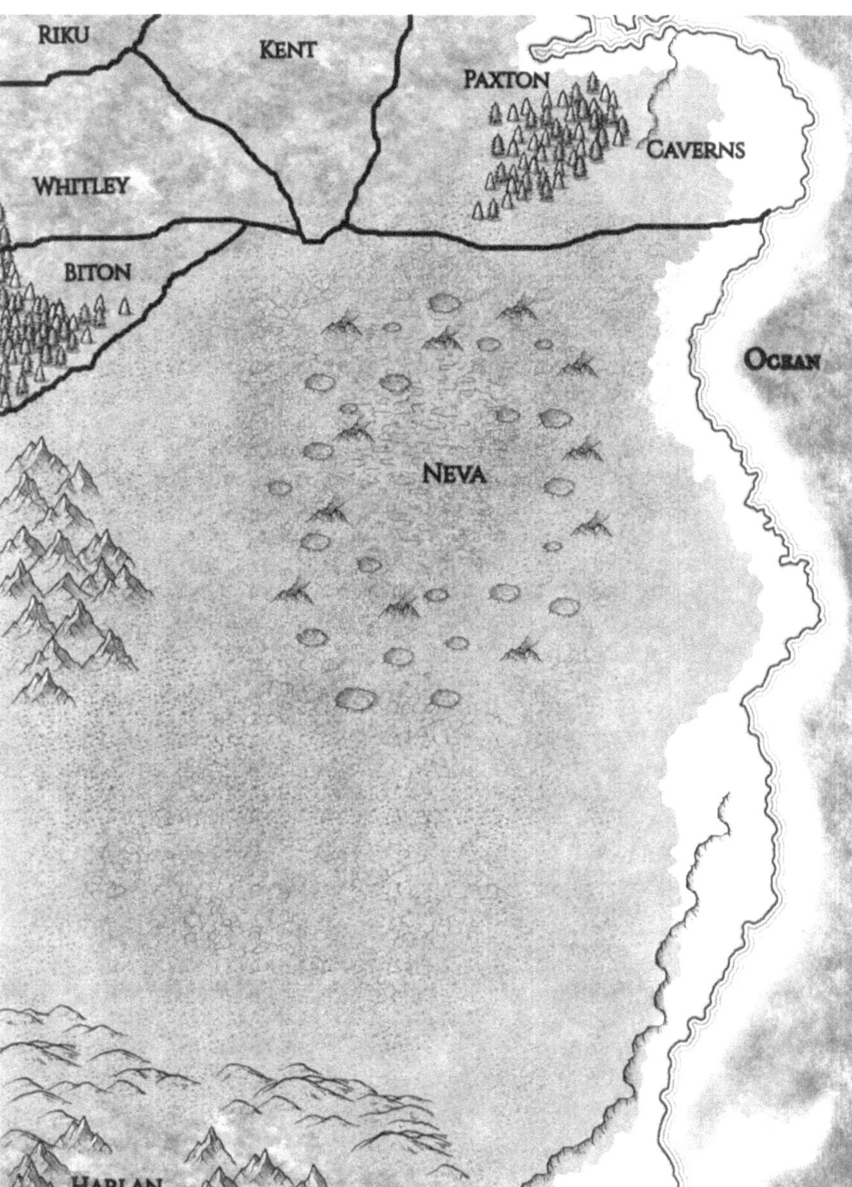

RIKU
KENT
PAXTON
WHITLEY
CAVERNS
BITON
OCEAN
NEVA
HARLAN

Acknowledgements

Wow! Where to begin? First, thank you to all who took a chance on a new author. I sincerely hope you enjoyed the journey. It was a thrilling experience to see the story taking on a life of its' own. With the unexpected twists and turns, I can't wait to see where it goes next! We are not done yet!

A big THANK YOU to my family and friends, who's belief in me sparked enough confidence to chance showing my work to someone unknown. What a journey this has been. A big thanks to my mom, for sharing the creative juices that flow in our veins. To my dad, thanks for being the pause to my thoughts and actions, challenging me to think it through again. To my sisters, and that one friend, thanks for loving me enough to be honest in reading my rough drafts and giving me pointers. I especially thank you for the final kick in the pants to show my book to the world. I needed your gentle critiques and encouragement. To the rest of my sisters, and sole brother (lucky guy that he is), thanks for helping to shape the human I became through our childhood. To my second round of siblings, you got this.

Warning, I'm about to gush on my hubby and kids. Ryan, thank you for supporting me in whatever creative outlet I try my hand at. Knowing how much I love to get lost in a great story, you gave me the peace I needed to not feel guilty for pouring myself into my writing. I want you to know how much I appreciate how hard you work to support our family, even if it means we miss you too much. Fire wife or not, being your wife was one of the best decisions I've made. Love you babe. To my kiddos, you are my motivation, you are my heart outside my chest. Mommy life put a pause on this book being printed for seven years, but I still sometimes wish I could hit pause now because you all are growing up too fast. It is my honor to be your Momma. I love every minute of watching you grow into the humans you are becoming. Selfishly, I want to keep you small longer, but the world needs you, so I am preparing my heart for the day you fly from my wings and find your own way.

To Pig Pen Publishing and the zany women who own it. I am forever thankful our paths crossed. I still get embarrassed thinking of the first draft I turned into you for potential publication. Thank you for seeing the story within the mess of this first-time writer. I love that we got to learn and grow together, building a friendship in the middle of all this. Your desire to see me succeed only matches my own, for Pig Pen to shatter ceilings. Here's to reaching for the stars. To Brevity Photography, thanks for capturing a bit of me in my photos. I love them. To Alyssa May, thank you for taking the idea from my head and creating it perfectly on the cover. You Rock! Thank you, Jaqueline Clotfelter, for weeding through the story and adding your editing touches. It has been surreal working with all of you wonderful, powerhouse, women.

Last, but certainly not least. Thank you to my God. I am still dumbfounded by all the ways You love me. May my life reflect you, Abba. In the obvious and expected ways, but especially in the unexpected. We need to be reminded of the God that we sometimes forget. The humorous Father and grieving friend, the Redeemer and Judge, the Lord over the chaos and the beauty, and my favorite, almighty God and gentle Father. And yet, You are so much more. Thank you for loving me enough to send your Son. Thank you, Jesus, for loving me enough to come. And thank you Holy Spirit for sticking with me through it all. This whole triune God thing still blows my mind. Thanks for being a God beyond comprehension. May I never put You in a box. Help me Lord, to live a life outside expectation so I never put myself in a box

About the Author

S.L. West has always loved being transported to different worlds and experiencing different cultures through the written word. She is a firefighter's wife, mom of three, and loves God with her whole heart. When she is not taking care of her family, her sassy animals, or finishing a home  improvement project you will find her cuddled up with a blanket, a cup of tea and a good book.

THE PADRE

ALEX DAVIDSON

Praise for **THE PADRE**

"As soon as you begin Alex Davidson's 'The Padre', you're pulled into a world of deep and vibrant character, mystery, unapologetic reality, and heart-racing action. With a hero as emotionally complex as any I've read in years, I simply couldn't put it down, and I couldn't get enough. About halfway through you start to figure out that you just might be witness to the birth of a next great voice in American fiction. It's that good. Alex is that good."

— **John Glenn, screenwriter, director, producer, and showrunner — whose credits include EAGLE EYE, THE LAZARUS PROJECT, NBC's ALLEGIANCE, and CBS's SEAL TEAM.**

"Alex Davidson is an important new light on the literary scene."

— **Grady Harp, Hall of Fame and Top 100 Amazon Reviewer.**

～

Praise for **BLACK RIFLE**

"An effective, fast-paced murder mystery that looks at gun culture in America from both sides of the political fence. A treat for Robert Ludlum and Joseph Wambaugh fans... 4.5 stars (out of 5)."

— **IndieReader.com**

"Jaw-dropping... With rapid-fire dialogue, larger-than-life characters, and a sinister but believable conspiracy, Black Rifle hits the mark as a high-powered thriller with some trenchant commentary on the country's darker impulses. ★★★★½"

— **Self-Publishing Review**

"Well-written. Pieces of it remind of Algren."

— **Robert Teitel, producer of MEN OF HONOR, the**

BARBERSHOP franchise, NOTORIOUS, SOUTHSIDE WITH YOU, and THE HATE U GIVE.

"Guns... are the third protagonist in Davidson's gritty tale, playing as important a role as the humanity of Cal, and the burning ambition of Lopez. With haunting characters and memorable action, readers will be glued as Cal and Lopez get closer to cracking the murder, their drive leaping off the page to the very end... Fans of tightly written thrillers with memorable detectives will enjoy this noir-tinged page-turner."
 — **BookLife by Publishers Weekly**

"Davidson manages to build up an intricate portrait of the United States that highlights the intersections of corruption, religion, and government power and explores right-wing extremism, the radicalization of White youth, and the United States' lax gun laws. In the end, the author presents an often powerful indictment of American gun culture in all its facets as it follows the titular rifle, an AR-15 that changes hands over the course of the story."
 — **Kirkus Reviews**

A Novel

PROLOGUE

E va watched the blade plunge into the pregnant woman's belly.

There was a communal gasp. Like the air had been sucked out of the room. A shock so deep and sickening it chilled the bone, jolted the heart, turned the stomach.

There are sights so terrible and jarring in this world that they are not only burned into memory but etched into the soul.

The Twin Towers on 9/11. The hundreds of thousands of empty shoes at Bełżec. The gassed bodies of Syrian children in Ghouta.

A Mexican cop stabbing a pregnant woman's womb on a busy street in Downtown Mexico City.

Passersby stopped, but no one intervened.

Moments earlier, Eva had been walking down the street in Centro Histórico, Mexico City's Downtown district. It was Friday night and the streets were alive. She moved in her tight dress and wedges through the crowds, past bars and nightclubs with lines snaking down the block.

The pregnant woman was walking in front of her. Eva

thought it was foolish for her to be out this time of night, looking the way she did — done-up in makeup and a skimpy dress that hugged her swollen belly. Two cops stepped in their way. They assumed Eva and the pregnant woman were together. They ordered them to stand against a wall.

The pregnant woman shook like a leaf.

Be cool, puta, Eva thought. Crooked cops fed off of fear. The trick was to stand strong, firm, and unafraid. You didn't want to be an easy mark. You wanted to make yourself unworthy of their trouble. Otherwise, they were liable to take liberties.

The first cop was a sleepy-eyed guy with a goatee. He shone his flashlight in the pregnant woman's face. It was the face of an eighteen-year-old Mexican woman. Plain, not pretty, not ugly. Entirely forgettable under normal circumstances. But tonight, it was a terrified face. Eyes on the ground, lip quivering under the weight of the interrogatory light.

"Why does your lip quiver?" the sleepy-eyed cop asked in Spanish.

The woman struggled but failed to steady her lip. The cold, intimidating Mexican police officer eyed her belly, which ballooned beneath her party dress.

Eva watched the interrogation without emotion.

"Look me in the eyes," Sleepy Eyes said to the pregnant woman, but she could not bring herself to look at him. Sleepy Eyes gently reached out his hand and slowly caressed the woman's inflated belly. Predatory. Erotic. The woman's horrified gaze darted up to meet the cop's eyes.

"How many months pregnant are you, mami?" the officer asked.

The other cop was a short, round, bald guy. *Chonchis*, Eva named him. Chonchis inched closer to Eva to make sure she didn't try to run.

The pregnant woman shook her head helplessly as the cop continued to fondle her inflated belly. The woman backed away, becoming more and more upset. Sleepy Eyes took a step toward her.

Suddenly, the woman pushed forward, knocking Sleepy Eyes off balance. She ran, but Sleepy Eyes tackled her to the ground. The pregnant woman bit Sleepy Eyes's forearm. Hard. Tearing flesh and drawing blood. He yelped and released her. She stumbled to her knees and pushed forward as Chonchis grabbed her by the arm and swung her back. The pregnant woman shrieked, kicked, and flailed as Chonchis restrained her by the arms from behind.

Just as Eva was about to use the opportunity to flee, something stopped her. She noticed that the woman's inflated belly was exposed. She watched worriedly as Sleepy Eyes rose to his feet, his forearm dripping blood, his eyes overflowing with hate. She watched him approach the pregnant woman — slowly, menacingly. She watched him raise his bleeding arm to the pregnant woman's face.

The pregnant woman wept hopelessly, no longer struggling as Chonchis restrained her.

Sleepy Eyes pulled out a knife. Sleek. Shiny. Evil.

"Pinche puta!" he said, and he plunged the knife into her belly.

Then, there was terrible silence. The worst kind. It was silence without action. The world stood still, and no one did a thing to intervene.

The pregnant woman slowly, sadly lowered her eyes and looked down at the knife stuck in her belly.

The sleepy-eyed cop pulled the knife out of the wound.

The blade was clean.

Then white powder poured out of the puncture. Neither cop was surprised.

"Congratulations," Sleepy Eyes said. "It's cocaine."

. . .

The pregnant woman, no longer pregnant, sat on the ground, handcuffed. A punctured stomach prosthesis and a kilogram of cocaine lay next to her.

Now it was Eva's turn to be interrogated. She stood where the pregnant woman stood before, facing the sleepy-eyed cop. With hostility, Sleepy Eyes shone the flashlight in Eva's face, but Eva remained calm.

"Look into my eyes," Sleepy Eyes said.

"I can't," Eva replied.

"Why not?" Sleepy Eyes asked. "You have something to hide? Something illegal?"

"No," Eva answered.

Sleepy Eyes produced his knife and caressed Eva's cheek with the blade. "Then why can't you look me in the eye, niña?"

Eva raised her head and squinted into the bright flashlight. "You're shining that light in my face. I can't see a damn thing."

The sleepy-eyed cop chuckled and turned off the flashlight. Eva passed the test. She was allowed to leave, unmolested, aside from the two cops' leering glances at her bulging c-cups.

The thing was…

Eva knew the pregnant woman. Her name was Juana, and earlier that evening, Eva had told her she was stupid to think her pregnancy prosthesis would fool anyone on a Friday night in Downtown Mexico City.

And also, Eva was really an a-cup.

PART I

THE FATHER

1

———

The sun rose on the cramped, labyrinthine settlement of worn and decaying structures just outside of Mexico City. The barrio woke up.

A mother bathed her infant outside in a rusted steel tub.

Police covered the dead body of a gunshot victim.

Rival cliques talked shit.

An old woman took ragged clothes off of her line.

There was a decrepit Catholic church, walls crumbling in places, undermined by a new frame being erected from the decay, and a lone figure perched, wielding his hammer, rebuilding the sacred structure.

He was rugged. Weathered.

He paused his labor to watch the sunrise. Peaceful and content. He calmly put down the hammer, hopped down from the church frame, and leisurely scooped up a nearby soccer ball.

In the crumbling concrete courtyard, he played fútbol with the poor neighborhood kids. They laughed and cheered and then whined when he told them he had to go. But they knew they would see him again tomorrow and the next day and the next.

He walked through the barrio. Impoverished and crime-ridden. Graffiti and junk. The ever-present smell of garbage Residents lit up when they saw him. They waved and smiled and they called out, "Hola, Padre!" He greeted everyone he saw with warmth.

He entered a gardening store. Various plants, flowers, and tools lined the walls. The owner was a skinny, lanky man with blurred tattoos lining leathery skin that reminded The Padre of a raisin. His eyes were set deep in his bony face. The Padre did not know his name. The locals referred to him simply as El Floristerío, the Florist. He gave The Padre a cold nod from behind the counter. This was about as friendly as The Florist ever got. The Padre nodded back, selected various packets of vegetable seeds from a rack, as well as a large bag of fertilizer. He paid The Florist and exited out onto the street.

The community garden was a beacon of light amid the urban decay. Señor Vasquez was a kindly old gardener. Skinny and ragged. "Hola, Señor Vasquez," The Padre said as he approached with the bag of fertilizer and seeds.

Señor Vasquez smiled kindly, revealing missing teeth. The Padre gave him the seeds and the fertilizer, then told him, "I got something special for you today." He handed Señor Vasquez a package of garlic seeds.

Señor Vasquez's smile widened. "Gracias, Padre!"

The Padre smiled and continued on his way.

On the main thoroughfare, hawkers advertised their items with street cries. A young, mean-looking gangbanger operated a stand. Knockoff designer junk, cheap gangster bling, Santa Muerte and Grim Reaper statues. He was selling amphetamines to a colgado as The Padre approached.

The kid grinned. "Padre!" They slapped hands and embraced.

"Hola, amigo," The Padre said. "What do ya' got for me?"

The kid reached into a nearby cardboard box, removing bootleg DVDs. "*Lawrence of Arabia, Gone with the Wind,* y *The Godfather.*"

The Padre accepted the DVDs. "Gracias."

"Also, just got these in," the kid said. He showed off his collection of handmade fireworks. Professional grade. Tubes painted in the green, white, and red stripes of the Mexican flag. "You haven't seen real fireworks until you've seen Mexican fireworks, Padre. You could use them on holy days."

The Padre handed the kid some pesos for the DVDs. "Maybe next time."

Just then, he spotted Eva across the street. She was entering a ratty, brown stash house. Barely seventeen and all business. She carried herself with the austerity of a hard life. And despite her best efforts to the contrary, she was beautiful.

The Padre moved toward the stash house, and the DVD Kid's clique leader stepped in his path. His face and body were inked with demonic tattoos. His eyes were black beads of hate. They burned into The Padre. Murderous and distrustful.

And The Padre darkened.

The Padre casually took out a pack of cigarettes, put one in his mouth, placed one at the foot of a nearby Santa Muerte statue, and held the clique leader's gaze. The clique leader saw something in The Padre's eyes. Something he identified with. Something cold, something empty. He accepted the cigarette, gave The Padre a firm nod, and let him pass. Respeto.

The Padre arrived at Maria's home at around noon. The two-room domicile was composed of dull brick walls and a rusted, corrugated tin roof. Inside, Maria was sleeping.

The Padre had known her back when she was beautiful, but her beauty had withered like a flower in winter. She lay in her bed, forty going on eighty. He hated the air in here. Death had a sour smell. Not like kill. Kill smelled fresh, like ice and steel. But death is sour, acidic, spoiled. The Padre left the door open because there were no windows to open.

Maria awoke with a start and found the Padre by her bedside. He smiled kindly. "It's only me."

Maria was relieved to see him, but her relief was only

momentary. As she gathered her bearings, her eyes scanned the room and filled with worry.

"Dónde está Eva?" Maria asked.

"Eva will be home soon." The Padre picked up a nearby book. *Harry Potter y El Prisionero de Azkaban.* He opened it to a bookmarked page. "Where were we?"

The Padre read to her in gringo-accented Spanish. He read for hours, and for a while, Maria forgot her pain. Forgot that she was dying.

The sun was setting outside when he finished the book. "El fin," he said. "Should we start the next one?"

The Padre moved to the bookshelf, where there were more Harry Potter books.

"Dónde está Eva?" Maria asked again.

The Padre pulled *Harry Potter y El Caliz de Fuego* from the bookcase. As he did, various watercolor paintings fell to the floor. He bent down and picked them up. Each painting depicted a different land or cityscape — some he recognized from the barrio — framed through a window.

"What are these?" The Padre asked.

Maria saw the paintings and grinned affectionately. "Mis ventanas."

"Eva painted these?" The Padre asked, impressed.

"What are you doing?"

The Padre turned and found Eva standing in the doorway. Her arms were folded across her chest and her face formed an angry scowl. He put the paintings in a neat pile, placed them back on the bookshelf, and marched to the door like a scolded schoolboy.

"I told you to stay away!" Eva said once they were outside.

"You left her alone all day. She kept asking for you."

Eva lowered her eyes.

"I know where you were. Just like I know why a girl from the slums of Mexico City can speak English," The Padre said. "Your mother needs comfort."

"She doesn't need you. She's going to be fine. Just leave us alone!" Eva said, slamming the door in his face. She treaded softly and made her way to the kitchen. Opened a cabinet. Inside were letters, a postcard of the Statue of Liberty, and a small vase.

"Eva?" Maria called from the other room.

"Sí, mama?"

Eva picked up the vase. Inside was a roll of cash. She added the money she earned tonight to the vase and closed the cabinet.

"¿Dónde estabas?"

"Estoy aquí ahora, mama," Eva said as she crawled into bed next to her sick mother.

It was dark by the time The Padre arrived home. The neighborhood kids had long since vacated the courtyard. Scooping up the soccer ball, he made his way into the half-constructed church.

He climbed up to the second floor to the room where he slept. He hung one of Eva's watercolors on his wall. It was a painting of the Mexico City skyline framed through a window.

He popped the DVD of *Lawrence of Arabia* into his DVD player. He reclined on his cot next to a half-built wall and watched the movie on his old school box TV.

Outside, gunfire rang out through the barrio as naturally as crickets on a hot summer night.

He just appeared one day. This gringo, squatting in the old church. Fixing it up. The people of the barrio took to calling him The Padre, though he was no priest. They didn't know what he was, where he had come from, or where he was going. To them, he was just The Padre.

But this had not always been his name.

He was once called Cal. Back when he was paid to kill people. But he never did it for the money. Cal possessed what shrinks call a "process addiction." The brain is malleable. Neuro-plastic. It can change its own structure. Through training and experience, the perfect interplay of nature and nurture, the brain can be rewired. The US government had trained Cal to be a killer. Trained him so that his brain rewarded violence the way a junkie's brain rewarded heroin, or the way a faithful person's brain rewarded going to church. Cal read once that two-thirds of a shark's brain is dedicated to sensory perception. Sight, sound, taste, smell, touch. Everything needed to hunt and kill, leaving little room for anything else. That sounded about right.

After a long career in Special Ops, Cal entered the private sector. He worked for a man named Pat Roti, a private military contractor who handled the blackest black ops for the highest bidder, including the CIA. In other words, Pat Roti ran assassins.

Ultimately, Cal's humanity abounded. It could be caged but not extinguished, and it chipped through its prison walls. Cal didn't want to kill anymore. He no longer wanted to be a pris-oner to his addiction. He wanted to live.

But you don't just get to quit. Not the type of job he had.

Cal knew that he was a loose end. That Pat Roti would try to find him. Try to kill him. But he was not worried. Pain is inevitable. Suffering is a choice. And, as he often told himself, *If I perish, I perish.*

Until then, he would live.

Until then, Cal would be The Padre.

2

One of the first people Cal met when he arrived in the barrio was a thirty-four-year-old homeless man named Ángel. Cal climbed up a nearby telephone pole, retrieved a pair of Nikes that were hanging up there by their laces, and slid them onto Ángel's dirt-caked and blistered feet.

Ever since that day, Ángel served as Cal's translator. Cal was proficient in Spanish, but he was not fluent. He relied on Ángel to capture the spirit of his words. The nuances and inflections that only someone from the barrio understood.

On Sundays, Cal had church. His congregants would sit in a circle on foldout chairs in the dusty nave.

"Thank you all for coming," Cal said. Ángel sat next to him, translating his words. "I see a lot of new faces today. I, like many of you, have struggled with addiction."

The attendees were locals. Paisas. Living from hand to mouth. Damaged and disenfranchised people, just trying to survive.

"But addiction is just a symptom of a deeper problem," Cal continued. "The question is not why the addiction? It is why the pain?"

Ángel spitfired Cal's words in Spanish.

"Until you identify what that wound is and heal it, you will always fill it with the wrong things. With addictions."

A squat man in work boots, denim jeans, and a faded flannel shirt — an out-of-work day laborer, Cal guessed — raised his hand and asked a question.

Ángel translated, "He wants to know how you stop yourself from using?"

"Whenever I am tempted, I remember what is important."

"Qué?" the man asked.

"That's the question, isn't it?" Cal said. "For me, it is all of you. Mi familia. Mis amigos. Mis relaciones."

A short, round woman in her fifties interjected. "We have no jobs. No way out of poverty," Ángel translated.

"If you're poor and you believe wealth will make you happy, it won't. Money is just another addiction," Cal said. "All people really have is each other."

"What do we do when there is no hope?" the day laborer asked in Spanish.

Cal thought about it.

"You find it."

Eva entered the post office and approached the postal clerk behind the counter.

"Box 117," she said.

The postal clerk found the mailbox, removed a letter, and handed it to Eva. Eva read the return address on the envelope and her face illuminated. She rushed home.

"We received a letter from Aunt Sylvia and Uncle Hector," she exclaimed as she burst into her mother's house.

She sat next to Maria on her bed, tore open the letter, and read, "Dear Maria and Eva. We have finally settled in Houston, Texas. I pray that one day both of you will be able to join us. Love, Sylvia and Hector."

Eva happily daydreamed for a moment.

"Very soon, I'll have enough money."

There was a knock at the door. Eva answered to find Cal standing on her doorstep. Her face dropped.

"I wanted to return this," Cal said, handing Eva the watercolor he took.

Eva snatched it. Surprised.

"It's very good," Cal said.

Eva nodded. Reserved. She was about to close the door.

"Why a window?"

"My mother can't leave the house," Eva said.

"So, you gave her a view." Cal smiled. Eva remained aloof. Uncomfortable. Distrusting. She closed the door.

Cal returned to the church and packed up his box TV set, DVD player, and a cardboard box of bootleg DVDs. He lugged them across the barrio to Maria's house. He knocked on the door, and again, Eva answered. She saw the TV, DVD player, and bootleg movies. She looked at him, taken aback. She stepped aside so Cal could bring the items into the house. Maria grinned when she saw Cal.

"Window," Cal said, indicating the TV. "Ventana."

Cal set up the TV and DVD player. He dug through the box of DVDs. "How about *El Mago de Oz*?" He fished *The Wizard of Oz* out of the box, put it in the disc tray, and pressed play. Eva watched Cal, uncertain.

After the movie was set up, Eva said she had to go to work. Cal walked her outside.

"I'm sorry for the way I spoke to you yesterday," she said. "It's just, when she sees you, she thinks she is going to die."

"I understand," Cal said. "Why'd you stop hanging your paintings for her?"

"Because it's not going to change anything."

"I think it helps."

"She has no one to help her. My father left before I was born. I need to get her to the United States."

"Why?"

"Because in the North, they can cure her."

The Padre bit his tongue. Eva's cell phone buzzed. She read a text. "I'm late. I've got to go."

"I'm rebuilding the church," Cal said. "I can't afford stained-glass windows, so I was thinking of doing murals on the walls instead. Saints and holy pictures. If you paint them, I'll match whatever the narcos are paying you."

Eva looked at him with sad eyes. "Padre, you can't afford me." She began to walk away.

"Eva..." She stopped and looked back at him. Cal stammered. He didn't know how else to say it. "Your mother is very ill."

Eva shook her head. Denial. "I can save her," she said and then marched away, determined.

3

M aria did not fear death.

She was thirteen when she met Rodrigo. He had thick dark hair, the face of a boy band singer, designer clothes, and a motorcycle. He was also almost ten years older than her.

Maria's mother knew it was inevitable. Looking the way Maria looked. A beautiful girl on her way to becoming a knockout of a woman. She only wished Maria had more time to grow up before she caught the attention of a narco. The best she could hope for now was that the narco treated her well.

And Rodrigo did. He took her to the most exclusive restaurants in Mexico City. Gave her money to shop at the most expensive stores. He was head-over-heels for her and, likewise, she for him. He asked her to marry him and she said yes. They planned a big, expensive wedding.

But there was trouble at work. It was the nineties. Sinaloa was at war with Tijuana, and proxy battles were being fought all over the country. Rodrigo was an up-and-comer, respected, and most of all, loyal. He stuck with the losing side and wound up dead.

The new regime respected Maria's fiancé for his loyalty to his boss, and the new leader did not believe in killing women or children unless absolutely necessary, so he spared Maria's life. But as the fiancé of one of his enemies, she had to be punished. He sentenced her to work in one of his brothels. It was an expensive place he kept for VIPs — politicians and lawmakers and anyone else he wanted to reward or blackmail. They called the brothel *Celestial*. Only the most beautiful women worked there, and they were all well taken care of. Relatively-speaking.

After losing Rodrigo, Maria was incapable of feeling love. She had no respect for life. She felt like she was already dead. So, she accepted the job. She let *Celestial* have what was left of her soul.

She existed like this for several years. Every day, she visited a local Santa Muerte shrine. She'd kneel before the robed skeleton, give an offering, light a candle, and pray for the Bony Lady to either give her a reason to live or take her life. Finally, she could take her Saint's silence no more. She visited the shrine and prayed for what she said would be the last time. That night, she intended to end her life.

She kept a nickel-plated .38 in her bedstand. She loaded it with a single bullet. She was about the bring the barrel to her temple when there was a knock at her door.

A man stood in her doorway. Although later, she would believe that he was not a man at all. He moved without feeling. There was something missing. He was empty. Or lost, maybe. Lost, like her.

She brought him to her room as she had so many times with so many other men before. His skin was white and cold like snow.

He disrobed and she fell back on the bed. He entered her. It had never been like this. She left her body and went to a place of bright colors and flowers and sweet smells.

He never said a word.

It was two months later that she learned she was pregnant. It was a miracle. She was told she was barren. She *was* barren. But she was pregnant.

The brothel had protocols for these types of situations. A doctor for the girls to see. But Maria refused. She was told that if she chose not to see the doctor, then she was no longer allowed to work. They controlled her bank account. Maria still had a few more years left in her sentence and there was no withdrawal for early retirement. If she wanted to keep her hard-earned, hard-fucked money, she had to see the doctor. *Why not?* they ask her. *Why does she want to keep some stranger's baby?* But she could not abort it. It would be sacrilegious. Santa Muerte had given her this child.

Eva. She was a miracle.

Maria left the world's oldest profession and raised her daughter penniless. She worried about Eva, as any good mother would, but she never truly feared for her. Which was why she did not fear death. She did not fear leaving Eva. Because she knew Eva would be okay. Eva was tough and resilient, but that was not all. Eva's father was not a man; rather, he was a vessel of divinity.

Maria did not fear death.

Because she knew that Santa Muerte would look after all she had here on Earth.

Eva wore makeup, a mini skirt, and a tank top. She exited the stash house with Javier. He was a man in his twenties. Handsome, in jeans and a leather jacket. They loaded into a Chevy Suburban.

When the sun set, Downtown Mexico City came alive. The air filled with music and neon lights. Rowdy tourists crowded the streets, drunk and debauched.

The Suburban cruised. Javier behind the wheel. Eva staring unfeelingly out the passenger side window. All business.

A police cruiser hit its lights behind them. Javier glanced worriedly in his rearview. Pulled over.

Two Mexico City cops got out of the cruiser and

approached either side of the Suburban. They tapped on the windows with the butts of their flashlights. Javier and Eva rolled them down.

"Hola," said the cop on the driver's side. He was short and stout with a Pancho Villa mustache.

They spoke in Spanish.

"Good evening, sir," Javier said.

"Where are you headed tonight?" Pancho 'Stache asked.

"The club."

Eva stared straight ahead. Cool. She could feel the leering eyes of the tall thin Mexican cop at her window. He wore aviator sunglasses, even though it was night.

"This is a nice car for two young kids," Pancho 'Stache said.

"It's my father's," Javier replied.

"Yeah? Who's your father? Tomas?"

Javier's eyes darted to Pancho 'Stache at the mention of Tomas's name.

"That prick owes us a lot of money," Pancho said.

The cops opened the car doors. "Get out."

Javier and Eva stepped out of the Suburban onto the sodium-lit street. The cops patted them down. Pancho 'Stache found a .38 handgun in Javier's waistband.

"What's this?" he said, pulling his cuffs from his belt.

As Aviator Sunglasses patted Eva down, he gave her ass a squeeze. Eva gritted her teeth.

Pancho cuffed Javier and searched the Suburban. "Where's the shit?" he asked.

"What shit?" Javier said.

Pancho 'Stache struck him in the diaphragm. Javier keeled forward, arms cuffed behind his back. He sucked in air.

"Don't play games with me," the cop said.

"Yes. We know Tomas," Eva interjected. "But we are not working right now."

Pancho 'Stache glared at Eva, trying to read her. He grimaced. Turned to Javier. "Let's see how Tomas likes bailing you out for an unregistered firearm, asshole." He pulled Javier toward the police cruiser.

"What about the girl?" Aviators asked.

"Does she have anything on her?"

"No."

"Then leave her."

The two cops got in the cruiser with Javier and drove away. Eva climbed behind the wheel of the Suburban. She drove to a nightclub. Parked across the street. Got out of the Suburban and approached. There was a line curled around the block, but the Mexican meathead in the too-small suit guarding the door knew Eva. She walked right in.

Inside, EDM blasted. Scantily-dressed females grinded to the music. Hugo Boss and Diesel-clad D-bags circled like scavengers desperate for scraps. Eva pushed through the crowd.

The owner's office overlooked the party below. The club owner was a Mexican man in his thirties. Well-dressed. Playboy vibe. He was sitting behind his desk, doing a line of cocaine, when Eva was escorted in by a bouncer. The owner eyed her.

"I'm waiting," he said in Spanish.

Eva took off her shirt, exposing her firm, young body. She removed a half-a-kilo of coke each from false nipples concealed beneath her bra and put them on his desk. She turned to exit.

"Wait a minute," the owner said.

Eva stopped and looked back at him. He grinned. "We have to make sure it's good."

The club owner stuck a pocket knife into one of the half-kilos, scooped out some powder, and offered it to Eva. Eva shook her head, no.

"You don't try it, I don't accept delivery."

Eva shrugged, took back the two half-kilos, and headed for the door.

"Whoa. Wait a minute." The owner headed her off. "Why are you so tense?"

He put his hands on her shoulders. She pulled away. He

grabbed her, so she pushed him. In a coke-fueled rage, he back-handed her across the face. Hard. She fell to the floor.

"Fucking bitch!"

Eva crawled on all fours away from him. He undid his fly. Grabbed her. Lifted her and slammed her face down over his desk. He reached up her skirt and tore down her panties. Prepared to enter her, as—

Eva spotted the coke-dusted pocket knife on his desk. Grabbed it. Swung around wildly. The blade lodged in his cheek. He screamed. The knife jutted out of his cheek and blood flooded down his chin. Eva pulled up her panties and sprinted to the door.

She rushed across the dance floor of grinning drug-fueled idiots. She ran out of the club, across the street, jumped in the Suburban. Turned the ignition and sped away. Eyes on her rearview.

The Suburban tore through the barrio and screeched to a halt outside of Maria's house. Eva got out of the vehicle and sprinted inside.

"Mamá! Nosotras tenemos que ir!" she said as she burst through the door. She stopped dead in her tracks. Cal sat by the bed next to Maria's lifeless body. He looked at her, sadly.

"She went peacefully," Cal said.

Tears filled Eva's eyes. She shook her head. "No. No!" She rushed to her mother. "Despierto! Por favor, mamá! Tienes que despertar!" Eva collapsed on top of her mother. Cal gently stroked her head as she wept.

Outside, car headlights approached. Cal slowly rose, leaving Eva to grieve with her mother's body.

There was a black Escalade parked outside. Cal stood in the doorway outside of Maria's home. Two Mexican men approached. The first one had a tattoo of a serpent coiled around his face. The second had a mouth full of gold teeth. Both men carried pistols.

"Is that little bitch in there?" Face Tat said. "Out of the way, Padre."

Cal stood his ground, raised his arms. "I am a man of peace. Please. Lower your weapons."

Gold Teeth shoved his gun in Cal's face. "Get the fuck out of the way."

Cal grabbed the muzzle of the gun, struck Gold Teeth's wrist with his forearm, and stripped the gun from his grip. Before Face Tat could raise his weapon, Cal had the pistol pointed at his forehead. Face Tat and Gold Teeth were shocked. How did the Padre know how to move like that?

Gold Teeth sucked his teeth at Cal. "This is not over." Gold Teeth and Face Tat retreated to the Escalade and drove away. Cal looked back at the house and saw Eva standing in the doorway, watching him.

Tomas gnawed on a cigar. He was five-foot-five and one-hundred and thirty pounds of pure rage.

"Fucking what? You got told off by fucking who?" he shouted in Spanish at Face Tat and Gold Teeth when they returned to the stash house.

Tomas gathered his men. They loaded pistols, rifles, and shotguns.

Cal brought Eva to the church. She sat on Cal's bed. Cal stood by the crumbled wall. He watched Tomas outside approach with his armed posse. Tomas pounded on the church door.

"Stay here," Cal said to Eva. He marched downstairs, crossed the nave, and answered the door.

"Give her to me," Tomas said.

"I can't do that."

"That man she attacked has very powerful friends. This must

be answered for," Tomas said. He stuck his Beretta in Cal's face. "Give her to me."

"Do you really want to be seen doing that?" Cal said.

Tomas looked around. The people of barrio had taken notice. Tomas knew how well-liked Cal was. Shooting him in the open would be a mistake. He lowered the gun.

"Some huevos, Padre," Tomas spit and lowered his gun. He and his men retreated.

Cal returned to Eva. She was still sitting on the bed by the crumbled wall.

"They're gone," Cal said. "You should get some sleep. It's a long way to Texas."

"I can't go to Texas. Not yet," Eva said. "I don't have enough saved."

"Don't worry about the money."

Eva's eyes narrowed. "Why are you doing this for me?" She shook her head, unable to hold back the tears. "I don't deserve it. Why waste your time? I couldn't save her. How the fuck am I supposed to save myself?"

Cal embraced her as she cried. "It's okay."

She wept all night. She wept in his arms.

The next morning, they had a small funeral behind the church. Maria had always kept to herself. She did not have many friends in the barrio, but people still showed up to help bury her. Eva bawled as Maria's casket was lowered into the ground. She grabbed Cal's hand and squeezed it.

Across the cemetery, Cal spotted Gold Teeth and Face Tat, watching them.

After the funeral, Cal walked Eva to the bus depot. They got in a line of immigrants to board a beat-up bus.

"Come with me to El Norte," she said to Cal.

Cal shook his head.

"You think Tomas will just forget about you? He won't."

Cal stared off distantly. Ghosts in his eyes. "I can never go back."

The Coyote in charge was a small, cocky man in his thirties. "It will be 55,000 pesos," he said in English.

"That will get her to Texas?"

"Sí, señor. No problem."

Cal paid the Coyote. He turned to Eva and handed her a cell phone. "Once you're across the border, take a bus to your aunt and uncle's house. Call me when you're there."

Eva nodded. She was next to board the bus. Just before she got on, she turned back and gave Cal a big hug. "Thank you," she said.

She let him go and boarded the bus. He watched her take her seat. He waved goodbye and the bus pulled away.

On Cal's walk back to the church, he wished he could have gone with Eva, but he knew it was impossible. Not only because Pat Roti was hunting him, but also because Tomas was hunting her. He had to stay behind not to protect himself, but to protect Eva.

Gold Teeth and Face Tat stepped in his way. Glared at him toughly.

"She's gone," Cal said. "It's over."

Cal walked past them. They watched him go. Grinning.

4

———————

Eva slept, her head propped against the window. The cramped bus bumped along. Outside, it was dark.

Suddenly, the bus jerked to a stop. Eva awoke.

They were parked outside of a nondescript building. No windows. No roads. They were in the middle of the desert. A dozen or so men — stable boys — emerged from the building. The driver opened the bus door.

"Everybody out! Move it!" the driver shouted in Spanish.

The stable boys boarded. They herded Eva and the others off of the bus.

Eva and the other immigrants stood in a line outside of the nondescript building. Eva looked around nervously.

Across from them was a luxury bus, the type professional sports teams rode in.

A fifty-five-year-old gringa woman in riding boots, a field coat, and Stetson hat walked down the line. The stable boys called her Ma. She looked and carried herself like the type of person who trained million-dollar thoroughbreds.

Ma appraised each of the immigrants. She stopped at a young man — sixteen, boyish and innocent-looking. Ma clicked a clicker counter, and a stable boy grabbed the young man by the arm and led him toward the luxury bus.

Ma continued down the line, studying each immigrant. She stopped again at a pretty, twenty-one-year-old woman. Clicked the clicker counter. A stable boy escorted the young woman toward the luxury bus.

Ma continued. Arrived at Eva. Eva lowered her eyes. Ma's gaze assaulted her, then — *Click.* Eva was chosen. A stable boy took Eva by the arm and escorted her toward the luxury bus.

Eva looked back. The immigrants that weren't chosen were herded back onto the shitty bus. This didn't feel right. Scared, Eva pulled away from the stable boy. Ran through the dark desert. Frantically dialed the phone that Cal had given her.

He was in his room in the church. His ringing cell phone woke him. He saw the caller ID.

"Eva?" Cal said.

"Padre. Something is wrong."

Cal heard shouting voices on the line in the background.

"Tell me what's happening," Cal said.

"They took us off the bus, and all of the young people, they're transferring them onto this other bus."

A stable boy shouted in Spanish into a bullhorn. "There is nothing but desert for fifty miles. Without us, you will die."

"I don't want to go with them!" Eva whispered into the phone.

The beam of a flashlight caught Eva. "She's over here!" a stable boy shouted in Spanish.

"Eva. Listen to me," Cal said. "I'll bring you home. I promise you."

Stable boys grabbed Eva. "Let me go!" she screamed.

"I'll bring you home!" Cal shouted. The line went dead.

Cal rushed down to the bus depot. He found the Coyote loading another bus with hopeful immigrants. Cal marched up to him.

"The girl I was here with."

The Coyote looked confused. "Qué?"

"The girl I paid you to take across."

"Lo siento. No Inglés."

"What? La niña! La niña!"

"Lo siento, señor. No sé quién eres."

Cal grabbed him by the shirttails, and immediately, the Coyote's guards pointed their pistols and rifles at him.

The Coyote grinned. "You should go now, Padre."

Cal eyed the guards surrounding him. He released the Coyote and marched away.

He returned to the church. After her mother died, Eva did not want to take anything from the house. She didn't want to keep any painful reminders. But Cal managed to smuggle her watercolors out. He sat by the crumbling wall of his bedroom and looked at them. The Mexico City skyline. A snowy mountain, a pastoral landscape, a tropical jungle, the ocean, the desert, outer space. Windows to a world which she was deprived.

His eyes darkened. Something was awakening in him.

Something dangerous.

5

———————

The stash house was where Tomas processed his products into smaller eight balls and dime bags for the local street dealers.

A Mexican man with a sawed-off shotgun guarded the door. At the sorting table, a man with an eyepatch worked with Face Tat and Gold Teeth. They bagged retail quantities of cocaine, crystal, Mexican mud, and MDMA.

Tomas sat at his desk in the back of the room with his muscled bodyguard, counting cash.

When Cal entered, the man at the door trained his sawed-off on him. Everyone stopped what they were doing and looked his way.

"I sent her away," Cal said. "You could have told your people anything you wanted."

Tomas shrugged. "The Coyotes are not so much coyotes as they are rabid dogs."

"What did you do?"

Tomas grinned cruelly. "Padre, Padre, Padre. This is what everyone calls you, yet no one knows your real name, who you are, where you come from."

"Where did they take her?"

"I wouldn't tell you, even if I knew," Tomas said. "There are far worse things in this world than me, señor."

"I know," Cal said, lowering his eyes. That latent darkness boiling to the surface. "Do you want to know how I know?"

"How?"

"Because I see it, every day, every time I look in the mirror."

Cal grabbed the barrel of the guy with the Sawed-Off Shotgun sneaking up behind him, jerked the gun forward, and blasted a hole in Face Tat's chest, then drove an elbow into Sawed-Off's nose, tearing the shotgun from him and firing it into Sawed-off's throat.

Eye Patch charged, slashing a knife, which Cal coolly dodged. His movements were calm and calculated, a rhythmic poem of death. Cal caught Eye Patch's wrist, snapped it, and drove the blade into his heart.

The muscular bodyguard lunged at him. Cal grabbed a nearby kilo of cocaine, sliced it, and smashed it into Muscles' face. Muscles fell back, coughing, wheezing, discombobulated.

Tomas reached for his pistol, raised it, but Cal easily disarmed him, pointed the pistol at Tomas.

"Wait," Tomas said.

Cal shot him before the word was barely out of his mouth. No hesitation. No ceremony. Cal turned the gun on the wheezing Muscles and mechanically shot him dead as well. Gold Teeth cowered in the corner, his hands raised.

"Please!" Gold Teeth begged. "You said you were a man of peace!"

"No peace without war," Cal said, and he pulled the trigger.

Cal strutted out of the stash house, leaving destruction in his wake.

6

It was midday. Cal glassed the bus depot with an ACOG scope. He watched the Coyote speak to one of his guards then walk over to a nearby table, where there was a bottle of tequila. He took a swig, then disappeared into the main building. Cal counted seven armed guards. Each sipped from the communal tequila bottle as they patrolled. One of the guards escorted a man in metal handcuffs toward a garage. Cal lowered the scope.

Down the street, a gringo with dreadlocks watched Cal.

He watched him outside the bus depot, then he followed him to the black market, where he watched Cal talk to the DVD kid at his stall. Cal handed the kid some pesos and received a bundled package.

From the black market, the dreadheaded gringo followed Cal back to the decrepit church. He hid in an alleyway outside, as Cal entered. Thirty minutes later, Gringo Dreadhead watched Cal exit the church. He no longer held the bundled package. Instead, he carried a heavy-duty steel briefcase.

Next, Dreadhead followed Cal to the gardening store. He

waited across the street while Cal went in. Moments later, Cal reemerged with a bouquet of flowers.

It was a short walk back to the church.

Dreadhead spied on Cal in the cemetery behind the church. He watched Cal place the flower bouquet on Maria's grave.

Dreadhead trailed Cal from Maria's grave through the cemetery, keeping a safe distance. He lost sight of Cal behind a mausoleum. Dreadhead pulled a Glock and approached then turned the corner.

In a flash of movement, Cal disarmed the gringo dreadhead and shot him in the foot with his own gun. Dreadhead yelped and dropped to one knee.

"Hey, Tony," Cal said casually.

Dreadhead, or "Tony," gripped his wounded foot by the ankle, looking up at Cal through pained eyes.

"Hey, Cal."

"They don't call me that anymore," Cal said. "Sorry about the foot."

Tony shrugged. "Hazard of the job, I guess."

"Roti promoted you?"

"Yeah. I'm a hitman now."

"Congrats."

"Thanks." He indicated the church. "Nice hideout. A contradiction if I ever saw one."

Cal smiled sadly. "How'd you find me?"

"Roti's got everyone scouring the globe looking for you. Someone was bound to catch up to you eventually."

Cal nodded.

"I saw you casing the bus depot," Tony said. "You know it's a trap, right? They know you're coming."

"I know," Cal said. "Hey, Tony?"

"Yeah?"

"You're no good at this." Cal shot Tony through each of his hands. "Find a new profession." Cal took out the mag, tossed the pistol, picked up his steel briefcase, and marched away, leaving Tony moaning in pain.

By the time Cal got back to the bus depot, it was night. He slid a sewing needle beneath the skin of his inner wrist, then raised his scope and surveyed the depot. The same seven armed guards were on patrol. Cal observed them for nearly an hour, memorizing their patrol routes, then he stealthily approached the compound.

A guard with an old AK-47 and camo tank top stopped to take a piss. Cal snuck up behind him. Just then, a guard in a *Club de Fútbol América* jersey shone his flashlight. Cal ducked behind a pile of tires.

"Hey! What're you doing over there?" Fútbol Jersey shouted in Spanish.

"Taking a piss," Camo Tank Top said. "Why? Are you trying to see my dick?"

"It's a flashlight, not a microscope."

Camo Tank Top laughed. "Asshole."

Fútbol Jersey turned off the light and continued his patrol. Once the coast was clear, Cal circled around the side of the compound's main house. He spotted the communal tequila bottle a few feet away. He peeked in the window.

Inside the house, the Coyote watched soccer and sipped beer. Cal set down his steel briefcase and stealthily snuck toward the door. He arrived just outside and prepared to breach—

One…

Two…

Three!

Cal kicked the door open and rushed in. The butt of someone's rifle greeted the base of his skull with a concussive crack, and everything went dark.

"Salut!"

Cal came to. Eyes groggy. Head splitting. He was bound to a

chair. His hands were cuffed behind his back. He was in one of the bus garages. Nearby, the Coyote and his guards downed glasses of tequila.

"Hola, Sleeping Beauty," the Coyote said, approaching Cal. "You didn't even have a gun when we caught you. What were you going to do? Pray us to death?"

His men laughed. "Sí. I recognize you," the Coyote said. "You are that gringo they call 'Padre.' Pero, you are not really a padre."

The Coyote snickered maliciously.

Cal had been disarmed. The money belt he wore around his waist, filled with hundred-dollar bills, was on the floor in front of him. It was his petty cash for his return journey to Los Angeles.

The Coyote grabbed the bottle of tequila. "Would you like a glass of tequila? From my brother's distillery. Premium shit, güey."

The Coyote put the lip of the bottle to Cal's mouth. Cal turned his head away.

"I really recommend you have some, señor… For what comes next," the Coyote said with mock concern.

But Cal would not drink. "Suit yourself," the Coyote said, then took another swig. "Do you know how they make tequila? It comes from the agave plant."

The Coyote raised a coa blade — a sharp machete with a rounded tip — and traced it over Cal's chest. "They must take out its heart."

The Coyote glared at Cal, toughly. Cal was unfazed. "With a coa blade, the agave is stripped. The heart is removed and baked. Its sap is fermented." He raised the bottle. "And this is its blood." He drank.

"I've got a recipe of my own," Cal said.

The Coyote chuckled arrogantly. "He speaks!" the Coyote said. "Okay, Padre who is not a padre. Go ahead. Tell us your recipe. After, I will cut out your heart and drink your blood."

"It comes from a plant native to Guayabitos and La Penita. It's called the castor bean plant. You pluck a bean, remove its shell, cook it, mash it, filter it and add solvents. Do you know what you have?"

The Coyote grimaced. A pain in his stomach.

"Ricin," Cal said.

Three hours earlier, Dreadhead Tony had followed Cal to the gardening store. He waited across the street, and after several minutes, he watched Cal exit with a bouquet of flowers for Maria's grave. He did not see what else Cal had bought in there — what the lanky, tatted-up Florist kept behind the shop in what he lovingly called "la casa del veneno," the house of poison.

This was where he grew hemlock, nightshade, white snakeroot, castor beans, rosary pea, and oleander.

In his spare time, The Florist would obsessively grind up apple seeds, hundreds of thousands of them, to yield cyanide.

For the right price, he would even construct a fertilizer bomb for you.

When Cal exited the gardening store with flowers for Maria, Dreadhead Tony was unaware that while he was in there, Cal had also bought a vial of something special from The Florist.

The Coyote and his men were feeling it. Unmistakably. The poison burning in their stomachs.

"There were too many of you for me to take on directly. You were too well-protected," Cal said from the chair. "But your tequila wasn't."

One hour earlier, Cal had been just outside of the Coyote's door, preparing to breach. But before he did, he had poured the contents of The Florist's vial into the guards' communal bottle of tequila.

Now cuffed to a chair, Cal picked at the threading needle hidden beneath the skin of his wrist.

"The question then became, how do I get to you before the poison? A concentrated dose of ricin, like the one I gave you, kills within hours, and you're no use to me dead," Cal said. "So, I let you catch me."

Behind his back, Cal removed the needle he hid under his skin and picked the handcuffs. The Coyote hollered, enraged, and brought the coa blade down on Cal. Cal swung his arms around and caught the blade between his palms. The Coyote's eyes widened. Cal rose, shoved the weakened Coyote to the ground. All around, the guards were dropping to the ground, deathly ill.

Cal knelt by the agonized Coyote. "You only have minutes to live," Cal said. "Tell me what I want to know and I will give you the antidote."

"Fuck you!" the Coyote yelled.

"Then adios, 'Sleeping Beauty.'" Cal turned and began to march away.

"Wait," the Coyote said. "What do you want?"

Cal showed him a photograph of Eva that he took from Maria's house. "The girl. Where did you send her?"

The Coyote grunted in pain, grasping his stomach. "All of the buses stop near the border, where they are sorted. Syndicates in El Norte pay a lot of money for young and attractive people. The girl would have been picked."

"And sent where?"

"I don't know."

Cal turned to leave. "Wait! I swear! I don't know!" the Coyote said. "I am just one link in a long chain."

"I believe you."

"So, give me the antidote!"

"There is no antidote." Cal marched away as the Coyote and his guards died painful deaths.

Outside in the bus depot yard, Cal picked up his steel briefcase, right where he left it. He got in line for a bus. Hopeful immigrants pack inside like sardines. Standing room only. Cal boarded. The other riders looked at him strangely. Who is this gringo?

The bus departed into the inky night.

7

I t was still dark outside when the bus jerked to a halt outside the same nondescript building in the middle of the desert. Cal gripped his briefcase as he and other immigrants were ushered outside.

He stood in a line, holding his steel briefcase. Across from them was the luxury bus.

Ma walked down the line, appraising each immigrant. Clicking her clicker counter. She arrived at Cal. Eyed him up and down. Ma turned and whispered something to one of her stable boys, then moved on down the line.

The stable boys roughly grabbed Cal. Took his briefcase. Searched him. Found the picture of Eva. Handed it to Ma.

Ma studied the photo, then looked at Cal. "Take him to holding," she said.

The stable boys brought Cal inside the nondescript building. The place was an open warehouse. Various pistols, rifles, explosives, bricks of powder and packages of pills brimmed from shelves or pallets. Stable boys were hard at work, scurrying through the rows of shelves like rats in a maze. Scanning QR tags and loading boxes and crates with guns or drugs. It was like a black-market Amazon fulfillment center.

Cal was placed in a chain-link pen with other prisoners. Ma stood in the doorway of the cage, flanked by her men. She looked at the picture of Eva. "I remember this one. Pretty," she said.

Ma took Cal's steel briefcase from one of the stable boys and fiddled with its lock. "Got some serious security on this thing." She offered the briefcase to Cal. "Open it."

Cal did not take the briefcase. He kept his gaze on her.

"We were told that an American had killed a bunch of Coyotes down in Mexico City," Ma said. "We were asked to keep our eyes open."

Ma handed the briefcase over to a baby-faced stable boy. "Open it." Babyface nodded and ran off to fetch his tools.

"What do I care about a couple of Coyotes getting offed?" Ma said. "They knew the risks when they entered this business, just like we all do."

Babyface returned with a power drill. He drilled the briefcase's lock.

"But then I saw you. Cal." Ma gestured at the sorting facility abuzz around them. "Guns. Drugs. Flesh. This is where things are sorted to their final destination. But I'm afraid this is as far as you go."

The drill bit smoked against the lock.

"Pat Roti has placed a lot of money on your head."

Babyface stopped drilling. Ma looked at him. He shook his head, no. The drill wouldn't penetrate the lock.

"What's the combination, Cal?" Cal remained a brick wall. "Well, now you've got my curiosity," Ma said. "Tell you what, give me the combination, and I'll kill you quick Otherwise, I take my time."

Cal remained silent.

"Left eye," Ma said to Babyface.

Ma's men restrained Cal. Babyface turned on the power drill and inched it toward Cal's left eye.

"We're gonna get it open. Save me the trouble. Give me the

combination." Just as the power drill was about to penetrate his iris, Ma raised the photograph of Eva. "Otherwise, I track down your girl and introduce myself."

Finally, Cal spoke. "Six. Six. Six."

Ma grinned. "Scary," she said mockingly.

Babyface turned off the drill. The men released Cal and joined Ma. Ma entered the combination into the briefcase's lock. Cal squeezed his eyes shut. Ma opened the briefcase, revealing—

Green, white, and red tubes. The DVD kid's Mexican fireworks.

The wicks had been shortened to the nub and as the case opened, a small copper rod sparked against a piece of flint, lighting the wicks.

A massive blast of blinding vibrant colors. Deafening screams and booms. Burning heat.

Ma and her men were blown to the ground. Blind and deaf.

Chaos. The detainees fled from the cage. The rest of Ma's stable boys didn't know what the hell was going on.

Cal calmly marched through the smoke and fireworks. He carefully selected a Mossberg pump shotgun off of a pallet, calmly loaded it as—

A stable boy charged toward him—

Boom! — Cal fired, blowing the stable boy out of his shoes. Cal finished loading the shotgun. Cocked it.

He grabbed a duffel bag and went shopping as chaos reigned all around. A Skorpion SMG, some boxes of ammo—

Boom!— Cal blew away an armed stable boy and cocked the shotgun with one hand as he continued filling the duffel.

An AKM, M4 Carbine, Glock 22, Walther PPQ. Stable boys opened fire. *Boom! Boom! Boom!* Cal cut them down, continued—

Grenades, Semtex, bulletproof vest. *Boom! Boom!* Cal dropped the Mossberg. He grabbed a red incendiary grenade, a flammable hazard icon on its face, pulled the pin and tossed it behind him as he marched toward Ma. She was lying disoriented on the ground. Her face red and raw, eyebrows burnt off. Cal searched her and took back his photo of Eva. All around, the facility burned. Ammo crates exploded.

Cal raised the photo of Eva. "Where did you send her? Tell me, or I leave you here to burn."

Ma released an ugly laugh. Cal got a sinking feeling in his stomach, fearing what her answer would be. "Where did you send her?" Cal asked again.

"Los Angeles," Ma said. "Your girl belongs to the L.A. Syndicate now."

Cal took this in. It was the last thing he wanted to hear. L.A. was where Cal was running from. L.A. was where he would be easiest to find.

Outside, stable boys and detainees fled into the desert as the building was consumed by flames and explosions. Cal marched, carrying Ma over his shoulder. He dropped her in the dirt. Took her car keys. Walked around the corner of the building where various cars and truck were parked. Cal pressed Ma's key fob. A Ford F150 honked.

Cal got in the pickup. The vehicle roared to life. Cal sped off into the dark desert, leaving the burning building in his wake.

8

────────

Cal was able to pick up the path. Faint tire treads in the sand through tumbleweed and cacti and desert bramble. He followed it in the F150. After about six hours, the Rio Grande river appeared on the horizon, glimmering like a mirage beneath the morning sun.

As he cruised toward the Rio Grande, he spotted a beat-up bus parked on the banks of the river, off-loading immigrants. Cal put the truck in park, judging it safer to allow the smuggler to cross with his human cargo before proceeding. He watched from a distance through his scope.

The immigrants formed a line and followed the smuggler into the river. It got deeper and deeper. An old woman struggled to keep her position in the line. She began to fall behind. Suddenly, the current swept her away. Cal watched her flail and scream for help. The others stopped, but the smuggler yelled and gestured for them to continue. The immigrants reluctantly kept moving, abandoning the old woman to her fate.

Cal put the F150 in gear, angled downriver, and floored it. The truck tore across the desert, kicking up a sandstorm. The truck arrived on the river bank. Cal jumped out and leaped into the river.

He spotted the old woman. She was drowning. The current was strong here. Cal swam as hard and fast as he could, reached her, lifted her above the water. She sucked in air.

Cal struggled with the old woman to the opposite riverbank. Her frail body collapsed in the mud. He tended to the old woman as she wheezed, catching her breath. He knew they could not stay long. This river was patrolled by US border agents. He helped the old woman to her feet and guided her to the nearby woods.

They hiked under the cover of cottonwoods, Texas ashes, and mesquite trees. The old woman did not say a word. She reserved all of her strength for the journey. Cal guided her along. Up ahead, there was a clearing. Cal gestured for the old woman to duck behind a nearby tree.

In the clearing, Cal spied a white-and-green Border Patrol SUV parked in the tall grass like a predator lying in wait. This place was remote. There were no roads. The vehicle struck Cal as strangely out of place. Cal cautiously crept toward the dormant vehicle. He could not see anyone inside, but as he approached, he noticed that the SUV was shifting on its axles.

He peaked in the window. A man was prone, his pants around his ankles. A woman was beneath him, her eyes wide with terror. Her eyes landed on Cal.

Cal quickly ducked.

"What is it?" the man said, looking back over his shoulder. "You see something?" He yanked up his pants, opened the door, and climbed out of the SUV, still buckling his belt. He wore a forest green Border Patrol uniform. Shaved head. Pants tucked into his boots. A Wannabe Marine.

Cal hid in the tall grass, just short of the cover of the woods. The border agent scanned the clearing for any sign of life. He spit and turned back to the woman in the back seat.

"Alright. Come on out." The eighteen-year-old Mexican girl climbed out of the back seat. She sadly pulled up her jeans with cuffed hands.

"Welcome to America, darlin'," the border agent said as he removed her cuffs. "Now, get."

She fled as fast as she could. The agent scanned the woods one last time, making sure he was not seen. That's when he spotted the old woman in the woods, glaring at him from behind the tree. Outrage in her eyes.

The agent pulled his sidearm. "Come on out now, ma'am. Hands where I can see 'em. I ain't gonna hurt ya'."

But he was. And Cal knew it. Cal sprung from the tall grass and sprinted the remaining five feet to the old woman and tackled her as the agent launched a barrage of bullets their way.

Cal helped the old woman to her feet, and the two of them scurried through the brush and bramble. The border agent followed their path. He spotted them and opened fire, narrowly missing the old woman as she disappeared behind a boulder. The agent circled around, following her, and Cal struck him in the throat. The agent dropped his gun and gasped for breath as Cal slammed the agent's head against the boulder, knocking him out.

Cal had hoped to avoid surface streets until he was further from the border, but the desert and woods were not safe — not for him, but especially not for the defenseless old woman. He walked with her down a blistering desert road. They were tired. The old woman's shoes were worn through the sole. They were completely exposed, but at least here, there were cars whizzing by. Witnesses.

A passing Border Patrol SUV spotted them, hit its lights and pulled over. A Latino Border Patrol agent stepped out, smiling politely.

"Hola," he said kindly. "May I see your papers, please?"

9

The immigrant detention center was made up of austere buildings nestled behind chain-link, barbed-wire fences. The Border Patrol SUV passed through the guard station and parked outside the processing building. The Latino border agent got out, opened the back door, and ushered Cal and the old woman out of the back seat.

The processing building smelled like sweat and desperation. The air was so thick it seemed chewable. Hundreds of immigrants were crowded in chain-link pens.

The agent in charge of this facility was in his forties, 5'7", and fit. A trim and muscled body beneath a starched army green border agent uniform. Shirt tucked into trousers tucked into combat boots. He was clean-cut, with a thick mane of hair and a face shaved smooth. Joel Osteen meets G.I. Joe.

G.I. Joel noticed the white man being brought in by the Latino border agent. He watched as his men separated the white man from the old Mexican woman and herded him into one of the male holding pens. Once inside, Cal moved from detainee to detainee with the photograph of Eva, asking if they had seen her. They shook their heads or shrugged him off. G.I Joel slammed his baton against the chain-link and hollered at a detainee, "Fingers off the cage!" He called out to Cal, "Hey, you. Move to the gate."

Cal met G.I. Joel at the gate. "Feel like I'm playin' a game of 'which of these things is not like the other,'" G.I. Joel said. "The hell you end up in there?"

"I lost my passport," Cal said.

"You got a social?"

Cal nodded. Joel unlocked the gate and let him out. "This way." Cal followed Joel to his desk. Joel slid into a chair and logged into his workstation. "Social security number?"

"043-68-0286." It was a fake social, one of many that Pat Roti had set up for him. Cal hoped it was still active, even though using it would alert Roti to his whereabouts.

G.I. Joel typed the number into the computer. Cal's photograph and information loaded onto the screen. "There you are," Joel says. "Now, let's see about getting you out of here."

Moments later, Cal was walking toward the door. A free man. But his problems were only beginning. Using the fake social had undoubtedly pinged on Roti's radar. Now every killer in the area looking to collect whatever fat reward Roti had placed on his head would be on their way. He had to get the hell out of dodge. And fast.

That was when the Wannabe Marine walked in. The right side of his face was gashed from where Cal smashed him against the boulder.

Too late to change course now. Not without looking suspicious. Cal lowered his eyes and continued toward the door. It was just a few feet away. The Wannabe Marine glanced at him as he passed. Did a double take. Cal was at the exit when the Wannabe Marine stopped and turned back. "Hey, you. Hold it." The guard at the door stopped Cal. "Turn around."

With no other choice, Cal complied. Wannabe Marine saw Cal's face and pulled his sidearm. "Don't you fucking move!"

Other agents took notice and converged on Cal. "What the hell's going on here?" G.I. Joel asked.

"This man assaulted me!" Wannabe Marine said.

G.I. Joel considered Cal. "You sure it was him?"

"He was with an old Mexican woman," Wannabe Marine said.

G.I. Joel shrugged. "Put him in solitary."

Two Border Patrol agents grabbed Cal by either arm, walked him to the solitary confinement wing, placed him in a six-by-eight-foot, windowless cell and slammed the door. Cal had a dirty metal toilet and a concrete slab for a bed.

And time.

Every second that passed, his enemies got closer and Eva got further away.

Seconds became hours. Cal had no way of knowing exactly how much time had passed, or whether it was day or night. He sat on the slab as calm and focused as a Buddhist monk. Mindful meditation. He knew that solitary breaks a man's mind. He had to keep his strength. Before him was the photograph of Eva. His focus. His mission.

His cell door clanged open and G.I. Joel strutted in with a shit-eating grin on his face. He stood in the doorway, tapping his baton in his palm.

"Now why would a man need to enter his own country illegally?" Joel asked. Cal remained seated. "Just got a call. Turns out Homeland Security's real interested in you. Sending a couple agents to pick you up first thing in the a.m. That's, oh, about, four hours from now."

It was Pat Roti. His CIA connections could easily get him phony Homeland Security credentials. In the morning, there would be federal agents to pick him up, only they wouldn't be federal agents. They'd be Roti's guys. They'd be what he used to be — highly skilled assassins, on Roti's payroll. They'd load him in the back of a black SUV and it would be the last ride he ever took.

G.I. Joel sized Cal up with curiosity. "So, what are you? Some kinda terrorist?" Cal was silent. G.I. Joel shrugged, took out a cell phone, dialed a number. "Fella at Homeland wants to talk to you." He handed the phone to Cal.

The line trilled, then a voice answered. "Hello, Cal." It was Pat Roti. Cal remembered his former boss. The old guinea, always put together in a crisp Italian suit. His eyes were dazzling blue. Hurricanes seen from space. He was always meticulous, always in control, never a shadow of weakness. The Gangster Philosopher. Too smart for organized crime. Too dangerous to be part of legitimate government. He lived in the shadow state.

"Pat," Cal said.

"Figured you'd have gone to Mexico. Your old stomping grounds. You could disappear down there. You shouldn't have come back," Roti said.

Cal was silent.

"I'm very disappointed in you, Cal," Pat Roti continued. "I don't know what happened to you. How you lost your balls. Your principles. Your honor. It's a shame, it really is. But you knew the rules."

"I did," Cal said.

"This was your choice."

"It was."

"Once you're in, you're in. Now there's only one way out."

"There's two," Cal said.

Pat Roti paused, not expecting this. "Yeah? How's that?"

"I could kill you before you kill me."

Pat Roti chuckled. "I told them to make it painless. Goodbye, Cal."

The call was ended. Cal handed the phone back to G.I. Joel.

"You ain't killing no one, son. You're staying right here for the next four hours, then you're someone else's problem." G.I. Joel said, then stepped out of the cell and sealed the door behind him.

Cal did not know what he was going to do. He was locked in a concrete box with no plan and only the clothes on his back. He cleared the useless emotions from his mind — anxiety, apprehension, panic, fear — and focused. He counted the seconds in his head until Roti's hitmen would arrive. At three hours, forty-one minutes and twenty-two seconds, his cell door quietly creaked open, and the Wannabe Marine slipped inside.

Cal pocketed the photograph of Eva protectively and glared at Wannabe Marine, ice cold.

Rapist motherfucker.

"I heard the bigwigs are taking you outta here," Wannabe Marine said, looking worried. "Look. I'm sorry you saw what you saw. See, it don't matter what these wetbacks say. They're illegal. No one'll listen to them. They don't have a voice. But a fella like you, well—" Wannabe Marine pulled a shiv. "I ain't gonna end up on CNN."

Cal had never been a very spiritual person. He had always believed in psychology. But every once in a while, he wondered how different meditation really was from prayer. If psychology was just another pathway to this notion of something called God.

He had been going over it in his mind, over and over again, wondering how he was going to get out of his cell before his executioners arrived. Then in walked this man. Cal didn't know whether it was divine intervention or natural selection, but either way, this man's stupidity just made Cal's morning a whole lot easier.

Cal calmly rose and faced Wannabe Marine. He reached his arms over his shoulders and took off his shirt.

Wannabe Marine frowned. "The hell you doin'?"

"Take off your uniform," Cal said.

"What?"

"Take off your uniform."

"Why?"

"Because I don't want to get blood on it."

Wannabe Marine tensed. He was taken completely off-guard by Cal's cool confidence. Suddenly, Wannabe slashed a shiv. Cal caught his wrist, snapped it, and grabbed the shiv. Wannabe Marine yelped and cradled his wrist. Stunned, his eyes widened as Cal approached, grabbed his head and shoulders, and snapped his neck.

Cal exited the cell, wearing Wannabe Marine's Border Patrol uniform. He sauntered to the security gate, took out Wannabe Marine's keyring, and fiddled with the keys. There were dozens on the ring. Cal tried one after another with no luck.

A portly, bald border agent approached on the other side of the gate. He squinted at Cal. "I haven't seen you before." Cal looked at Portly. He noticed the yellow-and-red button marked "DURESS" on the wall to Portly's right.

Portly smiled. "Took me forever to learn the keys here, too." Portly opened the gate for Cal. "Don't worry. You'll get the hang of it." Portly let Cal through the gate, then continued on his way.

Cal waited a few moments for Portly to disappear down the hall before he pressed the Duress button. Alarms screeched and LED lights strobed throughout the building.

In the main holding area, immigrants were herded out of their pens by Border Patrol agents. Cal calmly navigated the chaotic crowd, exited to the parking lot outside, and surveyed the rows of parked vehicles. He found the vehicle FOB on Wannabe Marine's key ring, pressed the "Unlock" button, and a Harley Davidson Sportster chirped. Cal saddled up. Turned the ignition. Drove past the crowd of immigrants pouring from the flashing, screeching detention center. He waved to the guard in the guard station, pulled out, and cruised away.

When he was about a half-mile away from the detention center, he noticed a black Chevy Suburban following him.

10

———————

There was no way to be inconspicuous. Not out here. Not with nothing but flat American desert surrounding them. There were two of these so-called "Special Agents" in the Suburban. Pat Roti's assassins. They were both built like combat soldiers. Lean and muscled. One had spiky hair. The other, a military crewcut.

Cal was unarmed. Wannabe Marine only had a quarter of a tank in the Harley. Outrunning them was out of the question. Cal cruised at sixty. Spiky Hair and Crewcut maintained a safe distance.

There were still occasional pedestrian vehicles whizzing past. They'd want to get him alone. He could keep to main roads and highways. That would keep him alive, but it would also reveal where he was going.

No. He'd have to lose them in Texas. Get them alone. Spin the chamber. *If I perish, I perish.*

He led them down a desolate desert road. The heat made it hard to think about anything else. The sun was blinding.

Behind him, he heard the Suburban's engine roar. The Suburban charged. The gunfire started. Screeching over his back.

Cal accelerated. Glanced in his mirror. The black beast

loomed. He wouldn't outrun it. He jerked the handlebars left, sped off the road and into desert chaparral. His tires bounced over stones and shrubs, slipping in the sand. He was launched over the handlebars. His body smashed into the dirt.

He glanced over his shoulder. The road was fifty feet behind him. The black Suburban had stopped there in the wavy heat like a stalking predator. Spiky Hair and Crewcut disembarked. Cal watched them circle around to the back of the vehicle and arm themselves with rifles. He scrambled into the forest.

He ran for hours. When he reached the Rio Grande river, he thought that maybe he had lost them. Then he heard movement in the brush. A snapped twig. A branch brushing. His hunters were still out there.

He jumped into the river and dove underwater. He heard muffled popping sounds. Bullets hissed by him. His lungs burned, but he could not come up for air. Not yet. He swam harder. His vision was cloudy. He pulled himself up onto the opposite bank and ducked behind a tree as Spiky Hair and Crewcut opened fire, peppering the tree with lead.

The assassins slung their rifles over their shoulders and swam across the river. They climbed up the opposite bank.

They looked behind the tree. Cal was gone. Spiky Hair nodded at Cal's tracks. They followed them away from the river into a desert clearing.

The F150 was right where Cal had left it when he abandoned it to save the old woman in the river. He sprinted like hell toward it. Spiky Hair and Crewcut opened fire. Cal zigzagged across the desert, the bullets barely missing him. He took cover inside the F150. The assassins took aim at the tires and engine block and unloaded their magazines.

Cal tried the F150's engine. It choked and died.

The assassins dropped their empty rifles and pulled their pistol. They silently crept toward the bullet-riddled pickup. Spiky Hair gestured for Crewcut to hold back. He approached the truck but couldn't see Cal through the spider-webbed windows, so he reached for the driver's side door handle and pulled it open.

Cal was lying across the seat, a Mossberg pump leveled. Cal pulled the trigger. The volley tore through Spiky Hair's chest and launched him off his feet.

Before Crewcut could react, Cal rose, propped an M4 carbine on the dash and held the trigger. A loud and steady stream of 5.56×45mm rounds shattered the windshield and cut Crewcut down where he stood.

Cal stepped out of the F150 with the big bag of guns that he got at Ma's black market fulfillment center. He slung the duffel back over his shoulder and began the long trek back to the United States.

11

A ndrés always looked angry. His brow was naturally furrowed. His face rested in a scowl. The plug earrings, eyebrow and cheek studs, bull-ring, and lip piercing didn't help to soften his edges. Of his many tattoos were the numbers "666" across his knuckles, a black scorpion on his neck, and a swastika on his chest. He wasn't really sure why he had gotten the swastika. His brown skin didn't exactly scream Aryan, and he wasn't a member of any white nationalist or neo-Nazi groups. For some reason, he just identified with it. It symbolized hate, and he had plenty of that.

Andrés was born in Texas of Mexican descent. A "Latino American" or "White Hispanic." Not white enough to be white, not Spanish enough to be Mexican.

The Mexican Mexicans would laugh at him because he couldn't speak Spanish. They would call him a pocho, a fake Mexican. He'd also been called a wetback and a beaner by non-Hispanics on more than one occasion. He didn't know which identity he was supposed to hate more.

He'd see his mother around town sometimes. She moved out when he was five, and she had kids with three other men in town before he was even a teenager. He wasn't even sure if she recognized him anymore.

His father was a truck driver and when he was a kid, he'd travel across the country with him on his routes. Sleeping in a small bed in the back of the cabin. Seeing the country. He loved it. His father was a good dad, at least for a while. But then he started using crank to help him stay awake for the long deliveries. Andrés watched helplessly as the drug decayed his father's mind. Andrés loved his father, but by the time the meth was done with him, he was pimping Andrés out at truck stops for dime bags. Andrés was twelve.

That's when he learned that people were just meat.

His father ended up going away on drug charges and Andrés was put into state care. The first time Andrés tried pookie was from his father's stash. After his father went away, Andrés maintained the habit. He swore he'd never let it destroy him the way it had his father. Hell, that Adderall shit that all the college kids took was just another form of meth, and they seemed to be doing alright.

But by sophomore year, Andrés had dropped out of high school and run away from his foster home. He did odd jobs — unskilled labor — with mostly undocumented workers from Mexico. That's where he first heard the term "pocho."

When he slept, which was becoming less and less frequent, he stayed at friends' places, and then, after his drug use alienated him, on park benches, in homeless shelters, or in unlocked cars. He panhandled on the streets and he became a regular at the local pawn shop. He stole and sold anything that wasn't nailed down. Anything for another dime bag. He was sixteen years old and his life was petty crime for cheap drugs.

That's when he met Ma.

She used the local drug dealers to spot talent. Addicts were good candidates because they were desperate. They would do whatever she said, no matter the risk. No questions asked. And they always needed cash. The job criteria was simple — all a person needed was a valid US driver's license and a bank account.

Andrés did well as a smuggler. His job was to pick the migrants up when they crossed the border, avoid local law enforcement, and bring them to a stash house. He didn't handle Las Sementales, the stallions. The young people like Eva. They were big money investments. Border guards were bought and paid for. Andrés got los pollos and los chivos, the chickens and the goats.

The way he saw it, the US building a wall on the border was fine with him. Wipe the smile off these shit-talking Mexicans' faces. Pocho that, motherfuckers. Besides, a wall would be a goldmine for the coyote business.

By the time he was twenty-one, Andrés was in charge of his own stash house. His job was to hold the migrants in El Paso until their next payment was wired from their relatives or friends in Mexico. He fed and watched them until they were picked up and brought on the next leg of their journey.

Andrés was making decent money. He didn't feel the need to be high all the time anymore. He curbed his meth intake to the level of recreational use. He credited Ma with all of it. Before he was introduced her, he had nothing. She gave him a job. She put money in his pocket. But most of all, she gave him what he never had and always longed for.

She gave him someplace to belong.

So, when Andrés heard about the attack on the fulfillment center, he got in his dark blue Dodge Ram and sped across the border.

The building was reduced to smoking rubble and ash. A black pockmark on the desert floor. Andrés found Ma lying in the dirt, burns on most of her body. She tried to speak, but he softly shushed her.

He gently lifted her into the bed of the pickup and drove her to the University Medical Center in El Paso. She was severely dehydrated and was suffering from both sepsis and hypothermia.

She told him about the man called Cal. She told him about Eva and how she was sent to the L.A. Syndicate. How Cal was determined to get her back. She told him about the five-million-dollar bounty on Cal's head. Andrés didn't care about the money. This man had burnt her. Left her to bake in the desert. No. This wasn't about money.

Ma died after two days in the hospital. Andrés was by her side.

Andrés had spent the last six years working with the Juarez Cartel and local street gangs. He knew the life, and, like any good Texan, he knew his way around a gun. With Ma gone, he didn't want to work for anyone else. He had put away a decent amount of cash working as a coyote over the years. He'd been a rancher. Now he decided he wanted to try his hand at hunting. So, he packed up his guns and his meth and he headed west.

Cal had been to Slab City before. He passed through on his way to kill an overweight pimp named Kilo who was hiding out in a camper in the middle of the desert.

He was on the last leg of his long journey from Texas to Los Angeles, and he figured it was the perfect place to stop and rest for the night. Slab City was two hundred miles outside of Los Angeles. An off-the-grid squatter city on a rundown, decommissioned military base. Drug addicts, artists, fugitives, and people just down on their luck. There was no law here. It was where the lost went to not be found.

The desert sun had set and it was getting cold. Cal walked the Harley through the complex of tents and campers and rusted shacks. Somewhere, a folk singer strummed his guitar and a tweaker mumbled to himself in the shadows. Up ahead, Cal spied a campfire.

A dreadlocked woman with nose rings, hairy armpits, and B.O. sat on a rusted lawn chair beneath a blanket. An emaciated man with face sores sat across from her on a stained and torn-up sofa. She took a hit from her glass pipe, then passed it to her accomplice.

"You know what you look like?" Hairy Armpits called out to Cal. "Like you've been through the desert on a horse with no name."

Cal approached, parked his bike. "Would you share your fire?"

"You don't gotta ask, man," Face Sores said, exhaling marijuana smoke. "Post up." He offered Cal the pipe. Cal politely declined.

"Here," said Hairy Pits, handing him a blanket. "It gets cold out here this time of year." Cal nodded his thanks, wrapped himself in the blanket, and lay next to his bike, using his duffel bag of weapons as a pillow.

Face Sores and Hairy Pits continued their conversation. "What I was saying, think about it," Face Sores said to Hairy Pits. "You go to Vegas — you look at the strip — it's like, you can go anywhere in the world — Caeser's Palace, Paris — they got castles, circuses, Treasure Island— all different places and time periods, but what's missing?"

"I don't know," Hairy Pits said. "What?"

"Outer space," he said. "Imagine it. A casino shaped like a space ship at Cape Canaveral, pointin' up at the stars. And where's it going? Into the sun. Celebrate tonight. Ain't gotta worry about tomorrow."

Cal had drifted off to sleep.

He dreamt of the night he met Maria seventeen years ago. He was twenty-six, just quit Special Forces. A hired gun for the Cartel. His boss was a faithful Santa Muertero. A devotee of the Most Holy Death.

And Death was all Cal knew. It made a lonely companion.

On the night he met Maria, he remembered the overwhelming need he felt to be with someone. To feel life. If only for a few hours. As the boss's top hitman, Cal had a lifetime pass to *Celestial*. He went there only once. And that was where he met Maria. In her bed. Without words. She meant nothing to him. At the time, at least.

He learned she was pregnant, but he left Mexico to work for Pat Roti. To travel the world, killing people. He left and he forgot about her. A decade and a half later, he didn't want to kill anymore. He went looking for his soul. He went looking for her.

When he returned as The Padre, Maria recognized him right away. She was not mad at him for leaving. She knew that she was dying. She knew that the Holy Death had sent him to look after Eva after she was gone.

She did not tell Eva who he was.

Cal awoke to shouting. "Get out of here with that phallocentric bullshit!" Hairy Pits yelled. "A rocket into the sun? Dicks and destruction. This is why the world is in such a state. We need to be like the bonobos."

"The what?"

"Bonobos. Like chimpanzees."

"Monkeys kill each other all the time."

"Apes, not monkeys. And not the bonobos. Their society is ruled by females. They rule through sex. They fuck men, women, children. They have huge orgies. Free love, not destruction. That is how me must live."

"I ain't fucking no kids," Face Sores said, hitting the pipe.

Addiction is just a symptom of a deeper problem, Cal thought. *The question is not why the addiction. It is why the pain?*

Identify the wound and heal it, otherwise you will only fill it with destructive things. Addictions.

Cal understood that Eva was his wound. Without her, he was

capable of anything. An addict. If he was ever going to save his soul, he had to first save her.

He also knew that his rehab was unique. Because he must indulge in his addiction in order to beat it. He understood that his journey to save Eva had placed him on an inevitable collision course with more violence. Could he crest just close enough to the edge without falling over? Could he touch the point of no return without crossing it?

He had no choice. He had to keep going, even if it was a death sentence. Because behind him, there was nothing to live for.

PART II

THE DAUGHTER

12

Eva had been locked in the luxury condo for nearly a week. She was a thousand feet above the streets. Her floor to ceiling windows overlooked Downtown L.A. She could see the people down there, in a city with a daytime population of over 200,000, yet she was completely alone. Her only contact with the outside world were the maids, none of which would speak to her, and a mute, stone-faced Mexican man in a designer suit with a long, braided ponytail named Delfino. He brought her meals. Fresh wild salmon. Filet mignon. Gourmet chicken. Everything was chef-prepared and paired with expensive wine. She ate like a queen.

There was always a bottle of veuve clicquot brut kept on ice. Delfino also furnished her with designer beauty products. Kiehl's, La Mer, Elizabeth Arden, Tom Ford. And she was never without fresh towels still warm from the dryer.

The condo had a full cable package but no internet access. A small gym and hot tub. It took her a while to figure out the bidet.

Eva spent her days drinking champagne to calm her nerves and watching the sun cross the sky from her 360-degree, panoramic-view windows. On a clear day, she could see the

Hollywood sign in the north, LAX in the south, and sometimes even as far west as the Pacific Ocean.

One day, Delfino entered and said, "Come with me." It was the first time he had spoken to her all week. He escorted her into the elevator, which opened directly into the condo and was accessible only by key card. They rode the elevator down to a garage. She never saw another living soul. He walked her to a black Mercedes Benz E-Class and opened the back door for her. Eva looked around. Nowhere to go. Pointless to run. She got in.

Delfino closed the door. The back windows were tinted, the door handles had been removed, and the doors were locked. There was a privacy wall separating the back seat from the front. She heard Delfino climb into the driver's seat.

It took them a little over an hour to get to San Pedro. Delfino pulled around behind an industrial building and idled outside of a large, overhead commercial garage door. After a moment, the door raised and Delfino pulled into the warehouse. He parked, got out, and opened the back door of the Mercedes for Eva.

They were in an empty windowless garage. A woman dressed like a nurse in green scrubs, a face shield, and a medical mask was waiting.

"Follow me, please," she said. Eva hesitated. Delfino nudged her. She followed the nurse down a dim, featureless hallway into what appeared to be an examination room. There was a scale, eye chart, sink and soap dispenser, examination table, stethoscope, otoscope, and various other medical tools. Eva looked at the nurse, frightened. The nurse handed her a medical gown. "Put this on, please."

"What's going on?"

"The doctor will be in to see you shortly."

"Wait—"

The nurse left, closing the door behind her. Eva tried the knob, even though she knew the door would be locked. She felt it rushing up from her stomach — the panic. She concentrated on her breathing and pushed the fear back down where it came from.

Now is not the time to lose your shit. Think, she told herself. *It is pointless to resist. At least, right now. Bide your time. Appear cooperative, get their guard down. Wait for your opening.*

She stripped and put on the medical gown. She waited in the examination room for about thirty minutes. Finally, the door opened and a doctor entered. He was clinical and cold in his white lab coat. The nurse trailed behind him with a clipboard. The doctor was short and round, bald with a white crown of hair, and yellow teeth. He did not introduce himself. Did not even acknowledge Eva. He merely studied her through bifocals like a test subject. His breath was sulfurous. He got to work.

The doctor photographed her. Shined a pen light in her eyes and mouth. Checked her blood pressure with a stethoscope. He drew blood with a syringe, weighed her, performed an extremities exam. All the while, the nurse took notes. Finally, the doctor peeled off his medical gloves and tossed them in the trash.

"Grade A," he said.

The nurse recorded the rating and followed the doctor out of the room. Eva sat there, scared and alone.

Delfino drove Eva back to the condo and her routine resumed. Nice meals. Luxury amenities. No contact with the outside world. One morning, while zoning out over a glass of champagne, she considered trying to break one of the windows. To escape. She looked down the side of the building. Slick and ledgeless glass.

Who am I kidding? she thought. *There's no escaping that way. But there is another option. I could always jump.* She shook the notion out of her head like water in her ear. *Keep it together.*

Several more days passed, then Delfino spoke to her again. "Go into the bathroom and strip down to your bra and panties," he said.

Eva felt dread rising in her stomach like vomit. Suddenly, she regretted not breaking the window and leaping.

Delfino read the reluctance in her eyes. He unfolded a knife, shiny and evil in his hand. "Do it, or I'll do it for you," he said.

Eva walked to the bathroom like she was at her own wake. She locked the door behind her and cried. Then she breathed.

Crying won't save you, she told herself. *Think.*

She pulled herself together. Took inventory of the bathroom. She lifted the porcelain lid off of the toilet. It was heavy and hard. She took a few practice swings. Shook her head. Too clumsy. She'd never get close enough to use it. She rifled through her beauty supplies. Perfume. It was flammable. She could douse him. Light it. But how to light it? No. Something small. Sharp. Tweezers? Nail clippers? *The fuck am I gonna do with that? Think!* Nose and ear scissors. *Yes.* They were small, they were sharp. If Delfino got close enough to her, she could stick them into his windpipe or his eye socket, grab his key card and escape. But she'd have to lure him close, very close…

Eva undressed down to her bra and panties. Held the small scissors in her hand. Where to hide them? She tried her brassiere, her panties. Too conspicuous. There was a bathrobe hanging on the hook by the door. She put it on, slid the scissors into the pocket. Kept the front open. Looked at herself in the mirror. Showing just enough skin, just enough to lure. She was a predator mimicking prey.

She looked at her face in the mirror, readied her mind, steeled herself, and spoke her truth.

I'm gonna kill this motherfucker.

When Eva stepped out of the bathroom, she was all nerves. Delfino stood in the corner of the room and she gave him her best "fuck me" eyes. Then, as she fully entered the room, she saw the two people sitting on the sofa.

One was a woman in her early-thirties. 5'4", tatted-up, and toned. HBIC vibe. She wore a tight red dress with pumps. She was sitting on the sofa with her legs crossed. She perused a file on her lap, and didn't even look up when Eva entered the room. She was all business. The other person was a large, white man with a warm smile. He was dressed in a conservative black suit. He was built like an NFL linebacker. He had a splash of flamboyance and the cuddly air of a puppy. He nodded kindly at Eva.

Eva stood in her bathrobe in front of them. Unsure. Delfino lurked in the corner of the room, not moving. Finally, the woman finished looking over the file on her lap, removed her Tom Ford reading glasses, and looked up at Eva.

"Eva. Good afternoon. My name is Giselle." She gestured at the three-hundred-pound puppy dog standing next to her. "This is Teddy. Teddy will be your chauffeur and bodyguard."

"Enchanté," Teddy said.

Giselle put her reading glasses back on and scanned the file. "Your blood work looks good." She nodded at Teddy. "Proceed."

Teddy approached Eva and gently removed her bathrobe. Eva was frozen. She stood there in her bra and panties.

From the sofa, Giselle examined her body. "You'll need to tone up. We'll provide a personal trainer."

Eva stood there. Vulnerable. Humiliated.

"The perks of this job are good," Giselle said. "We only work with A-list clientele. You receive a ten percent commission. Free health care."

"Please. Let me go," Eva said.

Giselle paused, removed her reading glasses, stood, and casually circled Eva. "Do you like this condo?"

Eva stifled tears.

Giselle spoke firmly. "I hope you do. Because it's yours. Well, not yours. It's where you will be living. It could be a lot worse. Remember that." She returned to the sofa, crossed her legs. "Now all that's left is the brand." Giselle snapped her fingers.

Delfino approached. He wore nitrile gloves. He pressed a stencil against the side of Eva's neck. Eva pulled away from him.

Giselle softened. Moved to Eva. Gently took her hands. "Honey. Where are you from? It's okay. You can talk to me."

"Mexico City," Eva said.

"I know how scary it is to come to a new town all by yourself. I moved here when I was only sixteen from a cow farm in Nebraska."

Giselle nodded to Delfino. Delfino raised a tattoo gun and began his work, needling a tattoo onto the side of Eva's neck. Eva whimpered. Giselle held her gaze, distracting her, comforting her. "We raised dairy cattle, as opposed to beef cattle," Giselle said softly "Dairy cows live long happy lives because they give milk."

The tattoo began to take form. It was a QR code. Giselle's voice hardened. Her warm embrace of Eva's hands became a vice grip. "This brand means you are one of mine. It means no one can fuck with you. You can do very well. As long as you remember one thing — you are no longer a person. From this moment onward, you are livestock. You can be milked or you can be slaughtered. The choice is yours."

Giselle released Eva's hands and moved to the door. "Go to work each day, take it up the ass for a paycheck. Do it long enough and maybe you'll retire in semi-comfort. You wanted the American dream? Honey. This is it."

Giselle swiped her key card, boarded the elevator, and disappeared behind its doors.

Teddy shook his head and chuckled warmly. "She's actually from the Valley," he said.

Eva held back bitter tears as the tattoo needle tore into her skin.

13

It ain't who you are, it's who you know.

And if you were a criminal in Los Angeles, Sly was the muthafuckin' man.

If you could find him.

Sly liked to do his business in the tunnels. There are miles of abandoned tunnels beneath the streets of Downtown L.A. Old subway stations, equestrian tunnels, underground speakeasies from the 1920s. On any given day, you could find Sly among the crumbling brick and rusted machinery, tagging the tunnel walls with his street art.

There was no law in the tunnels. The deeper you went, the darker it got. The tweakers tweaked, the junkies shot. Occasionally, if you went deep enough, you found a body.

But Sly was clean. He didn't kill and his only drug was coffee. Sly hustled. They called him "Customs." Say Joe Schmo wanted to clip John Doe or some heist crew from New York was in town and wanted to knock over a jewelry store. They'd talk to Sly. Sly ran it by the local bosses. The Russians and Eastern Europeans, Asians, Mexicans and South Americans, and so on. Out-of-towners knew to clear their L.A. business through Sly first, so they wouldn't end up starting a war or dead.

Sly was the guy you saw to clear it with L.A.'s upper management.

Getting a work permit, they called it.

Sly didn't have a lot of power, and nobody feared him, per se. He was skinny and brainy in a comic book nerd sort of way. He wore glasses, gauge earrings, and he was covered in skater tattoos. But it wasn't about who he was, it was about who he knew. When a guy knew everyone, he was bound to have a friend or two to fear.

Sly was untouchable because he served a purpose.

He was like a living, breathing social network for bad guys. He kept the lines of communication open. He kept the order, the balance, the peace. Most importantly, he kept the black market money machine oiled and running.

No one would dare harm a hair on his head.

"You local or just visiting?" Sly asked, barely even glancing at the man with the mutton chops who had just approached him. Sly was spray-painting a dope-ass sea life mural, which made the dark and grimy, old tunnel feel like the bottom of a coral reef.

"Visiting. I need a work visa," said Muttonchops.

"Type of work?"

"I'm here to kill Vinny Amato."

"I'll forward your request," Sly said "Come back tomorrow." Muttonchops nodded and began to lumber away. Sly called after him, "Service fee still applies. Regardless."

Muttonchops grunted his disapproval and handed Sly a hundred-dollar bill.

An hour later, Sly exited from a tunnel onto the dry, paved bed of the L.A. River. The sun was just rising. He climbed up toward the streets. He was in the Arts District of Downtown L.A. He passed galleries, hipster coffee shops and bakeries, and abandoned twentieth-century industrial buildings.

Sly unlocked and pulled open a rusted gate, and walked across the vacant lot inside toward a ratty, abandoned warehouse. He unlocked another lock, heaved open a heavy steel door and entered.

Sly lived in what appeared to be an abandoned industrial warehouse. Despite its worn and shabby upkeep, Sly took the security of this place seriously. Every inch of the property was covered on a bank of security monitors. State-of-the-art computer mainframes and equipment contrasted with the grungy, industrial setting. A halfpipe and arcade games. He was a weird mix of skater and techie.

Sly filled a Moka pot with grinds and water, and placed it on a burner. He turned away and sat down in his gamer chair. He logged on to his workstation. Sly worked at his terminal. Behind him, the Moka pot gurgled as it brewed.

It was easy for him to hack the L.A. Department of Water and Power to keep the lights and water on in the place. Sly noticed that the door to his bathroom was ajar and the light had been left on. He peered curiously. Sly was a creature of habit. Like a lot of hackers, he was borderline OCD about certain things. He wouldn't have left the bathroom door open, and he absolutely never would have forgotten to turn the light off. Sly picked up a can of pepper spray and approached.

He stepped into the bathroom. There was a faint layer of fog on the mirrors, but not enough to make them opaque. This room had previously been an employee locker room. Showerheads lined the left wall. One of them dripped. There was a puddle beneath it. He felt the drain. The water was still warm.

Someone had showered recently.

Suddenly, in the other room, the Moka pot stopped gurgling. Sly turned away from the showers and marched back toward his work station. He found Cal, freshly showered, pouring two cups of coffee from the Moka pot. Sly's eyes widened with fear.

"Nice place," Cal said. "Looks like being an errand boy for killers, drug traffickers, and pimps pays alright." Cal handed one of the coffees to Sly. "Do you know who I am?"

Sly slowly nodded.

"What's the price on me up to now?"

Sly cleared his dry throat. "Was just upped to ten million."

Cal raised his eyebrows in a look of surprise. "That much?"

"They say you killed two guys down on the border. Pros."

"It seems the more I kill, the more I'm worth." Cal took a slow sip of his coffee, never taking his eyes off of Sly. "I need you to find someone." Cal showed him the photograph of Eva. "She's from Mexico City. She was taken last week."

"That's not how it works. I need to clear it—" Cal threw his hot coffee in Sly's face. Sly shrieked and frantically wiped his eyes.

Cal placed his cup down and heaved his duffel bag onto the counter. Unzipped it, revealing the war chest inside. "You're a painter, right? Like street art and shit?" Cal pulled out the Mossberg. "Let's see you paint with no hands." He kicked Sly to the floor, stepped on his wrist, and pressed the barrel into the palm of his hand.

"Wait! Please! I'll find her!" Sly said. "If they brought her to L.A., she'll be in the database. On the dark web. It'll say who owns her now."

Cal removed his foot from Sly's wrist. "Her name is Eva."

"It doesn't matter what her name is," Sly said. "They give them new names for the clients. Internally, they identify them by assigned numbers."

"So, how will you find her?"

"Is this picture current?"

Cal shrugged. "Current enough."

Sly scanned the photo with his smartphone and ran a search. A hit came back on his computer monitor — Eva looking miserable in the photograph that the doctor took during her physical.

"That's her," Cal said.

Sly read her case file. "It looks like she belongs to Giselle."

"Who?"

"She's a madame. Not someone you want to fuck with."

"Okay. Now tell me how to fuck with her."

"She's holding an event tomorrow night," Sly said. "Private ranch out in Malibu. High security. Lot of VIPs."

"The address."

Sly wrote it down for him. Cal raised his shotgun.

"I don't deserve this," Sly said. "I'm an artist."

"You help people who traffic flesh."

"I can change." He fell to his knees and blubbered. "If you let me live, I swear, I will change." It was a familiar scene. Cal had seen it many times before. He had never been moved. Even in this moment, he was not moved. But something made him pause.

He was an artist. So was Eva.

He knew it was foolish to leave a witness. A rookie mistake. The second Cal left, Sly could call Pat Roti, tell him that Cal had been there and where he was going. Cal was untrained in mercy. Untrained and unpracticed.

So, why did he hesitate to pull the trigger?

It was faith. Faith and hope. He wanted to believe that people could change. That he himself could change.

"Please," Sly begged. "I will change." He squeezed his eyes shut, anticipating the bullet.

If you can change, then so can I, Cal thought.

Sly opened his eyes and Cal was gone.

He waited about twenty minutes before he called Pat Roti.

14

He wasn't sure how it would go. He knew she blamed him for the death of her girlfriend. And she was right to. It was his fault.

Last year, they were uneasy allies on what turned out to be Cal's last professional job. Their mission was to find the killer of Senator Marco Barros's daughter. Cal discovered the man's identity — a disturbed Marine vet named Wyatt Lemieux — but he kept it from her because, as an ATF agent, she would have arrested Lemieux, and Cal had been hired by an outside party to kill him. Because he withheld this information, Lemieux was able to break into her apartment and kill the love of her life. He tried to make it right. He helped her get justice.

But he was pretty sure Miranda Lopez still hated him.

He was sitting across from her on a white sofa in her loft in Downtown L.A. The place was bare and stunningly white. Not a scuff on the walls, nor photo or painting. It was like nobody lived there. Cal knew how hard Miranda worked. It left little time for a home life.

"So, you're not dead," Miranda said blankly. This was the first time she had seen Cal since he had vanished in a forest fire in Virginia a year and a half ago. The day he left his old life, quit Pat Roti, let people assume he was dead, and went on the run.

Miranda crossed her legs. "You said you have some information for me?"

She was as tough as he remembered. But it was a different kind of tough. Not the young woman with the chip on her shoulder and the fuck-yourself attitude he met a year and a half ago. This was the type of tough the comes from a deep wound healing into a permanent scar. She had come far and lost much since their first meeting.

"A major human trafficking ring. VIP clientele. Corrupt politicians, lawmakers, people in positions of power," Cal said. "It would be a huge bust. It's happening tomorrow night at this address." Cal placed a piece of paper with the Malibu address written on it on the coffee table.

"And you're bringing this to me, why?"

"I can't go to local police. They're compromised. This ring is protected."

"Human trafficking isn't ATF," she said, sliding the piece of paper back to him across the coffee table.

Cal gave her a confused look. "They take kids." He showed her the photograph of Eva. "Fucking teenagers. Don't you care?"

Miranda scoffed. "Am I supposed to believe that you care? That you're bringing this to me out of, what, the kindness of your heart? I know you, Cal. You have no heart. I do care, but I don't trust you."

Cal lowered his eyes. "She's my daughter," he said, his voice cracking.

Miranda's eyes widened. She wasn't expecting this. "What?"

Cal shrugged. "Well, she might be," he said. "After the Barros job, I realized I couldn't do it anymore. So, I left. I tracked a woman down that I had known many, many years ago in Mexico City. Her daughter was born around the time I left. Her name is Eva. I was just starting to get to know her. She doesn't know who I really am."

"What happened?"

"Eva was in trouble. She had to get out of the country. But the coyotes trafficked her."

Miranda lowered her eyes. She looked at the photograph of Eva. She remembered Senator Barros's daughter, Arianna. Another innocent young woman victimized for the sins of others. She was already dead when Miranda got to her. Miranda couldn't save her.

But this one, she was still alive.

Miranda sighed. "I can bring it to my SAC. But I doubt he'll go for it. If it's as big as you say, maybe I can convince him to run something joint with the FBI. Is there a number where I can reach you?" Cal gave her the number to the burner phone he bought before coming here. "I'll be in touch," she said.

Cal got a room at a cheap motel where he could pay cash and didn't have to show ID. He didn't carry any credit cards. In major cities across the country, the US intelligence apparatus has scanners hidden in high-traffic areas that can pull the information from your credit cards, driver's license, and smartphone. Walk under the wrong street light or through the wrong subway turnstile, and you ping on their radar. Cal couldn't leave a speck of digital dust. Not with Pat Roti watching. He changed burner phones every twelve hours. Wore a cap and sunglasses to neutralize facial recognition and adjusted the way he walked so that he could not be identified through gait analysis biometrics.

Brave new fucking world.

Sly was sitting at his work station, rubbing aloe vera on his coffee-burnt face, when someone pounded on the warehouse door. He looked at the security monitor and saw a man with brilliant red hair. "Yeah?" he said into his intercom.

"Pat Roti sent me," the Redhead said.

Sly heaved open the heavy steel door. "It's about time," Sly said.

The Redhead calmly entered the warehouse. He was built squat and strong. His skin was pale, which made his hair look like fire, and his face seemed stuck in a perpetual, devious smirk. But there was something dangerous behind the smirk. The way he carried himself, his air, reminded Sly of a cross between The Terminator and Puck from *A Midsummer Night's Dream*.

"You seem nervous," the Redhead said.

"Don't worry about me," Sly said. "You have the money?"

"What money?"

Sly tried to appear outraged even though he was afraid. "The ten million dollars for giving you this guy."

"That money is a bounty. It is for killing him. Did you kill him?"

"No."

"So, why would you think I have money for you?"

"I don't kill people, man. I tell you where he is going to be so you can kill him. That's what you're paying for."

"This country. Everyone so entitled. Everybody wanting something for nothing," the Redhead said, shaking his head. "Where's he going to be?"

"Where's my money?"

The Redhead smiled a cold smile. He took a few steps toward Sly. Sly shrank back.

"Forget it. Here," Sly said, writing out an address. "It's a ranch out in Malibu. There's going to be a lot of security. He'll be there tomorrow night." He handed the Redhead the address. The Redhead snatched it. His smirk widened into a grin.

"That was easy," the Redhead said.

"You're welcome."

"And this address is?"

"A brothel."

"How do I know you won't warn them?"

"Why would I do that?"

The Redhead indicated Sly's blistered face. "Judging from your sunburn, Cal came here looking for information. I assume it was this address?"

Sly lowered his eyes.

"What was it? A hot cup of coffee in your face and you told him what he wanted to know?"

"That and the threat of a shotgun blast."

"So, how do I know that the second I leave here, you won't betray me? Just like you betrayed Cal?"

Sly swallowed. He didn't have an answer.

"What is your mantra?"

"My what?"

"We, human beings, we think we have a *right* to live. We do not. We must earn our time on this Earth. Prove we belong here. What do you live for?"

Sly stammered. He didn't know what to say.

"I will answer for you. You live for survival. You live to avoid dying. But do you know what I've found? The harder you try to avoid something in this life, the more inevitable it becomes." The Redhead pulled out his Glock and pointed it at Sly.

"My art," Sly shouted. "I live for my art."

"Your art?" the Redhead said. He considered Sly's answer for a moment, then he lowered his gun. "Your art... Okay. I can work with that." Sly exhaled a huge sigh of relief. "Like the pen is mightier than the sword?" the Redhead asked.

"Yes." Sly said. "Well, more like a spray can in my case, but it's the same idea."

"Let me see them."

"You want to see my spray cans?"

"Sure."

Sly lifted a milk crate full of different colored spray cans onto his desk. "How much time do you have? This is just one crate."

"Wow," the Redhead said

Sly smiled proudly.

"So, 'the spray can is mightier than the sword.' This is your mantra."

Sly thought about it. "I like it. Sounds cool."

"Cool," the Redhead said. "Let's test it out."

"Wha—"

The Redhead shot Sly twice in the chest and once in the head.

"Turns out, the sword is mightier, after all," the Redhead said to Sly's corpse. "Your mantra is bullshit."

Miranda's SAC was a man named Mark Scarpelli. He'd sidelined her last year on the Barros case, but then soaked up all the accolades when Miranda brought it in on her own. She didn't like him before the Barros case, and now she could hardly stand to be in the same room as him.

"Who's your informant?" Scarpelli said.

"Private investigator."

"You trust him?"

"I've worked with him before."

"On what?"

"Barros."

The Barros job had been a political minefield. Scarpelli understood that it was only through pure luck that he had come out looking so good. Pure luck, and Miranda Lopez. Scarpelli was a bureaucrat with political aspirations, and bureaucrats didn't like taking chances. There's no telling who might be at this high-class whorehouse, and Scarpelli was in the practice of making powerful friends, not powerful enemies.

"Where's his evidence?" Scarpelli said.

"I figured that given his track record—"

"I'm not going in there off of the word of one informant."

"They're trafficking fucking teenagers."

"Show me the evidence."

Miranda called Cal and gave him the update. Cal told her

about Sly and his computers. "Guy like him can be compelled to cooperate," Cal said.

Scarpelli, Miranda, and Cal met outside Sly's hideout. The gate was unlocked. So was the steel warehouse door. They exchanged a look. Not a good sign. They drew their sidearms and entered the warehouse, where they found Sly's body splayed-out on the concrete. "Is that our guy?" Miranda asked.

Cal nodded.

They cleared the rest of the warehouse, then they examined Sly's computer system. "I'm no expert, but this looks like a pretty serious set-up," Miranda said. "I doubt our forensics techs will be able to get anything off of it by tonight. I'm sorry, Cal, but it doesn't look like the Feds are going to be able to help you out on this one."

Cal returned to his shithole motel room. He kept the Do Not Disturb sign on his door, but in a place like this, it kind of felt like he was stating the obvious. He sat on the stained mattress. Thought about Sly. *It was Roti*, Cal thought. *I gave Sly a chance to change, and he called Roti. People don't change.* Cal reached under the bed and heaved his heavy duffel bag onto the mattress.

The Feds wouldn't help him. A bag full of guns would have to be enough.

15

———————

al was on a public computer on the third floor of the central public library in Downtown L.A. He typed the address Sly had given him into Google Earth. A three-dimensional satellite image of the property appeared on the screen. It was a large, beachside Mediterranean-style mansion. A brick barrier wall surrounded the perimeter. Cal approximated the wall at twelve-feet. There was a guard station at the entrance to the drive and flood lights around the estate. He could assume there would be armed private security patrolling the grounds.

Back at his shithole motel room, Cal emptied his duffel onto the bed. He repacked it with a TAC vest, a Ka-Bar knife in a calf holster, a Beretta M9 pistol with a silencer, a suppressed M4 Carbine, and extra magazines of ammunition.

Finally, he fit a brick of Semtex plastic explosive with a cell phone and an electric blasting cap that he had swiped from a construction site off of Grande Avenue. He taped it all together and fastened it to a small industrial magnet.

Eva was in the master bathroom of her luxury condo. She slid on a corset, pulled on tights, and applied lipstick to her lips. She stepped into a pair of heels and slid the pair of hair and nose scissors into her waistline

Eva, dolled-up in her panties and a corset, entered the living area of the condo. Teddy was waiting. He smiled, pleasantly. "You look lovely." He held open a robe for her. She moved to slip into it, then quickly pulled the scissors from her waistband, and lunged forward.

Teddy caught her wrist. Twisted it. She yelped and dropped the scissors. Teddy looked at her, disappointed. "Oh, sweetie," he said, then he brutally slugged her in the stomach, knocking the wind out of her. She gasped for breath.

"You're okay. Just breathe," Teddy said, holding her up, helping her.

After she caught her breath, Teddy brought her down to the garage and loaded her into the back of the Mercedes.

It was just after noon in Malibu. Cal pulled off the Pacific Coast Highway and parked his bike outside a small sporting goods store. He went inside and bought a wetsuit, a two-person inflatable kayak, a sea scooter, and a fishing rod from the old hippie surfer dude behind the counter.

Cal changed into the wet suit in a public restroom on the Malibu pier. He lugged his duffel bag of guns, inflatable kayak, and fishing rod down to the beach. He used the included foot pump to inflate the kayak. After it was inflated, he used a wire to attach the sea scooter to the front of the kayak and set it in the front seat. The ocean was calm today. He walked the kayak into the water and placed the duffel bag and fishing rod in the front seat. He hopped into the back seat and paddled off.

It was a few hours before the sun began to set. The sky was bruised in brilliant purples and reds and oranges. Cal had paddled several miles up the coast. He idled approximately three-hundred yards from the beachfront Mediterranean mansion. He cast a fishing line into the water and glassed the mansion with his ACOG scope.

The party had not yet begun. Serious men in dark suits — private security — patrolled the grounds, looking for any vulnerabilities. Cal lowered his scope and returned his attention to fishing.

When the sun had finally set, Cal switched his scope to night vision and glassed the beach again. It looked like the men had settled in to their assigned posts. There were only two guards stationed on the beach. They looked bored. No one was expected a naval attack.

The problem was the three-man patrol making its rounds around the estate. At approximately every four-and-a-half minutes, the patrol passed the beach. If they saw two dead guards, the party would be over and Eva would be whisked away to wherever they were holding her prisoner.

Suddenly, Cal's fishing rod jerked. He quickly set the scope down and spun his reel. The fish was a fighter. It pulled and swam. Cal watched the line, making sure it did not become too taut. Giving and taking, giving and taking. Finally, the smaller animal ran out of strength. Cal lifted a white sea bass into the kayak. He looked at the animal. Its eyes were wide with panic and fear. Its gills desperately pumped for life. Cal pitied it. He unhooked the lure from its lip, and threw it back into the ocean.

Then he pulled his suppressed M4 Carbine from the duffel and got ready to kill a lot of people.

Cal attached his scope to the M4. He paddled until he was about a hundred yards away from the shore. The darkness of the night concealed his approach, but just in case, he kept his fishing rod propped between his legs. If they saw him coming, he wanted them to write him off as some eccentric night fisherman. Once he felt he was close enough, he raised the rifle and traced his crosshairs over the first of the two guards on the beach. It wasn't the distance that was tough, it was his precarious footing.

He was sitting on an air-filled kayak on a bobbing ocean. Keeping the crosshairs steady was like trying to thread a needle on a rollercoaster.

He waited for the three-man patrol to arrive and pass. Then he started the timer in his head and pinched the trigger. He launched three 5.56×45mm rounds toward the beach. They lodged in the first guard's diaphragm and put him down. Cal quickly swung the rifle to his next target, who was just noticing his fallen partner. Cal had to put him down quick. He held down the trigger and fired seven suppressed shots. They peppered both the sand and their mark. The second guard fell.

Cal quickly paddled to shore. He jumped out of the kayak, dragged it onto the wet sand, unzipped the duffel in the front seat, and grabbed the silenced Beretta M9 pistol. He marched up to the first target. The man had three bullets in him but was still alive, struggling to breathe through bloody lips. Cal pointed the Beretta down at him and shot him in the forehead. Cal checked the second target. He was dead.

Cal quickly dragged the two guards' bodies and piled them into the kayak. He picked the sea scooter up out of the front seat, turned it on, and dropped it in the water. It slowly dragged the kayak with the two dead bodies out to sea.

He kicked sand over the bloodspots on the beach. Then, he grabbed his duffel bag and rifle and took cover in the shrubbery between the beach and the estate. He unzipped the duffel bag, slid on his TAC vest, strapped his Ka-Bar around his ankle, and holstered his Beretta. He put the Semtex bomb in one of the ammo pockets on his TAC vest.

It had been four minutes.

From his hiding place, he looked out at the ocean. He watched the kayak trudge away. Still visible. He heard the voices of the three-man patrol team as they approached the beach. He held his breath.

"Where the hell are those two?" one of them said.

The three men scanned the beach. The kayak was just barely visible. Would they see it?

"They got the shit detail. Nothing going on," another said. "They're probably inside, trying to score blowjobs."

"Did you see that blonde in the blue?"

"I go more Asian."

Cal watched the unit move on.

The party was tastefully appointed but with an edge. Burgundy leather, mahogany, and gold. Well-dressed men and women gambling at tables or enjoying bespoke cocktails or something stronger. Cocktail servers wearing nothing but body paint roamed with fruit and cheese plates, bacon-wrapped dates, olives and hummus, crudités, trays of ecstasy, eyedroppers of GHB, and punch bowls of cocaine and crystal. A small orchestra played something Ramin Djawadi-esque.

Eva stood anxiously with other attractive young male and female sex workers. On display.

A white-haired man in Hugo Boss with dilated pupils and a small Hitler mustache of cocaine approached Aksana from Belarus. "Hey, baby." He raised his phone. She pulled her hair back, revealing the QR code tattooed on her neck. The man scanned it. This is how he would be billed. He took Aksana by the hand and led her off to one of the mansion's bedrooms.

Lulu, another worker, in her thirties, glanced at Eva with concern.

"Pull it together," she whispered. "You're only as valuable as how badly they want you."

"I have to use the restroom," Eva said, her voice cracking.

Lulu looked at her, feeling pity. "This way." Lulu took her by the hand and led her away.

In the bathroom, Eva stood before the mirror. Panicked. Dizzy. Not able to breathe. She lashed out, punched her reflection. The mirror shattered. Glass everywhere.

She looked at one of the glass shards.

Cal circled around the northeast edge of the property toward the front, looking for a way in. He had to remain undiscovered until he could get close enough to learn Eva's exact location inside the mansion. He glassed the entrance to the mansion with his scope. He watched guests pull up in their BMWs, Teslas, Audis, and Mercedes. The valets took the keys and steered the guests' vehicles around the side of the mansion to a makeshift parking lot. Cars parked tightly row by row. Suddenly, Cal had an idea.

Cal was about to move out when something caught his eye. A black Mercedes with tinted windows pulled up to the entrance. When the valet approached, the driver refused to hand over the keys. A bodyguard got out of the front passenger seat, circled around, and opened the back passenger door. Pat Roti stepped out. The old guinea. The Gangster Philosopher. The man trying to kill him. The bodyguard walked with Pat Roti into the mansion, while the other bodyguard drove the Mercedes around the mansion toward the parking lot.

Cal wondered if anyone at this party knew who Pat Roti really was. These people considered themselves powerful. State politicians and lawmakers. Celebrities and CEOs and tech billionaires. But Pat Roti ran with heads of state and warlords. He knew things that not even the President of the United States knew. He was here for Cal. There was no other reason a man like Roti would slum it with people like this.

By the time Eva returned from the bathroom, all of the others had been chosen.

"Hey, hun," Teddy said. For once, he was not smiling. "Giselle's not happy." Eva's eyes met Giselle's, glaring from across the room. "You need to get to work now, okay?"

The party was kicking into full swing. Old dudes with big

bank accounts and wives and kids at home, dosed with tina or GHB, wide-eyed and frenzied, pounding partners a quarter of their age until their backs gave out. Eva frantically scanned the room. Dizzy. Looking for a way out.

"Hello, my dear." The voice was refined and respectful. So was the man. He was impeccably dressed. Even though he was nearly ninety, his Sicilian skin was without wrinkles. His eyes were piercing blue like a white wolf's. He had that air of a bygone era. Of gentlemanliness. She immediately sensed that he did not belong here.

Roti nodded to his bodyguard. The bodyguard scanned Eva's QR code. Roti gently took her hand and led her away. She glanced across the room, where Giselle was watching her like a hawk.

It was good that Roti was taking her someplace private. It would be easier to use the glass shard hidden in her corset.

Roti led her to a library. He sat in a wingback chair and gestured for her to take a seat on the leather sofa across from him. The bodyguard closed the library door and stood guard.

"Better in here, don't you think? People like that." Roti said, nodding back toward the room from which they came. "No class."

Eva swallowed hard and nodded. Roti spent his life analyzing people. Within a minute of meeting someone, he assigned them an animal that he thought best summed up their character. Eva was a doe. A baby deer in wolfskin.

Cal snuck toward the cramped valet parking lot. The vehicles would provide cover for him to approach the mansion. He army-crawled beneath the luxury cars. Beneath Pat Roti's Mercedes. The driver sat inches above him in the driver's seat.

Cal entered the mansion through the basement.

. . .

From his perch on the ridge outside the mansion's security wall, the Redhead watched Cal through his scope. He was smiling, entertained. Cal infiltrated the mansion in exactly the same way that he would have. It made the Redhead proud. He almost regretted that in an hour, Cal would be dead and he would be the one who killed him.

The Redhead called Pat Roti. "He's in the building."

"I'm afraid I don't have much time," Roti said to Eva in the library.

Roti didn't have to be here. He could have set an ambush for Cal. He knew Cal was coming, but his problem was that he didn't know *why* he was coming. To Roti, intelligence was the ultimate currency. But this young woman sitting before him, this doe in wolf's clothing, she was an unknown. He had no idea who she was and why a man as cold and unfeeling as Cal would risk everything to rescue her. It didn't add up. She was an x-factor and in Roti's world, x-factors were dangerous.

"First of all, I'm not going to touch you. It's a filthy business. Necessary. There's a reason why it is 'the world's oldest profession.' But filthy," Roti said. "All I need from you is information."

Eva relaxed some, nodded.

"Do you know this man?" Roti showed her a military photo ID of a younger-looking Cal on his smartphone.

Eva paused. "If I tell you, can you help me get out of here?"

"That's not my place," Roti said.

Eva lowered her eyes. "I know him," Eva said.

"Who is he to you?"

"To me? No one. Just some gringo that showed up in the barrio one day. Lived in the old church. He helped me."

Roti perked up in his chair. "Helped you?"

"Well, he tried. I was in trouble and he got me out of Mexico, but I ended up here."

"Why did he help you?"

"I don't know." Eva shrugged. "Some people are just good."

If she only knew how ridiculous that statement was, Pat Roti thought. Cal was a born sociopath. And he received extensive training to reinforce and cement his antisocial nature. His personality became his greatest asset, and it made him the perfect weapon. Unfeeling, even craving the thrill of the hunt, the kill. Moral judgements like "good" did not figure into Cal's programming. His mind was incapable of such concepts.

That's when Roti got the call. It was the Redhead. "He's in the building."

Pat Roti tucked his phone back into his pocket and turned to his bodyguard. "We need to go."

Roti moved briskly to the door with his bodyguard.

Cal was in the wine cellar. His plan had been to knock out one of the servers and steal their uniform. Then he saw what the servers were wearing. Body paint. Fucking California.

It looked like this would be one of those guns-blazing kind of jobs.

The shooting started before Roti made it out. He could hear Cal somewhere in the mansion, carving his path of destruction. He and his bodyguard followed a trail of dead security guards.

Roti wasn't Cal's priority. Outside, the Mercedes was waiting. Roti's bodyguard ushered him into the back, then climbed into the front passenger seat. Roti glanced back at the mansion. He thought of Cal inside taking out a small army of security guards. He considered the doe in wolfskin who had called Cal "good." As the Mercedes whisked Roti away, he was more confused than when he arrived.

. . .

Inside the mansion, all hell had broken loose. Cal took security by surprise. On jobs like these, their main task was to keep out gawkers. The most they ever had to worry about was some guest getting too fucked up and roughing up one of the girls.

It was a cakewalk. Easy money.

Enter Rambo in a wet suit.

Eva was still in the library when she heard the shooting start. Alone, she cracked the door open and peeked out. She watched the frantic security guards with their Uzis and walkie-talkies, rushing toward the front of the house. This was her chance.

Cal moved into the main room. It was tastefully constructed to be what architects would call a "conversation pit," which Cal gunned-down guards into. Giselle rose from behind the bar with a Mossberg that was almost the same size as her. Cal ducked behind a sofa. Her volley sent cushion feathers into the air.

While Cal was predisposed, Teddy charged like a linebacker and tackled him from behind. Not so gentle anymore. He screeched, maniacal and high-pitched, like a banshee, as he brutally pummeled Cal with cinder-block fists.

Eva stepped over bodies and past bullet-riddled walls. She arrived at the end of a hallway leading to the main foyer. She moved toward the front door, glanced into the main room. She saw Teddy bludgeoning a man in a wet suit and TAC vest. She looked ahead. The front door was right there. The coast was clear. She might never get this chance again.

She looked back one more time at Teddy and his victim. One more time at the man in the wetsuit's bloody face.

She pulled the shard of glass from her corset, moved away from the door, approached Teddy from behind, raised the shard of glass to stab Teddy, and—

"What do you think you're doing?" Giselle said, catching

Eva's wrist. She twisted the shard free, and kicked her to the ground.

Cal attempted to block Teddy's blows with one arm as his other inched toward his ankle holster. The Ka-Bar knife. He slid it out and plunged the blade between Teddy's ribs. Teddy shrieked and grabbed his side. Cal slid out from under him.

Giselle kicked Eva in the ribs. Over and over. A hundred and ten pounds of angry madame. She heard Teddy shriek. Saw him crumble to the ground, cupping his side, saw Cal rise, and grip his pistol.

And she ran.

"Are you okay?" Cal asked, helping Eva up.

Eva looked at him with wide, disbelieving eyes. "You came."

"We have to move." They rushed to the front door. Outside the mansion was chaos. Panicked guests flooded the crammed parking lot, blaring their horns, crashing into one another, trying to escape.

"How are we going to get out of here?" Eva asked.

Cal had a plan. The guard post and exit were just ahead. "This way—"

He felt the bullets before he heard them. Two of them. High-caliber. They lodged in his chest with so much force they knocked him onto his back.

He coughed blood. Vision cloudy. He heard Eva's muzzled cries. Like being underwater. She knelt over him, frantic.

Cal watched the ghost emerge from the darkness in front of him. A nightmare from his past. His darkest parts incarnate. Pale skin. Dead eyes. And a shock of bright hair. The Red Devil was smiling.

Cal knew Victor wanted him to see his face. Wanted Cal to know it was him who did this. Victor had made Cal, and now he was unmaking him. Victor shoved Eva aside, looked down at Cal, and said, "Those who have crossed with direct eyes, to death's other Kingdom, remember us— if at all — not as lost, violent souls, but only as the hollow men."

The Redhead named Victor raised his rifle, and pointed it down at Cal for the kill shot.

16

———————

Seeing Cal again had dredged up the past. Miranda couldn't stop thinking about Camilla — her girlfriend, who had been killed during the Barros case last year. Back then, Camilla helped Miranda to see beyond her limited perspective. It was because of Camilla that Miranda finally got justice for Arianna Barros.

Camilla would have wanted Miranda to get justice for Eva, as well. Arianna Barros was already dead when Miranda got the case. Eva's was a life that Miranda could still save. A chance to not repeat the mistakes and tragedies of her past.

Miranda keyed the address that Cal wrote down into her iPhone, grabbed her car keys, and rushed out the door of her apartment.

She knew it was probably a mistake to go. She told herself it was because she knew Cal would probably do something stupid and violent tonight. So, she would be there just in case that happened. To stop people from getting hurt. After all, that was her job, wasn't it? To protect and serve.

But secretly, she knew that some dark part of her wanted to live vicariously through Cal. Wanted to see those people punished. But she knew she couldn't be the one to do it. After all, actions have consequences. She had a job and responsibilities. There were laws and right and wrong to consider.

She didn't have a plan. She was sure there would be security. Her badge wouldn't help her, not without a warrant. She couldn't be there as a Fed. Without probable cause, she wasn't even a cop. She was the fucking neighborhood watch. A nosy neighbor with a Glock 22.

She parked down the road from the mansion, considering her next move. It was dark. She saw the guard house — manned by three men with walkie-talkies and the conspicuous bulges of metal firearms beneath their blazers.

A little after midnight, she noticed something was wrong. The guards in the guardhouse received a call on their walkie-talkies. Looking frantic, they drew their machine pistols and rushed toward the house.

Hello, Cal, she thought.

She heard the crack of gunfire. Distant but distinct. And frequent. There was her probable cause. She drove up to the gatehouse, lifted the gate, and let herself in.

What she saw inside was chaos. Guests — many of whom she recognized from TV — running for their lives, charging into a parking lot brimming with vehicles packed inches apart, trying to get their cars out. Others just saying "fuck it" to the whole thing, taking off on foot out the gate and down the street. Miranda was just another face in the crazed crowd.

There were two more gunshots. Louder this time. Close. The crowd screamed, dropped to the ground. Miranda spotted the shooter. A red-haired man with a rifle. She saw his victim. It was Cal, lying on his back. She watched the Redhead approach him, throw Eva out of the way, say something to Cal, and raise his rifle.

"Federal agent!" Miranda screamed, raising her sidearm and badge. The Redhead froze. Miranda was ten feet to his right. She had him dead-to-rights. "Put down the rifle!" Miranda said. The Redhead didn't move. "I said put it down!"

"Okay," Victor said, and while his right arm gripped the rifle, his left snuck to his chest holster and slipped out a Walther P22 pistol. He leaned down to place the rifle on the ground, and, without turning to face her, opened fired over his right forearm with the handgun. Miranda ducked and wildly returned fire, not knowing if she hit anything. By the time she got her bearings, the Redhead was in a full sprint.

Miranda ran to Cal.

"I'm okay," he grumbled, still catching his breath. Victor's bullets had lodged in his TAC vest.

Miranda rose and scanned the property line, but the Redhead was gone.

Cal stumbled to his feet. "This way," Miranda said. She led Cal and Eva out past the gatehouse to her Prius. The three loaded in.

From the dark woods, Victor watched them. He memorized Miranda's license plate as she sped away.

Miranda drove Cal and Eva back to her apartment in Downtown L.A.

She considered calling in the shooting at the mansion, but what was the point? She knew how it would go down. The party never happened. The private guards, they were never there. As far as their files were concerned, they died in Iraq, or Afghanistan, or Niger, or whatever warzone private security contractors like that can earn a buck. The whole thing would be covered up and forgotten, and she'd have only put a target on her back.

And Eva? She had witnessed some very rich and powerful people engaging in illicit drug use and what basically amounted to rape. There was no way Miranda could turn her over to the Feds.

When Miranda first became a Fed, she thought she could fix the system from within. But ever since the Barros case, Miranda had been feeling more and more like the system was beyond repair. The only way to exact real justice required a radical approach.

Miranda grew-up in East L.A., in a poor Latino neighborhood. Racial profiling and harassment were a way of life. The police were not your friend. They were a menace, to be avoided at all cost. They'd plant drugs on suspected criminals, stop people they suspected were undocumented without cause. Breaking the law to uphold the law, they called it. Their law was racism. Hers was justice. Critics might ask what gave her the right to decide what justice was? And maybe they had a point. But, fuck it. Someone had to.

Something had to change.

So, Miranda allowed Cal and Eva to hideout in her apartment.

Cal tore his TAC vest off, set it on the kitchen table, and peeled off his wetsuit. The spots where the bullets impacted his chest were painted like a Rorschach test of black and blue bruises.

"Who was the man with red hair?" Miranda asked.

Cal darkened. "They call him 'The Red Devil.' His name is Victor Xano," Cal said. "We served together in Special Forces. He was my team leader. He trained me. After our stint in the military, we went our separate ways. For a time. We both went into the private sector. I found work in Mexico. He went to work for Pat Roti. He's the one who told Roti about me. He brought me in."

"What was it that he said to you?" Eva asked. "Just after he shot you…"

"Some stupid poem. Didn't mean anything. Victor just thought it sounded badass. He used to call our unit 'The Hollow Men.'"

It was almost three a.m. They decided it would be best to get a few hours of sleep, then decide on a plan of action in the morning. Eva took the sofa. Cal was fine with the floor. Eva lay awake while the others slept. She watched Cal in the darkness.

Who is this man?

He appeared in the barrio one day without explanation. He visited her mother every day. He knew his way around a gun. Why would he travel all of this way just to help her?

Her mother had never talked about her past, but Eva had heard the stories. How she'd loved a man. How he was killed. How after losing him, hopeless and depressed, she worked at a cartel brothel. How she got pregnant with Eva and left that life. Her mother never had anyone to save her. She prayed to her mother for strength.

Eva got up from the sofa and went to Miranda's laptop. Miranda had given Eva her password so she could use the internet. Eva googled "The Hollow Men." Clicked a link. The poem by T.S. Eliot appeared on the screen. She read the words and saw a lonely world, filled with haunted, empty people, and she understood Cal.

And she understood herself.

They woke around ten a.m. Miranda went out and got food. It was Eva's first time out of Mexico City, her first time in the United States. Miranda was hoping the In-N-Out Burger truck that sometimes parked outside Ernst & Young would be there, but it wasn't, so she picked up Shake Shack instead. Nothing says USA like milkshakes and greasy burgers. Eva loved it.

Miranda and Cal decided that the people looking for Eva would most likely have their eyes on the border. They agreed that the best course of action would be to lay low for the next week or so.

The hot sun hammered the asphalt. Andrés pulled his 2011 Honda Accord into a gas station. Just another stop off the long desert stretch of the I-10E to Los Angeles.

"Another scorcher today in the Coachella Valley," the weatherman on his car radio said. "Highs in the 110s. If you don't have to go outside, don't. It's dangerous out there..."

Andrés pulled his Honda up to pump number two. A cartoonish decal of a naked lady with huge tits, an AK-47, devil horns, and an angel's halo on his bumper. Andrés was wearing jeans and a B.O.-soaked, sleeveless black T, which revealed lanky, inked-up arms. He scooped the blade of his car key into a dime bag of crystal meth and treated his nostril to a generous bump, then he pulled a balaclava over his pierced face, grabbed a tire iron from the back seat, and marched toward the gas station mini mart.

"Get on the fucking ground!" he screamed.

Andrés went berserk, smashing everything in sight with the tire iron. Refrigerator glass shattered. Potato chips and Ho-Hos flew through the air. Patrons screamed and ducked.

The overweight clerk at the register raised his hands in a sign of surrender. "Empty the fucking register! Do it!" Andrés threw a backpack at him. "Put it in the bag! Hurry the fuck up!"

The clerk emptied the register into the bag. "And cigarettes!" Andrés screamed.

The clerk obeyed. Andrés snatched the loot and headed for the door, but before he exited, he stopped to grab a bag of Flaming Hot Cheetos, and through the convex anti-theft mirror, he noticed the clerk press the silent alarm beneath the counter. He turned back. "What the fuck did you just do?"

The clerk was paralyzed by fear.

"You hit the fucking alarm? You think you can fuck with me? I was out of here! You want to fuck with me?" Andrés jumped the counter. The clerk collapsed, terrified.

But Andrés didn't touch him. Instead, he turned on the gas pumps outside. He marched to one of the pumps, pulled the fuel trigger on a nozzle, locked it, and dropped it on the ground. Gasoline streamed onto the asphalt and concrete.

Andrés lit a zippo. "Teach you to fuck with me..." He dropped the lit zippo and sped away in his Accord. The gas station erupted in a fireball behind him.

Andrés had never killed anybody. Sure, he'd seen people die. In a lot of ways, it took a stronger stomach to let someone die slowly from sickness or exhaustion than to actually kill them. It happened sometimes when he was running the stash house. Mostly to the elderly. They'd arrive in the States, exhausted and in bad shape. If they wanted, he would take them to the hospital, but they usually refused because they knew that going to the hospital meant deportation. He'd seen many people die in his stash house.

Every once in a while, he'd get someone in his stash house with a price on their head. His bosses would find out and send sicarios — hitmen — to pick them up. Andrés had always wondered if he had what it took to be a sicario, so he went with them once just to see. They drove a guy to another stash house — this one empty — and shot him. Then they shrink-wrapped his body and plastered it behind one of the walls. Andrés found it thrilling. He wondered how many bodies lived within the walls of that house.

In his quest to avenge Ma's death, Andrés had driven from Texas to California. He was told the girl was taken to Los Angeles, so that was where Cal would have been headed. It was a big city, but Andrés wouldn't rest until he found him.

Andrés didn't think he would have any problem summoning the willpower to kill Cal, but the fact still remained that murder was an act he had never performed before. He would have felt far more confident about his mission if he had a little more experience.

So, he blew up a gas station.

He figured there were probably four people inside when it went up. Killing them was way easier than he thought. A great fucking high.

He looked forward to seeing Cal.

18

———————

Over the next few days, Miranda would go to work in the morning, leaving Cal and Eva alone in her thousand-square-foot apartment. They spent their days reading or watching TV. She remembered how back in Mexico City, Cal had no problem chitchatting with the locals and her mother, but around her, he seemed to be a man of few words.

"I don't even know your real name," she said.

"I'm Cal," he replied.

Eva tried her best to learn more about the man. He didn't have a favorite movie, favorite book, a favorite color.

"Who are you?"

"That's a broad question."

"Okay. Where are you from?"

"I move around a lot."

"Where were you born?"

"Boston."

"Why did you help me?"

Cal simply shrugged and said, "Because you needed it."

And that was the extent of what she learned about him during their time together in Miranda's apartment. He was Cal from Boston.

Eva knew the world of the Hollow Men. Knew the feeling. It was why she painted. Art was her escape. Cal had helped her, and she wanted to help him.

It was in the pop-up galleries in cinder block warehouses on the industrial outskirts of Mexico City or in the centuries-old Spanish colonial fortresses of Centro Histórico that Eva met the work of artists like Damien Hirst, Ed Ruscha, and Miguel Calderón. Art was her window to the wider world. It offered relief from her dismal and limited existence in the barrio. It gave her hope. It made her whole.

Back in Mexico City, she had heard people talk about the Broad contemporary art museum in Edward Ruscha's hometown of Los Angeles. It was free to the public. All you had to do was go online and sign-up. She reserved two tickets under false names.

"Absolutely not," Cal said when she invited him. "And you're not going either."

"Oh, I'm not?" Eva said, challenging him.

"It's not safe."

"It's never been safe. Not for me," Eva said. "There is a difference between living under a threat and living in fear. I have lived under threats my entire life, but I refuse to live in fear. Because once you do that, you are no longer living. No one can take your heart and your soul from you. It can only be forfeited. That's what fear does."

Victor had traced Miranda's address back to her apartment. He ruled out an assault on the apartment as too risky. Cal would have his guard up now that he knew Victor was hunting him, and Pat Roti wasn't going to kill an ATF agent if he didn't have to. So, Victor sat concealed in the apartment across the street with a directional mic, eavesdropping on the happenings of Miranda Lopez's apartment. Waiting for his opportunity.

When he heard Eva talking about The Broad, he had an idea.

Pat Roti had been building an army. On Facebook. On Twitter. On the dark web. There was no shortage of fucked-up people for Roti to manipulate. Conspiracy theorists, political radicals, the mentally unstable. He used social media to empower and embolden them.

Nowadays, all you need to create a mass shooter is an internet connection.

The project was called the U.I.N, or the "Useful Idiot Network."

When Victor overheard the conversation about Cal's trip to The Broad, he figured he could use the U.I.N. Now that Cal was aware that Victor was after him, Victor knew he would have to hit Cal in a way that he'd never see coming. And Cal would never expect to be taken out in a public place like a museum.

So, he looked to the U.I.N. for some local talent. He decided on:

STEPHEN WILLIAM ANDERSON. BORN APRIL 10, 1966. CURRENT RESIDENCE: MESQUITE, NEVADA. PROFESSION: SOFTWARE DEVELOPER. RELIGIOUS AFFILIATION: ATHE-IST. MARITAL STATUS: NEVER MARRIED. NO CHILDREN.

NOTES: HOBBIES INCLUDE VIDEO GAMES AND ASTRONOMY. NEIGHBORS DESCRIBE HIM AS MILD-MANNERED, WELL-SPOKEN, AND VERY POLITE. LARGE DIGITAL FOOTPRINT ON CONSPIRACY WEBSITES. AVID BELIEVER OF 9/11 CONSPIRACY THEORIES, MOON LANDING CONSPIRACY THEORIES, AND THE REPTILIAN CONSPIRACY THEORY.

Victor rendezvoused with Anderson in a remote area of Griffith park. He was fleshy and balding with glasses. He wore knee and elbow pads over painter's coveralls.

Victor had told Anderson that the museum was really a

reptilian brain-washing site. The art housed within was sublimi-nally turning male homo sapiens gay, so that they would no longer breed with women, thereby allowing the reptilian over-lords to swoop in and plant their seeds in the wombs of human women, thereby populating the Earth with more Reptilians. They were building an army.

He drove Anderson downtown, parked across the street from The Broad, and waited.

Cal and Eva walked toward the white, honey-comb-faced museum. Cal did not notice Victor and his useful idiot, who were staked-out in the van across the street.

Cal and Eva entered the cavernous lobby. They took the esca-lator up to the second-floor galleries. Victor and his idiot entered a short while after them.

On the second floor, Cal walked with Eva through the galleries. They stopped in front of a giant, mirror-polished, stain-less-steel sculpture of a magenta balloon dog.

"It just looks like a giant balloon dog to me," Cal said skep-tically.

Eva perused the sculpture's information panel. "It says it's meant to memorialize icons surrounding birthdays and holidays. The artist is trying to capture a moment of nostalgia."

Eva was rapt, soaking up each morsel of information. Cal watched her admiringly. Eva took one last meaningful look at the balloon dog, then moved on.

In the next gallery, there was a nearly ten-foot tall, wooden dining room table and four

equally large chairs. Eva chuckled gleefully. She and Cal walked underneath it.

"I feel like a kid again!" Eva said, grinning. She looked like a kid, too. Cal smiled sadly.

Eva's face illuminated when she saw the name on the next gallery. "Ed Ruscha. He's one of my favorites."

They stood before Ruscha's *Azteca / Azteca in Decline*. A depiction of decaying Mexican murals. Eva studied the work deeply. And Cal studied Eva deeply.

Then he spotted Victor.

And the Red Devil smiled.

And hell broke loose.

19

———

The gunfire was loud and terrifying and relentless. Chaos reigned as civilians fled, hiding behind Jeff Koons's *Tulips*, or beneath Robert Therrien's *Under the Table*, while Anderson fired willy-nilly, and bodies fell, and art was defiled, and the brilliant white walls were dusted with the pink-mist vapor of blood, and the polished concrete floors were sullied red with creeping pools.

Victor had equipped his agent with only what could be smuggled in unnoticed by museum staff, and only what could be bought by civilians at a gun store or over the internet. He needed this piece of work to look amateur, like a random mass shooting by an everyday nutjob, not the distraction orchestrated by a special-ops mercenary that it was. Anderson wore a bulletproof TAC vest with extra magazines beneath his sweatshirt. Victor had equipped a Heckler and Koch SP5 — the semiautomatic civilian version of the MP5 submachine favored by law enforcement and security forces — with a bump stock. The weapon was small, compact, and with the bump stock, fully auto. Anderson smuggled it in beneath a light parka. He may have looked overdressed for L.A. weather, but there was no law against that.

He had synched his watch with Anderson's. The shooting started right on time. Right as Victor let Cal see him.

Right when The Red Devil smiled.

For Cal, time slowed. He watched Victor reach into his coat. Cal grabbed Eva by the hand. Civilians screamed and scrambled all around them. Victor calmly stalked Cal and Eva through the galleries.

Cal and Eva could hear the gunfire behind the thin white gallery walls. They moved from gallery to gallery, avoiding the shooter like they were playing a lethal game of Pac-Man.

Within minutes, the second floor was quiet. There were bodies strewn across the floor. Most of the crowd had escaped to the first floor. Cal and Eva moved cautiously through the maze of galleries.

Somewhere, Victor called out. "So, what was it, Cal? Attack of conscience? You go looking for something else? Something better? Maybe you go to Mexico, fall in love with a girl half your age?"

Cal's and Eva's eyes met. Eva scowled.

"No. That's not it. Doesn't suit you," Victor continued. "An illegitimate child, maybe?"

Cal lowered his eyes.

"I don't care who she is. I know all I need to know. She is why I am going to beat you. Because you care about her, and I only care about the mantra. Do you remember our mantra, Cal? You betrayed it, and now you and this young woman will pay the price."

Cal and Eva made it to the escalator. They stealthily rushed down a cave-like tunnel toward the first floor.

When they emerged into the lobby, it was teeming with terrified people trying to file out through the narrow exit doors. Cal and Eva joined the crowd. People pushing and shoving. Tumultuous waves of fear and desperation. Cal was gripping Eva's hand, trying to keep her close, when she was torn from him. Cal turned, and, in the chaos, he glimpsed Victor carrying Eva, kicking and struggling. They disappeared into the crowd. Cal pushed after them, the current of the crowd impeding his progress.

Victor dragged Eva down an empty hallway. Cal spotted Victor just as Victor disappeared into the cinema room. Cal cautiously followed him into the dark and ghostly, multi-screen maze of various projections of classic Western films. Randolph Scott, John Wayne, and Gary Cooper. Tough talk and gunshots echoed throughout the cinema graveyard. Cal treaded carefully.

Victor hid in the darkness, muffling Eva's mouth with his hand, waiting. Cal approached, blinded by a projector.

Victor raised his gun. Eva struggled. Cal was ignorant to their presence. Moving closer. Closer.

Eva bit Victor's hand and screamed, "Cal!"

Cal ducked out of the way.

His cover blown, Victor shoved Eva aside and scanned the darkness for any sign of Cal. "What are you doing, Cal? Trying to be the good guy? You know better. You and I, we're enlightened." Victor gripped his Walther P22 and lurked through the dancing projections of light and shadow.

"People may tell themselves they're good. Maybe they go to church on Sundays. But those six other days of the week, they're worshipping death. They worshipped it in the Roman Colosseum, they worshipped it at Golgotha. They worship it on their televisions. In their music. In their books. On the news. They go to the movies and watch Keanu Reeves kill a hundred people in ninety minutes and cheer while he does it."

Behind Victor, Rooster Cogburn shot it out with Ned Pepper in the finale of *True Grit*.

"People hero-worship men like us. They wish they had the ability to do what we do. To live and act without fear, hesitation, or remorse. To be incapable of feeling guilt. To be free of conscience," Victor said. "Whether they want to admit it or not, deep down, every person wishes they had what it takes to be a mass murderer.

"We are Supermen."

Cal sprung from the darkness. He brought his left hand up and placed his index finger at the side of Victor's weapon. Moving the weapon in a straight line to his right, he brought his left shoulder forward, blading his body, as he pushed the Walther down and away. He twisted Victor's wrist, wrenching the gun from Victor's grasp, sending it skittering across the ground.

Victor hooked Cal's temple with his left fist, freeing his right arm from Cal's twisted grip.

They fought, hand-to-hand, just as they'd sparred so many times in the past. Fists and elbows. Knees and legs. Dodging and blocking and brutally retaliating. Each anticipating the others' movements. Each knowing the other as they knew themselves. It was a dance, a seduction, a re-recruitment.

Cal grunted and growled. His pupils dilated with rage — big, black, dead, shark-like. Victor grinned, invigorated. Urging him. "Come on!" High on all of it. Ecstatic in violence. And bringing Cal down the rabbit hole with him.

Then, Eva said, "Cal." And the light came back to Cal's eyes. He turned and looked at her. "We have to go," she said.

"We're not done yet," Victor said. Cal glared at him. Eyes darkening.

"Cal," she said again. He looked at her. Her eyes were wide and worried. Cal softened, stepped away from Victor. "This is why you will never be able to beat me," Victor said. "She holds you back." Cal moved to the door with Eva.

"You can't save her," Victor called after them. Cal and Eva retreated out the door. Victor searched the darkness. Found his gun.

Outside, the LAPD had formed a perimeter. Terrified museum goers evacuated the museum and were directed to EMTs.

A SWAT team snaked toward the entrance of the museum, as Cal and Eva moved through the gift shop toward the exit.

"Hands where I can see them!" an officer screamed as the SWAT team entered the lobby. Cal and Eva raised their arms. A SWAT officer rushed them outside and handed them off to a uniformed LAPD officer.

The street was crowded and hectic. Cops trying to keep things organized, no one knowing what was what. The LAPD officer brought Cal and Eva to line of ambulances.

"Wait here," the officer said. "An EMT will be with you shortly." The second the officer turned her back, Eva and Cal disappeared into the chaos of the crowd.

Upon seeing the SWAT team, Anderson fled up the stairs to the third floor, where he found Victor. "The reptilian enforcers have arrived!" Anderson said, wide-eyed and frantic.

Meanwhile, SWAT cleared the first floor. A terrified young couple hiding in Collection Storage. Three teenagers in Yayoi Kusama's *Infinity Mirror* room. Two women in their mid-twenties hiding in a stall in the woman's room.

Once the floor was deemed safe, uniform cops entered in the SWAT team's wake and secured the area. The SWAT team snaked toward the stairs.

On the third floor, Victor and Anderson were cornered. They could hear SWAT finishing up below them. Anderson looked at Victor, wide-eyed. "The reptiles! They're coming!" They could hear the SWAT team's boots stomping up the stairs. "Where are our reinforcements? You said—"

Victor calmly raised his Walther and shot Anderson in the head.

The SWAT team stormed up the stairs and Victor dropped his gun. The SWAT officers screamed at him, "Show us your fucking hands!" "Don't fucking move!" Victor raised his arms and dropped down to his knees.

Victor was unruffled. "I am a professional soldier. I am licensed to carry a firearm," he said.

A SWAT officer cuffed Victor's arms behind his back. After they cleared the third floor, they brought Victor down to the lobby, then to the station for questioning, where Victor gave him the fake name and social security number that Pat Roti had issued for him.

Victor's story and credentials checked-out. He was a decorated, ex-special forces soldier now working for a private military company. He had a conceal carry permit for all fifty states. The cops ruled his shooting of Stephen Anderson lawful self-defense.

Victor knew there was still going to be a long and detailed, multi-agency investigation into The Broad shooting. He knew that eventually, someone would see security footage or hear witness testimony about how he hunted a man and young woman through the museum as the shooting unfolded, but none of that mattered. By then, Victor would have disappeared.

All that concerned him was that the mission had failed. Cal was still alive.

20

———————

The ATF's Los Angeles branch was front and center of the sweeping multi-agency investigation into the mass shooting at The Broad. It was all hands on deck in Miranda's office.

They'd identified the shooter as a paranoid conspiracy theorist from Nevada named Stephen Anderson.

One of the many questions investigators were asking themselves was Anderson's motive. What had made this man drive 350 miles to shoot-up The Broad?

Of course, Miranda knew. Cal had come back to her apartment after the shooting. It was the only place he could think of to bring Eva that was safe. Miranda didn't mind. Cal told her all about Pat Roti's Useful Idiot Network, but Miranda knew she had to tread carefully. If she made an accusation like that without proof, she'd look just as crazy as Anderson.

"That's what Pat Roti and Victor Xano do," Cal had told her. "They find the devil in you and nurture it, make it strong, until that is all you are."

21

———————

Andrés had been in L.A. for a little over a week, working his contacts. He was just a low-level coyote from Texas, but he knew people a little above him who knew people a little above them and so forth. Eventually, he heard about what happened at the Malibu ranch. He begged his contact's contact's contacts to get him a meeting with Giselle. He said, without thinking, that he had "an offer she couldn't refuse." This elicited laughter from his Mexican colleagues. "Pinche pocho." Andrés grit his teeth.

Eventually, Giselle agreed to give the persistent coyote from Texas five minutes of her time. He met him in her office off of Wilshire in Downtown L.A. Teddy lurked in the corner of the room.

"I'm hunting the man who attacked you in Malibu," Andrés said. "I heard that he has someone who belongs to you. If you help me, I will kill this man, bring your property back to you, and split the reward."

"And what do you need from me?" Giselle asked.

"Funding."

"Do you know how much this bounty is?"

"Ten million."

"That's a lot of money. Enough to attract the best mercenaries in the world. You come in here with trashy tattoos, piercings straight out of Hot Topic, and in desperate need of a shower. Why would I ever think you'd be qualified to do something like this?"

"These two need to get out of the country, and I know how smugglers think. I've been a coyote since I was sixteen years old, and I have never been caught. The best mercenaries are looking for them, but have they found them? I know nearly every smuggler in the country. I know how to find them because if the shoe were on the other foot, I know how I would get them out of the country."

Giselle considered the wiry, grungy coyote. "Would you bet your life on it?"

"What?"

"If I agree to finance you, would you still take my money with the knowledge that if you do not find them, I will order Teddy here to track you down and beat you to death with a baseball bat?"

Andrés glanced at Teddy. Teddy shrugged innocently.

"Yes," Andrés said.

"Tell Teddy what you need get started," she said. "Now, if you'll excuse me. I'm late for my cardio Muay Thai class."

And with that, she marched out of the room.

22

———————

They couldn't stay in L.A.

Luckily, Cal was good at disappearing. Trained in it. Eva had never been out of Mexico City. She was capable but inexperienced in the ways of the world outside of the barrio. Cal, on the other hand, had resources. There were a million different ways to disappear. They couldn't go back to Mexico. Roti had found him there. The barrio was compromised. And Eva didn't have a passport, so air travel would be tricky.

So, Cal looked to Canada.

He knew a place up there where they could lay low for a while as they figured out their next move.

He told Eva his plan. She didn't exactly have many other options, so she agreed. Miranda bought them some winter jackets. Cal thanked her for everything, and they set out.

It took them three days to get to Michigan, staying in motels that took cash and didn't require ID. It was snowing outside of Detroit. Large fluffy flakes danced on crisp breezes. Eva was elated. She'd never seen anything like it.

Cal was supposed to meet his contact in a bar in a suburban town north of Detroit. Cal parked the bike in the icy, mostly-empty parking lot in front of the bar, and he and Eva entered.

The place was quiet. It was something between a sports bar and a hunter's lodge. ESPN played on televisions behind the bar. There was a dart board and pool table. The walls were decorated with wood carvings, four-point buck antlers, and various wall-mounted animal heads. Neon signs advertised Bud Light and Pabst Blue Ribbon.

They found a table in the corner and the bartender said she'd be right over. On one of the bar televisions, the news was reporting an update on the mass shooting at The Broad. Cal spied a man at the bar in a Cabela's cap angrily shaking his head as he watched the report. Thankfully, the news made no mention of him or Eva being sought for questioning.

A man entered and doffed his grey North Face jacket. He looked to be in his late-sixties. He was 5'8" and lean. His white hair was thinning. He wore khakis, loafers, and a tucked-in, striped button-down shirt, like he was dressed for Sunday mass. He scanned the bar, spotted Cal and Eva at the corner table, and approached. "Mr. Payne?" the man asked. Cal nodded. It was one of his many fake names.

"I'm Jim Snodgrass." Snodgrass firmly shook each of their hands, making sure to maintain eye contact. He came off as very old-fashioned.

He took a seat at the table and ordered a Shirley Temple. "My wife has supper waiting for me at home," he explained. "But feel free to order anything you want. My treat."

Eva was famished and wanted to take him up on his offer, but Cal declined. He didn't want to stay here one moment longer than he had to.

"I must say, you don't look like my typical clients." He paused expectantly. Cal let the silence hang.

"This is my uncle," Eva said. "My name is Isabella. We are trying to get to Canada because I am illegally in this country and I do not want to be sent back to El Salvador."

"I'm sorry," he said. "I didn't mean to pry."

"That's okay. We have nothing to hide," Eva said.

"So, where are you staying?"

All of the local motels required identification. Cal could use a fake ID, but it would ping on Roti's radar. He'd have to find a flophouse in the city. "Detroit," Cal said.

Snodgrass grimaced. "That might be a problem. You see, how I work is I monitor the coast guard channels. We'll have to be ready to move within thirty minutes of my say-so. My clients usually stay at a local stash house, but I understand why you might not be amenable to that." He glanced at Eva, then back at Cal — the insinuation being that a place where arms or sex workers or drugs or fugitives were being held might not be the best environment for his young "niece."

"I usually don't offer, but you're not my usual kinds of customers," Snodgrass said. "I have a spare bedroom and a pull-out sofa in the living room. You're welcome to them."

Cal didn't like it, but it was the best of only bad options. "Okay," Cal said.

Snodgrass threw a few bucks down for the Shirley Temple, and Cal and Eva followed him out to the parking lot. They got on the bike and trailed Snodgrass's Jeep Cherokee. They parked in the snow-shoveled driveway of his two-bedroom colonial. Cal and Eva got off the bike and followed him into the warm home.

Jim Snodgrass's wife was named Sally. She was in her early-sixties. She was slightly overweight, a housewife on the tail end of empty nester syndrome. She was thrilled by the news of dinner guests. Eva introduced herself and her "uncle." Cal remained aloof.

They took seats around the dining room table. Sally placed a piping hot casserole dish of cheese, macaroni product, and veggies in the middle.

Snodgrass tilted his head. "Where's the beef?"

"I made fresh vegetable lasagna. It's vegan."

"So's cardboard," Jim said. "I thought we were having spaghetti and meatballs?"

"You keep eating meatballs, you're going to turn into one."

Jim shrugged. "Better than a vegetable," he said, winking at Eva.

Eva chuckled.

"You need to start eating healthier. You're not getting any younger."

Jim feigned playful offense. "I'm not old."

"You just quoted a Wendy's commercial from the 1980s," she said, as she flopped a piece of vegetable lasagna onto his plate. "They say you should think of food the same way you think of drugs. Both affect your body in similar ways. For example, red meat raises testosterone, causing aggression. When has aggression ever been beneficial to society?" she said.

"God help me!" Jim said.

Sally chuckled.

Eva indicated a framed photograph of a young man in a graduation robe and cap on a wood bureau in the corner of the room. "Is that your son?" Eva asked.

"Yes. That's Conor at his graduation from U of M."

"U of M?" Eva asked.

"University of Michigan, honey," Sally said.

"He lives over in Deerfield now with his wife," Jim said. He rose from the table and grabbed another framed photo from the bureau. "And this is our grandson," he said proudly, handing the photograph of his infant grandson to Eva.

Eva smiled warmly at the picture. "You have a beautiful family."

"Thank you," Sally said. "What about you, Isabella? Do you have family back in, where was it? El Salvador?"

"I have a mother, but she is very sick," Eva said. Cal looked at her out of the corner of his eye.

"It's a very hard thing to go through," Sally said, lowering her eyes. "We went through the same thing a few years ago with Jim."

Jim looked flummoxed. "Now, honey, they don't want to hear about that."

"No. I do," Eva said.

"He had cancer," she said.

"Skin cancer," Jim added. "Squamous cell. Wouldn't have been anything serious, but I didn't keep up with my doctor visits, and by the time they found it, it had gotten into my lymph nodes. To tell you the truth, I'd had the feeling that there was something wrong for a while, but I kept putting off going to the doctor because I was afraid of what they might find. Silly, right? I learned the hard way. The longer you don't face up to a thing, the worse it'll rot inside of you."

"But you survived," Eva said.

"I did. With the love and support of my family." He put his palm over his wife's hand. "And I came out stronger."

After a dessert of homemade apple pie, Eva retired to the spare bedroom.

"Try to sleep," Cal told her. "You'll probably only be able to get an hour or two before we have to leave."

"What was my mother like when she was younger?" Eva asked.

Cal froze. Caught completely off-guard. He narrowed his eyes. "What makes you think I knew her when she was young?"

"Are you saying you didn't?"

Cal paused. "Get some sleep." He moved to the door.

"The longer you don't face up to a thing, the worse it'll rot inside of you," Eva said.

Cal stopped momentarily in the doorway, then walked out, closing the bedroom door behind him.

23

Cal woke Eva at four a.m. Snodgrass said they had to move fast. They piled into his Jeep Cherokee, and Snodgrass drove down back roads and turned onto a dirt path. After about two miles, he pulled off of the path and parked in a copse of maple trees. They got out of the Jeep. He opened the back, removed camo netting, and pulled it over the Jeep, concealing it.

"This way," Snodgrass said.

They hiked for about forty-five minutes through the snowy, dark woods to a remote beach. "Watch your step," Snodgrass said. He led them down a rocky outcropping. He pulled a ghillie net off of a duck hunting boat. Then, all three of them boarded the vessel. Snodgrass sat at the stern of the boat, started the outboard motor, and guided the vessel over the smooth lake.

Eva had never tasted air so fresh as she did while speeding across Lake St. Clair. The cold, clean lake water kissed her face in icy sprays. Up ahead, the warm sun was climbing over the snowy, tree-lined horizon.

Snodgrass pulled the duck boat up to the shoreline of Walpole Island.

"You know where you're going?" Snodgrass asked Cal.

Cal nodded.

"Thank you for helping us. And please, thank Mrs. Snodgrass for me, as well. The vegetable lasagna was delicious," Eva said.

Snodgrass smiled kindly. "It was our pleasure."

Eva hopped out of the boat and trudged through the cold water toward the shore. Cal gathered his duffel bag.

"Good luck to you. Your niece really is quite a young woman," Snodgrass said, as he turned back to look at her.

That was when Cal shot him in the back of the head. The bullet from his Beretta M9's barrel exited through Snodgrass's right eye and lodged in the shallows. His body fell facedown into the lake.

Eva screamed. "Why did you do that?"

Cal scanned the shoreline, grabbed a multifunctional shovel from the boat, then got out and pulled Snodgrass's body toward the beach. "I had to."

"He was a nice man!"

"How do you think I found him?" Cal said. "He knows Pat Roti. Sooner or later, he would have heard that Roti is looking for us. He would have heard about the bounty and sold us out."

Cal began to dig a hole on the beach.

"You don't know that."

"Eva. He's a smuggler. He traffics women from Asian and Eastern Europe. Fentanyl. Military-grade weapons. Whatever pays. The world is better off without him."

Eva shook her head. "I thought I left all of this back in Mexico."

"You thought you'd leave the barrio and what? That the world would be nicer? Ugliness does not respect borders," Cal said as he continued to dig Snodgrass's grave.

24

They hiked through the cold woods in silence, blinded by sunlight magnified by the icy, pure-white snow all around them. There was no singing or cooing of birds overhead, only the sound of their shoes crunching over the brittle snow.

After forty-five minutes, they emerged into a clearing of four trailers. Unfriendly-looking Ojibwe, Potawatomi, and Odawa men idled around a fire burning in a rusted steel drum, smoking, drinking, or playing cards in the cold. Upon seeing Eva and Cal, one of the men rose, went to the largest trailer of the four and rapped on the door.

After a moment, a short and wiry Native American man stepped out of the trailer. His face was long and vulture-like and he had eyes like two black pebbles. His little black eyes landed on Cal. He spit and approached.

"What's up, chief?" he said. "Welcome to the rez. Did you bring the money?"

"To whom am I speaking?" Cal said.

The man flashed a yellow smile. "I'm Little Feather."

Cal handed Little Feather a bundle of hundreds. Little Feather checked it and nodded.

"Kirra," Little Feather said, and an angry-looking Ojibwe

woman in her twenties approached. She wore worn jeans, beat-up work boots, and a winter jacket. A tight braid yanked back her scalp in a way that looked painful. Her face, though pretty, was always frowning.

"Take them," Little Feather commanded.

The woman gestured for Cal and Eva to follow. She led them through the woods without speaking a word.

After a twenty-minute hike, they arrived at a solitary and secluded, old wood cabin with a rusted, corrugated tin roof. The woman led them inside. "There is a wood-burning stove for cooking and heat," she said, her first time speaking. "An outhouse out back. No running water. It is a five-minute walk to the lake."

The place was a single dusty room, still lived-in from the last person who had hidden out there. Consumed bottles of Canadian whiskey and empty cans of various foods lay around. The sheets on the single bed had once been white, but were now tinged yellow. Eva rifled through the kitchen area.

"There is a supply of canned food in the cupboard," the woman said. "I will check on you once a week. You tell me what you need, I tell Little Feather, and he will handle it. Other than that, you are to avoid contact with the people of the First Nations. My name is Kirra. I am to be your sole contact. As far as anyone else is concerned, you are not here. Any questions?"

"No," Cal said.

"Laundry detergent?" Eva asked. Kirra looked at her. "I don't see any in the cupboards. And some bars of soap. Basic household cleaning supplies..."

"I will forward your request to Little Feather."

Outside, Cal checked the cabin's sightlines. It was elevated over its surroundings. He would be able to see people coming. That was good.

• • •

Eva stripped the dirty sheets off of the bed, wrapped herself in her winter jacket, and slept on the bare mattress. Cal made do with the hardwood floor. The next morning, Eva awoke to a loud cracking sound. She went outside and found Cal methodically chopping wood.

"Do you have to do that so early?" Eva said.

Cal did not acknowledge her presence. If he even knew she was there, he did not show it. He just went on chopping. Eva sighed, frustrated, and marched back into the cabin. She was dozing when Cal awoke her about an hour later. He was rifling through his gun bag. He took out an AKM rifle and checked its mag.

"What are you doing?" Eva asked.

"Going hunting."

"What am I supposed to do?"

Cal shrugged. "You can come, if you want."

Her eyes scanned the dreary cabin, then she rose from the bed and followed Cal out the door. She walked with him through the woods, her feet crunching in the snow.

"Watch where you walk," he said.

"What?"

"Move close to the ground. Like this." Cal crouched slightly. "Engage every muscle as you move. Distribute your weight." Cal slowly and deliberately moved through the snow. He didn't make a sound. Eva tried it.

"Better," Cal said.

They moved like this through the woods. Eventually, Cal picked up a trail. Hoofprints in the snow, which wound through the brush. They followed the path and came upon a pile of deer droppings. Still steaming. *Looks like frijoles*, Eva thought.

The ramble ahead opened onto a snowy clearing. Thirty yards away, a skinny doe grazed for dead grass in the snow. Cal offered the rifle to Eva. Her eyes darted to him. She shook her head, but Cal shoved the rifle into her arms anyway.

"Crouch," Cal whispered. She gripped the rifle reluctantly

and bent down to one knee. "Aim," Cal whispered. She hesitantly raised the rifle. "Support your elbow with your knee. Aim just behind her eye." Eva glassed the doe through the rifle's scope. The crosshairs wavered anxiously. "When you're ready, inhale. Fill your lungs, hold the air in your chest, stay as still as you possibly can, and pull back on the trigger."

Eva slowly inhaled, then pinched the trigger. The bullet smacked into the doe's shoulder. The doe frantically limped away. Eva lowered the rifle, looking at Cal with upset eyes. "It's hurt."

"Come on," Cal said.

They tracked a crimson trail through the cold, white snow and found the wounded animal lying in the brush, bawling terribly. "Do something," Eva begged.

Cal unholstered his Ka-Bar knife and offered it to Eva. "The throat," Cal said. Eva looked at him, wide-eyed, and shook her head. "I can't."

"She's suffering."

"Help her, please."

He dropped the knife onto the ground and stared at her. The doe continued to squirm and cry in agony. "She's suffering because of you," Cal said. "Because of your weakness." Tears welled in Eva's eyes. She grabbed the knife out of the snow, went to the doe, pressed the blade under its chin, and slid it across her throat. The doe fell silent.

Eva turned to Cal. "Fuck you!" she said. She dropped the knife and stormed away.

Cal field-dressed the deer and brought the carcass back to the cabin, where he hung it from a thick tree limb to allow the meat to cool and tenderize.

Eva didn't return until after the sun went down. She saw the doe hanging from the tree limb and grimaced. She entered the cabin, shivering. The wood-burning stove was burning. Cal was cleaning and oiling his Beretta M9 pistol at the table. He glanced at her. She glowered, marched to the mattress and laid down on it.

After a moment, Cal rose and went to the wood-burning stove. There was a venison steak simmering on the burner. He placed the steak on a plate, grabbed a knife and fork, and set the meal next to her on the bed. She looked at him bitterly. She hadn't eaten in two days.

"You only get more of what you resist," Cal said.

"Whatever that means," she said, and she picked up the knife and fork and devoured the steak.

25

Eva awoke in the middle of the night and wasn't sure if she was dreaming — or rather, having a nightmare. She heard movement in the snow outside. She crept to the window and in the pale moonlight, she spied a grey wolf feeding on the hanging deer carcass. Its teeth tearing through red flesh. Its snout was caked with sinew. The beast saw her through the window and licked its blood-drenched maw.

Eva was awoken early again to the sound of Cal chopping wood outside. She angrily stormed to the door.

"I think we have more than enough wood," she yelled to him. Yesterday, he had split enough logs to last them two weeks.

Again, Cal did not react to her. He seemed entranced.

Eva slammed the door and went back to bed. When she awoke again, Cal was gone. She went outside to where the deer hung. There were bloody pawprints in the snow circling the mangled deer carcass. Eva shivered. Her eyes scanned the woods apprehensively.

She went back into the cabin, took a Glock 22 from Cal's gun bag, slid it into her waistband, and walked through the snowy woods, not sure where she was going. She wandered for several miles, through coniferous trees and over icy sandstone. The only sound was the whipping of wind.

After a few more miles, the wind carried the sound of a man bellowing. Not in pain nor fear. It was rage.

Eva followed the sound to a rundown, clapboard house at the foot of a snowy escarpment. She crouched in the brush and spied a tall, heavy man. He was not First Nations. He was swarthy but looked to be white. He stood completely naked in the cold in a suit of black body hair. He looked more like a bear than a human.

Steam rose off of his fleshy, sweaty body as he yelled and violently whipped a half-naked woman with a belt. Her nude body was covered only in a bedsheet. The woman simply lay in the snow and accepted the abuse. Then, the large man grabbed the woman by the hair and pulled her head upward, and Eva saw her face.

It was Kirra.

Without thinking, Eva rose from her hiding place. Spotting her, the bear man froze. He glared at her, full of menace. Kirra calmly rose to her feet, blood trickling from a split lip. She marched up to Eva and roughly grabbed her by the arm. "What the fuck are you doing here?"

"You need help," Eva said.

Kirra shoved her. "Get the fuck out of here!"

Eva hesitated. She looked into Kirra's furious eyes. As she reluctantly retreated, she glanced back over her shoulder at the bear man.

He was staring at her like she was dessert.

26

When Eva got back to the cabin, Cal was baking a can of beans over the wood stove.

"Looks like we have a wolf," he said.

Eva slid off her boots, left them by her bedside and lied back on her mattress. She thought about Kirra and she thought about what Cal had told her. *Ugliness does not respect borders.*

"How long do we have to stay here?" Eva asked.

"Until it's safe."

"When will that be?"

Cal shrugged. "Days, weeks, months." He removed the can of beans from the stove and shoveled a spoonful into his mouth. "You don't have to stay."

"What choice do I have?"

She awoke that night to the wolf howling somewhere nearby.

In the morning, Kirra made an unexpected visit to the cabin. Her lower lip was swollen purple. She gave Eva the laundry detergent, bars of soap, and house cleaning supplies that she had requested. But she would not meet Eva's eyes.

Kirra asked if there was anything else they needed. Cal requested a sleeping bag, instant coffee, socks, thermal underwear, toothpaste, shaving cream, razors, and other sundries. Eva asked for books. Whatever Kirra could find. Kirra said that she would return within a week with their requested items.

As Kirra headed for the door, she glanced at Eva. Eva followed her outside.

"You are not one of us," Kirra said when they were out of earshot from Cal. "You are not supposed to be here. This is your only warning. Do not intervene in our lives again."

"He shouldn't get away with that," Eva said. "Who was he?"

"Did you hear a word I just said to you?"

"I don't care if they kick me out."

"Kick you out? No. If you intervene again, you will be killed. And there is no 'they.' There is only me. If Little Feather orders me to, I will kill you myself. I am not your friend. Do you understand?"

Eva nodded.

"No one asked for your help," Kirra said, then she turned and marched away.

Eva watched her go, then went back into the cabin. Cal was loading a magazine. He said he was going hunting. "I'll go with you," Eva said, picking up the AKM rifle.

It was Eva who tracked the deer this time. A four-point buck. When she and Cal came upon it, it was eating leaves from a low-hanging oak branch. Eva crouched down on one knee, took aim at the deer's eye, inhaled, and pulled the trigger. The bullet struck the buck's head, killing it instantly.

"Nice shot," Cal said.

They approached and she watched Cal field-dress the deer, cutting and removing its entrails. The gore made Eva nauseous, but she would not let herself look away.

They got back to the cabin around noon. Cal carried the

carcass. He butchered a couple of steaks for that night's dinner, then hung the carcass from a tree branch. Higher this time, so that the wolf would not be able to get at it.

That afternoon, Eva went down to the lake. She stripped and walked out into the icy water. She shivered violently and sucked in the freezing air. She scrubbed the dirt and deer blood off of her trembling body and out of her caked and dirt-licked hair with the bar of soap Kirra had brought her. She washed her clothes and bedsheets in the lake with laundry detergent, then marched back to the cabin in only a towel.

The cold reminded her that she was still alive.

27

———————

Andrés figured that there was no way Cal would risk going back to Mexico, so he looked north. He may have overstated his smuggler connections in his pitch to Giselle. Sure, he knew pretty much every smuggler on the southern border, but in the north, Andrés knew exactly one.

Alistair Cathey ran a lumberyard just south of Vancouver. He was a Scotsman in his sixties, rugged, with a grizzled, grey beard, and he was never without his proud Scottish military tam o'shanter. Andrés drew looks from Alistair's Gaelic, blue-collar workers as he marched across the muddy work yard. Alistair took one look at the skinny, tatted-up Mexican with face piercings and scoffed. "And what're you supposed to be?" he said in his Scottish brogue.

"I'm Andrés. We spoke on the phone."

Alistair nodded. "Andrés, yes. Do you have the money?"

"I do."

"Well then. Step into my office, laddy."

Alistair led Andrés into a cluttered mobile office trailer. Alistair sat behind his desk while Andrés remained standing.

"There have been others coming around with similar inquiries. But I told them nothing. The only reason I'm talking to you is because we're in the same business, and your reputation precedes you. I hadn't anticipated you looking like something out of a freak show, but I've been told you're a hell of a smuggler, and that you can be trusted."

"I'm looking for a white man in his forties and a Mexican woman in her teens. They probably crossed into Canada within the past two weeks."

Andrés showed a photograph of Eva that was provided by Giselle. "This is the girl."

"Most smugglers deal with people coming into the US, not out," Alistair said with a chortle. "Personally, I am not aware of anyone who matches their description crossing recently. But I know every smuggling operation worth a damn on the Canada-US border. I can put you in touch with other smugglers. If those two crossed, someone is bound to know something. Of course, it'll cost you."

That was where Giselle's purse came in handy. Andrés paid off the Scotsman and received a healthy list of northern smuggling operations.

Over the next week, Andrés contacted each one. It was exacting work. He had to bribe the boss of each operation, only to learn that they had no knowledge of the two people he was looking for. Giselle was less than pleased that the coyote was burning through her money with little to show for it. But Andrés remained dedicated. He would get justice for Ma.

Or die trying.

Mrs. Snodgrass reminded Andrés of Ma in a lot of ways. Not the tough Ma. The woman who headed a Mexico-United States border smuggling empire. No, Mrs. Snodgrass reminded him of the Ma that took him off the streets, gave him a job, a life. To those who knew her best, Ma had a nurturing side. If you were loyal, she took care of you like you were family. That's why it hurt Andrés to see Mrs. Snodgrass in mourning the way she was.

Andrés had tried calling Jim Snodgrass, but his cell phone

was turned off. Luckily, Alistair's list had Snodgrass's home address. Andrés visited one afternoon. When she answered the door, Mrs. Snodgrass paused at the sight of the wiry Mexican with face piercings.

"Good afternoon, ma'am," Andrés said. He would have smiled, but that wasn't something he did. "I'm looking for Jim Snodgrass."

"He's not home," Mrs. Snodgrass said.

"Do you know when he will be back? I have a business opportunity for him."

"No. I don't." Mrs. Snodgrass's eyes watered. "I'm sorry. Have a nice day." She tried to close the door, but Andrés held it open.

"I think may be I can help you," he said.

Mrs. Snodgrass looked into Andrés's eyes. Uncertain but desperate. "Who are you?"

"I guess you could say I'm a bounty hunter. I'm looking for a man. White, forties. He is traveling with a young Mexican woman."

Mrs. Snodgrass's eyes widened and she stepped away from the door. "Come in."

She served slices of apple pie with coffee. "This was the last thing I ate with him. This apple pie, the night before he left." She sadly shoveled a forkful into her mouth. "He went missing last week. He took a man and a young Spanish woman out on the lake and he never came back."

"Where was he going?"

"What do you know about what my husband does for a living?" Sally Snodgrass asked.

"I am a smuggler, too," Andrés reassured her.

She nodded. "He never tells me much about his work. Doesn't want to worry me. But if I had to guess, I'd say he was bringing them to Walpole Island. The First Nation Reserve. It's an Indian reservation. They call them 'reserves' in Canada.

"All I know for sure is that those two needed to get out of the country. Jim took them across the lake and he never came back. They seemed like decent enough people. The young woman in particular." Mrs. Snodgrass's eyes welled.

"Looks can be deceiving," Andrés said. "If your husband is alive, I'll find him."

"God bless you."

He took a bite of his pie. "I've never had anyone give me homemade pie before. Thank you."

"You're very welcome, young man," Mrs. Snodgrass said. "All I want from you in return is a promise."

"Name it."

"If you find out that someone harmed my husband, you'll bring me back their fucking scalp."

Walpole Island had a marsh and river system that made it a premiere destination for duck hunting. For a hundred dollars a night, Andrés was able to secure a bed in a lodge right in the middle of the wetlands.

It was not a big island. He figured he could hike about twenty miles a day. If his targets were still on the island, he would stumble upon where they were hiding.

And soon.

28

———————

Kirra had brought Eva a bunch of books from the free book basket at the local library. A children's book with a sad-looking cartoon bunny in children's clothes on the cover called *The Night Dad Went to Jail,* a picture book on feline energy-field dynamics called *Dancing with Cats,* a book called *Does God Love Michael's Two Daddies* by Sheila K. Butt, *Love and Marriage* by Bill Cosby, and *Dating for Under a Dollar: 301 Ideas* by Blair Tolman. After the "so-bad-it's-good" novelty wore off, the only book that managed to somewhat hold Eva's attention was a dated reference book on virology.

She'd pass her days, bundled up on the beach of Lake St. Clair, reading about Ebola, AIDS, the Hantavirus, Bird Flu, Marburg, Lassa, Junin. Diseases which should have sounded terrifying, but seemed mild in the hindsight of a post-COVID world.

It was a particularly cold afternoon. The usual paddling of ducks was bobbing in the surf.

"What is a virus?" she read to the ducks. "At once parasite and predator. Neither alive nor dead. Opportunistic. Hiding and always awaiting the right conditions to fulfill its one, single, monomaniacal goal: to infect. To consume. To spread.

"Ebola Zaire. 90% human mortality rate. For the past forty years, this virus has emerged sporadically, killed thousands, then returned to its hiding place.

"It starts with a headache, which progresses into a fever. Over the next week, the virus liquefies the organs. Clots form in the veins, blood becomes hemophilic.

"The virus erases any form of identity, but it keeps its host alive. It needs to finish its work, which is to turn its host into itself — into virus — and after it has done that, the host goes off like a biological bomb, crashing and bleeding out."

"Kind of makes you wish you were a duck, doesn't it?" The voice came from behind her. She jolted and turned and was surprised to see a skinny Mexican guy. Tattoos peeking from his neck collar and coat sleeves, face blemished with piercings. "Sorry. I didn't mean to startle you."

"You didn't," she lied.

"You know, I read somewhere that in five billion years, the sun will die and explode and destroy the Earth. So, whenever I feel anxious or upset, I tell myself, 'It's okay, because in five billion years, it's all going to end anyway.'" A smile snuck across Eva's face. "It actually makes me feel better," Andrés said.

Many people would've felt uncomfortable alone in the woods with a guy that looked like Andrés, but Eva was so lonely, she had been talking to ducks. She welcomed the company. Besides, he seemed nice enough. Living in the barrio, she'd learned that you can't judge people by the way they look.

"Five billion years. Is that true?" she asked.

"It is."

"Huh." Eva's eyes became distant as she looked across the lake. "That is, unless Ebola doesn't get us first." Another small smile from Eva. "Or nuclear war, climate change, asteroids, super-volcanos, artificial intelligence, Al-Qaeda, zombies, Hitler clones, Al-Qaeda Hitler clones."

Eva laughed.

And then Andrés did something he never did. He smiled.

"I'm Andrés," he said.

They talked until the sun went down. She told him her name was Kirra and that she lived on the island. She tried to remain elusive about the details of herself without seeming suspicious. She knew she shouldn't be talking to him. But weeks alone in the wilderness with only Cal and a paddling of Canadian ducks to talk to would make even the most taciturn person feel chatty.

"Do you live nearby? I'll walk you home," Andrés said.

"No. That's okay."

"Are you crazy? It's cold and it's dark and there are wolves and grizzlies and who knows what else out there. I'm sticking with you as long as I can."

She lowered her eyes and smiled. "Okay. Thanks."

On the walk back, Andrés pointed out different constellations in the sky. Orion, Hercules, Scorpius.

"You know a lot about astronomy."

"My old job had me out late at night. A lot of down time. I'd look at the stars."

"What did you do?"

"Transport."

The cabin was about thirty yards ahead. Cal was outside, butchering venison steaks. "This is me," Eva said.

"That's where you live? Cool."

"No, you don't have to—" But Andrés was already approaching the cabin.

Cal stood perfectly still as the skinny young Hispanic man emerged from the brush. Andrés took a few steps toward Cal, his eyes studying him.

"Hell of a buck, sir," Andrés said, nodding at the butchered deer. Eva trailed behind Andrés, looking at Cal worriedly.

"You a hunter?" Cal asked.

"Me? Oh, no, sir. I've never even fired a gun. Not sure I'd have the stomach for it," Andrés said. "I was out on a hike when I ran into your—"

"Niece," Eva said.

"Your niece here. Just wanted to see her home safely."

Cal gave a neighborly smile. "Thanks very much."

"Okay then. Have a nice night, sir," Andrés said.

"You, as well," Cal said.

Andrés turned around, "See ya', Kirra."

"Bye, Andrés," Eva said. Cal and Eva locked eyes, as Andrés walked back the way he came.

Once Andrés was out of sight, Cal marched into the cabin and pulled the M4 Carbine from the gun bag.

"No!" Eva said, blocking his path out the door.

"He saw our faces."

"He's just some hiker."

"We can't take that chance."

"I won't let you do this. Not again."

"Get out of the way, Eva," he said, pushing through her.

"If you do this, there is no way I can stay here with you anymore."

Cal paused. "This is a mistake."

"No. It's not," she said. "We don't have to be as ugly as the world."

Cal knew Andrés was out of place. There was a chance he wasn't after them, Cal thought, but the safest thing would've been for him to put a bullet in Andrés right then and there. But then he looked into Eva's eyes and stayed his hand.

He sighed and returned the M4 to the gun bag.

Andrés didn't have a gun.

So, when he returned to the lodge, he told the manager that he was interested in doing some duck hunting, but he didn't have a rifle. The manager corrected him, explaining that a shotgun, not a rifle, was used for duck hunting. The manager thought it was strange that this young man would travel all the way out here to go hunting without a firearm, but then again, there was much about the young man that the manager found strange. The manager was able to secure a twenty-gauge for the young man to rent for twenty dollars a day.

Andrés had never fired a shotgun, so he hired a guide to take him duck hunting. The guide explained that he had chosen to visit Walpole Island at the end of duck season. Temperatures were dropping and the lake was starting to ice over. They spent most of their time among the cattails of the marshland behind a camouflaged duck blind by the water's edge. Andrés sat there all day, picking off unsuspecting ducks with the twenty-gauge. A black lab dutifully swam through the icy water to retrieve his kills. Andrés hardly thought it was fair. The ducks never saw it coming.

When they were done, the guide told Andrés that a snow-storm had been forecasted for the end of the week. Over the next several days, temperatures were expected to dip so low that the lake would freeze over with nearly ten inches of ice. The guide explained that while such conditions were not ideal for duck hunting, they were perfect for ice fishing. He urged Andrés to check with the manager for more details.

Andrés was already aware of the coming storm.

29

The shooter was smart. That was the last thing Cal thought before the shotgun volley tore into his side.

Eva had been dreaming about the wolf. She had heard it just outside the cabin. Its soft footfalls in the snow. Its teeth, yellow and slick and eager. Paws gently scratching against the creaking door.

It raised its chin and opened its mouth to howl and the shotgun blast woke her. She saw Cal's body in the firelight. Wrapped lifelessly in the sleeping bag. A large, bloody wound in his side where the round had torn into him. Blood-stained sleeping-bag feathers danced in the air.

One thing Andrés was good at was avoiding detection. He'd had plenty of experience herding immigrants across the border under the watchful eye of border agents. They never heard or saw him.

He waited for the storm. He knew that the howling wind would mask the sound of his approach. No one would hear him. Not until it was too late. Cal, the legendary assassin, never made it out of his sleeping bag.

Oh, yes. The shooter was smart.

Eva scrambled to her feet and Andrés swung the butt of his

rifle into the side of her head. She faltered as the room spun. He struck her again and the room disappeared.

Andrés had a 4×4 truck that he'd stolen from the lodge. With the lake frozen and the whipping snowstorm creating whiteout conditions, there would be little coast guard activity tonight. He figured he could drive across the frozen lake in a little over an hour.

When Eva regained consciousness, she was in the front passenger's seat of 4x4 pickup. Her head throbbed. Her hands and ankles were bound with zip-ties. Her body was buckled into her seat. Wind and snow lashed against the windows. Andrés drove blind, using the map on his phone to navigate the whiteout. They moved at a snail's pace. She squirmed against her restraints.

"Stop struggling," Andrés said.

And then it all came back to her in a dreadful rush. What had happened. How she had gotten here. "Where is Cal?" she said, her voice cracking.

"Dead."

Her eyes welled. "Why are you doing this?"

Andrés shrugged casually. "It's a job."

"Why did you spend all that time talking to me? Acting like you liked me?"

"I do like you, Eva," he said, using her real name. "I really do. But I'm not sorry. I'm not doing this to you. It's the world. You and me, we're both just in it. Now stop struggling or I'll hit you again."

Her lower lip trembled. "Where are you taking me?"

"Back to L.A."

And she realized just how truly helpless she was. Cal wasn't a saint, but he was not quite a monster. She had every opportunity to learn from him. How to fight, how to survive. She was wrong to think she could live apart from the ugliness of this world. And because of that, she was on her way back to the fate that seemed written for her. A fate worse than death.

Just give me death, she prayed.

At first, she thought it was a gunshot. A loud booming sound that reverberated through the truck. Then she felt the truck slide out of Andrés's control across the icy lake and she realized that one of the tires had blown.

"Shit." Andrés gently nudged the brake and slid the 4x4 to a stop.

He got out of the driver's seat with his 20-gauge and, bundled against the wind and cold, carefully plodded across the ice to examine the back right tire. "Fuck," he muttered under his breath as he knelt down for a closer view of the flat tire. He found a perfectly circular 5.7-millimeter hole in the tread.

A bullet hole.

Andrés's eyes widened. He gripped the shotgun, stiffened, and scanned the horizon. He was surrounded by a thick blanket of white. He circled around the truck and searched the other side of the lake. He could not make out the shoreline, a tree, a single figure. Only any infinity of white.

In the truck, Eva writhed in her seat. She kicked open the glove compartment. Maps and receipts and other documents spilled out. Among them was a retractable utility knife.

Outside, Andrés returned to the flat tire. In the ice a few feet behind the truck, he noticed another bullet hole. A missed shot, he guessed. He raised his shotgun and nervously trekked out into the snowstorm, moving unsteadily over the ice. Snow-blind and deafened by howling wind. After another few feet, he found another bullet hole in the ice. The shooter had struggled to hit his mark in the whiteout. It would have been a difficult shot even without the snowstorm. The shooter had to be close by. Andrés felt like he was being watched. It was two degrees Fahrenheit, but Andrés felt a nauseating warmth. He was flushed with anxiety.

A few dozen yards after the last bullet hole in the ice, the snowstorm revealed an abandoned scoped M4 carbine with a suppressor. There was a trail of blood on the ice, leading away from the rifle. Andrés swallowed hard and, shotgun raised, followed the red trail.

After about fifteen painstaking minutes, he realized he was following the trail in a circle. He heard movement behind him and turned just as Cal tore the shotgun from his skinny arms and cracked him in the jaw with the butt. Andrés fell down onto the ice.

"You're a good smuggler. But a lousy hunter," Cal said, blood dripping from a steaming wound in his side. "You don't shoot men with the same weapon you use to shoot ducks. You hit me with birdshot."

Yeah, the shooter was smart.

Until he wasn't.

"It typically takes more than one shot to kill a man with bird-shot from a 20-gauge." Cal pointed the gun downward and shot Andrés in the gut. Andrés hollered. "See?"

"Who else knows we're here?" Cal said.

"No one."

Cal shot him again. Andrés bellowed in agony.

"No one," Andrés said. "I work alone. The job was to kill you and bring the girl back to L.A. I didn't tell anyone because I don't trust anyone. I didn't want any surprises."

This seemed to satisfy Cal. He aimed his shotgun higher on Andrés — damage the young coyote wouldn't recover from. He heard someone approaching and saw Eva emerge from the white, having freed herself with the retractable knife. Cal froze, the shotgun pointed down at Andrés. He and Eva locked eyes.

Then, Eva gave the slightest nod.

Cal bent forward and pressed the barrel of the shotgun to Andrés's throat.

Andrés's eyes filled with hate. "Fuck you—"

Cal fired and Andrés was dead.

• • •

Luckily, the cold had caused Cal's wound to coagulate. He wound not bleed to death. He trekked to Little Feather's camp and told him about the coyote's body. Little Feather sent his men to take care of it. He also gave Cal a first aid kit of gauze, rusty tweezers, and a bottle of Canadian whiskey.

Back at the cabin, Cal lay on his side as Eva sanitized his wound with the whiskey and plucked the tiny pellets out of his flesh with the rusty tweezers.

Cal wondered if they should move. He believed the coyote when he said that he had not told anyone else where they were hiding. The kid wouldn't have wanted it to get out. He was an amateur, and the last thing he would have wanted was professional competition.

The coyote's appearance on Walpole Island may have raised Little Feather's eyebrow, but Cal decided that this was still the safest place to hide. The community was so insulated that Little Feather's gang was one of the few criminal organizations in the world that was ignorant to who Cal was and how much he was worth. Of course, if Little Feather ever found out, everything would change.

The burning logs cracked in the cast iron stove as Eva did her work. Silent and diligent. He had almost lost her. She was a strong person, Cal thought. But no one can do it alone. Maybe Victor was right. Maybe she was his weakness. Maybe she would be the death of him.

And maybe that was okay.

"I have nothing to give but death," Cal finally said. "This is all I can teach you."

Eva paused.

"Okay," she said.

30

———————

They started on a Monday. Cal set up a shooting range behind the cabin by placing cans on stones and snowy tree branches. He started her with the M4 Carbine. Demonstrated how to disassemble and assemble it. How to clean it. How each part worked.

But when it came time to shoot, she missed. She tried to remember what Cal had taught her. How to aim. How to breathe. Cal watched the gun barrel tremble in her grip.

He took the rifle from her, led her to the woodpile. "Chop," he said.

"We have more than enough firewood."

"It's not about the wood."

Eva looked at him, confused.

"It's about the mind." He offered her the ax. She reluctantly accepted it. "Be present. Only in the here and now. Just you, the ax, and your target."

She raised the ax, brought it down and split the piece of wood. She placed another log on the chopping stump and repeated the process.

After thirty minutes of this, she returned to the shooting range.

She couldn't miss.

That afternoon, Cal led her on a two-mile run, followed by push-ups and sit-ups in the snow until her muscles failed.

She slept well that night. She did not hear the wolf howling outside of her door.

On Tuesday, Cal awoke to the sound of Eva chopping wood. After, he trained her with the AKM rifle. Disassembling, assembling, shooting. Running, push-ups, and pull-ups in the snow.

On Wednesday, it was the Mossberg pump. He showed her how to pull the butt tightly into her shoulder to absorb the kick as she blasted the bark off of tree trunks. The lake had begun to thaw. She swam five-hundred yards through the icy water.

On Thursday, it was the Walther PPQ. Friday, the Skorpion SMG. Saturday, the Glock 22. Running, swimming, push-ups, pull-ups.

On Sunday, she was allowed to rest.

It was like this for the first four weeks. Firearm training in the morning. Strength and endurance in the afternoon.

Kirra visited every week with supplies, including more and more ammunition for Eva's training. Some days, Kirra looked okay. Others, she didn't. A bruise or a slight limp or the smell of liquor on her.

She wouldn't meet Eva's eyes.

Eva was running one afternoon when the wolf cornered her. She'd never seen it this close-up before. It looked well-fed. It did not seem hungry, but it was ravenous all the same. It snarled and inched toward her. Eyes dark. Fangs sharp and yellow.

Eva froze. Her legs stiff. Heart racing. Unable to breathe.

Cal, who happened to be on his way back from the lake, fired a single rifle shot into the air and the wolf fled.

"A wolf without a pack must be extra ruthless to survive," he said.

On the fifth week, Cal upped Eva's training. Mornings were dedicated to Krav Maga. Hand-to-hand and knife fighting. Afternoon endurance sessions included Navy SEAL exercises like drown-proofing and underwater knot-tying.

On Sundays, Eva would take the M4 Carbine or AKM from Cal's gun bag, attach the ACOG scope, and go on hikes. She treated them like recon exercises. In the woods and marshes of Walpole Island, she honed her stalking skills. The island was approximately fifty-three square miles. Much of the reserve, she deduced, was composed of honest, hardworking people.

Then there was Little Feather's gang. They ran guns, they ran drugs, they ran organs, they ran people. She learned the location of Little Feather's stash houses, as well as the points of embarkation from which he shipped his contraband across Lake St. Clair into the States.

She tried to stay away from the clapboard house where she'd seen Kirra and the Bear Man, but willful resistance does little more than make the will grow weaker, and one Sunday, Eva could no longer resist.

She patiently surveilled the site from the escarpment. Unlike Little Feather's other stash houses, there were a dozen or so cars parked out front. From her elevated position behind the house, she identified a hatch in the sealed crawl space beneath the structure. She descended the rocky, snow-covered face. Sticking to the shadows, she crept toward the hatch. A padlock restricted it from opening. She had come prepared. Cal had taught her how to pick handcuffs with both arms literally behind her back. The padlock was a piece of cake. She used a bobby pin to remove the lock and army-crawled beneath the house.

The ground was cold and dry. It was dark. She used what little daylight peaked through the ajar hatch. As her eyes adjusted to the dimness, she discerned a pair of duffel bags about ten feet away. She crawled over and unzipped them. One was filled with cubes of shrink-wrapped cash. The other contained various rifles and handguns and ammunition. They were items one would expect to find hidden beneath the floorboards of a gang stash house. Or whatever this place was.

Eva took a .38 Special from the bag, loaded it, and slid it into her waistband. Just in case.

She reached up above the bags and felt the dark ceiling. It was just as she expected. Another hatch. She gently pushed, peeked, then crawled up through the hatch in the floor into a dark closet. She pressed her ear to the closet door, then turned the doorknob and carefully peeked out into an empty hallway.

Eva crept into the hallway. At one end, there was a closed door. She wasn't about to blindly open doors without knowing what was on the other side, so she went the other direction. She could hear muted sounds and shuffling above her. She reached the end of the hallway. Around the corner was a kitchen, and in the reflection of the kitchen window, she spied a man whom she recognized as one of Little Feather's goons. He was standing with his back to her at the refrigerator. He pulled a bottle of Molson out of the fridge, cracked it open, took a swig, and turned in her direction. Eva quickly and quietly retreated unseen back down the hallway toward the closed door. She could hear the man crossing the kitchen, moving in her direction.

With nowhere else to go, she prayed the room would be empty, pushed open the door and slipped in.

A room full of ten men stared back at her. They did not look like natives, more like townies and tourists. Visitors. They sat on the sofa and in easy chairs or leaned against the walls.

A husky white man in a green John Deere cap grinned at her. "Hi there. What's your rate?"

Eva faked a smile and moved across the room. She turned a corner into a foyer, which led to a staircase. She silently ascended the stairs. There was another long hallway with doorways branching off of it leading to what she assumed were bedrooms. All of the doors were closed. It was cold and dry outside, but up here, it was sweaty and hot. It was clear now what the muted sounds and shuffling she had heard downstairs were.

A cacophony of yelps and ecstatic moans. Some of the women were good actors, but most weren't. The men, well, they didn't have to act.

She could hear the sexploits occurring behind each door except one. A doorway at the end of the hall. She pressed her ear to the door and heard the muffled sound of a television playing somewhere in the room.

Just then, a door opened down the hall. Eva, cornered yet again, twisted the doorknob of the TV room and ducked inside. Five young Native children, aging from four to ten, looked up at her from their Disney Channel cartoons. Eva moved a finger to her lips. *Shh.*

She peeked back out the door. A First Nations woman in a negligee was just finishing up with big, dumb-looking country boy.

"Thank you," he said sweetly as he leaned in for a kiss. The woman artfully turned her face and accepted the kiss on her cheek. He took out his wallet.

"Not me. Kirra," she said.

The man nodded. Eva's heart pounded as she watched the man walk down the hallway toward her. He arrived outside the door adjacent. Knocked. Kirra answered. Unlike the woman in the negligee, she was dressed in jeans and a sweater.

"Finished?"

Big Dumb Country nodded.

"It's gonna be a hundred."

Eva watched the man pay Kirra. She silently closed the door and looked back at the children, whose curious gazes hadn't left her.

Eva stood there, frozen for a moment, rage bubbling up inside of her. Then she pulled the .38 from her waistband.

Fuck it.

She marched across the hallway, kicked open Kirra's door, and pointed the revolver at her. Kirra rose from behind her desk, stumbling to her feet. She put her hands in the air.

"Put it down," Kirra said.

"Why would I? Why shouldn't I shoot you right now?"

"I know what you think. You think you'd be helping these women."

"You keep children here!"

"To look after. You have no idea what you're talking about. Do you know how many women disappear on Native American reserves? You don't. Because no one does. Tribal police don't investigate. No one gives a shit. Those kids are the children of women who have vanished. We look after them Would you please lower the gun so we can talk?"

"What, like friends? You're not my friend. You'd kill me yourself. Remember?"

"I told you that so you would stay away. I already have enough girls to protect."

"You call this protection?"

"There's strength in numbers."

"Who was the man I saw?" Eva didn't have to elaborate. Kirra knew exactly who she was talking about. The Bear Man.

"This isn't a door you want to open. Just walk away." Eva held the gun on her. Kirra sighed. "His name is Rocky Sciarrone. He works for a syndicate out of Detroit. He uses Little Feather to run arms and drugs. He visits the island about twice a month. He always stops here after his business is concluded. His is a big account, so Little Feather tells me to give him and his guys VIP treatment. The only thing is he likes to get rough. His first visit here, he killed a girl. Beat her to death. I couldn't let him see another of my girls after that, but Little Feather still insisted he get the VIP treatment."

"So, you…"

Kirra lowered her eyes. "I do what I can to protect them."

Eva lowered the gun.

31

———————

"Y ou only get more of what you resist.

"Do not resist fear.

"That is not to say embrace it.

"Be aware of it. Feel it.

"And deal with it."

Cal handed her his Ka-Bar knife. Today was the final day of her training.

"I located the wolf's lair near Goose Lake," Cal said. "Do not come back until you have killed it."

Rocky Sciarrone was never so calm as he was after beating a woman.

That's why he liked to take the ferry back. To take a moment, savor the little things. Cool off, so to speak.

He'd always been an angry guy. Since before he was cut from JV baseball, his mother had been telling him he wasn't good enough. Back when he was an amateur bodybuilder, he'd hear his mother in his head, calling him weak, a nobody. Eventually, he tried to squat more than his body could handle and permanently injured his back. It ended his bodybuilding career before it started. Years of steroid abuse had left him with only one testicle, a gut, flappy bitch tits, high blood pressure, and too much body hair.

Plus, he could never get it up. Not the traditional way.

At first, he felt bad after beating a broad. But then he'd remind himself that these dirty bitches don't love him. They probably talked bad about him when he wasn't around, just like ma used to. May she rest in peace.

Besides, beating them was the only way to make his little one-nutted pecker stand up. He didn't know why. Anger made him feel like a man.

He stood on the deck, calmly smoking a cigar in the brisk cold air. This redskin cooze named Kirra, she really did it for him. Could take a beating like a rented mule.

He took another puff of his cigar, feeling the mild nicotine high wash over him like a warm bath.

He was standing at the railing at the front of the ferry. Half a dozen cars were parked behind him. The two guys he traveled with — his soldiers — they knew to leave him alone on his ferry trips, that he liked to "ponder things" or some shit. That was fine by them. They didn't need to freeze their nuts off on the ferry deck. Let the skipper do his pondering. They stayed in the Chrysler with the heat blasting.

Rocky liked to stand at the front of the ferry on account of the view. Behind him was Canada. Ahead of him, the U.S. of A. Land of opportunity. He was always a forward-thinking guy, and he also used these short ferry rides to think about his future. He was a capo in the Detroit mafia. He hated making these fucking bimonthly trips to Canada, thought it was beneath him, but he knew that the money he was bringing in through his smuggling deals with Little Feather had every other capo in the organization green with envy. Give it a couple years, boss would either step back or get put away, and he was a shoe-in.

Then someone else could make these trips to the redskin ghetto.

Maybe he'd bring Kirra with him. Not many women could take a punch like her. It was truly fucking impressive.

He looked ahead at the coast of Algonac, Michigan. American soil. Yeah. His future was bright.

The knife blade entered the right side of his neck and then pushed forward, severing his esophagus and trachea. He never saw it coming. He never knew who killed him.

He died in Canada.

Cal had given Eva the knife and told her to kill the wolf, but on her way to the wolf's lair on Lake George, she found herself detouring to the old clapboard whorehouse. She didn't know why she went there. She didn't have a plan.

Not at first.

She wondered if Rocky Sciarrone was there tonight.

She was just about to leave, when a black Chrysler pulled up and parked outside of the house. Rocky sauntered out of the vehicle with two other men. They looked Italian and reminded her of the Cartel guys she knew back home. The same thuggish swagger. The same gaudy flash.

Eva watched them enter the whorehouse. She went to their Chrysler, not sure what she was looking for. She saw a ferry ticket on the dashboard. They had arrived on the morning boat.

It was about a two-hour hike to the ferry station, but Eva was able to make it in ninety minutes. She only hoped that Rocky and his goons could last that long.

Kirra had said Rocky always stopped by the brothel after his business was concluded. If he took the ferry that morning, finished his business that day, there was a chance he would be taking the ferry back that night.

So, Eva staked-out the station, and it wasn't long before her hunch proved correct. The black Chrysler with Rocky and his two goons pulled up, paid, and waited for the next ferry.

The ferry itself was not large. It could transport no more than a dozen cars at a time. It was eight dollars per vehicle, two for a walk-on. Eva bought her ticket with a twenty she managed to find among the fifties and hundreds in Cal's cash belt. She was told that the ride was approximately seven minutes long, and that she should have her passport prepared for US Customs on the other side.

She boarded the ferry.

The wheelhouse was elevated over the ferry deck below, creating an awning of sorts. Eva found a seat under its shade. It was not too cold today, about forty degrees and sunny. The lake was calm.

The Chrysler was parked parallel to where Eva was sitting. A red Volkswagen sedan acted as buffer between where she was sitting and her target's vehicle. She watched Rocky Sciarrone exit the Chrysler, go to the front of the ferry, and light a cigar.

The ferry cast off. Seven minutes to the other side.

Eva rose to her feet, glanced at the Chrysler. The two goons were in the front seats, chatting. They weren't paying much attention to anything going on outside of their vehicle, but, still, Rocky was in their sightline. They would see her approach.

The clock was ticking. Her heart began to pound.

She closed her eyes for a moment and imagined she was chopping wood, just her in the present moment and nothing else. She opened her eyes and felt the cool wind in her hair, the vibrations of the ferry buffeting against the waves, the sun as it moved across the deck.

Five minutes.

The ferry was moving northwest across the river. It was late afternoon and they were moving toward the sun. The awning's shade gradually receded as the ferry's angel changed in relation to the sun.

Four minutes.

The sunlight was creeping over the hood of the Chrysler now. Eva moved toward the front of the ferry.

Three minutes.

She timed it. The glare reached the Chrysler's windshield and Rocky's goons turned their heads away, just as Eva descended on Rocky with the stealth of a jaguar. No one saw her slide the Ka-Bar into the side of Rocky's neck and tear out Rocky's throat.

Rocky's guys pulled down the car visors and saw was Rocky keeled over the railing. At first, they thought he was just sea sick.

By the time they got out of the Chrysler and realized that their boss had been assassinated, Eva was long gone.

After she stabbed him, she had jumped over the side of the ferry. She would have to swim strong and fast, and remain underwater to avoid detection. The underwater knot-tying, the drownproofing, the SEAL training coupled with the shot of adrenaline after killing Rocky made her escape a piece of cake.

Once on the shore, she immediately found a secluded area and started a fire. Her teeth chattered and her body trembled. She stripped off her wet clothes and let them dry.

Ninety minutes later, she was dressed and hiking through the forest. The air was crisp and woody. She took a moment to view the clear night sky, dappled with hundreds of burning stars.

When she spoke with Andrés that day on the beach, he told her how some stars had burnt out years ago, but we could still see them because they were so far away that their light was only now reaching Earth. Like ghosts.

She continued south, and as the cabin came into view, she saw the wolf prowling on the outskirts, sniffing the air. The deer carcass was hanging out of its reach. The wolf's dark eyes landed on her. He lurked toward her.

Eva held the Ka-Bar knife at her side. The wolf stood in her path, hair raised, teeth borne. Eva took a step toward him. Never breaking eye contact, gazing deep into its dilated pupils. The wolf growled fiercely. She gripped the knife and moved into striking distance, prepared to fight.

The wolf flattened its fur. It returned her gaze and lowered its head. Then it turned and disappeared into the dark woods.

Cal was grilling venison steaks with canned green beans and sweet corn. When Eva entered, he looked at her expectantly.

"The wolf is dead," she said.

Cal only nodded. She sat at the table and he plated a venison steak for her. When he placed it on the table, she sprung from her seat and pressed the Ka-Bar to his throat.

"You used her and you left her! Like a piece of meat!"

Cal glared back at her with cold eyes. "You're right. I did." The knife pricked his skin, drew blood. Eva's hands trembled as she held the blade against Cal's throat.

Finally, she lowered it and collapsed down into the chair, her eyes wet and distant.

Cal sat across from her at the table. "When I went to the brothel, your mother was the only woman I saw. We spoke very little. We were just two sad and empty people. One day, she told me that she was pregnant and that that she was leaving. Although we did not speak much, she told me she felt connected to me. She said she did not know who the father of her child was, but that she prayed it was me."

Eva did not say a word. She just gazed down sadly at the meat on her plate, getting cold. Cal plated the other venison steak with green beans and corn and ate his dinner.

32

———————

Little Feather was sleeping off a hangover when someone rapped on his trailer door. He groggily rose to his feet, crossed the trailer on shaky legs, and answered. A pair of rough hands grabbed him, yanked him outside, and threw him onto the ground.

Little Feather looked up at Rocky Sciarrone's goons. A wiry thug in a gold chain and track jacket glared down at him with wild eyes, while a dead-eyed pitbull in a sport coat trained a shotgun on his guys.

"What's the problem, chief?" Little Feather asked.

"You know what the fucking problem is," Track Jacket said.

"Afraid I don't, chief."

"What? You don't watch the fucking news?"

"You're on the rez. We're lucky if we get clean drinking water, much less CNN."

"There was a problem on our ferry ride home." Track Jacket said.

"What kind of problem?"

"The type of problem that cut out Rocky's throat," Pitbull said, holding his shotgun firm.

"Did everything but scalp him," Track Jacket added.

"Wasn't us, chief."

"Bullshit."

"What do we have to gain from killing one of our best clients? This is a loss for us, too."

"Here's how it's gonna go, Tonto," Track Suit said. "We're going to come back in forty-eight hours with some guys, and one of two things is gonna happen. Either you will have found out who whacked Rocky and hand them over to us, or we're turning your whole fucking camp into Wounded Knee."

"I'm impressed by your knowledge of Native American history, chief. And they say Detroit schools are failing."

"Shut-up!" Track Suit said, backhanding Little Feather across the face. A trickle of blood flowed out of his mouth and down his chin. None of Little Feather's men moved a muscle. They just stood there, neutral and stoic.

Little Feather glared at Track Jacket, then grinned a bloody grin. "Okay, chief. You win."

"Forty-eight hours," Track Jacket said, then he and Pitbull Sport Coat walked back toward their Chrysler.

That was when Little Father gave his guys the nod.

Little Feather's men converged on the two Detroit goons. Quiet, calm, and fast. They overtook Pitbull first, tearing the shotgun from his grip. Track Jacket reached for the Beretta in his waistband, but they caught him by the wrist and knocked the gun from his hand.

The sound of someone being beaten to death by bare hands is terrible. There is nothing more primal. Nothing more violent and profane. Before it was over, both of them called out for their mothers.

Little Feather had their bodies buried in the woods.

It wasn't that Little Feather thought they were wrong. It was how they came at him. Yes, the Detroit guineas did lucrative business, but Little Feather was still living in a shit trailer on an impoverished reserve.

See, Little Feather had bosses of his own. Guys running hotels and casinos on other plots of First Nations land. Little Feather ran smuggling on Walpole Island, but he was basically a lieutenant in the larger scheme of the organization. Losing the Detroit goombas would do little to better or to worsen his personal situation either way.

The punks should have known their audience.

When it came to Rocky Sciarrone, Little Feather had a good guess as to who was responsible. First the pierced-faced Mexican kid, then that sadistic, hair-covered whop. The only variable that had changed on the island since those two died was the arrival of his two cabin guests.

Little Feather decided to dig a little deeper into exactly who he was hiding out there in the woods.

33

S pring was coming. The days were longer and warmer. Kirra made her weekly visits, dropping off supplies. Cal requested that she drop off copies of USA Today and other news-papers so he could stay connected to the outside world. She and Eva never discussed Rocky Sciarrone's disappearance. Cal had also asked for fishing rods, and he and Eva spent much of their time at the lake. Walleye, Yellow Perch, and Smallmouth Bass. They'd grill them up outside over an open fire.

Most evenings after dinner, they'd walk on the beach and watch the sunset. By now, Eva was used to the solitariness of this place. Even fond of it. She felt like she could live here forever.

Things were happy for a while. Their lives were peaceful.

Then one day, after Kirra had made her weekly delivery, Cal was perusing the week's USA Today when an article crossed his eyes. "ATF AGENT KILLED IN CAR ACCIDENT."

A photograph of Miranda stared back at him. According to the article, she had swerved into oncoming traffic and collided head-on with a dump truck just outside of Chicago. She was killed on impact. Sources said they were still awaiting the results of the Miranda's toxicology report, but Cal knew it was no accident.

A few weeks ago, Cal had seen another story in the paper. Miranda had held a press conference, naming Victor Xano and Pat Roti as persons of interest in The Broad shooting. It was a bold move. Had Cal been there, he would have advised her against it. Pat Roti was a dangerous and powerful enemy to have. But Cal also knew that Roti wouldn't kill a Federal agent unless he was absolutely compelled to do so. There had to be more to the story. What did Miranda uncover that got her killed?

Call shook his head, still trying to process it.

Miranda was dead.

Roti, he thought. *He had gotten her.* And Cal realized just how temporary his and Eva's happiness was. Roti was still out there, and sooner or later, he would get to them just like he had gotten to Miranda. They couldn't hide forever.

And that had never been the plan, Cal had to remind himself. The plan from the beginning had been for him to prepare Eva. To teach her how to survive life without him.

To be, no matter how briefly, something like a father. If such a thing was possible for a man like Cal.

He'd done that. He'd prepared Eva the only way he knew how. But now it was time to return to L.A. To deal with Roti once and for all.

"We need to talk about going home," Cal said to her on one of their evening walks.

"Is it safe?"

Cal paused.

"Then we stay," Eva said.

"We can't stay here forever," Cal said.

"Why not? Why can't we make this place our home?"

"Because we're not living here. We're hiding."

"They'll kill you."

"You only need to worry about yourself now."

"What?" Her eyes welled. "Why are you doing this? You don't even know that I'm your daughter. Odds are I'm not."

Cal lowered his head. "Come with me," he said.

He led her down the beach toward Goose Lake. "Quietly," he said, and they both expertly crept through the woods.

He led her to a large oak tree. The ground beneath had been excavated. Ropy tree roots draped down like tentacles. Inside, a mother bear, skinny from her long winter's hibernation, was grooming her cubs.

"She's a killer," Cal said. "But still, she has the instinct to protect her cubs." Cal looked at Eva.

"Instinct, Eva. That's what I have."

34

———————

As Cal and Eva approached the cabin, they spotted Little Feather and five of his guys staked-out, hiding in the brush. That only meant one thing. Little Feather had figured out what he had out here in the woods. He'd learned that Cal was worth far more to him dead than alive.

"This is my fault," Eva said. Cal looked at her. She shrugged. "I may have killed a guy on a ferry."

"Why?"

"Long story."

Cal shook his head. "I told you we had to keep a low profile. You disobeyed me. We're going to discuss this later," Cal said. He realized how he sounded. Like a parent scolding his teenager. What was he gonna do, ground her?

"They haven't seen us yet," Cal said. "We can turn around right now. Just walk away and never come back."

Eva thought about Kirra and the women in the brothel. She thought of the orphaned children watching their Disney cartoons.

"No. We can't," Eva said.

. . .

Little Feather and his men watched Cal and Eva approach the cabin. Once they were inside, his men spread out. Two approached from the left flank and two approached from the right. The fifth was a Native man with a serious face and a long, braided ponytail. He was armed with a Remington model 7600 pump-action rifle. He approached the front door, leaned back on his left heel, raised his front foot and prepared to front kick the door open when—

A volley of buckshot tore through the door like tissue paper and ripped into the serious man's chest, launching him off of his feet. He lay on the ground gasping, a dozen metal pellets lodged in lungs torn to ticker tape.

Eva stepped through the blast door. She had the AKM and M4 carbine crossed over either shoulder. She held the Mossberg pump in her hand. She aimed the shotgun down at the dying man and fired a second volley, putting him out of his misery.

Eva calmly walked back into the cabin and closed the shotgun-blasted front door behind her.

Little Feather stood back from the cabin, watching in disbelief.

His men raised their deer rifles at the cabin. Their muzzles exploded with gunfire.

Inside, Eva and Cal took up positions by the windows on either side of the cabin, ready to defend. Cal trained his Glock on a large Native man armed with an AK-47. Cal fired and clipped him in the neck.

But the lumbering giant didn't go down. It was like a wasp stinging a bull. The big man plugged his neck with one hand and angrily unloaded his AK-47. Cal ducked for cover.

On the other side of the cabin, Eva took aim at two more of Little Feather's men. She fired her Mossberg twice. One of the men was grazed in the side with a volley but remained standing. Eva ducked down and took cover as the men returned fire.

The four men converged on the front of the cabin. The

injured giant cautiously approached the front door of the cabin with his AK-47 raised. The other three gunmen watched the windows. The giant tried to open the door, but it was barricaded.

The giant slammed his massive shoulder into the door, cracking it. He slammed again. And again. The door was giving. It cracked open and the giant found himself looking down the business end of Cal's Glock — *Bam!* — The giant was shot point-blank in the head. The other men watched in anger as the giant crumbled to the ground, dead.

The white noise roar of brutal gunfire as Little Feather's men angrily and haphazardly unloaded on the cabin. In the cabin, Eva and Cal lay prone, covering their ears as lethal bullets violently whistled past, splintered wood, shattered glass, toppled chair, and tore the whole fucking place apart.

Outside, the gunfire ceased. Ears ringing. The pungent smell of Nitroglycerin hanging in the air. The cabin riddled with bullet holes. Little Feather's three remaining men approached the front door. Opened it. Inside, they found Eva waiting for them. The AKM in one hand and the M4 Carbine in the other.

Little Feather watched his men disappear into the cabin. Then he heard a loud, short exchange of gunfire.

His three men had walked into the cabin. Only Eva walked out. She had a rifle in each hand. She was about twenty yards away. Her eyes landed on him. Little Feather got a sinking feeling in his stomach. He turned and ran back toward his '85 Ford pickup. Eva quickly closed the distance and raised her rifles as Little Feather turned the ignition. Eva fired on the fleeing pickup. 5.56×45mm and 7.62x39 mm rounds tore through the truck like tin foil.

Cal watched it all from the cabin. He watched her rain lead and hellfire down on the traffickers when they burst through the cabin door. Watched Little Feather run from her in fear. Watched Eva unload into the fleeing pickup until it lost control and drifted into a tree. He watched Eva march toward the crash site, fearless. Watched a wounded Little Feather stumble out of the pickup truck about to beg for his life. Watched Eva gun him down before the words were even out of his mouth. No hesitation. No fear. No ceremony.

He almost felt a tear come to his eye.

He'd never been prouder.

PART III

THE MOTHER

35

The iPhone's illuminated face cut through the darkness at 5:30 a.m. Instead of an alarm, Johnny Nash's "I Can See Clearly Now" hummed through the iPhone's speaker. A finger swiped the phone's gorilla glass, silencing it.

Miranda rose from her bed with alacrity.

She moved into the area of her apartment that others might call a living room, but the set-up had changed slightly since Cal's and Eva's stay. Where there was once a television, Miranda had hung a heavy bag. Where there should be a sofa, a bench press.

Every morning, Miranda worked-out as the city slept.

Because if she was taking on Pat Roti, she knew she'd better stay in fighting shape.

During the winter that Cal and Eva spent up in Canada, life at the ATF trudged on. The shooting at the Broad was eventually blamed on a mentally-ill conspiracy theorist and closed, but Miranda could not let it go.

Scarpelli had been riding high ever since Miranda brought in the Barros case last year. He finally received his long-sought promotion.

Good riddance, Miranda thought.

The new SAC was a guy named Louis Shackelford. He was a short, stout baby-faced black guy from Philly. He grew up blue-collar. His father had been a fisherman. He was in his late-thirties. Young for an SAC. Miranda wasn't yet sure if she could trust him.

The Broad shooting haunted her. She was the only one in the office that knew who was really behind it, but she had to be careful. The name was poisonous, but it was always on the tip of her tongue.

Pat Roti.

He didn't show up in any of the Federal databases. Hell, she didn't even know if Pat Roti was his real name.

She had footage of Victor Xano from The Broad's security cameras, but she could not get a facial ID match. It made sense that any information about the man would have been scrubbed.

No, there was no way she'd ever be able to find Victor or Pat Roti.

Her only choice was to make them find her.

She wouldn't be able to do it alone, so she decided it was time to see just how much she could trust SAC Shackelford.

Miranda never trusted a man that wouldn't drink. So, when Shackelford accepted her Happy Hour invitation to talk about a case, she took it as a good sign.

"You hear the one about the kid, went to the local mafia boss and asks, 'What's it take to be a gangster?'" Shackelford said, as he took a sip of his Guinness. He was sitting across from Miranda at a high top at a local sports bar.

"The boss says, 'Well, being a gangster is about running your neighborhood. You collect payments from the local businesses, you keep outsiders off your turf, and you take care of your crew.' Couple weeks later, the kid comes back, says he's a gangster now.

"Boss asks what the hell he's talking about. Kid says he took a piece from his classmates who play dice for baseball cards on the playground, beat a couple of shine boys from the next neighborhood with his Little League bat when he caught them on his street, and he lied to the school principal about who was passing notes to get his friend out of detention. The boss says, 'You mean to tell me you shook down a gambling op, clubbed a couple niggers and framed an innocent guy? Congratulations, kid!' Kid asks, 'So am I a gangster now?' Boss replies, 'No. You're a Philadelphia Police Officer!'"

Miranda was unsure how she was supposed to react, so she stayed pokerfaced.

"That was a joke from back in my father's day," Shackelford said. "In short, that's why I became a cop."

Miranda nodded. "Change the system from within?"

Shackelford returned the nod. "Shake shit up."

Miranda decided to take a chance. "What do you know about a man named Pat Roti?" she said.

She knew that it was a dangerous question. Simply uttering the name could put both her and Shackelford in the crosshairs of one of the most dangerous people in the world.

Miranda told Shackelford about Pat Roti, his private military company, and the Useful Idiot Network. She told him she wanted to go after Roti for what he did at The Broad. Shackelford was resistant. The case had been closed and they weren't in the business of unsolving crimes. He was new and young. He was under immense pressure to perform. His every move was being scrutinized. Besides, based on what Miranda had told him, it was going to be next to impossible to prove Roti's involvement in The Broad.

"We won't know until we look," Miranda said. "As far as I can tell, no one has ever investigated this man. Guy like that has to have any number of skeletons in his closet. We can get him on something. I'm sure of it."

Shackelford didn't look convinced.

"Why did you say you became a cop again?" Miranda asked.

A small smile flashed across Shackelford's face.

"So, let's shake shit up," Miranda said.

Victor was in Boston chasing down a lead on Cal when the press conference aired. Images of his and Pat Roti's faces showed on the television screen in his hotel room. Special Agent Miranda Lopez of the ATF stood behind a podium, addressing a room full of press.

"The ATF is seeking these two men for questioning," Miranda said. "The first is Victor Xano. He is considered armed and dangerous. If spotted, do not approach him, and immediately call the authorities. The second man goes by Pat Roti. Both of these men are persons of interest in The Broad shooting."

This was going to severely hamper Victor's ability to hunt for Cal for a while. He glared daggers at Miranda on the TV and imagined all of the violent things he wanted to do to her.

Pat Roti was having dinner at Mastro's in Beverly Hills with a twenty-two-year-old Belarusian woman from Giselle's stable. Pat Roti only ever really had the time and the temperament to date professionals, but he still believed in acting like a gentleman, even if he was paying for the company. His smartphone vibrated and he read the news about Miranda's press conference. He saw that he was named as wanted for questioning. He did not seem bothered. In fact, he did not seem to react at all. He simply slipped the smartphone back into his blazer pocket and returned to his meal and conversation with Aksana, seemingly forgetting about the news as quickly as he had read it.

Miranda was sitting in her apartment when the press conference aired. This was typically the time of night she would be relaxing with a glass of red wine. Instead, she was oiling her service weapon. She finished reassembling it and took a deep breath.

Now all there was left to do was sit back and watch the world come undone.

36

A romantic violin concerto played low. The flicker of candlelight on the white tablecloth was enough to make any girl consider giving it up. Miranda hoped that that was where this was headed. She was definitely out to impress with this restaurant.

They'd met at a kickboxing class at Equinox. She used to take the class with Camilla and even though it had been a year, Miranda still wasn't ready to end the tradition. Her date's name was Alexandra. She liked that about her, that she went by "Alexandra," not "Alex" or "Allie." That, and the fact that she was twenty-three, fit, and had never been with a woman before.

The death of Camilla last year had left Miranda broken. She was not sure she was capable of ever loving anyone again. Alexandra didn't know what Miranda really was — a wolf, seeking only to devour.

Alexandra. The name sounded as elegant as the concerto.

The date ended with tiramisu, a short drive to Alexandra's home, and a kiss on the cheek. Miranda wanted more, but Alexandra said, "Not tonight." Miranda gently ran her hand through Alexandra's hair, said she was worth the wait, and that she'd text her. Baby dykes like this needed to be wooed.

Miranda parked in the garage beneath her apartment building. On the elevator up to her apartment, she remembered that she was out of coffee. She already knew she'd be bitter tomorrow because she was waking up alone. Add the absence of caffeine into the mix and a lousy morning could transform into something truly terrible. She decided to avoid that and walked down the street to the local Starbucks to pick up a bag of Pike Place.

When she returned to her apartment building with her bag of coffee, the doorman was away from his desk. She pulled out her building key, unlocked the door, and slipped into the lobby. As the door closed behind her, she was startled by a man standing outside. He seemed to have appeared out of nowhere.

He was white. Average height. Average build. Entirely forgettable. Except for his eyes. They were dark brown, large and intense and seemed to vibrate in their sockets.

"I just moved in and forgot my keys," Crazy Eyes said. "Could you let me in?"

Miranda shook her head. She had become extra cautious since last year, when a man named Wyatt Lemiuex broke into her apartment and killed Camilla. "I'm sorry."

"Seriously?" Crazy Eyes said.

Miranda moved away from the door. Maybe she was being paranoid. Maybe the guy was just a perfectly harmless new tenant and she was being a bitch.

But that was okay.

Miranda was used to people thinking she was a bitch.

In the morning, Miranda had a meeting at LAPD headquarters. She had fed them intelligence on Giselle's organization and urged them to crack down on sex trafficking. The department was less than receptive. Apathetic at best, complicit at worst. They said they'd look into her claims, but nothing ever came of it. Miranda had kept pushing. Today, she was meeting with the Chief of the Los Angeles Police Department. A man named

Leslie Boyle. He was a large white guy, a hardened career cop in his sixties. Despite his age, his hair and mustache were more brown than grey. At over six feet, two hundred pounds, and lean, this was a grandpa you'd think twice about tussling with.

Boyle rose from his desk and shook Miranda's hand as she entered. "Agent Lopez. I'm Chief Boyle. Nice to meet you."

"Thank you for making the time," Miranda said.

"Not at all," he said. "Please, have a seat." She sat across from him at his desk. "What can I do for you?" he asked.

"I'd like to know what's being done about the city's sex trafficking problem?"

"Right. We received your intelligence. It's been forwarded to our Human Trafficking Section."

"Why haven't they moved on it?"

"It's tricky. These people came here illegally. Most of the time, they don't even want our help. We've got enough to worry about protecting the rights of actual citizens."

"Spoken like a true asshole," Miranda said. She knew she needed to get better at making allies out of people, but she just couldn't help herself. It was the East L.A. in her.

Boyle grit his teeth and forced a smile. "Was there anything else, Agent Lopez?"

Miranda got out of the meeting at around 11:00 a.m., crossed 1st Street and approached a great food truck she knew about for an early lunch. Tamales just like mom used to make. She ordered a chicken tamale and a coffee and scrolled through emails on her phone while she waited.

Behind her, the art deco monolith of Los Angeles City Hall towered pristine and untouchable over a small park. The park's manicured green lawn was blemished with unsightly patches of dirt. The homeless were sprawled out like ragged sunbathers at the beach.

In the middle of the small park was the Frank Putnam Flint Memorial Fountain. It was made of marble from the same quarry as the Lincoln Memorial. It no longer ran, however. Instead of water, it was filled with old newspapers and discarded fast food containers.

The only reason Miranda looked away from her phone and turned around was because a homeless man asked her if she could spare some change. As a rule, Miranda didn't give change to panhandlers. It wasn't because she was callous. In L.A., if you gave change to every person that asked, you'd be broke in a week. She was about to tell the homeless man, "Sorry," when she spotted him by the Frank Putnam Fountain.

Crazy Eyes.

Watching her.

Miranda's body stiffened. She quickly reached into her pocket and handed the homeless man whatever loose change she had, then walked away from the food truck without receiving her tamale.

LAPD Headquarters was a fifteen-minute walk from her apartment, and she hadn't brought her gun. She could try to make it back to her apartment, but by now, Crazy Eyes had to know he'd been made. He was liable to do something, well, crazy.

Pat Roti had guys willing to shoot up a major modern art museum in broad daylight. Who knows what Crazy Eyes was capable of?

Crazy Eyes knew Miranda would have remembered him from last night, so when she spotted him in the park, he decided he wouldn't get another chance. It was now or never. He adjusted the Desert Eagle pistol in his coat pocket and trailed Miranda as she walked north up Spring Street. Funny. He figured she'd head south. Her apartment was south.

It didn't matter. She was in his sights and she wasn't going anywhere. He was closing the distance. Once he got within five feet of her, he'd pull out the Desert Eagle and blast her to kingdom come.

He was about ready to make his move when Miranda beelined up the stairs of City Hall's west courtyard. Crazy Eyes lost her for a moment among Greco-Roman columns and tiled mosaics. Then he spotted her again, walking briskly through the west entrance of city hall.

Crazy Eyes followed her into the yellow lit, golden art deco lobby. There were two cops and a metal detector. Miranda had already passed through the security checkpoint when Crazy Eyes entered.

Clever.

As Miranda approached the elevator bank, she looked back. Crazy Eyes stood on the other side of the metal detectors like a dog that had been abandoned by its master. She watched him turn and walk back outside, presumably to ditch whatever weapon he was carrying. All she'd done was buy herself some time. He'd be back.

She was counting on it.

Crazy Eyes ditched his Desert Eagle behind a bench in the west courtyard and reentered City Hall. He emptied his pockets — car keys, wallet, coins — into a tray and passed through the metal detector.

Most of City Hall was off-limits to the public. He figured that the observation deck was really the only place she could go.

He passed through the metal detector. "How do I get to the observation deck?" he asked one of the police officers as he retrieved his items from the tray.

"Take the elevator to the twenty-second floor. Cross the hallway to another elevator. You're gonna take that to twenty-six. There'll be a stairway that leads up to the observation deck. But you're gonna need a visitor's badge."

Crazy Eyes gave the police officer his name and ID. The police officer gave him a visitor's badge.

Crazy Eyes went to the elevator bank, pressed the Up button, and boarded one of the elevators. The inside was paneled in gold metal and glass. He pressed 22 and the elevator ascended.

When the elevator opened on the 22nd floor, Miranda was waiting.

"It would have been easier if you'd have just let me keep my gun," Crazy Eyes said, stepping off of the elevator. "Easier on you, I mean."

Miranda was petite, but that had never stopped her. She could do some real damage in a fight and had taken down guys three times her size. Crazy Eyes looked to weigh about a buck sixty.

He marched toward Miranda. She attempted to throw a jab. Crazy Eyes leveled her with a spinning wheel kick to her jaw.

Crazy Eyes happened to have a black belt in Taekwondo.

Miranda spit blood onto the tile floor and crawled to her feet. This was a fight she wasn't going to win. She retreated to a stair-case. Crazy Eyes grinned and calmly stalked her. He entered the stairwell and dodged the fire extinguisher that Miranda tried to smash into his face. He punched her in the throat and she dropped the fire extinguisher and gagged for air. She stumbled up the stairs. Crazy Eyes followed her. Taking his time.

She burst onto the 26th floor and shuffled up a short staircase, past a bust of former L.A. Mayor Tom Bradley's head, through a grand dining room with white tablecloths and long, ruffled burgundy curtains, and emerged onto the observation deck. The open-air deck gave a 360-degree view of the city. But there was nowhere to go but down.

Crazy Eyes followed her onto the deck like a dark shadow.

Survival is not neatly choreographed like a John Wick film. Survival is messy. Miranda had nowhere to go. She turned and faced her pursuer.

Who was he? Another member of Roti's Useful Idiot

Network? Another limp-dicked nobody bent on gunning down anything he disagreed with?

Fuck him.

In the movies, this was the part where the good guy overpowered the bad guy, hung him off the building ledge, and demanded, "Who sent you?" and the big, tough bad guy, facing the prospect of a four-hundred-foot drop, sang like a choirboy, but any real-life cop will tell you that the job is rarely like the movies. So, Miranda didn't waste any time or effort trying to choreograph the complicated hang-him-by-his-ankles-until-he-snitches scene. Instead, she charged wildly like a cornered animal and shoved the asshole with everything she had off of the side of the building.

Crazy Eyes fell thirty-two stories and smeared the pavement below. Shackelford had Miranda's back, but even he was going to have trouble weathering the scrutiny of one of his agents pushing an unarmed civilian off of the top of City Hall in broad daylight. But then they found the Desert Eagle stashed behind the bench in the west courtyard. Prints on the gun were eventually matched to what they were able to spatula from the concrete-grease-spot remains of Crazy Eyes's body.

But Miranda didn't wait for all of this. She didn't even wait for the authorities to arrive and turn the area into a crime scene. The first thing she did after Crazy Eyes's flight fail was go down to the lobby, show her ATF credentials, and ask to see the names of everyone that had been issued a visitor's badge that day.

One name in particular stood out. It was the name, she assumed, of the man with the crazy eyes that she had no less than five minutes ago shoved off of the side of that building.

His name was Carlo Roti.

37

C arlo Roti was born January 12, 1985 to Francesco "Frank" Roti and Fiona (née McIlhenny) Roti at Northwestern Memorial Hospital in Chicago.

Records show his first arrest at thirteen-years-old for shoving lit fire crackers up the asses of stray cats. What followed was a sheet of misdemeanors and felonies as long as a phonebook. His present place of employment was listed as ABB Construction, where he collected a paycheck as an engineer, even though he had no prior training or work experience in engineering.

Carlo's father, Frank, was an alleged member of the 26th Street Chinatown crew. See, while New York had five families, all with any number of their own crews, Chicago had five crews that made up one single family, and that family was called the Outfit.

Frank Roti was born in 1953 on Taylor Street to dirt poor immigrants from Abruzzi, Italy. His father made a living as a ditch digger. Frank cut his teeth on jewelry store robberies and drive-by shot-gunnings. He was looking at life without parole when he went missing. The cops assumed he had lambed it until they found his naked body hung by the asshole from a meat hook. His killers had taken a blow torch to his face. His skin was charred, his eyeballs popped, and his lips and ears were seared off. The cause of death was ruled asphyxiation from screaming. It was assumed that the deed was done by his own friends, guys he had known since he was a kid, because they were afraid that he might make a deal with the Feds, give them up for a reduced sentence.

Hell of a thing, the Chicago Outfit.

Anyway, at the time of Frank Roti's death, there was a rumor going around that he was going to take a deal. It was later revealed that Frank had no intention of snitching and that the rumor was spread by the FBI in an effort to pressure Frank to cooperate. That was the beginning of Carlo's lifelong hatred for the Feds. So, imagine how Carlo felt when he saw some ATF cooze on the TV badmouthing his Uncle Pat.

Carlo was mad in both senses of the word. Mad enough to drive to Los Angeles from Chicago. Mad enough to pay a Russian hacker to get him Miranda's home address. Mad enough to kill the bitch.

Or try.

It was going to be a closed casket funeral.

Records on Frank's lesser-known, or maybe just lesser-notorious, older brother were murky. He was born Pasqualino Roti some-where around 1941. No criminal record. He earned a Purple Heart and a Distinguished Service Medal in Vietnam. Throughout the seventies, his name popped-up here and there on declassified CIA briefs on operations in South America, the former Soviet Union, and the Middle East. By this time, he was going by Pat.

But after 1981, there was nothing on Pat Roti. No home addresses, no bank records, no tax returns, not even a parking ticket.

How did this seemingly good guy become the world's premiere recruiter of sociopathic killers? Miranda wondered, as she sat at her desk, perusing the files on the Roti clan. *What changed him?* The answer had to be somewhere in his past.

Carlo Roti's funeral was tomorrow. Miranda was booked on a 6:45 flight to Chicago that night. She figured the funeral would be a good place to gather intelligence on the elusive Pat Roti. She tried not to think of the old crime scene photograph she'd seen of Frank Roti's body hanging from the meat hook like charred fish bait. If these guys could do that to their friend, what would they do if they caught her?

Shackelford had tried to talk her out of it. He said he'd back her no matter what, but guys like Pat Roti don't go down. And he didn't want to see her get hurt.

Maybe he had a point, but despite all the reasons not to pursue this case, she had to keep going.

Why was that? she wondered. *Why did she have to do this?*

She thought about Cal and Eva, wherever they were.

And she thought about her childhood, growing up in East L.A. with her mom and four sisters. Her mother struggling every day to make ends meet. Hating the father she never knew, but at the same time knowing she would forgive him in an instant if he walked through their door. Wishing every day that this man she didn't know, this man that she hated, would walk through that door so that she could love him.

Now Eva had that chance. With Cal. Miranda could help spare Eva the pain she suffered never knowing her father. All that stood in the way was Pat Roti.

Miranda was packing up her files when Shackelford came to her office door.

"Got a walk-in. You should handle the interview," he said.

"Seriously? I'm on my way out the door."

"You're gonna want to handle this interview."

"I doubt that."

"It's Pat Roti."

38

P at Roti was pissed.

Not at Miranda or the ATF. He was pissed at Carlo. See, Roti never saw Miranda as a serious threat. At most, she was a pest. A little fly, buzzing. And Roti was prepared to let her buzz. He knew that the ambitious young agent could not touch him. He had not paid much attention to her at all, much less sent an assassin to kill her. But that's exactly what someone had tried to do. And that someone happened to share his last name.

He knew what was going through the dumb kid's head. It was supposed to be an honor killing. Old school guinea vendetta bullshit carried out by a mentally unstable guy who viewed his lowlife father as a "Man of Honor" and had seen *The Godfather* one too many times.

If Agent Lopez hadn't thrown Carlo off a building, Pat might have killed him himself.

He sat patiently in the FBI interview room with his hands resting on top of the silver lion's head of his cane. He wore a refined Hugo Boss navy suit with silver cufflinks and a blue and black paisley silk pocket square.

Miranda entered and stared at him with a mixture of suspicion and malice.

"You must be Special Agent Miranda Lopez," Pat Roti said, smiling at her. It seemed genuine. Not a hint of irony or arrogance. The old man used his cane to rise to his feet and offered his hand. Miranda shook it. His grip was firm.

"Where's your lawyer?" Miranda said.

"Oh, I don't think that's necessary, do you?"

Miranda shrugged. She dragged the chair opposite Roti out from under the interview table. It scraped against the linoleum floor. She sat across from him at the table. "We've been looking for you, Mr. Roti."

"I've been out of the country for work," Roti said. "I came as soon as I could."

"For work? Where?"

"I'm afraid I'm not at liberty to say."

Miranda scowled.

"As I'm sure you are aware, I own and operate a private military company," Pat Roti said. "We regularly subcontract to the DoD and the CIA, and, legally, there are some things I cannot disclose. You understand."

"Oh, yes. I understand a lot," she said, her glare cutting into him.

"No. I'm not sure that you do."

"Oh?"

"You think that I had something to do with my nephew's actions. I did not. He is a very disturbed individual."

"Was," Miranda said. "I threw him off a building, so he isn't anything anymore. He *was*," she said sharply.

Pat Roti smiled, unruffled. "Of course. 'Was.' Anyway, I'd like to apologize on behalf of the Roti family and let you know how extremely upset I am about this whole thing."

"What do you know about the shooting at The Broad museum in Downtown Los Angeles?"

"Only what I saw on the news. A mentally ill individual concluded that the only way to express his discontent with the world was through bullets and murder."

"Why did he choose The Broad museum?"

Pat Roti shook his head. "How should I know?" Pat Roti paused, tilted his head quizzically. "If you suspect that I have some sort of inside information about this tragedy, please present me with your evidence, so that I may clear it up immediately."

Miranda clenched her jaw.

"I know who you are," Pat Roti said. "That is to say, I'm familiar with your work. The Barros case last year. You did something truly heroic. I'm on your side, Agent Lopez. I understand and share your disdain for senseless violence."

Beneath the table, she squeezed her hands into fists. It was all she could do to keep herself from diving across the room and strangling him.

After the interview, Miranda walked Roti out. "Quite a show you put on in there," Miranda said to him once they were outside the ATF building.

Roti looked at her. "That wasn't a show. I meant every word of it."

"I know you were behind The Broad shooting. The only reason I can't prove it is because Cal would never testify against you." Miranda shook her head. "You're doing all of this to silence Cal when Cal has already proven that he won't talk."

"I don't expect you to understand it, but everything I do, ultimately, is for the greater good. That is all that motivates me."

"How does killing Cal fit into that?"

"It's a question of mathematics. Sixteen people were shot at the Broad. Seven of them died. Cal knows things that, if they ever got out, could start wars. Would you kill seven to save thousands? How about hundreds of thousands? How about millions? Wouldn't it be immoral not to?"

"Cal won't talk."

"I wish I could take that chance," Pat Roti said, as his Mercedes pulled up to collect him. "Cal knew the deal. He knew what he signed up for."

Pat Roti's driver, a six-foot soldier in a dark suit, circled around from the driver's side and opened the back door for him.

"And what about you and I?" Miranda asked.

"Don't go to Chicago," Pat Roti said. Miranda was taken aback. How did he know she was going to Chicago? It could have been a lucky guess, but probably not.

"Is that a threat?"

"God, no. You have nothing to fear from me. But those people — my family — they are thugs. You can keep coming for me, Agent Lopez. You're not the first and you won't be the last. And in a way, I admire you. I admire your heart and your values, naïve and misguided as they may be. But you won't succeed. You won't even come close. And it would sadden me to see you get yourself hurt over the pursuit of something so futile."

Pat Roti sat down in the back of the Mercedes and looked up at her. "But it is a free country and you will do what you will do. I only ask that you think about what I have said to you today. Good day, Agent Lopez."

And with that, the driver closed the door and circled around to the front of the Mercedes, sat behind the wheel and drove away.

After Pat Roti's Mercedes disappeared down the street, Miranda took out her cell phone and checked-in for her flight to Chicago.

39

No one could nail Pat Roti because no one knew anything about him. After his stint in the CIA, he didn't exist. There were virtually no records pertaining to Pat Roti after the mid-1980s, and even before that, his history was spotty. Heavily-redacted by the Company.

It was a cliché, she knew, but it was true. Pat Roti was a ghost.

So, Miranda's plan was to start at the beginning. To go back to where Pat Roti came from. Pat Roti grew-up in Chicago on Taylor Street in a place that used to be called "The Patch." It was once an Italian enclave but was now mostly eaten up by the University of Illinois Chicago campus. Today, it was more of a tourist attraction. Chicago's Little Italy.

Miranda walked beneath green-white-and-red tricolor flags and past Italian restaurants, pizza shops, and gelato stands peppered between Starbucks, Subway Sandwich Shops, and CVSs. A Middle Eastern restaurant. A Thai food joint.

Miranda had tracked down the address of the house Pat Roti had grown-up in. When she arrived, she found a row home with a sign out front that read: "JANELLE'S AFRICAN AMERICAN HAIR BRAIDING." Miranda wasn't sure if it was a licensed business or just something the homeowner had started on her own. As she entered the row house, she was eyeballed by a room full of clients.

There was a single, heavyset black woman working at a barber's chair in the living room. "Are you Janelle?" Miranda asked.

"I got nothing to say, officer."

Miranda smirked. "Is it that obvious? You're not in any trouble." Miranda showed the woman her shield. "I'm with the ATF."

"Damn," came a voice from the other room. "They send a Fed to bust me for operating without a license?" A pretty African American woman in her thirties stepped into the room through a beaded curtain. "Ya'll ain't playing."

"Janelle?"

"You got a warrant?"

"No. Like I said, you're not in any trouble. I need your help. Hear me out? Please?"

Janelle sized Miranda up, then pulled back the beaded curtain and gestured. "Step into my office."

Miranda walked through the beaded curtain into the kitchen.

"Have a seat," Janelle said. Miranda sat at the kitchen table. "What's this about?" Janelle asked.

"According to property records, your family bought this house in 1987."

"My daddy did," Janelle said.

"I'm investigating the family that lived here before you."

"Don't know nothing about them. I was just a child."

"And your father? Where's he?"

"Died a few years back."

"Is there anyone else in your family I can talk to?"

"Afraid not. It's just me."

There was a racket at the front of the house. "Afternoon, ladies. Everyone please stay seated," a man's voice said.

Janelle sighed. "Jesus. Again?" She reached above the refrigerator and removed a coffee can.

"Cook County Treasurer's Office," the man's voice called. Two Chicago Police Officers peeked their heads through the beaded curtain. They were in their thirties. One was white and the other was black. They didn't give Miranda a second look.

"This is the second time this week, fellas," Janelle said, as she fished a few twenties out of the coffee can.

The white cop flashed a shit-eating grin. "You know what they say about death and taxes."

"Wouldn't want to have to shut you down," said the black cop. Janelle glared at them as she shoved the money forward. The white cop took it, smiled, and nodded. "See you next week," he said, then he and his partner walked back the way they came.

Miranda rose from the table. "Don't cause trouble for me," Janelle said. Miranda grimaced and moved toward the door.

The two police officers crossed the street outside of Janelle's house and approached their parked cruiser. Miranda marched up behind them.

"Excuse me, officers?" Miranda said. The two cops turned back around and faced her. "What are your badge numbers?"

The two cops exchanged devious glances. "You want our badge numbers?" the white cop asked. They approached Miranda menacingly. "Now why would you ask for that?"

Janelle and her clients had gathered on her stoop to watch the showdown.

"Because I just witnessed you soliciting a bribe," Miranda said.

The two cops looked astonished. A little entertained. "You're not from around here, are you?" said the black cop.

"Look. If you knew what was good for you, you'd turn around and walk away right now," said the white cop.

"Badge numbers," Miranda said.

The white cop gritted his teeth and glanced at his partner. The black cop shrugged. "Alright. Hands behind your back," the white cop said. He reached for Miranda's wrist. Miranda caught his forearm, pinned his arm behind his back, kicked the back of his knee, and slammed his face against the hood of his cruiser. Blood gushed from his face.

The black cop drew his firearm and leveled it at Miranda. "Let him go!"

Miranda raised her badge. "ATF!"

The black cop hesitated. "Shit." The black cop glanced at Janelle and the half-dozen other witnesses standing on the stoop across the street.

"Lower your weapon," Miranda said.

The cop reluctantly lowered his gun. Miranda released the white cop. He wiped the blood from his face with his shirt cuff and rose to his feet.

"You're going to let my friend, Janelle, run her business in peace," Miranda said. "If you ever bother her again, I'll have you both brought up on corruption charges. Am I understood?"

The two cops glared at her murderously and nodded.

"Get the hell out of here," Miranda said. The cops loaded into their cruiser and drove away. Miranda walked back to Janelle.

"Alright, girl," Janelle said. "This way."

Janelle led Miranda back into her townhouse and down a rickety staircase to the basement. She pulled the light chord and a single bulb swayed in the dark, damp concrete room. The room was cluttered with junk dating back to the Taft Administration.

"We ain't ever got around to cleaning this place out. Stuff's been here since before we bought the place. Maybe there's something that could help you."

Miranda nodded. "Thank you."

"Alright, then." Janelle headed back up the stairs. Miranda rolled up her sleeves and got to work.

After hours of searching through hand-me-downs, old Christmas decorations and other junk, the only real record of Pat Roti's existence that Miranda could find was an old trucker's license. Apparently, Pat Roti had gotten a job as a truck driver and for whatever reason — maybe he was underage — he had a fake license made and, boy, was it a doozy. The kid in the black-and-white photo looked nothing like Pat Roti. The hair color was listed as red and he had pale skin like he was just off the boat from Ireland.

That wasn't going to be a lot of help.

Maybe she'd have better luck tomorrow at Carlo's funeral.

40

The FBI agent assigned to surveil Carlo Roti's funeral was named Derek Kim. He was a baby-faced twenty-three-year-old fresh out of Quantico. In contemporary Chicago, the Outfit didn't ping high on law enforcement's radar anymore. They were relics and didn't warrant much manpower or attention. Agent Kim's job was to sit in a car outside of the funeral home and take pictures of the people who attended the funeral and then file a report that no one would ever read. But Derek Kim was a glass-half-full kind of guy. He was a first-generation Korean American. His father ran a grocery store on Chicago's South Side. He worked eighteen hours a day, seven days a week to send his boy to college. Derek Kim knew the value of going the extra mile. Where others might have seen pointless busy work, Kim saw opportunity.

That's why he got a warrant from a judge to plant a wire.

He had visited the funeral parlor a few days earlier, posing as a grieving son looking for a place to hold his mother's viewing. He had planned on asking to use the men's room and installing the bug in there, but the men's room was out of service that day. A broken pipe or something like that. But the funeral director was happy to let him use the woman's room. With no other options, he installed the radio frequency bug under one of the sinks of the woman's room.

It wasn't much, but it was something.

So, when Carlo Roti's funeral began, Miranda found herself parked across the street in the front passenger seat of Agent Kim's sedan

The funeral wasn't a big affair. The Italian Mafia wasn't what is used to be. Edged out by the drug cartels in the south and the Russian and Chinese syndicates from the east. Carlo's crew was there, of course. White boys that made their nut on juice loans, sports betting, and wholesaling coke, H, MDMA, and crystal. Agent Kim dutifully photographed each one with his telephoto lens.

"Fiona Roti," Kim said. "Carlo Roti's mother."

Miranda sat up in her seat. Fiona Roti walked toward the entrance of the funeral parlor. She was a dour woman in her seventies.

After Fiona, a couple of higher-ups made appearances. These were the guys that Carlo's father, Frank Roti, would have grown up with. Some of them may very well have been part of the crew that tortured and murdered him all of those years ago. They were geriatrics now, who had only survived this long because they'd spent most of their adult lives in prison. Nowadays, they were more icons from a bygone era than actual gangsters. They had their legit businesses and their fingers in a few illegal pies, but mostly, they liked for things to stay quiet.

"Carlo's wife," Kim said. "Inés Hernandez-Roti."

Inés was a pretty, Spanish woman in her mind-thirties. She marched toward the funeral home, bundled in her coat against the cold.

It takes huevos to be the only brown girl in a room full of gringo gangsters, Miranda thought.

As the funeral began, Miranda and Kim found themselves listening to a cacophony of chatter on an RF receiver. Only instead of drug dealers and wise guys talking about incriminating shit, they were overhearing mob wives and girlfriends in press-on nails in the woman's room yapping about where they got their hair styled, their Botox injected, and their tits done.

It wasn't until after about an hour of this that something interesting happened.

On the receiver, they heard someone enter the woman's room.

"Fiona. I'm so sorry for your loss," a woman's voice said.

Miranda and Kim straightened up in their car seats. "Carlo's mother is there," Kim said.

They heard Fiona thank the woman, then the woman excused herself and returned to the funeral. It was quiet for a few moments. Fiona was alone.

"It's me," Fiona said.

"Who's she talking to?" Kim asked.

"That little cunt Inés is here, licking her fucking chomps. Now that Carlo is gone, she's going to try to take a bigger piece."

"She's on the phone with someone," Miranda said.

They heard Fiona sniffle. Her voice cracked "I wish you could be here with me. What they did to our boy."

Miranda tilted her head. *Our* boy. Who was she talking to?

"It's not about the money, Frank," Fiona said. "Why should Inés get to take what our son built?"

Miranda felt a pit in her stomach. She and Kim exchanged grave glances. Could Frank Roti still be alive?

"She knows that with Carlo gone, there's no reason for us to keep her around. She knows we'll be coming after her. It's us or her. Her only choice is to try to bring us down." Fiona paused and listened to whomever she was speaking to on the other line. "I'll take care of it. Trust me. No one will miss her," Fiona said.

After the viewing, a gaudy gold casket with the remains of Carlo Roti was carried out of the funeral home and loaded into a hearse. Kim and Miranda followed the funeral procession to the graveyard.

. . .

When they got back to Kim's office, Miranda and Kim discussed who Fiona could have been talking to on the phone.

"We don't even know for sure that she was on the phone," Kim said. "Heck, I still talk to my dead dad sometimes. The simple truth is, we don't know what we heard."

He was right. She thought about all of the times she spoke to Camilla when she was alone. Wounds leave scars and ghosts stay with us.

41

I nés Hernandez-Roti owned and operated a taco shop called Chica Organica in Downtown Chicago. It was an adorable, sort of sexy Mexican cantina. Bright and colorful. Pastel art deco. A neon pink sign read "Chica's" above and an illustration of a woman Miranda assumed was "Chica" herself — a gorgeous brown-haired, tan-skinned flamenco dancer with luscious red lips, who beckoned patrons to enter with her fuck-me eyes. It may have been the cutest little taco shop she ever saw. And it stood out on the cold Chicago street like a wild flower in a snowy wheat field. Miranda never would have guessed it was a drug front. Agent Kim had told her about how the bureau suspected that the taco restaurant was how Carlo washed his drug money. Miranda stomped the snow from her boots before entering.

Outside, it may have been snowing, but in here, it was hot, hot, hot. Salsa music played. The place was hopping. And at the heart of it all was Inés. When Miranda first saw her outside of the funeral home, she looked cold and mean, but in this setting, she was a damn knockout. Her arms were full of plates as she ran food to tables with the grace and sensuality of Chica herself.

Her hips swung seemingly in tune with the music. Miranda had trouble taking her eyes off of her.

Miranda took a seat in an empty booth by the front window. Inés approached, pulled on the collar of the tight shirt that clung to her chest to let in some air. "Ready to order?"

"How are your tamales?" Miranda asked.

"Excellent. We make them fresh in house. Family recipe."

"Better than my mother's?"

"Depends. How much did you love your mother?"

"Very much."

"I can't compete with that," Inés said, smiling and holding Miranda's gaze. She did not seem like someone who had just lost a husband. But it was more than that. Miranda felt like she was picking up a vibe.

"I'll have the chicken tacos, please," Miranda said.

"Rice and beans?"

"Please."

"Coming right up." Inés smiled at her again.

After Miranda finished her tacos, Inés returned.

"How was everything?"

"Delicious," Miranda said. "How do you stay so thin, working here?"

"You see how I run around this place?"

Miranda chuckled. "Please give my compliments to your boss."

"You're looking at her."

"No? You're the famous Chica?"

Inés laughed. "No. 'Chica' was my grandmother. I named the restaurant after her. She passed when I was a child."

"Well, you've been gifted with very good genetics." Miranda indicated the sign. "Your grandmother was a very beautiful woman."

Inés blushed and ran a hand over the nape of her neck.

"Only thing that could make this meal better would be a nice margarita," Miranda said.

"Yeah. Unfortunately, we don't have a liquor license. But there's a cantina off State Street called Rosa's that does it right."

"Rosa's off State Street," Miranda said. "Will I see you there?"

Inés smiled. "After how busy we were tonight, hell yes. I could use a drink."

Drinks at the bar led to dancing, led to drinks at Inés's apartment, led to mota, led to sex.

Inés's weed was some good shit. It made Miranda feel like she was possessed by an angel. The bed covers danced around their naked bodies like soft clouds.

But even through the heavenly fog, the fact shown like a distant lighthouse. Inés was not Camilla. This was hunger — Miranda's greedy wolf-like will to devour.

Inés was just meat.

"So, who are you?" Inés asked. She was laying in bed next to Miranda. Miranda was enjoying her customary post-coital joint.

"You wouldn't believe me if I told you," Miranda said.

"Oh, really?"

"You'd be like, what the hell did I just do, bringing this person into my home? Me jodí. I fucked myself Is that something you do often, by the way? Bring home random customers? I mean, I'm not complaining about the customer service or anything."

Inés chuckled. "I just escaped a very bad marriage. I was feeling good tonight and I felt like fucking the first pretty thing I saw."

"And when that didn't work out, you settled for me."

Inés chuckled again. "You're beautiful. In a don't-fuck-with-me kind of way."

Miranda smirked. "You have no idea."

"You're dodging my question."

"I'm just someone in town on a job."

"What do you do?"

Miranda leveled her eyes on Inés. "You're not gonna like it," Miranda warned. Inés furrowed her brow. "I'm in importing and exporting," Miranda said.

"Why wouldn't I like that?"

"Because what I import and export is not entirely legal."

Inés took the joint from Miranda and smiled. "I see. The 'good shit,'" she said, then took a hit.

"No. Not drugs."

Inés tilted her head. "What then?"

"Guns."

"Bullshit," Inés said. She reached beneath the mattress, pulled out a handgun, and leveled it at Miranda. Miranda stared back at her coolly.

"Sig Sauer P 226," Miranda said.

Inés grinned. "Very good." She slid the Sig back beneath the mattress.

Miranda had told Inés that her name was Esperanza Del Castillo. It was an old cover that the ATF had created for her for undercover work. If Inés were to look into it, she'd find out that Esperanza Del Castillo was a known L.A.-based firearms trafficker.

"So, tell me about this marriage?" Miranda said.

"That was the technical term for it."

"What do you mean?"

"It was more like a business arrangement."

"What kind of business arrangement?"

Inés eyed Miranda with uncertainty. Miranda took a big toke from the spliff. "You certainly don't have virgin lungs," Inés said.

Miranda shrugged. "This is some good shit."

"What are you doing tomorrow night?"

"I could make myself available." Miranda tilted her head back and exhaled smoke. "If it's worth it."

Inés smiled.

42

Miranda went shopping for an evening gown at Prada. Given the event, nothing less would suffice. She chose a black silk dress with a square neckline and a floor sweeping hem. It wasn't the nicest dress in the store, nor was it the cheapest. It was simple and elegant and, most importantly, it did not draw attention. When it came to picking a handbag, she chose something slightly oversized. The sales associate tried to talk her out of it, but she needed something that could accommodate the recording device and Glock 42 that the Chicago FBI would be providing for her.

After her night with Inés, she'd briefed Shackelford about her progress, and Shackelford liaised with the Chicago FBI Field Office. It was agreed that Inés and anyone she was connected with would be their bust. Pat Roti was the focus of the ATF's investigation. He was their prize.

Inés sent a limousine to pick Miranda up at her hotel. When the driver opened the door for Miranda, Inés was already in the back seat. Miranda smiled as she ducked into the limousine and pecked Inés on the cheek.

"I looked you up," Inés said. "Turns out you're legit."

"What's that mean? You googled me?"

"I had my people do it."

"What type of 'people' does a taco shop owner have?" Miranda said, playing dumb.

At this, Inés chuckled, reached across Miranda's lap and clicked her seatbelt around her waist. "Buckle your seatbelt, baby," she said.

Miranda couldn't escape a feeling of déjà vu as the limousine pulled up to the Chicago Museum of Metropolitan Art. Images of the lurid crime scene after The Broad shooting flashed through her mind. The valet opened the limousine door and Miranda and Inés walked up the red-carpeted staircase toward the boxy concrete building.

Chicago's aristocracy was gathered for a private dedication ceremony. Champagne flutes. Tuxedos and evening gowns. Servers patrolled like sentries with trays of fancy hors d'oeuvres.

"Well, this is unexpected," Miranda said to Inés. They roamed the gallery. Miranda didn't get to museums much, but she recognized one piece for all the wrong reasons. It looked exactly the same, only the last time she had seen it, it was at The Broad, colored magenta, and dappled with bullet holes.

But this giant, stainless-steel balloon dog was orange. "I love this one," Inés said. "It's supposed to be a reminder of childhood birthdays. Cherished memories. You blink and they're gone. As time goes by, you cherish them more because they're gone. You miss it more, it grows bigger. Until it's a giant."

Miranda's eyes became distant. In every inch of the mirror-polished orange steel, she saw Camilla. "I know the feeling," she said.

Miranda and Inés moved toward the front of the room, where a museum official stood at a microphone, preparing to make an announcement.

"You know what it is to build a business. On your own, from the ground up," Inés said to Miranda.

"I'm sure owning and operating a restaurant is no picnic," Miranda said in a tone that was subtly belittling.

"The restaurant is not my only source of income," Inés said. "I am what you might call an entrepreneur."

"Oh?" Miranda said, feigning surprise.

Inés nodded toward the front of the room. "That man's name is Luke Corrigan."

Luke Corrigan stood before the gathered crowd with the museum official and his date, an anorexic-thin white girl. That malnourished look that high fashion loves. Luke was a white guy in his forties in a black Prada suit and a gold Piguet time-piece. He was handsome, built like a retired boxer. Scrappy, but a pound or two over being lean. The result of wealth and comfort. Miranda's immediate impression was that Luke wasn't born rich, but now he was and it had made him complacent.

"He gives himself too much credit," Inés said. "He is trying to edge me out of what I built. Men can be like that."

The museum official tapped the mic and the room grew silent. He spoke for a few minutes about the history of the room they were standing in and the various exhibits it had housed over the years. Then he spoke at length about their generous benefactor, Luke Corrigan, and how all this proud Chicago busi-nessman's many donations had benefited the museum.

"In thankful recognition of his many charitable donations over the years," the museum official said, wrapping it up, "it is my honor to officially inaugurate the Luke Corrigan Atrium."

The crowd applauded. Luke spotted Inés in the crowd. His eyes lingered on her.

After the speech ended, Chicago's high society went back to mingling. Luke glad-handed his way across the room to Inés like a man trying to put out a secret fire. "I wasn't expecting to see you here," he said.

"You invited me," Inés replied.

"Yes, but given Carlo… I'm so sorry, by the way."

"I got your flowers."

Luke turned to Miranda and smiled. "And this is?"

"My plus one."

"Esperanza Del Castillo," Miranda said, offering her hand.

"Pleasure to meet you, Miss Del Castillo," he said as he gingerly took her hand and kissed her knuckles.

"I've been trying to get a meeting," Inés said.

"Take a breath," Luke said.

"Business does not stop just because Carlo is dead."

Luke's eyes darted around, worried that his rich friends might overhear.

"If only they knew what you really are," Inés said, raising her voice slightly. "How long do you think until they see through this 'Great Gatsby' act?"

"Not here."

"It has to be tonight."

Luke sighed. "My office. One hour."

Inés nodded.

"It makes you look weak, you coming here like this. Enjoy the hors d'oeuvres." Luke said, then he marched away.

Luke's office was in a luxury building in the Loop. Inés and Miranda approached the security desk and gave their names to the guard on duty. A military-looking guy that on appearance alone struck Miranda as overqualified for night security work at a corporate office building.

"This way," the guard said.

Miranda and Inés followed the guard to a bank of elevators. The security guard approached one of the elevators, swiped his badge. The doors opened and Miranda and Inés entered. The security guard pressed the appropriate floor number and the elevator doors closed.

When the doors opened again, a bodyguard built like a boulder was waiting. Without a word, the Boulder gestured for Miranda and Inés to follow him.

Luke's office was expensive and modish. A large eastern-facing window offered a picturesque view of downtown Chicago and Lake Michigan beyond. Luke was pacing in front of the window speaking Mandarin into his Bluetooth when the Boulder escorted Miranda and Inés into the room. After a few more minutes of Mandarin, Luke ended the call and turned to his guests.

"You're a purist, if I remember correctly," he said to Inés.

Inés squinted. "Sorry?"

Luke moved to the wet bar in the corner of his office. "Fresh lime juice, Cointreu, tequila, and a splash of orange juice." He added the ingredients to a shaker as he spoke. "A true purist."

He salted the rims of three glasses, filled them with ice, shook the shaker, and poured the margaritas. "Cheers," he said, indicating for them to take a glass. Miranda and Inés reluctantly approached the wet bar and accepted their drinks. The Boulder loomed in the corner of the room like a grizzly.

"To Carlo," Luke said, raising his drink, a smug grin creased on his face. Inés did all she could not to scowl. The three of them tapped their glasses and drank. Luke moved to the window with his cocktail and slowly exhaled. He took in the view.

"You know, I grew up here in Chicago. Grand Avenue," Luke said. "I hardly recognize this city anymore. The streets, they used to sing with energy like improvised jazz. Now it's all soulless elevator music. Bloodless and superficial. Like plastic surgery on a corpse. There's nothing authentic about her anymore."

He turned back to face Inés and Miranda. "How's the family?" he asked.

"You mean, the Rotis?" Inés said.

"Yes. The family. They holding up okay?"

"I'm not here to talk about the Rotis."

"Well, in a way, you are. They certainly figure into this," Luke said. Then he glanced at Miranda. "Why's she here?"

"I'll get to that," Inés said. "It *is* a hell of a view." She gestured to the large office window. "Don't forget. You wouldn't have it without me."

"What you and Carlo started was mom-and-pop. I'm the one that turned it into Walmart."

"I can cause problems for you," Inés said.

"Goose feathers."

Inés flinched. "What?"

"Seventy percent of goose feathers in this country come from China. Some unfortunate chink mallard's about to bite the dust, they strip it for parts, bring the meat to market and ship off the feathers to the good ol' U.S. of A. to stuff our pillows and down comforters.

"It's a common misconception that we import most of our stuff from China. They're actually only responsible for about fifteen percent of the United States' total imports — on the licit market."

Luke smirked mischievously. "China is, however — and this is rough because economists can never be too accurate when it comes to the black market — but China is responsible for approximately eighty percent of the United States' supply of illicit fentanyl.

"For a humble import merchant like myself, that eighty percent, that's my nut. It's a business those Cartel fucks have been trying to muscle in on for years. Even tried to synthesize their own — at only a fraction of the purity." Luke grinned with gusto at this.

"The Mexican cartels are trying to move in. They want my connect. They want my business," Luke said. "I trusted Carlo. You just happened to be his wife and his business partner."

"So, you don't trust me because I am a woman or because I am a Mexican?" Inés asked.

"Both, *mamacita*. I am well-aware of your connections to the Sinaloa Cartel. So, I made a deal with the Rotis. You'll have to talk to them about where you fit into it."

"You think you can cut me out?"

Luke just shrugged. "Just business."

"What if I cut you out instead?"

Luke scoffed.

"Esperanza is a smuggler," Inés said.

Now Miranda knew why Inés had brought her along. It was a bluff, but maybe not such a bad one. If Luke researched the backstory of "Esperanza Del Castillo," he would see that she was an international arms smuggler. If someone like "Esperanza" partnered with Inés, they could potentially import their own drugs without him.

"You cut me out, I go directly to the Chinese, undercut you on price, and use Esperanza to import."

"Are you looking for a war?"

"Are you?" Inés said. "If I'm as connected to Sinaloa as you say, soldiers won't be a problem."

Luke paused. "Do the Rotis know about this?"

"I'm talking to you."

"What do you want?"

"Now that Carlo is gone, I absorb his share."

"The only person I answer to is Carlo's old man," Luke said. Miranda tilted her head. *Carlo's old man.* Yet another indication that Frank Roti was still alive. "I can't cut out the Rotis," Luke said.

"I'll handle the Roti family."

Again, Luke paused. He clicked his tongue, glanced at Miranda, and then back at Inés. "Okay. Talk to the Rotis. I'll respect whatever they decide."

After the meeting, Inés explained to Miranda that now that Carlo was gone, Luke (the broker) and the Rotis (the distributors) were trying to cut her out of the drug business that she had basically built for them. A Latina independent operator (her ties to Sinaloa were mostly bullshit) needed muscle. That's where Carlo and his crew came in. It was a marriage of convenience. A business arrangement. Carlo was stupid and crazy enough for Inés to manipulate to her ends. She built up a distribution network for coke, MDMA, heroin. Enter Luke with his China connect for fentanyl. That's when shit really took off. Luke got it into the States, but without Inés, he was like a twelve-year-old boy with his dick in his hands, didn't know what to do with it. Inés had the network. Inés made everyone rich —Luke, the Rotis — but now that Carlo was dead and the business was already established, Luke and the Rotis figured they didn't need the enterprising Mexicana anymore.

So, she brought Miranda, or "Esperanza," as she knew her, to the meeting. She bluffed and Luke flinched. Now all Inés had to do was go talk to the Roti family. She asked if Miranda would come with her. Her presence would strengthen the lie that they were in business together (and not just random fuck-buddies that had only met a day ago). Miranda feigned hesitance before accepting the invitation.

"Do you have a gun?" Inés asked.

"I can get one," she said, not mentioning the FBI-issued Glock 22 in her handbag.

"Good," Inés said. "Let's go see my mother-in-law."

43

———

After their meeting with Luke, Inés made a stop in Chicago's Little Village neighborhood. She led Miranda into a windowless, nondescript building. A skeleton draped in robes like the Virgin of Guadalupe stood at the front of the dim, candle-lit room. In one hand, she held a globe and in the other, a scythe. Inés knelt and placed a few folded hundred-dollar bills among the candy, cigarettes, nips of tequila, and other offerings at her bony feet.

There were different colored candles lit at the altar. Gold for money. Red for love. Purple for psychic insight. Green for justice. Blue for wisdom. White for purity.

Inés lit a black candle. Black for the destruction of her enemies. Black for protection against evil.

It was when they were leaving the Santa Muerte shrine that Miranda arrested her.

Miranda's undercover op was going better than anyone at the FBI had ever imagined it would. She'd already brought in Inés and incriminated Luke Corrigan. Those busts would be credited to the FBI. The agreement Miranda had made with the bureau in exchange for their help was that her case was Pat Roti and only Pat Roti. As for the FBI, they were over the moon. Luke Corrigan was no small fish and they had him on tape admitting to importing fentanyl. Miranda was beginning to close in on the Roti family, but she wasn't sure how much closer she was to Pat Roti himself.

She'd have to keep digging.

Miranda was in the viewing room at the Chicago FBI field office with Agent Kim. She watched Inés through the one-way glass mirror. Inés was sitting in the interrogation room, drumming her nails on the table impatiently. It was always awkward questioning someone you just slept with, but Miranda was well-practiced. Aside from maybe Camilla, she had never trusted anyone she slept with.

"We have you on Drug Trafficking, Inés. Dead-to-rights," Miranda said, as she sauntered into the interrogation room. "I was wired-up for your whole conversation with Luke." She remained standing, looking down on Inés.

Inés would not meet Miranda's eyes. She just kept drumming her nails.

"Luke. He's going to go down, too. And soon, we'll have the Rotis. These are dangerous people, Inés. People with reach. And because of you, very soon they will all be looking at long stretches in federal prisons. How do you think they're going to feel about that? How do you think they're going to feel about *you*? You need to help us so we can help you. It's your only option."

From Inés, nothing. Only the sound of her nails clicking on the table.

"Luke Corrigan said that the only person he answers to is 'Carlo's old man.' What did he mean by that?"

Finally, Inés stopped tapping her fingernails on the table. She shook her head and looked Miranda in the eye. "You stupid bitch. You have no idea what the fuck you're walking into."

She resumed drumming her nails on the table. She would say nothing else.

Miranda returned to the viewing room. "If Frank Roti is still alive, who was the guy found tortured and murdered back in 1967?" Miranda asked Kim. Inés was visible through the one-way mirror in the interrogation room, her mouth shut tighter than a steel trap.

Miranda and Kim decided to hold off on arresting Luke until after Miranda visited Fiona Roti. The only thing that Miranda knew for sure was that Inés was right. She didn't have any idea what the fuck she was walking into.

If she had, she would have been on the next flight back to L.A.

44

Fiona Roti lived in a middle-class colonial in the Chicago suburbs. The Chicago FBI had loaned Miranda an impounded BMW. She had to look the part. She parked the beamer in the driveway behind Fiona Roti's Cadillac. She got out of the BMW, approached the front door, and prepped herself.

When Fiona Roti answered the door, there were tears streaming down Miranda's face. Fiona watched her neutrally. If she was surprised, she didn't show it. She had a great poker-face. She was in her seventies, but looked younger. Her hair was colored dark brown and thinning on the top. Her skin was remarkably smooth for a woman of her age. Her body was round but hard. So were her eyes.

"My name is Esperanza," Miranda said through tears. "And I loved your son."

After a moment of coldly sizing Miranda up, Fiona stepped aside. "Please, come in, dear."

"I'm sorry for coming here like this," Miranda said, stepping into the house. "But I've been a mess since Carlo's death. I couldn't even go to the funeral."

"You were his mistress?"

"We were in love," Miranda said. "Carlo never loved Inés. He only stayed with her for the business."

"The business?"

"I'm not here about that. I'm not looking for money."

"Then why are you here?"

"I guess I don't know," Miranda said, lowering her head. "I just miss him so much." She continued, tears streaming down her face.

"That's okay, dear. Have a seat," Fiona said, indicating the living room sofa. "Would you like some tea? Something stronger?"

"Whatever you're having," Miranda said.

Fiona disappeared into the kitchen. Miranda's eyes quickly assessed the room. On a bookshelf, she spotted a photograph of a man that might have been a younger Pat Roti.

Fiona reentered the living room with two Irish whiskeys. She handed one to Miranda. "Something to warm you up." They clinked glasses and drank.

"How long were you with Carlo?"

"A couple of years. He was planning on leaving Inés as soon as he could extricate her from the business, but it was proving to be more complicated than he thought."

"She is a stubborn one," Fiona said. She took a sip of her whiskey. "So, what is it you want from me?"

Miranda shrugged. "Just to talk. I never got to meet his family. I miss him so much and I have no one to talk to about him."

"I understand, dear."

"Oh, is that Carlo's father?" Miranda said, indicating the photograph on the bookshelf of whom she suspected was a younger Pat Roti.

Fiona turned and looked at the photograph. A thin smirk crept across her face. She rose without answering and went to the bookshelf. She removed an old album and returned to

Miranda. "This is Carlo's baby book," Fiona said, opening the album on the coffee table. "I started it when he was born."

On the first page, there were prints of baby Carlo's hands and feet. A lock of his black hair. There were photographs of his first day of school, first communion, first trip to Disney World. His first lost tooth.

She saw a photo of a man that looked like a younger Pat Roti with who she assumed was the bad brother. Carlo's father, Frank. He had pale skin and red hair. "Who's that?" Miranda asked, indicating the photograph.

"That's Carlo's father, Frank, and his brother, Pat "

Miranda was confused. She already knew the photograph was of Frank and Pat, but when Fiona identified them, she got it backwards. She pointed to the red-haired man when she said Pat and the dark-haired man when she said Frank. Pat Roti wasn't a redhead.

Maybe she had made a mistake. So, Miranda tested her. "Carlo didn't inherit his father's red hair."

"Red hair is uncommon in Italy. Something like one percent. In Sicily, they call them *normanne*, or Normans," Fiona said, then her eyes darted to Miranda. "But Carlo's father didn't have red hair."

Miranda got a sinking feeling in her stomach. Remembered reading the autopsy of Frank's corpse, burnt beyond recognition. Not a hair left on his head.

And then she recalled something that was, in many ways, more frightening. She recalled young Pat Roti's trucker's license. The one she had found in Janelle's basement. She had assumed it was a fake because the boy in the photograph looked nothing like the Pat Roti she knew. His hair color was listed as red. What if it wasn't a fake? What if that was the real Pat Roti?

"Are you starting to figure it out, Agent Lopez?" Fiona said.

Miranda froze. It all made sense now — Pat Roti's uncanny ability to recruit and control sociopaths.

It was the story of two brothers. One good and one evil. So

evil that he was wanted for murder. He was looking at the death penalty. So the evil brother, in order to stay out of prison, hung his red-headed good brother from a meat hook and burnt off his hair, face, and fingerprints with a blowtorch. He stole his identity and shipped off to Vietnam where he made a name for himself as a sociopathic killer.

Yeah, Pat Roti was a ghost alright.

And Frank Roti was the motherfucker wearing his skin.

The room began to spin. Miranda reached for her handbag, but it was gone. Fiona must have taken it. When did she do that? Everything was getting foggy. What was happening to her?

"You must think we're really stupid," Fiona said. Her voice seemed distant even though she was sitting only a few feet away. "You didn't think I'd know the identity of the bitch who killed our son?" Fiona took a sip from her glass of whiskey and calmly crossed her legs. "So, now that you know who you are fucking with, I only have one question for you." She placed her glass on the coffee table and leaned forward. "How fast can you run?"

Miranda heard a car engine roaring down the street.

"That'd be the boys," Fiona said. "I texted them when I was spiking your whiskey with barbiturates."

Miranda looked at her empty glass with dread. She rose and shuffled toward the door.

She saw headlights approaching down the street like the eyes of a dragon. She stumbled to the BMW, swung open the door, and slid into the passenger's seat. She pressed the ignition button, turned the wheel, and recklessly reversed out of the driveway, kicking up grass and dirt and toppling Fiona's mailbox. She put the car in drive as a gunshot rang out behind her and shattered the Beamer's back window. The car's tires screeched and kicked up dust as Miranda floored it.

The road wouldn't stay in one place. Miranda struggled to hold the wheel steady and keep her head level. She fought back the urge to close her eyes. She could feel the barbiturates in her system dragging her down toward unconsciousness. She looked in her rearview mirror and saw a dark blue Suburban on her tail. A murky figure hung out of the passenger side window. Muzzle flashes illuminated the pistol in his hand.

Miranda swerved through the sleepy suburbs, down dimly-lit streets, toppling garbage bins and street signs. She slid her iPhone out of her pocket and divided her focus between staying on the road and dialing. Before she could finish dialing, her phone rang. The callers ID read: "UNKNOWN NUMBER." She ignored the call. Jerked the wheel, righting the car just before it drifted off the road. She resumed dialing, but was interrupted again by an incoming call. "UNKNOWN NUMBER." Her engine raged as gunfire popped behind her in vicious bursts. She answered the call.

"Hello?"

"Hello, Agent Lopez." Miranda wasn't sure if it was the drugs or if she was really hearing who she thought she was hearing. "It's Pat Roti," the voice said.

"Pat Roti was murdered in 1967," Miranda said.

The voice chuckled. "Am I my brother's keeper?"

"Fuck you," Miranda said. She hung up the phone and began to redial.

Behind, the Suburban roared like charging bull and slammed her bumper. Her neck snapped back, her head slammed against the headrest, and the phone slipped from her grasp. She shook away the haze, tried to focus. With one hand on the wheel and her eyes on the road, she bent forward and reached down into the darkness beneath her, searching for the phone. The Suburban slammed into the rear bumper again. Miranda's body was thrown back violently against the seat and she felt a sharp pain in her spine. The shooter hanging out of the window popped a new mag into his handgun and released another barrage of bullets. Bullets whizzed by her head, peppered her windshield. She felt her body jerk forward and a burning pain in her right shoulder. Her arm slid from the wheel. She could not move it. She saw the blood streaming down the right side of her body. She'd been hit.

And still, the drugs were willing her to sleep.

She jerked the wheel right and fishtailed up the exit ramp of I-290. She had to get off of these dark and quiet backstreets. Get someplace public. They weren't going to gun her down in a populated area.

Horns blared and tires screeched. She was speeding east on I-290 West, dodging traffic. The Suburban remained in dogged pursuit. She drifted over the median and merged onto I-290 East. She could see the cityscape of Chicago on the horizon, shining like a beacon. She sped recklessly. Where was fucking highway patrol when you needed them? Other motorists would be calling the police. She just had to hold on a little longer.

"Do not go gentle into that good night," Camilla said. Miranda looked at the seat next to her and saw Camilla staring back. Her hair was shiny and dark. Her skin black and smooth. She hadn't changed at all since the day Miranda lost her. She was glowingly beautiful. And for whatever reason, Miranda's doped-up psyche had her reciting Dylan Thomas.

Miranda's head began to droop. The car drifted back across the median and into the westbound lanes. "Rage."

Up ahead, Miranda saw a light.

"Rage against the dying of the light."

Miranda sped toward the blinding light.

"I love you," Miranda said to Camilla, as the beam of light split in two and a horn blared and Miranda closed her eyes.

Miranda drove headfirst into a dump truck. The truck had tried to swerve out of the way, but ended up crushing the BMW under its tires like a coke can, reducing the vehicle to a smoking jumble of mangled steel guts.

PART IV

THE HOLY REAPER

45

After Cal shot Jim Snodgrass on the shores of Walpole Island, he hid Snodgrass's duck hunting boat in the marsh. Cal and Eva used it to cross back into the United States. Once there, Cal used cash to buy a 1991 Ford F150 he had seen advertised in someone's driveway.

It was a two-day drive back to Los Angeles. When they arrived, Cal and Eva laid low in Sly's old warehouse. After Sly's murder, the ATF took his surveillance system as evidence, but the fortified doors and doorbell cam were still there. They also left the arcade games — Pac-Man, Space Invaders, Galaxian — and the halfpipe. Cal didn't know where Sly had been siphoning his electricity from, but the ATF hadn't turned it off. Cal went to the hardware store and changed the locks, and pretty soon he and Eva had their own fortress.

It was Friday night. Cal told Eva he was going out and he'd be back later. He drove to a burger restaurant and ordered a hundred burgers to go. He brought the burgers to Skid Row and handed them out to the people there.

Cal had known an ex-marine that lived on Skid Row. Cal would sit with him, sometimes for hours. They'd never exchanged a single word, but Cal felt that they knew each other. Really understood one another. They didn't need words.

That was how he now felt when he was with Eva. Their silences were comfortable. On the road back to Los Angeles, the two hardly spoke. They didn't need to.

When Cal returned to the warehouse, he found Eva methodically disassembling and cleaning her weapons. Watching her, she reminded him of himself. He had tried to make her self-sufficient, but he had made her just like him.

And that scared him.

Eva was aware of how Cal had changed her. She remembered her virology textbook and thought Cal was not unlike a type of virus.

Not good, not evil.

But contagious.

She remembered how she read that some scientists viewed viral epidemics and pandemics as nature's way of fighting back against humanity's overreach. Overpopulation and deforestation caused the right conditions for a virus to form and spread and kill like a form of population control, returning the environment to a level of stasis.

Cal was stasis. Cal was equilibrium.

Somewhere between a saint and a monster.

And now I am too, Eva thought.

Cal wasn't sure why he returned to Miranda's apartment. She was dead. He wasn't sure how he felt about that. It wasn't anything new. Death figured largely in his day-to-day life.

Part of him wanted to know why she'd been killed. What had she uncovered that so threatened Pat Roti? The news had been sparse on details, only reporting that an ATF agent had been killed in a head-on collision with a dump truck. She had been driving the wrong way down the highway. The authorities would not say whether or not she was intoxicated, only that the investigation was ongoing. Cal knew Miranda well enough to understand that this was no random accident.

He waited across the street from her apartment building. From here, he had a clear view through the building lobby's window of the front desk. A single doorman manned the desk. Cal waited until the doorman was called away, then he made his approach. The door required a FOB to enter, but it still had an old school key lock as backup. Cal had no problem picking the lock. He slipped into the building unseen and took the stairs up to Miranda's floor, picked the lock to Miranda's apartment and entered.

He wasn't sure what he was looking for. Some clue of why she died. What that might look like, he had no idea.

It didn't take him long to find a file box in the living room. As he fingered through it, the hairs raised on the back of his neck. The name, "Roti," over and over again. Miranda had been investigating everyone in Pat Roti's family.

Cal's eyes darted to the door. There were footfalls on the carpeted hallway outside, imperceptible to all but the most trained ear. The fact that they were so silent told Cal that this wasn't just some passerby. This was someone trying to conceal their approach. This was someone that was there for him.

Cal approached the apartment door, stood to the side, reached out and slowly turned the knob. He waited a moment. He knew the person outside would have seen the door knob turn and waited for the door to open. When it didn't, they'd worry that they'd been made. And that was exactly what happened.

The person outside kicked the door open. A man in a suit with a raised Glock 19M charged into the room. "Federal Agent!" he shouted. He spotted Cal over his shoulder, but it was too late. Cal twisted the man's wrist, disarming him of his pistol, and kneed him in the gut. The man in the suit keeled forward, gasping for air.

Cal marched out into the hallway. If this man really was a Fed, he would have called for backup before entering the apartment. Cal estimated the average police response time in this area to be approximately five minutes. Cal had more than enough time to get away clean. On the other hand, if the man was actually one of Pat Roti's goons, Cal could expect more resistance.

But nothing he couldn't handle.

Cal pulled back the slide on the Glock. He took the stairwell down to the lobby. It was quiet. Guy must have been ATF like he said, which meant Cal had plenty of time to leg it. He slid the Glock into his waistband and walked out onto the street.

The police cruisers came out of nowhere. They peeled up and surrounded him on all sides. The car doors opened and uniformed cops aimed their service weapons. Their police sirens were off, which meant when the ATF guy radioed them, they were ready to go. This wasn't just an ATF surveillance op, it was a sting. They were waiting for him. Cal was so focused on breaking into Miranda's apartment, he hadn't considered that he was walking into a trap. Why would he? Miranda was already dead. What reason would the ATF have for watching her apartment?

"Hello, Cal," Shackelford said as he approached. "We've been waiting for you."

46

They told Cal he wasn't under arrest, but they still cuffed him.

"For our safety," Shackelford said. "You have something of a reputation."

They led him to one of the unmarked ATF sedans. "Watch your head," Shackelford said as he guided him into the back seat and closed the door. Shackelford got into the driver's seat and drove Cal back to the ATF's field office in Glendale.

They led him into the interrogation room and that was where he saw a ghost.

Miranda certainly looked better than the BMW she had been driving, but not much. Both of her eyes were purple and her nose was swollen. She leaned on crutches because her right leg was broken. She wore a brace for her cracked ribs, and her right shoulder was in a cast.

"It looks worse than it is," Miranda said.

"Better than dead," Cal said.

"Misinformation," Shackelford explained. "To keep my agent safe. We arrested Fiona Roti, but we still can't connect any of this to Pat Roti, or 'Frank,' or whoever the hell he is."

"What?" Cal said.

"Long story," Miranda said.

"He's still out there," Shackelford said. "And as I understand it, he is beyond dangerous. I decided it would be better if he thought Miranda was dead. Otherwise, he might try to finish the job."

Cal nodded. "So, what do you want with me?" he asked Miranda.

"I thought you'd want to be here for it," Miranda said.

"For what?" Cal asked.

Pat Roti brought his lawyer with him this time. He waited in the ATF's interrogation room, tapping his foot impatiently.

"I don't have time for this!" he shouted to whomever was listening through the one-way glass. He was all worked-up. Angry and indignant. But when the interrogation room door opened and he saw Miranda standing there in her casts and crutches, he blanched. His eyes widened. He became very still and quiet.

Miranda limped across the linoleum floor, deliberately taking her time, and took a seat at the interview table across from Pat Roti.

"Mr. Roti," she said. "Pleasure to see you again."

Pat Roti's throat was suddenly very dry.

"I see you brought your attorney with you this time," Miranda said, nodding at the lawyer with a thin smirk. "I'm wondering if you might prefer speaking privately? You know, off-the-record?"

"Absolutely not," Roti's lawyer said. "What the hell is this?"

Pat Roti tried to speak, but he had to clear his throat.

"You sound parched. Would you like a glass of water?" Miranda asked. "Can we get Mr. Roti a glass of water, please?" she called to the one-way mirror.

Miranda leaned forward and tapped her pen on the interview table. "Now, Frank, as I was saying—"

"Pat," the lawyer said.

Miranda looked at him. "I'm sorry?"

"You called him 'Frank.' My client's name his Pat. Jesus. Do you even know what interview you're in? This is unbelievable!"

Miranda grinned at Roti smugly. "My mistake. *Pat.*"

Just then, the interrogation room door opened. Cal entered with a dixie cup of water. Roti's eyes focused on him like lasers. Cal gingerly placed the cup of water on the table in front of Roti.

"Get out." Roti was talking to his lawyer, but his eyes remained staring at Cal.

"Mr. Roti. I must advise against—"

"Get out!" Roti screamed. It was the first time Miranda had ever seen him lose his cool. The lawyer lowered his head like a scolded schoolboy, gathered his things, rose, walked past Cal and out the door.

Miranda nodded at the one-way mirror and the red power light on the camera in the corner of the ceiling turned off.

"Off-the-record," Miranda said to Roti.

"Nothing is ever off-the-record in a police station," Roti said. "But I think maybe we should have a discussion." He was still glaring at Cal.

"Here's what it is," Miranda said. "I know who you are. You're Frank Roti. You know that I know this. You know that I know about how in 1967, you tortured and murdered your own brother, stole his identity, and shipped off to Vietnam. I know that Carlo was your son, not your nephew. And that Fiona is your wife. How do you think she's enjoying lock-up in MCC Chicago, by the way?"

"That's quite a story," Roti said, taking a long, slow sip from the dixie cup. "And I'm sure you have evidence to back it up?"

"I understand now why you had Carlo cremated. Can't get DNA from ash," Miranda said.

"It will never stop," Roti said suddenly. He was talking to Cal. He was hardly bothered by Miranda. She was still just an annoying fly, buzzing. But Cal's presence in the room was weighing heavily on Roti. "Not because of what you know, but because of what you betrayed. You broke my heart."

There was a tense silent beat. Pat and Cal's eyes were locked in mutual anger. Finally, Miranda broke the silence.

"As I was saying, I understand why you had Carlo cremated. I also saw that you had your lawyers expunge Carlo's criminal record. Through what I assume was either some high-level backroom dealing or extraordinary cyber hacking, you managed to get Carlo's DNA removed from the FBI's database. I gotta say, I'm fucking impressed. I saw where you came from in Chicago. To be where you are now. Sitting here in a three-thousand-dollar suit. Powerful. Untouchable. That's no small thing."

"Are we done?" Roti asked impatiently.

"Almost," Miranda said. "After we arrested Fiona, we got a warrant to search her house and logged this as evidence."

Miranda placed Carlo's baby book on the table. Pat Roti's eyes widened as Miranda flipped the book open to the second page and he saw Fiona had saved a lock of baby Carlo's hair.

"How much do you want to bet that hair matches your DNA, Frank?" Miranda asked.

"First, you'd need to have my DNA—"

Before Pat could think to grab it, Cal snatched the paper dixie cup that Pat had drunk out of and dropped it into an evidence bag.

Miranda grinned. Pat Roti sneered.

"Now we're done," Miranda said.

47

Outside the ATF building, Miranda and Cal watched Roti's black Mercedes pull up. They watched Victor "The Red Devil" get out of the driver's seat, circle around, and open the back passenger door for Roti.

Victor locked eyes with Cal and grinned, then circled back to the driver's seat and drove away.

"Once we nail Roti, the contract on you won't be worth the paper it's printed on," Miranda said.

They went out that night, the three of them, to a restaurant called Yamashiro in the Hollywood Hills. The place was a re-creation of a medieval Japanese castle with spectacular views of the city. Miranda was surprised when Cal picked the place

"They filmed part of *Kill Bill* here," Cal said.

It felt fitting to dine there this night. Warriors celebrating their victory.

They sat at a table in the inner garden courtyard next to sculpted Japanese plants and a koi pond, and for a few hours, it was like Miranda hadn't been in a car wreck last week that nearly ended her life and given her a permanent limp, and Cal wasn't a sociopathic hitman on the run from his old boss, and Eva wasn't a budding young assassin being hunted by Los Angeles sex traffickers.

They were a far cry from the fucking Brady Bunch, but between the Mai Tais, Darth Vader rolls, and Himalayan salt plate steaks, they felt strangely like a family.

Miranda swore she even saw Cal smile.

Miranda let Cal and Eva crash at her place that night. Roti was on the ropes and Cal would soon be free. Without Roti hunting him, Cal would be able to do what he does best. He'd take care of the L.A. Syndicate and then Eva would be free too.

Miranda woke up at four a.m. Usually, she would use these early hours to exercise, but her recent injuries made that impossible. Miranda refused to sleep in though. It was important for her to stick to her schedule. Instead of weight-training or running, Miranda went for an early morning walk. She liked this time of day. It was the rare quiet hour on the streets of Downtown L.A. The shift change, so to speak. The junkies and freaks had crawled back into their holes, but the nine-to-fivers weren't up yet. The streets belonged to Miranda.

She limped down South Broadway. Decrepit movie palaces stood like mummified corpses. The ghosts of grandeur. *What a great city this once was*, she thought. *What a great city it could have been.*

If not for the rot.

She returned to her apartment around five a.m. Eva was still dozing, but Cal was awake and asked her if she wanted breakfast.

"That sounds great," Miranda said.

She showered, then the three of them had eggs scrambled with peppers, onions, and mushrooms with avocado, salsa, and a side of warm corn tortillas. Miranda was surprised. Cal was a hell of a cook. She supposed she shouldn't be surprised that Cal was good with his hands, but the food lost some of its appeal when she imagined how many bodies those same hands had disposed of.

After breakfast, she dressed in a navy-blue pantsuit and put on makeup. She hated wearing makeup, but today was a big day. Today was the day they got the warrant to arrest Pat a.k.a. Frank Roti for the torture and murder of his brother, along with the string of other murders Frank Roti had been charged with back in the sixties.

Today, she would excise the rot.

Miranda arrived at work around 7:30 a.m. Her meeting with Shackelford was scheduled for 9:00 a.m., so she was surprised when he called her to come up to his office. When Miranda limped into Shackelford's office, she knew right away that something was wrong. It was the look on his face. Like he just ate something foul.

"It's over," Shackelford said.

"What?" Miranda said.

"The Roti case. We've been ordered to drop it."

"That's bullshit. We have him."

"My hands are tied," Shackelford said. "This is coming from the top. We've been instructed to hand all of our evidence over to the Attorney General."

Miranda shook her head. "I won't do it."

"Miranda. This is coming from the fucking President of the United States. There's nothing you can do. Roti walks."

Miranda could feel the rage boiling up inside of her. Before she knew what she was doing, she smashed her crutch over one of Shackelford's office chairs, breaking the crutch in half.

Miranda limped pitifully out of the room.

48

That same morning, Eva took a walk to Grand Central Market. Cal offered to go with her, but Eva told him it wasn't necessary. As far they knew, Roti was done for and L.A. was a big city. The odds of running into Giselle were slim to none.

Besides, she could handle herself now.

Grand Central Market was an indoor, open-air market in the heart of Downtown L.A. It was nothing like the open-air markets she was used to back home. There were stalls for Thai, Chinese, Japanese, Peruvian, and Mexican food, and while the cuisine looked authentic, it was outrageously overpriced. There was a Jewish deli, a gourmet burger place, a place that only sold egg dishes called "Eggslut," a gourmet pizzeria, and a gourmet cheese shop. There were neon lit signs and wine bars and craft beer bars and juice bars and bespoke coffee bars. The place was much cleaner than the markets Eva was used to. Polished and sterile. Corporate and fake.

Eva had been in the United States long enough to know that she did not like norteamericanos. She found them disingenuous. Their values backward. Everything seemed artificial in the United States.

Their obsessions with tan skin, and straight white teeth, and smiling. Butt lifts and breast implants and Botox. Their body dissatisfaction and obsession with being thin. Losing weight was not so hard. Try moving to the Mexico City barrio.

And "speaking their truth." This was a term she had read about in magazines and heard over and over again on television since arriving in the United States. Also, "live your best life." It's mierda.

Truth is subjective.

Truth is deceptive.

And people can be conniving.

Do not these North Americans know that people hide ulterior motives?

No one is completely truthful.

And if you feel you need to "speak your truth," it is because you do not know what the truth is.

Pinche norteamericanos. Overfed and bored. Nothing else to do but whine, whine, whine.

She was standing at an overpriced fruit stand when the LAPD officer interrupted her thoughts. "Excuse me, miss?" he said. "I'm going to need you to come with me."

At first, she wasn't sure if he was talking to her. He was a gringo. Younger, maybe late-twenties. He smiled pleasantly. It made her tense. She did not trust a cop who smiled.

"Miranda sent me to get you," he said.

Eva relaxed when she heard this.

"This way," he said.

Eva followed him out of the market onto Hill Street, where a police cruiser was waiting. He opened the back door. The gringo's partner was sitting in the front passenger seat. He was a pocho. "Good morning," he said, as Eva slid into the backseat.

The gringo cop got in the driver's seat and headed north, the opposite direction of Miranda's apartment. "Where are you taking me?" Eva asked. "Miranda gave us an address to take you to. We don't know anything beyond that. Just following orders."

Eva felt the tension return, and she immediately regretted getting in the car. She sat rigidly in the backseat. She played it out in her head. They both had guns and they had the size advantage, but they'd likely underestimated her. She'd have the element of surprise. She was pretty sure she could take them.

But hopefully, it wouldn't come to that. Hopefully, they were telling the truth and Miranda really had sent them.

The cruiser pulled into an underground garage and circled down the ramps to the ground floor, which was empty except for a matte, bright pink Cadillac Escalade limousine.

Funny, she couldn't see Miranda driving one of those.

But, Giselle. That tacky bitch sure would, so it made sense when she climbed out of the back of the vehicle with Teddy, who was looking fabulous with his FN F2000 bullpup rifle, and four other armed goons.

The police officers got out of the cruiser and the pocho cop approached Eva's door.

Two cops were one thing, but the addition of Giselle and Teddy and an entourage of submachine-gun-toting mercenaries kind of threw a wrench into Eva's escape plan.

But what the hell.

The pocho cop opened the door and Eva hammer-punched him in the balls. The pocho cop gasped and keeled over. Eva slipped out of the cruiser and the gringo cop dashed toward her. She squatted, rapidly twisted her body, whipped a fist into his ribcage, and heard something crack. He bent forward and covered himself. Eva would have turned and run, but Giselle's goons were already on her. She was quick and wiry and slipped their grapples and bounced off their punches.

Teddy cracked her in the temple with his bullpup. A hot, dizzying pain rattled her skull, and she fell to the ground. Giselle's goons pinned her.

"Well, that was unexpected," Giselle said. Eva struggled hopelessly in their grip. "I got the address of where you were staying from Pat Roti. I'd brought the extra guns on Pat Roti's advice, just in case you had your friend with you. He recommended that we wait until you were alone to snatch you up. I thought it was overkill, but goddamn, girl. I'm glad I listened."

They dragged Eva into the back of the pink Escalade limo.

And just like that, Eva was a prisoner again.

You only get more of what you resist.

49

"It will never end."

That was all Cal said when Miranda told him the news about the charges against Roti being dropped. Roti himself had called Cal only moments earlier to tell him what he had done to Eva. How he had fed her to Giselle.

Cal walked out of the apartment without saying where he was going.

50

———————

The matte pink Escalade limousine winded up Mulholland Drive in the Hollywood Hills. Eva sat pinned in the back-seat between two goons. Giselle was seated across from her next to another gunman. Teddy sat behind Giselle in the front seat next to the driver.

"I thought you were a lamb," Giselle said. "When I first met you, I never thought you would last. How wrong I was.

"People used to think I was a lamb. Maybe lamb isn't the right word. More like a toad." Giselle smiled. "When I was younger, I had bad acne all over my face. I never liked to be out in public because if someone looked at me, I'd always think they were looking at my acne, and if someone didn't look at me, I'd think they didn't want to look at me because of my acne. As I grew, my skin cleared and men began to find me attractive. I started to like to go out in public because if a guy looked at me, I knew it was because he wanted to fuck me. If a woman looked at me, it was because she wanted to *be* me. And if they didn't look at me, well, it was because they didn't want to get caught looking."

The limo banked a sharp left, and everyone's bodies leaned right. "When a man would take me to bed, he thought he was fucking me, when really, I was fucking him. If he was a rich man, I was fucking him out of his money. If he was an influential man, I was fucking him out of his power. The whore he kept on the side, his dirty little secret, his secret was my leverage. That's the secret of life. What nobody will tell you: Fuck, don't get fucked. Simple as that."

Giselle paused and stared at Eva for a moment. "I was brought into this profession in much the same way you were. Without getting into the gritty details, it happened against my will. The woman who forced me into it was a much-feared Salvadoran they called La Loba. The she-wolf. At first, I hated her. I'd fantasize about all of the ways I would have liked to murder her. I'm sure she could see it in my eyes, much in the way I can see it in your eyes right now. But then, a strange thing happened. I grew to respect her. Eventually, in a twisted way, I guess you could say I even grew to love her." The limo followed Mulholland up a steep left curve. Eva felt herself thrown off-balance.

Giselle lit a cigarette and rolled down the window. "La Loba. The she-wolf. Did you know that among wolves, the competition to become alpha female is fiercer than it is for alpha males? The males sort out status through threats, but the females, they draw blood. The male alpha, he knows when he is beat, when to lie down and submit, but the queen will not give up her crown until she is dead. And no matter how much the new alpha loves the old queen, respects the old queen, she knows it must be done. Because there can only be one La Loba."

Giselle's eyes moved out the dark window. They became distant. "I poisoned her. It was terrible to watch. She suffered horribly before she died. I didn't want that. I knew it had to be done, but I never wanted her to suffer. I'll never forgive myself for it, but I suppose it was the only way."

Her eyes refocused on Eva. "Yes. I thought you were a lamb." She cracked her window and ashed her cigarette. "But as it turns out, you are a wolf." She took a drag. "And I respect you for that. But I will not make the same mistake I did with La Loba," Giselle said. "I'll make it quick. You won't suffer."

Eva decided her best chance at escape was to get her hands on one of these goons' submachine guns and light the Escalade's cabin up like a firecracker. It wasn't going to be easy. Eva's advantage over her much stronger adversaries was her speed, which was pretty much neutralized by the confined space of the Escalade cabin. These thugs were on high alert after they saw what she did to those two LAPD assholes.

She would wait for the next sharp turn that Mulholland Drive threw at them. When the goons were off-balance, she'd make her move.

They rode the next few moments in silence, the limo traversing the Santa Monica mountains ridgeline. She stole periodic glances over Giselle's shoulder through the windshield at the road ahead. Biding her time. Finally, up ahead, Eva saw her opportunity. The road banked upward, left, then right.

She timed it out in seconds in her head. 5… 4… 3… 2…

"What the hell are you looking at?" Giselle said, glancing over her shoulder and out the windshield.

1.

The limo climbed and turned left. Eva shot her elbow into the cheekbone of the guard on her right, then drove her right fist into the jaw of the guy on her left. She grabbed for the submachine gun slung across his chest. The goon across from Eva sprung forward, tackled her, twisted the submachine gun from her grip. She squirmed helplessly beneath his grip.

Giselle smirked. "I can still change my mind about the suffering."

The biker wore a black modular helmet with a tinted face shield. He sped down the winding, mountainous road, overlooking the Los Angeles skyline. Luminous and vast. The Harley's engine rumbled as he closed in on the pink Escalade limousine. The biker wondered if they'd spotted him in their mirrors yet.

"Teddy?" Giselle said.

"I see him," Teddy said from the front seat. He readied his bullpup. "Any idea who it might be?"

Giselle had an idea. "It's the guy Pat Roti warned us about. Gotta be. He's come for her again." Giselle glared at Eva, whose arms were now bound behind her back.

"How the hell did he find us?" Teddy said.

"Doesn't matter now. Don't mess around with this one."

"Copy," Teddy said. "Gentlemen, light him up!"

The biker was approximately twenty feet behind the Escalade. The gunmen hung out of the vehicle's windows like parasites and opened fire. Bullets danced on the pavement and whizzed over the biker's modular helmet like Blue Angels.

The biker sharply jerked his handlebars right, dodging the onslaught. The bike skidded off the road and down a steep rocky ravine and disappeared into a thick copse of sycamores.The shooters climbed back into their seats.

"That was easy," Teddy said.

Eva looked back worriedly at the copse as it disappeared around the bend.

The biker dusted himself off, lifted and remounted his Harley. The bike growled as it climbed its way up the rocky ravine back onto the road. This part of Mulholland Drive was remote, but soon the Escalade would reach the more populated areas. His window of opportunity for a rescue was closing fast.

The biker twisted the throttle. His Harley screamed full speed ahead, tearing down the winding, twisting road at speeds beyond dangerous. Speedometer cresting 100 miles per hour. It seemed as if he could launch off the road at any moment.

The Escalade appeared ahead like a lazy water buffalo in the path of a charging lion. The Escalade's windows descended once more and the gunmen protruded like dog fangs. The biker raised a Skorpion machine pistol and peppered the Escalade. Bullets sparked off of pink steel and shattered tinted window glass.

The parties exchanged fire as they sped beneath stilted houses and the HOLLYWOOD sign. They weaved through traffic and blaring car horns. Their lethal parade entered a small neighborhood of cramped streets and walled-off homes and tightly-packed parked cars, which lined either side of the road.

The Escalade plowed through plastic garbage bins parked at the mouth of a driveway, forked left, and was met head-on with SUV headlights. The driver of the Escalade quickly whipped the wheel right and swerved off the road. The biker remained in stubborn pursuit. Guns blazing as the Escalade bumped over rocks and dirt, through trees and brush.

The biker pulled up alongside the SUV, extended his machine pistol toward the driver's side window. The driver of the Escalade whipped the wheel left, slamming into the biker. Jousting for dominance.

The biker sent a barrage of bullets toward the Escalade. The driver whipped the wheel and sent the Escalade spinning head-on into a thick oak tree. Its metal body wrinkled upon impact and the engine groaned and smoked and died.

The biker sped past the Escalade, struggling to stay upright and steer straight. No longer driving the bike — the bike driving him.

From the back of the crashed SUV, Eva lost sight of the biker over a rise, then heard a loud crash.

Giselle, Teddy, and their men cleared out from the wreckage of the Escalade. Giselle surveyed the wreck and shook her head. "I loved that fucking car," she said. "Go find that asshole and kill him, please."

Teddy nodded. He opened the back of the Escalade and handed out walkie-talkies. He left one man behind with Giselle and Eva, then he and the three others pressed over the nearby rise. They found the burning wreckage of the biker's Harley Davidson. The Skorpion was on the ground, its mag empty. They scanned the wooded area around it.

Blood in the dirt.

He was hurt.

The trail led up ahead into an eerie settlement of abandoned structures. A ghost town. Or rather, a ghost zoo.

"It looks like he fled to the old L.A. zoo," Teddy said to Giselle through his walkie. "Sit tight."

An abandoned, graffiti-strewn zoo deep in Griffith Park. Rusty animal cages. Teddy and his men crept into the old zoo, guns ready.

"He's close," Teddy said. "Find him."

The men branched out.

Faux caves structured from concrete. Old newspapers and trash littered the ground. One of Teddy's gunmen patrolled the area. He scanned each cave entrance. He paid little attention to the filthy blanket lying on the ground among the trash. From underneath, the biker pounced, knocking the gunman out. He quickly laid the gunman down under the blanket.

The biker coolly marched into one of the caves, dropping the gunman's walkie-talkie at the mouth.

At the animal cages, Teddy spoke into his walkie-talkie. "Check in."

Teddy's walkie chattered in response.

"Becker, all clear."

"Sims, all clear."

"Moreno? You copy?" Teddy said into his walkie.

Nothing.

"I'll go check it out," Sims said.

Sims trekked into the cave exhibit. He spotted Moreno's walkie in front of the cave.

He approached, picked it up, looked at it quizzically, but

before he could call it in, the biker sprung from the cave and pulled Sims back into the darkness.

At the animal cages, Teddy was starting to look worried. "Sims? Where are you? Talk to me."

Sims was unconscious. The biker listened to Teddy's nervous voice through Sims's walkie-talkie. He moved through a service stairwell. Dark. Cavernous. Graffiti of every color lined the walls. Grunge chic.

"Sims, you read me?" Becker asked as he moved down the stairs. He heard someone whistle. Becker turned as the biker descended on him. The biker wrapped his arm around Becker's throat, cutting off his oxygen until his world went dark. The biker dropped Becker's body and grabbed his HK MP5 submachine gun.

The biker warily approached the animal cages, gun in hand. Teddy sprung. Knocked the gun out of his hand Grabbed the biker and yanked him into one of the animal cages.

The two men exchanged brutal blows in this tight space. Teddy was a bruiser, twice the biker's size. He threw a low hook, cracked the biker's ribs.

The biker was hurt. Teddy got him in a chokehold. Squeezed. The biker kicked and flailed, fading under Teddy's lethal grip.

The biker pressed his feet against the opposite wall and slammed Teddy back against the bars. Again. Again. Teddy's grip loosened. The biker slipped free. Wheezing beneath his modular helmet, he stumbled out of the cage, slamming the barred door behind him.

The biker grabbed a rusty lead pipe off of the trash-strewn ground and slid it into the cage door's handle, locking Teddy in. Teddy glared at the biker through the bars like a vicious animal.

The biker took off his helmet and the first thing Teddy noticed was his bright red hair. Victor caught his breath.

Teddy squinted through the bars. This wasn't the guy Pat Roti had warned them about.

Victor raised the MP5 and mercilessly fired into the cage, riddling Teddy with lead.

It was a nice night. The air was a refreshing sixty degrees and a cool, crisp wind blew through the trees, washing everything in the smells of nature. Giselle crouched in her tight silver dress behind a tree. She watched Eva, sitting alone by the crushed Escalade. The battered vehicle's headlights were lit like a beacon. After Giselle couldn't get Teddy on her walkie, she had hand-cuffed Eva to a door handle and retreated into the dark woods with her one remaining security guard.

The hunter was still out there. So, Eva would be bait.

Giselle watched the red-haired man emerge from the darkness. Watched him stand over Eva menacingly. Giselle recognized him. He was Pat Roti's man.

What the fuck is going on?

Giselle watched the red-haired man and Eva exchange words. Then the red-haired man pointed the MP5 down at Eva. Eva turned her head away and he pulled the trigger.

He fired a single, quick volley, which freed Eva's cuffed wrist from the car door. Then the red-haired man handed Eva the weapon. Giselle's brow furrowed as she watched Eva circle to the front of the Escalade and shoot out the headlights.

Then everything became very dark. Giselle couldn't see Eva anymore.

"Kill her! Go!" Giselle whispered to her last henchman, as she turned around and made a run for it. She heard a quick sputter of gunfire, looked back over her shoulder, and watched her last gunman fall down dead.

Giselle never got a chance to notice what a nice night it was. She was too preoccupied with fear. The taste of it. Like something bitter and black lodged in the back of her throat.

Giselle couldn't outrun it. Though she tried. She sprinted frantically and aimlessly through the dark woods.

She spotted Eva and the gun she was holding only a split second before the bullet split her forehead, but it was long enough for her to swallow that taste.

Eva looked down at Giselle's dead body, saw the fear frozen on her face, and decided that the bitch had gotten off easy.

Because it was a very nice night to die.

Victor emerged from the inky night and stood by Eva's side over Giselle's body. He slid his iPhone from his pocket, aimed the camera at Giselle's dead body, captured a picture, and sent it.

Cal had been hiding out in Sly's warehouse and that's where he was when his burner phone buzzed. He looked at the picture of Giselle on his screen. Eyes wide with surprise. A single red hole in her forehead.

Confirmation.

After Giselle took Eva, Cal had called Roti to make a deal. It was simple. *Me for her.*

In return for Eva's safety, Cal would hand himself over. But in order for Eva to be truly safe, Giselle had to die. Cal had just received confirmation that Roti had delivered on what he promised. Now it was time for Cal to hold up his end of the bargain. Because it would never end.

Not unless Cal ended it.

They devil must have his pound of flesh.

51

———————

Miranda found Cal at Sly's warehouse. He told her he had to go. He asked her to look out for Eva. Miranda followed Cal to the lot outside, where Cal had parked his F150.

"Where are you going?" Miranda asked.

Cal did not answer, but Miranda understood.

"Who is this girl to you? Why are you doing all of this for her?"

"It's not just for her," Cal said. "It's for all the ones I didn't save. And all the ones I could have spared." He looked Miranda in the eye.

"I fight for the dead."

52

I t was night. Victor waited with a group of armed men around their dark SUVs. They were parked outside of an old cabin at the end of a long road someplace deep in the woods of Griffith Park. Cal drove up in his pickup. He stepped out of the vehicle and raised his arms. One of Victor's men — a burly, bearded Slavic-looking guy — patted him down.

The Slav slid Cal's burner phone out of his pocket. Finding nothing else on him, he walked the phone back to Victor. Victor looked at the phone, somewhat disappointed that they hadn't found more. That Cal hadn't come to fight.

He felt let down.

He nodded to his men. They converged on Cal and brutally beat him. Cal fell to the ground and curled up, absorbed their blows. Victor turned and marched back toward the cabin. The men grabbed Cal by the arms and dragged him.

The cabin was empty, aside from a table, a couple of chairs, and a portable gas generator with jumper cables. They brought Cal in, threw him into a chair, and bounded his hands and legs.

Victor stood over him. "What is your mantra?" Victor asked.

Cal lowered his head and did not offer an answer. Victor grinned. "I was hoping you'd say that."

Victor went to work brutally beating Cal.

Eva returned to Miranda's apartment and found the place empty. She called Miranda and Miranda told her that she was at the warehouse. Eva took a bus to the Arts District. She banged loudly on the reinforced warehouse door. Miranda let her in and locked the door behind her.

"Where's Cal?" Eva asked.

Miranda looked at Eva sadly.

Pat Roti rode in the back of his black Mercedes down a wooded service road in Griffith Park. His cell phone buzzed and he accepted the call.

"I don't know how much longer he'll hold out," Victor said.

"I'll be there soon. Keep him alive until then," Pat Roti said.

Victor ended the call. He glared jealously at Cal, brutally beaten and tied to the chair. "You were always his favorite," Victor said. "The human body can stand roughly fifty volts of electricity." Victor picked up the jumper cables. "What is your mantra?"

Cal's eyes were distant. He slumped in the chair wearily, resigned to his fate, and said nothing.

Victor jammed the jumper cables into Cal's ribs, electrocuting him. Cal endured the torture. On the gas generator, the meter climbed to "30 V." Victor pulled the jumper cables away. Cal caught his breath.

"Before I end your life, I want you to know that the girl will die too," Victor said.

The life came back to Cal's eyes. He jerked his head up and glared at Victor. "You gave me your word," Cal said.

"And you gave me yours. What is our mantra? Say it!" Victor said.

Cal grit his teeth. Grimaced. "I will serve," Cal said.

"I will serve," Victor repeated.

Victor pressed the jumper cables to Cal's ribs again. Held them there. Cal's eyes watered, his veins bulged. His jaw clenched so hard it felt like his teeth might shatter. The meter climbed to "40 V."

"You betrayed our mantra, so I will betray you!" Victor shouted.

Victor pulled the jumper cables away. Agonized, Cal sucked in air, fought back the urge to pass out from the pain.

"The girl will die," Victor said. "And you will be the one who kills her."

Victor shoved the jumper cables into Cal's ribs. Cal screamed as the meter crested "50 V" and then he wasn't screaming anymore.

Because Cal was dead.

53

———————

Cal awoke in the barrio. At first, he did not recognize his surroundings. The buildings were restored. They stood bright and polished beneath a warm sun. The streets were clean and candlelit and lined with decorative altars flowered with Mexican marigolds.

There were residents. Made-up in sugar-skull makeup, flamenco dresses and flower crowns or mariachi ensembles and top hats or trilbys. They ate and drank and danced and celebrated and reveled.

And all Cal could feel was warmth. All he could smell were flowers and trees and the sweetness of life.

Here, not even tequila burnt.

The residents of the barrio smiled when they saw him.

"¡Bienvenido a casa, Padre!"

There were the kids playing soccer on a grass field. Not the kids he knew, but kids.

There was a man in Señor Vasquez's garden who looked like Señor Vasquez but was not. The garden, it was bountiful and overflowing.

There was a young man at the DVD Kid's stall, selling flowers, and candies, and tequila.

And then Cal saw Maria. She wore a long red robe and sugar-skull makeup and smiled warmly at him. She took Cal by his hand.

She led him away from the party and as they moved, he felt the warmth migrating away from him. He felt something cold in his chest. He felt it before he saw it.

The church that Cal had been rebuilding. It stood like a dark temple, shadowed and dilapidated. It gave off a flaring black light. Cal stopped where he stood. Maria looked back at him. Cal's eyes were wide like a frightened child's. He slowly shook his head. "I don't want to go in there."

"Mis ventanas," she said. She pulled Cal forward and though Cal tried to resist, he felt irreversibly drawn to that dark place. Like an alcoholic to the bottle, or the avaricious to money, or a moth to the flame. She led him into the dark church. She reached out her arm, curled out a finger, and pointed to the front of the nave.

There was a window.

Cal shook his head. "I don't want to," he said.

Maria smiled, gently took his hand, and led him to the window. Cal stood at the sill. He tried to resist, but it was futile. His hands moved to the handle, not quite with a mind of their own. Because it was his mind, just the part he could not control. His entire chest cavity was freezing. The smell of ice stung his nostrils.

He lifted the window.

The part of himself he could not control raised his leg over the sill and climbed through. Maria followed behind him. They stepped into a silent, black-and-white dungeon, like the chiaroscuro nightmares that have plagued clairvoyants even before the advent of film. She led him deep into that silent dungeon. He could not even hear his footfalls on the cold, hard ground and he realized that few things are more horrifying than perfect and absolute silence. The only thing to keep you company, your own thoughts. The greatest punishment for a sinner is to allow them only time and silence to fill their heads with their own reflections.

Maria led Cal down a staircase into a darker place. A place of sound. A place of black mirrors that reflected no light. Housing only shadows. This place was cold, but not in a sensory way. He'd describe it as atomic — if souls had atoms — the chill, a type of cold which no warmth could combat.

A cold of being.

"I don't want to be here," Cal said, frightened.

Maria guided him through the puzzled maze of dark mirrors. As they moved, the shadows in the mirrors gained dimension and mass. The uncharted cartography of their blurred visages sharpened into identities — maps of Cal's sins.

And those maps were faces. Victims. Each belonging to a life Cal had ended.

The murdered souls reached for him through their black mirrors with clawed and wiry fingers.

Maria ferried him onward. Cal's victims' clawed hands, reaching, and pulling him back. Their vengeful moans, unrelenting.

Maria's palm grew cold.

Black spikes protruded from her scalp. A gothic crown. Her skeleton sucked her skin inward in a slow and disgusting inhale. Her make-up fused with her bones until she was only a robed and painted skeleton, crowned in spikes and she was no longer Maria.

And she had never been Maria, Cal realized.

She led him to another window. It glowed with light in the dark place.

"They will be here," the Bony Lady said. "Waiting for you."

She released his hand. Cal looked back at his victims. He didn't want to say I'm sorry. What would be the point?

Besides, he wasn't.

Most of them deserved what they got. What he gave them. So, he said all he wanted to say. "I'll see you soon."

And then, he stepped through the lit window.

54

Cal sucked in a huge gasp of air. Victor's jumper cables had defibrillated his heart. He was still in the chair in the cabin. He guessed he had only been dead for less than a minute.

"You don't get to die that easily," Victor said.

Cal was dizzy, discombobulated, struggling to stay conscious.

"We know where the girl is. My men followed her to a warehouse in the Arts District. But the place is fortified." Victor dangled the cell phone over Cal. "Call them and tell them to let my men in, and all of this can be over. I will end your suffering."

"Let me talk to Pat Roti," Cal said through wheezing breaths.

Victor shocked him. He shrieked. The pain was unbearable.

"Do you know what this is?" Victor said, as he picked a pouch up off of the table and unzipped it. Inside were five syringes.

"Sure, you do. We used to use these in interrogations all the time," Victor said. "Adrenaline. Your heart won't stop. You won't pass out. You won't die. Not until I allow you to. You know how effective I am at 'enhanced interrogations.' My success rate is ninety-nine percent. Why don't you spare yourself the pain?" Victor offered the phone. "Call them."

Cal cringed and shook his head. "Where is Pat Roti?" Cal asked. Victor ignored the question.

"Ninety-nine percent," Victor said again. "Do you really want to end up like the one? You remember him, don't you? Munich. Five years ago. Some Jihadist fucker. We worked on him for days, but he wouldn't give up the other members of his cell."

Cal remembered the terrorist. He was young, maybe twenty-one. Iraqi. No matter what they did to him, he would not talk. Cal remembered the empty look in his eyes. Nothing behind them. Like a mall mannequin or a wax statue.

"Don't make me do to you what I did to him," Victor said, unsheathing a knife.

After four days of fruitless interrogation, Victor castrated the young terrorist.

"I'm not going to cut your cock off. Not yet. First, I'm going to cut out your tongue."

Out the window, Roti's Mercedes appeared at the end of the long road. It was approaching the cabin. "You wanted to talk to Pat?" Victor said. "Well, here he comes. Last chance. Make up your mind because in a minute, you'll no longer be able to speak," Victor said, wielding the knife.

He thought of the room with the black mirrors. All of the lives he had taken. *How many more?* he wondered. How many more would wait for him on the other side? Everyone dies.

"Okay," Cal said weakly. His voice cracking. "I'll call."

Victor smirked. Triumphant. This is what he wanted. Not just to kill Cal but to *break him.*

Victor's men unbound Cal's hands. Cal took the phone.

Miranda heard something outside. She looked through the doorbell cam and spotted Victor's men. There were five of them, armed with some serious pieces. She called it in to the ATF.

In the meantime, Eva told Miranda about Cal's gun bag. The two rifled through it. They may have been outmanned, but they sure as hell weren't going to be outgunned. Miranda armed herself with the AKM rifle. Eva had the M4 Carbine.

Miranda was shocked by the small arsenal Cal had been carrying around. Where the hell had he gotten all of it? There was enough illegal hardware to put him away for several life sentences. And that was without her even knowing about the Semtex.

The plastic explosive, invented in the late-1950s by two scientists in Czechoslovakia, was the bomb material of choice of Islamic militants in the Middle East, as well as the Provisional Irish Republican Army. It was relatively easy to use and sniffer dogs had trouble detecting it. In December of 1988, twelve ounces of Semtex brought down a Boeing 747 over Lockerbie, Scotland.

In short, Semtex had a reputation as the terrorist's explosive of choice.

So, it was good that Miranda didn't find the Semtex.

Victor's men unbounded Cal's hands.

It was good that Cal had fitted it with a cell phone and an electric blasting cap. Taped it all together and fastened it to an industrial magnet.

Cal took the phone.

It was good that Cal brought the Semtex with him to the Malibu ranch when he rescued Eva.

Cal dialed the phone.

. . .

And when Cal was in Malibu, it was good that he'd fastened the Semtex bomb on the undercarriage of Roti's Mercedes.

Cal pressed Send on the phone and prayed the bomb was where he'd left it.

Roti sat in the backseat of the Mercedes. He was in a gloomy mood. It was true that he had viewed Cal as something of a son. He never enjoyed killing his children.

Beneath Roti's feet, the Semtex bomb with the cell phone trigger received Cal's call and the Mercedes exploded in a massive fireball.

Roti was instantly vaporized.

Victor and his men ran to the wreckage. Twisted metal and burning oil. Charred corpses.

Victor took it all in. Shocked. Then—

A cruel smile creased across Victor's face.

Victor glanced back into the cabin, where Cal jumped out a window and fled into the woods.

"Find him!" Victor said to his men. "Kill him!"

Cal fled through the woods, snapping branches, tripping through brush, stumbling in the dark. Victor and his men chased Cal, blindly firing potshots in his direction.

Cal emerged onto a steep crag. Looked back. Victor and his men were closing in.

Cal took a step forward, stumbled down the rocky terrain. Victor and his men emerged from the woods. Watched Cal's body violently land in a rocky gorge.

Cal gathered what little strength he had left and pulled himself up. He stumbled to the nearby road.

An approaching Ford Mustang. The driver — a white dude with spiked hair— pulled over. "Hey, bro. You okay?"

Victor's men released a barrage of bullets from the woods. They missed Cal, flying over his head, and riddled the driver. Cal ducked into the Mustang.

Victor and his men watched helplessly as Cal sped away in the Mustang.

Then, strangely, Victor chuckled.

Victor's men looked at him nervously. "Boss?" one of them said. "Are you okay?"

"The king is dead," Victor said. "All hail the king."

55

After escaping the cabin, Cal was in bad shape. He barely made it back to the warehouse. He found five of Victor's guys outside, being questioned by Miranda and other ATF agents. They claimed they were employed as private soldiers. They had carry permits for their firearms, but that didn't explain what they were doing that time of night outside of the warehouse.

Eva spotted Cal parked on the street in the Mustang. Miranda stayed behind with her colleagues to question Victor's men, while Eva drove Cal back to Miranda's apartment.

She ran an ice bath for Cal. His swollen, battered body sullied the water pink with blood. She went back out and ditched the Mustang. When she returned to Miranda's apartment, Cal was out of the tub and dressed.

"We should return to Mexico," he said.

Eva shook her head. "I can't go back."

"Why not?"

"Because I got out. I got to the United States. This is my home now."

"Home is not a place. You can't leave it behind any more than you can outrun your own shadow. It will always be part of you,"

Cal said. "You can stay in Los Angeles if you want. I'm sure Miranda can help you with citizenship."

"What will you do?" Eva asked.

"I'll go where you go," Cal said. "It's your choice."

The next morning, Miranda brought Cal to the ATF office to meet with Shackelford. Now that Roti was dead, Shackelford wanted to know everything he could about this new guy. He wanted to know about "The Red Devil."

Cal's and Victor's mantra had been, "I will serve." They were Roti's servants. His angels of death. Like samurai loyal to their lord. But Cal had broken his vow. He broke it because he could no longer bear it. To kill without question, without knowing why.

But Cal still had his principles. Omertà. Roti had ingrained it in him. He'd often quote an unknown source, "Whoever appeals to the law against his fellow man is either a fool or a coward. Whoever cannot take care of himself without police protection is both. It is cowardly to betray an offender to justice, even though his offenses be against yourself, as it is not to avenge an injury by violence. It is dastardly and contemptible in a wounded man to betray the name of his assailant, because if he recovers, he must naturally expect to take vengeance himself."

Cal told Shackelford nothing.

Shackelford intended to keep an eye on Cal. That's why Cal didn't tell Miranda where he and Eva were going. Although, he was sure she could have guessed. He thanked her for everything and said goodbye. Miranda wondered if she'd ever see Cal again. Part of her knew it would probably be better if she didn't. But strangely, another part of her was going to miss him. She couldn't say exactly why. Maybe it was his loyalty to the girl. Maybe Eva was the one thing that was good about him. And she took comfort in the fact that as long as he was around, Eva would be safe.

Cal purchased two first class tickets to Mexico City. It was Eva's first time on an airplane. From up in the sky, the world looked like a painting. The pretty, young stewardess was so pleasant and nice. Eva wondered if she might be able to get a job being a stewardess, but decided like most things in life, it was probably only for people that had an education and she got down on herself.

But then she realized she *was* coming home with an education, of sorts.

How many high school students were proficient with a Russian AKM, an American M4, a Czechoslovak Skorpion, and so many other weapons? How many college grads knew Krav Maga or the location of every knockout pressure point on the human body?

For the first time in her life, she didn't feel like she was less than. She didn't feel powerless or disadvantaged.

She glanced at Cal from her cushioned airplane seat. It wasn't that he was an unhappy person. It was more like he was free from feelings entirely. Free from happiness or sadness. Anxiety or fear. And perhaps joy, too. Perhaps that was part of the bargain.

She sunk into her seat, looked out the window at the painted world sailing by below her, and she contemplated this gift that he had given her.

As they descended into Mexico City, the world got closer and the painting turned into reality. She could see the slums of cramped houses where she had grown up on the outskirts of the city. A gritty mazework jungle known only to the Initiated.

They landed at the Mexico City International Airport at six p.m. and took a cab to the barrio. Familiar faces gawked. "¡Bienvenido a casa, Padre!" They returned to Maria's house. Everything was just how they had left it. Eva went to the bookshelf of Harry Potter books and found the windows she had painted for Maria —"mis ventanas"— and her eyes welled.

It seemed like nothing had changed. And somehow, it seemed that everything had changed.

As the sun set, they walked over to the old church. It remained a work-in-progress. Only half-reconstructed.

Eva looked at Cal. "We should finish it," she said.

If there was a silver lining to Cal's betrayal, for Victor, it was what he stood to inherit after Roti died. Roti's real son, Carlo, was a thug, a drug trafficker. He wasn't qualified to run a billion-dollar private military firm.

But someone stood to inherit Roti's empire.

The way Victor saw it, it really came down to either him or Cal. They were the best of the best, Roti's most-trusted, and as much as Victor hated to admit it, he suspected that Roti favored Cal. He wasn't sure why, but he had his theories. He suspected that it was because Victor enjoyed his job a little too much. For Victor, the work was something he *wanted* to do. Whereas for Cal, it was something he *had* to do. Like breathing. It wasn't something he took pleasure in. Not like Victor.

Victor liked hurting other people. Victor enjoyed killing.

And now that Pat Roti was dead, Victor had just inherited the most powerful private military firm in the world.

After Roti's death, Victor put Cal out of his mind. Cal was Roti's problem, not his. Victor had more important concerns.

Like establishing himself as the new head of Roti's company.

But over the next several weeks, he struggled to get a foothold. He couldn't figure out why.

The Russians needed an FSB defector in London silenced and were looking to hire an outside contractor.

Members of the Saudi Royal family secretly wanted some Al-Qaeda leaders disappeared, but couldn't make a move without upsetting other members of the family.

And the CIA was a gold mine. No shortage of jobs in Mexico or the Middle East. And they always needed outside interrogators. Guys who could pull off the type of enhanced interrogations that they weren't allowed to.

But none of the contracts went to Victor.

Victor was wrong. Cal *was* his problem. Pat Roti left big shoes to fill. His reputation was outstanding and his control over his organization was absolute. But the man who killed him was still out there. Potential clients didn't trust Victor's operation. They didn't think Victor could control his men. What if another operator defected? The type of people that required Victor's services were also the type of people that couldn't afford to have their secrets getting out. They needed airtight security. They needed to know that the man in charge was in absolute control.

Cal was becoming a shining example of Victor's inability to manage.

Every breath Cal took was bad for business.

Victor called a meeting of his seven best hitters — ex-special forces from around the globe. Arguably the best killers in the world. They cost a few million each. But Cal was no easy mark, so Victor wasn't going to take any chances.

They all knew Cal, either from previous jobs or by reputation. After everyone was assembled and briefed on the op, Victor only had one question.

"When's the last time you fellas been to church?"

56

Cal and Eva had been living back in the barrio for several weeks. At first, Cal was very cautious. He did not know if Victor would come after him, but as time went by, Cal figured that Victor had moved on. With Roti dead, there was no longer any money to be gained by killing him, so what reason would Victor have to continue hunting them? Sure, there was the personal animosity. Victor felt betrayed by Cal. Felt that Cal had betrayed their mantra, but now that Roti was dead, Victor no longer had his mantra either. He was like Cal now. No one to serve. Besides, Victor was never too sentimental. Not when there was money to be made elsewhere. So, Cal wasn't surprised when weeks passed and Victor hadn't come for him.

Cal assumed he and Eva were safe.

Eva was walking up the street in paint-covered overalls. She was on her way back to the church from a supply run, carrying a gallon of paint in either hand. When she arrived at the church, she found Victor waiting outside, smoking a cigarette. He took a drag. The butt glowed as red as his hair.

Eva dropped the paint cans and turned to run, but she was seized by Victor's men. She kicked and flailed as they dragged her into the church.

Cal had been helping Señor Vasquez in the garden — they were going to make caldo de vegetales for the community meal center tonight — when the DVD Kid ran up and told Cal about the strangers that had been spotted in the barrio.

He told Cal what they'd done to Eva.

Cal became very quiet, and the DVD Kid saw that darkness in Cal's eyes again, bubbling to the surface.

57

His call sign had been Reaper. Victor was The Red Devil. Cal was Reaper. No two names were more feared and respected among mercenaries around the globe.

The assassin code-named Uriel patrolled the black market. He was equipped with a headset and an AN/PRC-126 radio. He wore a ballistic vest and carried an HK 416 rifle with a holographic sight strapped beneath his coat.

"Hey, gringo! I have what you're looking for!" the DVD Kid said, beckoning Uriel to his stand. He showed off his wares.

"I got uppers, downers. I can get you girls... guys. I got the new Nikes. How 'bout some bling?" DVD Kid showed off his gaudy, fake jewelry.

Uriel checked out the life-sized Santa Muerte and Grim Reaper statues that stood around the Kid's stand.

"Or a DVD? I got movies that aren't even in theaters yet."

Uriel grunted. "Piss off," he said, turning his back.

Suddenly, one of the Grim Reaper statues came to life, wrapping its hand scythe around Uriel's neck. The statue slit his throat.

. . .

Eva was cuffed to a pipe in Cal's room in the old church. Victor stood nearby at the crumbled wall overlooking the courtyard below, arms folded behind his back, chest puffed, like a general standing over a battlefield. His men were out there. Hunting.

Victor raised his radio to his lips. "Check in," he said.

His men responded from their various locations throughout the barrio with their call signs.

"Michael, all clear."

"Gabriel, all clear."

"Raphael, all clear."

"Selaphiel, all clear."

"Barachiel, all clear."

The assassin code-named Raguel was searching Señor Vasquez's community garden when Victor's call came in through his earpiece.

"Raguel, all clear," he said.

"Uriel, check in," Victor said into his radio.

There was silence. Victor grinned deviously. "Hello, Reaper," Victor said.

Throughout the barrio, Victor's men tensed as Cal's voice filled their earpieces. "You all know who I am," he said. "I only want the girl. I'm giving you all this one chance to walk away. If you stay, I will kill every single one of you."

"You really think you can pull that off?" Victor said into his radio.

"I'm standing behind one of your assassins right now," Cal said.

Victor's patrolling assassins checked their sixes in a flurry of frightened responses.

"Michael, clear."

"Gabriel. He's not here."

"Raphael. Not here."

"Selaphiel, all clear."

"Barachiel. Not here."

Leaving only—

Raguel, in the community garden. He slowly turned around and found himself facing—

A closed garden shed.

"Shit," Raguel mumbled.

Raguel unloaded his MP5 submachine gun into the shed, then he cautiously approached, slowly opened the door.

The shed was empty.

Raguel's face dropped. "Oh, fuck—"

Cal emerged from the cornstalks behind Raguel, still wearing the Grim Reaper's skull mask, wielding a pair of gardening sheers.

Raguel's horrified screams echoed through the earpieces.

For the listeners — Michael, Gabriel, Raphael, Selaphiel, Barachiel, and Victor — the reaction was uniform. Pure terror.

Their radios fell silent. Then Cal spoke. His voice sounded like something dragged across gravel.

"Welcome to hell," he said.

Victor's men regrouped outside of the church. Victor stood above them in Cal's room with Eva. "It's psychological warfare," Victor said into his radio. "Don't let him get in your head."

The mercenaries took up positions around the entrance to the church. If Cal wanted to save Eva, he would have to go through them.

They scanned their surroundings. They caught glimpses of the DVD Kid and his friends moving between the allies and narrow passageways around the church. The mercenaries were at the center of the mazelike barrio. A labyrinth of corrugated metal, black market shops, crumbling concrete, and urban decay. They were surrounded by the hurried and chaotic footfalls of locals.

"I don't like this," Raphael said. "What the hell are they doing?"

"Scurrying like fucking street rats. Forget about them," Barachiel said. "Does anyone see Reaper?"

And then all at once, the street lights went out.

The mercenaries equipped their night vision goggles. They scanned the perimeter of the church courtyard with their guns. "Anything comes this direction, shoot it," Gabriel said.

But everything had become very still and silent. There was no more movement between the alleyways. No more patter of sneakers on asphalt.

Cal appeared about thirty feet away from the mercenaries. He stood before the church in the skull mask, like some prophet of the apocalypse. In one hand, he wielded Uriel's HK 416 rifle. In the other, he raised Raguel's severed head.

The assassins froze in their places for a shocked moment. Then fireworks erupted all around them. A dazzling display of fiery reds and yellows. The DVD Kid and his clica had done well, scurrying between the alleyways, setting up fireworks all around the church. Cal had told them he wanted them to put on a show.

The fireworks caused the mercenaries' night vision goggles to bloom out. By the time the mercenaries tore the googles from their heads, Cal had gunned down Michael and disappeared back into the labyrinth.

The sky was on fire.

The fireworks cracked, deafeningly, like the bones of giants.

Barachiel's and Selaphiel's and Gabriel's and Raphael's senses were impaired by lights and sounds and psychological terror and—

An object sailed through the air and struck Selaphiel on the shoulder. Selaphiel turned and saw Raguel's severed head on the ground staring up at him.

Cal shot Selaphiel from an alley when he wasn't looking.

From the church, Victor watched Selaphiel fall and heard Cal in his ear. "You're running out of angels," Cal said.

Victor's face dropped. He could feel the walls closing in.

"Pull back," Victor said into his radio. Barachiel, Raphael, and Gabriel retreated into the church.

Cal marched across the courtyard and into the church. The dark, half-built nave glowed dark blue. Objects and walls were smashed, jagged, jutting outward at offensive and disorienting angles.

The walls had been painted with glow-in-the-dark paint to depict a nightscape. Deep blues and blacks and purples mixed to form something brooding, vast and beautiful. Eva had turned the place into an art exhibit.

Cal heard Victor on his radio. "Who is she, Reaper? Who is this girl to you?"

Cal trekked through the dark and dazzling maze of Eva's soul. Somewhere between a dream and a nightmare.

"This is how we found the place," Victor said. "The girl's got some talent. It's too bad. Too bad you came into her life. Too bad that everything you touch dies."

Cal ducked as Raphael rose from the darkness and fired suppressed shots from his HK 416. Cal rose, but Raphael had vanished back into the shadows.

"At least you got to see it," Victor said on Cal's radio. "There was no artwork hung on Daddy's refrigerator for her, was there? You were too busy killing anything with a heartbeat. I wonder how she felt being so alone in the world?"

Victor chuckled cruelly. Cal clenched his jaw — the killer instinct taking over. He sensed the smallest movement in the shadows. Raised his rifle and pressed the trigger. Raphael's gut-shot body stumbled into the blue glow.

Cal grabbed Raphael, slammed him against the wall, and

squeezed his trigger until his mag was empty. Cal screamed, enraged.

He heard Victor chuckle on his radio. "What's the matter, Reaper? Am I getting to you?"

Barachiel heard the shots. Trekked into the nave. Found Raphael's bullet-riddled body. Barachiel scanned the area around him. Deep, glowing blues and inky dark blacks.

Cal emerged from a dark corner behind Barachiel. The glowing, painted tableau, his camouflage. Cal slashed the tendons in Barachiel's legs and arms, pinned him against the wall.

Cal stabbed Barachiel in the heart, pinning him against the wall, then vanished back into the shadows as quickly as he had appeared.

Gabriel was with Victor and Eva in Cal's room. "We're on his terrain," Victor said. "He's got the advantage. We need the lights back on."

Gabriel nodded. He equipped his night vision goggles and descended into the nave. He trekked over Raphael's shot-up body. Passed Barachiel's sliced corpse pinned to the wall with a Ka-Bar knife.

Gabriel descended a dark staircase into the basement. It was pitch black. He fumbled around, feeling the walls, found what he was looking for: the circuit breaker.

Gabriel flipped the switches, turning the lights on, revealing Cal, lurking like a bat.

Flurry of fists.

Smack of flesh.

Crack of bone.

Cal and Gabriel fought, hand-to-hand.

· · ·

Upstairs in Cal's room, Eva struggled against the steel pipe she was cuffed to. Stomped it over and over with the sole of her foot, wishing Cal hadn't rebuilt the church with such a sturdy foundation. The pipe wouldn't budge.

"Stop it," Victor said, approaching her. She side-kicked him in the groin, knocking the wind out of him. He looked at her, eyes wide and surprised.

Eva resumed kicking the pipe.

Victor marched out into the nave. Stood over Raphael's bullet-riddled body. Saw Barachiel's impaled corpse. Looked out the door. Michael's and Selaphiel's bodies. Uriel's severed head. They were getting their asses kicked.

"Fuck it," Victor said.

He pulled the pin on a red incendiary grenade.

In the basement, Cal had Gabriel in a chokehold. He squeezed as the ceiling began to burn. Gabriel struggled, still some fight in him. The wood above them creaked, ready to give way at any moment. Cal jumped out of the way as the ceiling collapsed in a downpour of fiery detritus, crushing Gabriel.

Cal crawled through blinding and suffocating smoke into the nave. Fire raged all around him.

"Eva!" he screamed.

He heard her voice above him. Stifled by cracking flames. Cal squinted and stumbled through the fire, wheezing, running out of air.

In Cal's room, Eva coughed and squirmed as runners of smoke flooded under the locked door. She desperately kicked the pipe that her hand was cuffed to.

Cal, gasping, fading, barely able to stand. He reached for the doorknob. It singed his hand. He banged desperately on the burning door. Too weak to break through. His legs gave out. The fire cackled. He crumbled to the ground. His eyes closed.

And he could no longer breathe.

. . .

Outside the church, the residents of the barrio watched the church burn. They saw movement in the doorway. It was Eva, her wrist cuffed to a broken pipe. She was dragging Cal out of the church.

Cal slowly regained consciousness. "You saved me," he said, looking up at Eva. They shared a smile, and she helped him to his feet.

A bullet struck Cal in the shoulder. Another hit his hip.

"No!" Eva shrieked as Cal fell.

Victor marched toward him with a pistol. Tore Eva off of Cal. "You shouldn't have come back, Reaper," Victor said.

Cal looked up at Victor. "That's not my name anymore."

"That's right," Victor said. "Now you're nothing." Victor aimed his pistol at Cal's head.

"No," Cal said, staring through Victor. "I'm the Padre."

A bottle shattered against the back of Victor's head. Victor turned and saw the crowd. A gunshot sounded from somewhere. The bullet lodged in Victor's side, beneath his bulletproof vest. He dropped his gun.

Victor tried to raise his gun, but he was struck with a barrage of bottles, stones, pipes, knives, more gunshots. The DVD Kid, the tatted-up Clique Leader, the Florist, Señor Vasquez, the Neighborhood Soccer Kids and other familiar faces from the barrio fought for their Padre.

A potshot struck Victor's leg. He dropped to one knee.

Cal struggled to his feet, limped over. Picked up Victor's gun and pointed it down at Victor. Victor glared up at Cal and snarled.

"I will not serve," Cal said, and he pulled the trigger.

The fire burned through the night. Eventually, it simmered to a warm glow. And the night at last was peaceful.

58

Over the next three months, Cal and Eva rebuilt the church. At first, they toiled alone, but then a funny thing happened. The barrio pitched in.

By the time they were finished, it wasn't quite a church. Or rather, it wasn't *only* a church.

It was so much more.

Part community center. Part cultural museum. Part spiritual center. A place for residents to congregate.

Outside the front door, Cal posted the rules in Spanish: *1) No guns. 2) No drugs. 3) No violence.*

Inside the church, there were murals and cultural objects, specific to the barrio: Santa Muerte, Our Lady of Guadalupe, Jesús Christo, Jesús Malverde. There were grocery stands and old women playing cards. A tattoo artist had set-up shop in the corner. Mariachis performed. Sunlight shone through an opening in the roof on a community garden, which Señor Vasquez tended.

Outside, Cal played soccer with the Neighborhood Kids. Nearby, Eva finished a mural on the face of the remodeled church.

It was a depiction of the barrio — the good, the bad, and the ugly. Titled in large letters: "Hogar."

"Home."

EPILOGUE

Ray Valetta got the call at around four AM.

Another body had been found. This one in an inconspicuous warehouse near the airport. Boston Police were on the scene with a forensics team. The M.O. was the same. The victim was a white male in his sixties. He had been shot and quarters had been placed over his eyes.

It was the calling card of a man whom the FBI had dubbed the most brazen, yet elusive killer in US history.

Dado Veiga. "The Ferryman."

Ray Valetta was the Superintendent of the Boston Police Department's Bureau of Investigative Services, which was just a fancy way of saying Chief of Detectives. He'd issued special orders that he be notified immediately each time The Ferryman struck. No matter the time of day.

Valetta wasn't getting much sleep these days.

He trudged into the somber warehouse, sipping his Dunkin' coffee. CSU was pulling forensics from the crime scene. Valetta was preoccupied. Dunkin' had given him something flavored. French Hazelnut or some shit. He hated flavored copy. He took it black and unsweetened.

The CSU guys waved Valetta over. Valetta saw the victim's face and suddenly he looked nervous.

And Valetta *never* looked nervous.

"We pulled prints. Working on an ID," the CSU guy said.

"His name his Jack Caine," Valetta replied.

Valetta and the victim went way back. They were both born and raised in Boston. Jack in Southie and Valetta in the North End. They knew each other as kids. They served together in the military.

They were not friends.

But Valetta's daughter was missing. She was last seen with Jack Caine. Now, Jack was dead at the hands of one the most dangerous people Valetta had ever encountered.

And his daughter was still missing.

Valetta felt sick and it wasn't the hazelnut coffee.

"You know him, sir?" the CSU guy asked.

Valetta nodded. "He was a smalltime criminal turned journeyman boxer."

"Next of kin?"

"He has a son. A vet. His name is Caleb Caine."

"Caleb Caine?"

Valetta grimaced. "He goes by Cal."

Cal will return in
Bastard

See where it all began in *Black Rifle* (Caleb Caine Book 1)
ON SALE NOW

There has been another mass shooting in America, and thirteen people are dead. One of the victims is the daughter of Marco Barros, a powerful U.S. senator. The killer is still at large. Their identity and motive remain a mystery. Rookie ATF Agent Miranda Lopez's only lead is the murder weapon: an AR-15, a.k.a. the "black rifle."

Forced to work with Cal, a mysterious private sector mercenary hired by Senator Barros, Miranda's search for the rifle will take her across the country: from the crumbling city blocks of South Central, California to the frigid streets of South Side, Chicago to a sun-baked Arizona militia compound to the polished halls of power of Washington, D.C.

As they unravel a shocking grander conspiracy behind the shooting — a dark secret that the powerful will do anything to keep hidden — Miranda and Cal risk losing everything...

For updates, visit: Alex-Davidson.net

ACKNOWLEDGMENTS

I would like to thank my family.

I would like to thank my friend and collaborator, John Glenn, for donating his time and talents to making this book better, and for always supporting my work.

I would like to thank my sister, Annie Davidson, for her awesome editing skills.

I would like to thank the readers.

ABOUT THE AUTHOR

Alex Davidson is a multi-award-winning screenwriter, playwright, and #1 Amazon bestselling author. He earned his MFA in Dramatic Writing from NYU's Tisch School of the Arts in 2009.

Learn more about Alex and his work at: Alex-Davidson.net

ISBN-13: 978-1-7365196-5-3